Ruins of Sea and Souls

Fae Isles - Book 3

Lisette Marshall

ASIN: B0BHL9R2X4

Cover design: Saint Jupiter
Editor: Erin Grey, The Word Faery

www.lisettemarshall.com
www.facebook.com/LisetteMarshallAuthor
www.instagram.com/AuthorLisetteMarshall

To Steph,
who is of course the only goddess
who truly matters in this story

CONTENTS

Chapter 1

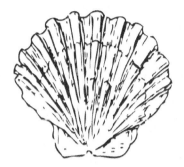

I'D FALLEN ASLEEP IN the library again.

I woke to find the room ominously silent, the fields beyond the arched windows dark, the endless bookshelves shrouded in shadow, illuminated by nothing but the twinkling orbs that hovered silvery above the reading tables. It took me a moment to figure out I'd inelegantly collapsed on one such table gods-knew-how-long ago, cheek to book, the itch of drool in the corner of my mouth.

A half-conscious groan escaped me. Thank Zera's merciful heart the encyclopaedia serving as my unwilling pillow wasn't some rare and ancient manuscript. Lyn would have my head for drooling on it.

Only then, having analysed and discarded that most urgent danger of the situation, did I become aware of the fingers prodding my shoulder.

I blinked against the darkness and then against Creon's winged silhouette towering over me. The tangled realm of my dreams was loath to let go of me, and reality seeped in slowly – a reality of towering piles of notes, ink-stained fingers, and frantic browsing through scrolls and leatherbound tomes. Dark room. Fingers. *Just a short trip to the reading hall*, I'd said. *I'll be back before the lights are dimmed*, I'd said.

'Oh,' I muttered groggily. 'What time is it?'

Creon's fingers vanished from my shoulder. *Late*, he dryly gestured.

I glared at him. 'I'd guessed that, thank you.'

He let out a silent laugh. *Coming to bed?*

With a muffled curse, I dragged myself into a sitting position, wincing at the objections of my stiff neck, my stiff shoulders, my stiff spine. Hours and hours hunched up on these rigid reading stools were starting to take their toll on my body. Before me, the open pages of my notebook were still painfully empty.

Perhaps I should have slept more than five hours the previous night, too.

'I'll be done in a minute,' I said, grabbling for my pen with clumsy fingers. 'Just need to finish this last summary, and then—'

Em. He sank to his knees next to me – the Silent Death, kneeling. Not so new a sight anymore, but it still shut me up annoyingly easily. His left hand moulded firmly to my bare knee as his right shaped his words; his eyes were as dark as the night outside, gleaming with what I could only describe as gentle menace. *Time to sleep. You did enough.*

'I'm almost done,' I said, with less conviction than I'd hoped. As the words fell from my lips, I was unpleasantly reminded that I'd told him the same thing last night, and the night before, and the night before that.

I *was* almost done, but somehow the definition of "done" kept changing under my hands, like a slippery fish that wouldn't allow my fingers to grasp it.

You're panicking, Creon informed me.

The fact that he was right annoyed me more than the problem itself. 'You're supposed to keep your shields up. Naxi will be displeased if you're sampling my emotions again.'

My shields are doing just fine. A wry smile grazed his lips. *But you're torturing yourself for the sole purpose of reading more Faerie texts. Don't need demon senses to tell something's wrong.*

I laughed, damn him. 'It's not that something's wrong. I'm just not sure if we've got enough to convince them.'

It's either enough or it isn't, Em. He pulled his hand from my knee, coming up to settle himself more comfortably on the edge of the desk. His dark wings spread restlessly behind his back, a shield between me and the world – hiding the two of us here in our cocoon of darkness, nothing but the silvery orb above our head to keep the shadows at bay. *There's nothing we can do in these last few hours that's going to make the difference.*

Which would have been a reassurance, if not for the nagging, aching suspicion that it simply meant I was doomed before I'd truly started. A few hours. And then our friends and allies would gather once again in the Wanderer's Wing, exchanging whatever plans and intelligence we'd found in these last two weeks ...

And I would have to make my proposal.

My desperate, impossible proposal.

I'd postponed it twice already. A month ago, I'd told myself I hadn't read enough, hadn't excluded the possibility there might be more information out there. Two weeks ago, I'd told myself I hadn't worked out a satisfactory line of argument yet, that no one would take me seriously with the garbled mess of troubles I was about to throw into their laps, and that I should at the very least present them with a *structured* mess if I wanted to cause a stir so badly.

Now I'd structured and planned, argued and counter-argued until my head spun, and it still didn't seem close to sufficient.

I don't suppose you'll suddenly agree with me that we don't have to inform them at all? Creon signed, reading my mind as usual.

'We can't do that,' I said sharply. If only we could – hell, how much I wished we could. 'You know how much they rely on me. If I suddenly disappear ...'

He shrugged. *You'll be back.*

'They won't know how to reach us. What are they supposed to do if anything happens in the meantime?'

Not an empty threat, and we both knew it – the tales Beyla told us at breakfast were more alarming with each passing day. The Mother's cronies visiting human islands, threatening death at every hint of treason. Alves on the northern isles arming themselves. Magical convoys visiting the Underground, negotiating new alliances. It could be weeks until the Mother would first strike – it could be days, if we were unlucky – and if our research of the past weeks was anything close to accurate, the Alliance may need me more than even they knew.

Sneaking away under those circumstances ... even the promise I'd made wasn't worth that much.

I know, Creon gestured before I could put any of that into words. *You want to ask them. Not saying that's a bad idea. Just ...* He hesitated, looking for the least offensive wording. *Remember that their disagreement doesn't have to be the end of the matter.*

Because they could hardly chain me to my bed. Because we could always ignore the opinions of our allies and trick our way outside, damn the war looming closer and closer.

'It would be a complication, though,' I said, drawing in a terse breath that itched to become a curse. 'So let's not risk it. I'll just finish this last summary, and then—'

He flipped my book shut.

'Hey!' I jolted up straighter. 'You don't get to send me to bed like some disobedient child, Your Highness!'

I'm not sending you to bed. He smiled, the gesture hawkish with the cold light and the sharp-edged shadows playing over his features; his wings unfolded farther, a lazy spread of silver-lit velvet. *I'm luring you to bed. An entirely different game.*

I scoffed, planting my elbows on the desk. 'So far you're mostly luring my fists to your nose.'

A grin flashed over his face. *That counts as foreplay, doesn't it?*

'Bastard.' The word came out a fraction too hoarse. 'Stop getting in my way. I'm doing this for you, in case you forgot.'

I haven't forgotten for a single heartbeat, he signed, the amusement dwindling. *And you know how grateful I am. If you try tomorrow and they don't agree, I'll still be more grateful than I'll ever find the signs to say.*

Signs. Not words. Because if I failed ...

Hell, I shouldn't think about that now. 'Then why won't you just let me finish this? I promise I'll come to bed as soon as I'm done.'

He hesitated, then rubbed a hand over his face, his left fingers locking tight around the edge of the table. There were traces of something dark under his nails – dried blood, I realised with a queasy feeling in my stomach. Perhaps I should have been more concerned about him joining Edored for training, even though the alf had sworn loudly and convincingly that he would do no lasting harm to the insufferable winged fucker who'd saved my life during the battle for the Golden Court.

'I just want to have done all I can do,' I said feebly. 'I don't want to have them reject the idea and feel like I might have done better if I'd just tried a little harder.'

The best you can do is sleep. He held up a hand, interrupting my sharp intake of breath. *Em, I've been doing this for longer than you've been alive. Scheming. Making plans. Trying to account for every variable, every stroke of bad luck. Lack of sleep has not once improved my chances of success.*

I tried to tell him I wasn't that tired and had to stifle a yawn. He demonstratively settled back on the desk, raising an eyebrow.

Well?

Something about the sight of him made the prospect of more endless Faerie literature look less attractive by the heartbeat. Hell, did I really need that bloody summary? I'd read the chapters on the last inhabitable days of the continent some five times. So had he. If he believed we didn't need any more detailed notes, who was I to object?

And soft blankets were waiting for me in his bed, strong arms and the soothing twinkle of his faelights.

'If Lyn or Tared or bloody Agenor asks for more information on Sophronia's study of the plague,' I grumbled, getting up from my stool, 'I'll know who to blame when I don't have the answer right at hand.'

Oddly, he didn't appear at all deterred by that threat. *I promise I'll beg for your forgiveness very convincingly.*

I tried to punch him anyway.

He didn't even dodge. No matter how fast I was, his fingers caught my wrist mid-air, halting my fist with two inches left between my knuckles and his sharp cheekbone. He swept his free hand around my waist next, shoving me flush against him; his thumb rubbed slow circles on my captive wrist, every caress prickling up my arm with taunting intensity.

Not my best move, I had to admit as warmth pooled at every spot where his hard body met mine.

'I thought you wanted me to sleep?' I got out between gritted teeth.

He released my waist, his fingers still tight as steel around my lower arm. *I thought this would be a kinder way of achieving that goal.* A chuckle. *But do tell me if you'd prefer me to drag you out of the library kicking and screaming.*

'Resorting to kidnapping again? How very fae.'

It's a subtle art few people appreciate. He somehow managed to look appropriately humble as he signed the words, a feat about as impossible as a prize bull's attempt to appear feeble. *You'll be glad to know you're my favourite victim by far.*

I snorted, the last of my resistance crumbling. 'Flatterer.'

He scooped me into his arms in response, cradling me against his hard chest so effortlessly I didn't even have time to squeak. His arms under my knees and back were a cage – a strong, safe cage, coaxing my weary limbs to let go, to leave the books on the reading table and focus on nothing but the slow pulse of his heart below his ribs and the warmth of his breath as he bent to kiss my forehead.

Dangerous surrender ... but my breath hitched and my body slumped in his hold.

Tucking in his wings, he navigated easily through the maze of bookcases and slipped out of the room without even the slightest creak of the hinges, through the deserted main hall and out of the library's front door. Into the public parts of the Underground, where only the dim alf lights in the corners kept the deepest of darkness at bay.

He never made a sound. Even carrying my added weight, his feet padded across the stone quietly like cat's paws, moving us from shadow to shadow with an ease that bordered on instinct. Safely in his arms, resting my tired head against his chest, it seemed I was floating along on wisps of darkness, as invisible as an evening breeze. A few dozen feet away, a rowdy group of alves crossed our path. A vampire sauntered past, a trail of goat blood dripping over his chin. None of them noticed us. Had we meant them any harm, they wouldn't have found out until Creon's knives already lay between their ribs.

Even here, surrounded by allies in the relative safety of the Underground, this would always be his most familiar role to play – a lone hunter, prowling through the night, owing obedience to no queen or crown.

He carried me until we reached the rune-covered front door of the Skeire family home, then set me on my feet and pulled out the key Tared had grudgingly given him on our return to the Underground three months ago. The living room was dark when we slipped inside, Beyla's maps and Lyn's books on the table evidence that I hadn't been the only one preparing for tomorrow's gathering. Nothing moved in the shadows, yet the ever-present threat of alf appearances had me tiptoeing a safe three feet behind Creon until we reached his room.

I moved to follow him only after a few wary glances over my shoulder. As far as I was aware, Lyn was still the only one who knew where I spent my nights – and if I wanted to have any chance at getting them where I needed them tomorrow, this would be the worst possible moment for the others to find out.

Em, Creon signed, eyes locked on my face. *Stop panicking.*

'I'm not panicking,' I whispered, throat clenching tight. 'It would just be damn inconvenient for Edored to fade by while I'm eating your face off.'

I can guarantee you he's seen worse in his life. His stance was so deceptively nonchalant, leaning against the wall, wings lying loosely over his back. His smile was so close to convincing. But he signed the words too quickly, and we'd had this conversation too many times before for me to believe it truly left him indifferent. *One day they'll figure it out anyway. Waiting is not going to make it any better.*

'But it might!' That, too, I'd said before – pleaded with him to understand. So much could change between now and the next few months. We'd have this mad mission behind us, or else we'd have given up on it entirely. Our allies might trust him better. They might develop a little more faith in my good sense.

We might have this entire damn war behind us, and then at least the fate of the world would no longer rest on my annoyingly thin shoulders.

His own shoulders tightened as he watched me, knowing the line of my thoughts without a word from my lips. They hated him anyway, he'd said. Couldn't we at the very least stop making things so damn complicated for ourselves, if the rest of the world was already happy enough to complicate life for us?

I didn't want to think about this now. Not with the next morning looming like an unmovable boulder on the edges of my mind.

'Shouldn't we just go to sleep?' I breathed. 'You wanted me to get my night's rest. There'll be better moments to talk about all of this.'

He sighed. But he held the door for me.

The room behind was soothingly familiar, a mixture of nondescript Underground architecture, alf furnishings, and brand new traces of fae magic. Most of the furniture had remained unchanged since our arrival months ago, rough wood and fabrics. The alf lights had vanished, though, and in their place, a serene glow now spread from behind the stained glass Creon had embedded in the ceiling vaults, drowning the room in smoky hues of indigo and dove grey. An impressive arsenal of weapons lay meticulously ordered in one corner; the desk and arm-chairs were besieged by the piles of books and scrolls we'd studied over the past weeks.

I swallowed another lump of nervousness. All that work, and it may just be for nothing.

Creon didn't immediately react as the feeling struck – another recent change. His shields were still up, then – up and strong enough to keep me out from such a small distance. On this occasion, it saved me for only a heartbeat or two: the moment he shut the door and turned back to me, his eyes narrowed at the tension on my face.

Still not convinced by the bottomless well of my wisdom? he signed.

I huffed a laugh. 'That same bottomless well which made you decide to go to training with Edored, of all people?'

Matter of precaution. He shrugged as he brushed past me and began unbuttoning his shirt with his left hand, fingers moving so fast it seemed the lines of ink were shifting under his skin. *Don't think he'll be at the meeting tomorrow.*

I stared at him.

He casually continued loosening his shirt at the front, then below his wings, and shrugged the dark cloth off his shoulders. Most days, the reveal of sinfully sculpted chest would be enough to distract me from the discussion at hand, but my lingering panic and the sense of alarm inherent in anything involving Edored momentarily blinded me to the taut ridges of ink-marred muscle.

'What?'

I'm not letting you do all the work, he dryly added as he flung the shirt over the nearest armchair.

'You ...' I sucked in a baffled breath. 'You got him to challenge you at training ... so you could ... do what? Bash his head in?'

He raised a scarred eyebrow, amused. *I'm more subtle than that.*

'So you could wound him subtly but unpleasantly,' I corrected myself, understanding dawning as I spoke the words, 'so that he'll drink too much to numb the sting as usual, so that he'll sleep too deep and wake too late tomorrow? Good gods, Creon.'

His smile reminded me, in a flash, why grown men shivered at the sound of his name in the world above. The Silent Death at work, again – I should have known. He hadn't survived a hundred and thirty years of thwarting the Mother right under her porcelain nose just to sit back when a handful of miffed alves threatened to render months of work useless.

'Well.' I fell down on the edge of the bed and began to loosen my braid with snappish yanks, sending him a wry grin. 'One less opponent to worry about. I'll just pretend that justifies the questionable methods.'

I don't think I ever claimed to be a male of spotless morals, he signed as he squatted to pull his knives from his boots, then loosen the boots themselves. For a few moments, his fingers were occupied with those tasks; then he added, pleasantly, *But if you feel very guilty about the bastard, you're free to wake him early with a fried egg and ginger tea tomorrow.*

I snorted. 'I'll sympathetically make him ginger tea when he wakes up two hours past noon and we have handled the discussion already. Anyone else you quietly chained up in unused rooms or knocked out in the fields?'

He sighed and shook his head as he shoved his boots aside, wings drawing taut behind his naked back.

'How very mild of you,' I said.

There was nothing mild about the gleam in his dark eyes. *Don't tell yourself it's a matter of kindness. I would get questions if half the group were to stay away tomorrow.*

'Mm-hmm,' I said, nodding earnestly. 'And if not for that bit of cold calculation, you'd end them all without a second thought for the sake of our plans, of course.'

Of course. He sank down on the bed beside me, crossing his legs as he met my gaze. The look in his eyes was half laughter, half bitter sincerity. *Sometimes it seems you don't take the depraved depths of my soul even half as seriously as you should, cactus.*

I cocked my head, my unbraided hair a mess of loose strands around my shoulders. 'Ah. That stone heart of yours, incapable of feeling love or any emotion of all? Silly of me to forget about that.'

He didn't smile. *Can't deny I'm a rotten bastard.*

'Of course you're a rotten bastard.' My dress smothered my words as I pulled it over my head; the green cloth smelled faintly of ink and sweat and the tea I'd spilled at my desk that morning. 'But that doesn't mean I didn't see you laugh at Hallthor's jokes at dinner.'

Now he did chuckle, even though there was little humour to the breathy sound. *His impression of Naxi is eerily accurate, admittedly.*

'It is. And you *do* like some of them, as much as you're trying to deny it.'

He closed his eyes. *Weren't we planning to sleep?*

'We were,' I admitted, pulling off my underwear and chucking it into a corner. 'Do you need any help getting those trousers off, then?'

He did not need help, but I took an unreasonable amount of pleasure in assisting him anyway, stripping off the sturdy black cloth to reveal inch after inch of muscular thighs and calves, kissing the spots where veins and tendons bulged below his skin. By the time I finally pulled the last of his clothing off, his half-hard cock had swollen into a full-fledged erection.

At the sight of his half-lidded eyes, my nervousness ached a little less painfully.

Sleep? he signed as I clambered into his lap, straddling him.

'Are you sure?' I murmured.

He kissed me.

Our tumble was quick and messy and somehow ended with me wiping seed from my left eye as we collapsed laughing and panting into our blankets. For a few moments, nothing else in the world seemed to matter, even the possibility of failure no more than an irrelevant note in the margins.

Then Creon darkened the lights with a few quick hand motions, and in the gloom of night, the urgency seeped straight back into the marrow of my bones.

I knew the feel of his body in my arms. Knew the way his chest rose and fell against me, knew the satin softness of his skin and the rough patches of his callouses, the rippling of his muscles as he shifted under the blankets. I knew the way he wrapped his wing around me, keeping me safe from the world outside, locking me forever in his grasp.

But most of all, I knew the silence.

In the darkness, the shapes of his fingers hidden from my eyes, he was once again fully and completely voiceless, nothing but the whisper of his breath and his hands on my body to tell me whatever was happening in that lightning-quick mind. And of course he never complained. Of course he told me not to worry. Of course he'd never repeated the confession that had escaped him in the water of the Sunstone Bay three months ago, that he *did* miss his voice, fiercely and desperately. But everything he wouldn't say echoed through the shadows of the night, and I lay asleep for far too long after his breath grew slow and shallow, my mind spinning, running over my plans and arguments again and again.

They might tell me I was being unnecessarily concerned.

They might tell me none of my theories made sense.

They might ...

But it was too late and I was too tired. A downy weight stifled my thoughts, lured them back into the territory of dreams; I fell asleep with my plans unfinished, slipping unnoticed into the day that might shatter my promises.

CHAPTER 2

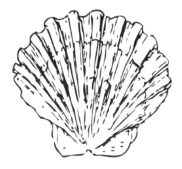

EVEN AFTER MONTHS OF meetings – even after moving heaven and earth to get Council permission for his presence at my birthday celebration – it was still odd to see Agenor in the familiar space of the Wanderer's Wing, Oleander wrapped around his shoulders, his silk shirt folding in all the right places. He stood browsing through some traveller's notebook when Beyla faded Creon and me into the light-drenched meeting room. Thorir, who had picked him up from the Golden Court for the occasion, was nowhere to be seen. In all likeliness, he had quickly returned to the castle to keep an eye on the other alves posted there.

'Morning, Em.' Agenor's smile was tired but genuine, a glimmer of softness that made me feel unsure of where to look. It slid off his face the moment he turned to Creon, though, who wasn't granted more than a terse nod by way of greeting.

'Morning,' I said. 'How are the ships?'

The ships were the Mother's Moon fleet, which had shown up around the Golden Court in the dead of night some three weeks ago and laid siege to the island. No new allies had managed to reach the castle since, which we suspected was the main intention of that silent guard; as both Creon and Agenor had predicted, the fleet hadn't made an attempt to attack the castle directly.

Yet.

'Peaceful as always,' Agenor said, shrugging as if a dozen warships locking him in were nothing of concern. 'The main challenge is to keep our alves from attacking them. What have you been up to these weeks?'

'Training. Reading.' *Breaking bindings* – but he'd hear all about that in a few minutes, and there was no reason to give the surprise away. The sheer inconceivability of my plans might be their best advantage. 'Nothing out of the ordinary.'

He looked like he was about to say something, but at that moment Naxi fluttered into the room in a storm of powdery pink and high-pitched exclamations, and he stepped past me with just a brief squeeze to my shoulder. Lyn and Tared appeared a moment later, accompanied by Cas, a gawky, freckled phoenix male in the early twenties of his current life. From their glances in my direction, I suspected they'd been discussing me, but Tared's quick grin and Lyn's bright greeting betrayed nothing of the reason.

My blood ran cold. Was there anything I'd failed to take into account?

With most of the Underground's unofficial government within hearing distance, this seemed a terrible moment to ask. I swallowed my roaring nerves and sat down next to Creon at the map table. He lounged in his chair with that carefully crafted air of indifference he always pulled up whenever I dragged him into a room with Tared or Agenor – a sense of lazy invincibility that rendered all scornful looks and sharp remarks useless in advance.

Valeska slipped into the room, purple hair swirling around the nymph's small antlers. Nenya followed half a minute later, looking stiffer than usual in her black lace-and-leather corset. There was a suspicious gleam in Creon's eyes as he followed her path to the table, a focus suggesting her rigid shoulders were symptoms of a larger problem – but before I could ask, Naxi swatted the fuzzy sleeve of her sweater at him and hissed, 'Shields!'

Creon rolled his eyes, and she laughed out loud, patting him patronisingly on the crown of his head. As if a little lamb was giggling at a sleek black panther, except that there was little lamb-like about the flash of sharp teeth in her smile.

'Can't start slacking,' she said brightly and then added in a lower voice, 'but yes, she is terribly upset about something.'

I glanced back at Nenya, who did not so much look upset as quietly furious, glaring at the map-covered walls with an unwavering determination. Behind her, Lyn turned away from her urgent whispering to Tared and Cas to meet my gaze. A lack of demon powers clearly hadn't stopped her from noticing the same thing.

'Shall we get started?' she said out loud, interrupting Valeska and Agenor's polite conversation beside the bookshelves.

Nenya jolted up, as if shaken awake. 'Aren't we waiting for Edored?'

Quite to my satisfaction, Edored had been absent at breakfast, and even Tared didn't sound suspicious when he grumbled something about honey mead and not going to risk his neck to wake half-drunk cousins. Nenya, however, looked thoroughly displeased at that explanation, her bright red lips so tight I could see the shapes of her fangs behind them.

'Do you have unpleasant news?' Lyn said, painfully cautious.

'Quite.'

The rest of the company quickly took their seats at that – Naxi and Valeska at Creon's side, Agenor and Beyla next to me, Lyn, Cas, and Tared on the other side of the table.

Nenya threw a last glance at the door, as if Edored might unexpectedly show up after all, and then said, 'I came back from Ubrit last night.'

One of the islands inhabited by remote vampire communities, and one of the few whose ruler had immediately agreed to join the fight against the empire, concerns for safety and retributions be damned. But the next thing Nenya said was a hoarse, 'The king is having doubts after all.'

Frozen silence was her only answer.

'I wasn't even planning to meet with him,' she said, closing her eyes as she sagged into her chair. 'But I visited a few other islands in the past three days, as you requested, and all of them were suddenly far more hesitant to pledge their support than a week ago. So I wondered …'

'Has the Mother been meddling?' Lyn said, her face more frown than freckle.

'No. Bakaru.'

The others stiffened collectively around the table – hell, even *Agenor* stiffened. Bakaru. A name I'd never heard before … but it fell from Nenya's lips like a curse.

'Who?' I said, feeling annoyingly young.

'His Majesty, Bakaru Sefistrim, King of Kings and theoretical ruler of all remaining vampire domains.' Nenya didn't look me in the eye. 'Also, as it so happens, my giver.'

'Your—'

'He made me a vampire,' she clarified, interrupting me with unusual impatience.

'Oh,' I said sheepishly. The tone of her voice suggested that relationship was not a source of much joy – *terribly upset*, Naxi had whispered. Were the complications for the Alliance the reason, or was the involvement of His Majesty himself the major problem?

'So he's still alive?' Agenor muttered, and Tared grumbled something that suspiciously resembled the word *unfortunately*.

Nenya sent the both of them a glare. 'He's spent the last few centuries in Gar Temen. Most of the time, he doesn't bother with worldly matters. I hadn't expected him to have opinions at all.'

'What is he angry about, exactly?' Cas asked cautiously.

'No idea. They were painfully vague at Ubrit, just kept repeating that new information had reached them and that they had to reconsider their commitments with a higher authority. It could be that Bakaru is unhappy about the plans themselves. Could be he's just annoyed I didn't come to him first.'

'Don't blame yourself,' Lyn said, rubbing her eyes. 'If you'd gone to him first, he'd have thrown a fit about you wasting his time. There was no way to predict he'd be interested in the matter at all, after he ignored the entire previous war.'

I glanced at Agenor. On his shoulders, Oleander had raised her sleek black head, tongue flashing in and out as she followed the conversation with her beady eyes.

'If he wasn't involved with the war,' I said, 'how do you even know him at all?'

Agenor shrugged; the gesture earned him an annoyed hiss. 'He was already sworn to Korok before I was born. Possibly quite long before I was born.'

Oh, gods help me. Life had been complicated enough without the existence of fickle godsworn vampire kings older than even the oldest fae male I knew – vampire kings disinclined to help us win a fight we desperately needed to win.

Next to me, Creon sat examining Nenya closely, and this time not even Naxi told him to keep his powers locked away.

'So what do we do?' Lyn said.

'We need the vampires,' Cas said, hunching up his bony shoulders with his usual awkward, apologetic expression. He had the kind of floppy red hair that made even an adult look boyish, and he'd never looked floppier than at this moment. 'The phoenix elders are still being ... how do I put this ...'

'Mind-numbingly unhelpful?' Tared suggested, glancing at me for some reason.

Cas followed his gaze, sending me an uneasy grin. 'I suppose that covers it, yes.'

They *had* been talking about me, damn them. I fell back in my chair and snapped, 'Does the unhelpfulness have anything to do with my person, or are you all just that eager to see my pretty face a little more often?'

'Em ...' Lyn said, but even her grin was too restrained, some untold secret shimmering through.

'Oh,' Valeska said, mousy face brightening. 'Good gods. She's been spreading the same story with the phoenixes?'

Tared snapped around. 'What? The nymphs too?'

'*What* story?' It fell from my lips sounding too shrill. 'Did I do anything I shouldn't have done?'

'No,' Lyn said bleakly. 'Or ... well, nothing that could be prevented, I suppose. But apparently the Mother's envoys have been going around telling people ...' Her eyes flashed to Creon, a look estimating a threat, and back to me. 'Reminding people not to forget that you're just a witless almost-human girl entirely under the Silent Death's traitorous influence, and that as much as they may dislike the empire, do they truly think it will get better with her son ruling it?'

I stared at her.

Creon – *ruling* anything?

Oh, fuck. And the poor souls would believe that story, wouldn't they? I would have accepted it without question a year ago, too. Of course the Silent Death was rotten enough to betray his own people over his unbridled lust for cruelty – who wouldn't acknowledge that? And all they knew about me ...

Silly little Emelin, fae whore. Imagine they'd accuse me of *thinking*.

Cas sat hunched up in his chair as if he expected someone to shout at him. Nenya looked ready to nibble someone's head off. Tared gave the impression that Lyn's presence was his last reason not to draw a sword and challenge his old enemy to a duel over my honour on the spot. But when I turned aside, suddenly excruciatingly aware of their gazes on every look we exchanged, Creon hadn't even sat up straighter, observing the company with cold, dark eyes.

No attempts at defence. By the faint sneer of satisfaction around his lips, I might have thought they'd complimented him.

'It's gotten the nymph isles all in a flurry,' Valeska said when he remained unmoving; she fidgeted with her sleeves as she stared at his hands. 'They haven't forgotten how you killed the queen of Tolya twenty years ago.'

Creon turned to Agenor, eyebrow raised in a wordless challenge.

'Ah.' At least my father had the good grace to look a little embarrassed as he cleared his throat. 'You might have to blame me for that particular incident. Not that that will mollify anyone, I suppose.'

I thought for a moment Naxi would bite him. Valeska bitterly said, 'But at least *you* didn't show up to chop up her fingers and then the rest of her.'

Thank the gods Creon had learned to shut out my emotions, because I wouldn't have wanted him to feel the cold shiver that ran through me. Cas seemed about to throw up. Beyla and Tared's faces were similar masks of cold alf fury, mirrored in the icy gleam in Nenya's eyes.

Chop the poor queen in question to pieces. What had it cost him to take that pain?

'Well, whoever is to blame, we'll have to do something about this situation,' Lyn said firmly, an obvious attempt at distraction before anyone could elaborate on nymph fingers. 'We don't stand a chance if all our potential allies decide they'd rather suffer the treatment of the empire for the rest of time than take the risk of joining our efforts. Should we ask Gish to go have a word with Bakaru, or—'

'Please don't ask Gish,' Nenya said brusquely. 'I suspect he's Bakaru's main source on the Underground. Don't give him more ammunition if you can avoid it.'

Agenor muttered a curse. 'We're talking about Gishkim, I presume? Shouldn't we do something about him, if he's feeding Bakaru information we don't want him to have?'

A reasonable question, I thought; disappointingly, Lyn pulled a sour face. 'Gish has always been loyal to our side. It just so happens he's also loyal to the vampire side, but that's hardly a reason to kick him out. We're an allegiance, not a kingdom.'

'Which does sound impractical to me,' Agenor said, raising an eyebrow.

'The alternative sounds unethical to me,' she shot back. 'Make your choice.'

He wisely shut up.

'I'll go,' Nenya said, jaw clenched so tight that the scars over her face drew taut. 'Don't worry about Gish. Bakaru will want to see me anyway, if he knows I'm involved with all of this – there's no sense in delaying it.'

The glance Lyn and Tared exchanged suggested they saw a lot of sense in delaying that visit, preferably forever. But before they could object, Cas mumbled, 'And the phoenixes? Drusa has been asking for you, Lyn. Perhaps you could—'

'Drusa,' Lyn said, paling a fraction, 'can go fuck herself.'

I realised in that moment that I had not the faintest idea of her history – that even after months in the same household, I didn't know how she had ever ended up with the Alliance, why she had moved into this buried place and for all intents and purposes joined an alf family from the other side of the archipelago. Apparently, I was the only one who didn't know; even Agenor's joyless smile showed a hint of understanding. 'If there are no objections I'm overlooking' – he was clearly not expecting to be overlooking anything – 'I might be able to help out?'

Cas blinked. '*You?*'

Agenor gave a shrug, ignoring Oleander's unamused glare. 'I've met with Drusa a handful of times. She may not be fond of me, but I think she knows that, with all due respect, I wouldn't join any attempts to get Creon on a throne.'

Is that what we call respect these days? Creon scribbled in his notebook.

'Do I need to remind you,' Tared said sharply, 'that we'd be in a lot less trouble right now if not for that reputation you so enthusiastically cultivated, Hytherion?'

I scoffed. 'You'd be in far more trouble if he'd refused to execute the Mother's orders and died a century ago. Are you going to blame me for surviving as a witless little human, too?'

'Oh, stop it!' Lyn burst out, flinging up her small hands. 'This isn't getting us anywhere, for hell's sake. I think Drusa respects you well enough, Agenor, so if you're willing to suffer their endless blathering for a good cause, try your luck. As for the nymphs ...' She met Valeska's gaze and grimaced. 'We'll probably have to think of a better solution than throwing more fae at them.'

'Why doesn't Em go have a word with them?' Beyla suggested, her voice as eerily light as her eyes and her silver-blonde hair. 'She's pretty good at looking clever. Might be the easiest way to convince them she's not under any fae thumbs at all.'

My heart skipped a beat. Oh, Zera help me. They weren't going to send me on some diplomatic visit *now*, were they? 'Well—'

'That does sound like a solid idea, actually,' Lyn said, her eyes brightening. 'Would that work for you, Em? If Naxi or Valeska is coming with you?'

'Oh, don't count on me,' Naxi said cheerfully. 'They don't trust me any farther than they can throw me. And their arm muscles aren't—'

'Look,' I interrupted, chest tightening in alarm, 'I understand this is all very urgent and of course I'd love to help out, but I've been looking into a couple of issues myself and I think ...' I sucked in a breath. Here it was, then. All or nothing, for all it was worth. 'I may have more important things to do at the moment. If you don't mind.'

That smothered all suggestions of diplomatic missions for a heartbeat or two.

'Ah,' Tared said, a spark of amusement in his voice as he combed a hand through his blond locks and leaned back in his seat. 'Are we finally getting to hear why you tried to skip training twice this week?'

'Only once,' I said indignantly. 'And that was more because you tore my biceps to shreds the day before than because I was so desperate to read my books. But yes – it's about the bindings.'

Agenor snapped his head around to me. I hadn't told him of my research yet, and deliberately so; I didn't need him to spend time thinking on the matter and conclude Creon's influence was all that had me working on this project.

'The *bindings*?' he repeated, a hint of bafflement in his deep voice.

'Yes.' I suppressed the urge to look at Creon for support, for approval, for help. We'd discussed the strategy. I was going to present this plan, I was going to make this argument, because enough of our audience would suspect selfish motives behind every word he spoke and believe my plea for the greater good much more easily. 'I've been looking into them, and from what I've seen so far ... I think we may have a bigger problem than we thought we did.'

Eyes narrowed. Fingers tightened. Nenya scoffed and muttered, 'As always.'

'Could you explain yourself, Em?' Lyn said, resting her chubby arms on the edge of the table and lowering her chin onto them.

'If I understand everything correctly ...' I slouched in my chair, a sudden calm sinking over me. To hell with it. I *did* understand everything correctly. Who was I trying to fool with my false modesty? 'So far we've always assumed the bindings simply protected the Mother, yes? Your magic can't hurt her, so none of you can storm into the bone hall and set her on fire – pretty straightforward, all in all.'

They waited, no confirmations or objections.

'Here's the problem,' I said. 'Ophion survived Creon's demon magic at the Golden Court. Lyn says she tried to send a burst of fire into the prick's face as soon as she saw him but didn't manage to – she thought it was exhaustion, so she nosedived into his back instead, which saved me anyway. But combined with the point of Creon's magic ...'

'You assume our bindings are protecting Ophion as well?' Lyn finished slowly, her amber eyes such thin slits they might have been closed.

'I think they're protecting everyone and everything close enough to the Mother to have direct unpleasant consequences for her. That the definition of "not harming her" is broader than we thought.' I braced myself and turned to Agenor, whose fingertips had stilled against Oleander's slender body. 'Have you ever tried to use magic against her close allies since you turned against her?'

'I ... no, but ...' He hesitated, then nodded at Creon. 'You killed Deiras. A few decades ago. Achlys and Melinoë definitely missed him, so that should have given you trouble, shouldn't it?'

Creon shrugged and tapped his knife. No magic involved.

'Ah.' Agenor let out a mirthless laugh. 'Still, if everyone in her personal circle is included in the bindings, that would mean that until recently the two of us should also have been protected by— Oh.' His eyes abruptly widened. 'Gods help us. *Wait.*'

'Any returning memories?' I said dryly. 'Creon had a few of those.'

Agenor parted his lips, then abruptly turned away, rubbing his jaw with too much force. 'There have admittedly been a few occasions where my opponents turned into remarkably poor mages, but I always assumed ...' His next glance at Creon was more bewildered. 'Fear and nervousness can have that effect as well. It doesn't *have* to be binding magic.'

Creon grabbed his pencil. *Your red was defective when you captured me below the Golden Court thinking I was there in her name. Do you usually lose your colours when you're scared?*

Agenor stared at him. 'Fuck.'

Creon chuckled.

'And it makes sense if it's never been very noticeable,' I said quickly. 'The Mother doesn't give a rat's arse about anyone but herself, so fae attacking each other rarely harmed her to the point of evoking the bindings – not as long as she had enough of them not to care about a few dozen lives more or less. The other magical peoples were only bound after the Last Battle, and most have never been close to the Crimson Court since. In the few cases where the bindings might have taken effect, the intended victims were arrogant enough bastards to believe it was their mere presence paralysing their opponents ...'

Tared huffed a laugh. Agenor gave me a dignified glare.

'But now it's war, you see?' I continued, ignoring them. 'Now she suddenly cares about losing armies and protecting herself, and who knows what effect that may have on the binding magic? Who knows if there are more people she actively wants to keep alive now?'

'Starting to see the problem,' Nenya said, her voice low and ominous. 'For all we know, the walls of the Crimson Court are binding-protected as well, if she'd dislike losing them. One unbound mage isn't getting us anywhere if she has to break through all defences single-handedly.'

'Exactly.'

Disconcerted glances crossed the table. I held my breath for four, five heartbeats, but still no one objected.

'I suppose you have a plan?' Naxi said, jolting straighter in her chair.

'Well ...' Bloody demon eyes. I had planned to introduce the next stage more carefully, but there was no escaping it now. 'Ophion's answers have been haunting me – he told us that the Mother is able to break a binding, so it must be possible *somehow*. But there's just too much we don't know – why she's taking a part of the people she binds, how the magic is contained, and if getting your powers back means you also get back whatever else you lost. So ...' Even though I'd accepted the hard truth weeks ago, it still hurt to say it out loud. 'So I don't have a plan to break them, per se.'

'Which is nothing to be ashamed of,' Lyn muttered – kind of her, because I knew she'd hoped for more, after weeks of answering my feverish questions. 'Hordes of us have looked into it. There's just not that much we can do.'

'I know,' I said. 'I had to acknowledge that, too. So my suggestion would be to ask the experts.'

'The ...' She blinked and raised her head to glance at Creon, as if he'd laugh and confirm I was joking. 'What are you talking about? There are no experts when it comes to binding magic, that's the entire point.'

'It's divine magic, isn't it?' I said.

She gaped at me with wide amber eyes for a full two heartbeats. 'Em.'

'You want to go ask the *gods* for answers?' Nenya said sharply. 'Hell take us all. Raising the dead might be just a tad ambitious, Emelin.'

'It might be,' I said, willing my voice to stay calm, 'if raising the dead is actually what we're talking about. Agenor? Do you know ...'

'Good question,' he said bleakly. 'Excellent question, really. If I had the answer for you, I don't think we'd be sitting here.'

'You don't know what happened to them either? The gods, I mean?'

'No. I ...' He cursed. 'Well, Korok is most definitely dead and not coming back. But the others ... I couldn't tell you for the life of me.'

We were silent for a moment.

'You were there,' Tared said, those few words a glaring accusation. 'The day she killed him and cursed the entire continent with that gods-damned plague. Aren't you supposed to know what happened, of all people?'

'I know *some* of what happened.' Agenor closed his eyes; whether he was trying to better see his memories or rather to avoid them, I wasn't sure. 'Their plan, if I understood the shreds they told me afterwards correctly, was to use Korok's life force to steal the powers of the other gods, essentially. If everything had happened as intended, Achlys and Melinoë would have wielded the magic of four deities by the end of that day.'

Cas blurted out a curse. Around us, most faces had gone pale; only Creon somehow looked like he wasn't in the least surprised by the story, even though I knew this was as new to him as to anyone else.

I'd never heard any of it, either – but it did make sense, so much sense.

'And that didn't work out as hoped.'

'No,' Agenor said wryly. 'It was all rather experimental, you must understand. They planned it alone – as far as I'm aware, no one else knew of their schemes until the moment everything went to hell. I like to think ... well.'

Liked to think he'd have done something if he'd known. Instead, he'd stepped aside while the Mother killed the god he'd sworn to protect, while she destroyed a continent he'd loved, while she started yet another war just as she'd won his coveted peace.

I let that point go.

'Good to know,' I said, and I said it firmly enough to distract even Tared from the sneer I knew he'd been about to utter. 'Because that lends a lot of credibility to Sophronia's theory that the plague is linked to divine magic.'

'The plague is most certainly linked to divine magic,' Agenor said, rubbing his eyes. 'Achlys and Melinoë assumed the powers were drained from the gods but didn't attach to anything else. So instead, that magic just ...'

'Went rogue.'

'Yes.'

'Destroying all life in its path. Becoming what we know as the plague.'

He sighed. 'Yes.'

'But that means all we know for sure is that the gods lost – well, some of their magic,' I said, weighing my words with painstaking care. 'It need not be all of their powers, and there's no particular reason to assume they *died* from the impact.'

'No,' Beyla said quietly, 'but that's a weak basis for a rather dangerous undertaking, wouldn't you say?'

'There's more,' I said, waving that objection aside. 'I found a travel report from an alf who tried to fade into Orin's mountains to find more alf steel. Didn't get far before the plague magic started burning him, but he does mention seeing two white wolves guarding the place.'

Agenor's breath caught. 'Oh, hell. Orin.'

'Yes. There are sightings of Zera's doves, too. Not that those are entirely reliable, because of course everyone would like to be blessed with lifelong love and happiness, but I found a few cases with multiple eyewitnesses, and in those cases the receivers of the blessings *do* appear to have lived surprisingly long and happy lives. Sailors sailing close to the Elderburg coast say they hear strange voices singing at night, which ...'

'Sailors' tales,' Nenya said sharply.

'What exactly are they supposedly singing?' Agenor said.

'Songs everyone on board is able to understand, even if they speak different languages. Which sounds like magic to me.'

He cursed again. 'Inika. Hell below. I had no idea.'

'So you agree it's possible?' It took every last shred of willpower to not shout the words, to not grab him by the shoulders of his frustratingly well-tailored blue shirt and shake him until he gave the answer I needed. 'That they're still alive?'

'I suppose so,' he said, still sounding dazed, 'but that doesn't mean you can just ...'

'Go look for them?'

'*Em*,' Lyn said.

'What?' I fell back into my chair. My heartbeat was a dizzying rattle against my ribs. 'If anyone knows how to solve this mess, it's the gods. For all we know, they'd be happy to receive a visit after all these years.'

'The continent is inaccessible,' Tared reminded me, his smile not as natural as usual. 'You'll have a hard time finding any gods if the plague burns your skin off your face before you take the first step.'

'But we just concluded the plague is divine magic.' I turned to Lyn. 'And according to the *Mage's Compendium* and that mouldy history of the pre-divine world you lent me, the only magic that could oppose the magic of the gods is ...'

She stiffened. 'Demon magic.'

Had Creon drawn a knife and killed them all on the spot, they couldn't have gone any quieter.

'So,' I hurried on, before they could regain their senses and bring up wise yet impractical concerns such as the point that I had not the faintest idea what I was doing. 'The plan is quite simple, really. Fly to the continent. Use demon magic to keep the plague at bay while we look for the gods. Find them and ask a few questions. Get rid of the bindings. Victory and eternal happiness for all, the end. Any questions?'

I hadn't expected Tared to be the first to speak, but he leaned forward so suddenly I jolted back. He settled his elbows on the edge of the map inlaid in the table surface as he slowly said, 'Who exactly did you have in mind with that *we* you're throwing around, Em?'

'Creon and me?' I said, praying he wouldn't make an issue of that if I looked hard enough like there was no issue to be made. 'I didn't think you could afford to send too many people from the Underground.'

'Well, time to think again.' His eyes shot to Creon, who'd gone dangerously, glacially quiet – like a sheet of ice hiding a brimming volcano. 'You're not going to—'

'Travel around with him alone?' I finished with a sharp chuckle. 'What do you think he'll do – look at my ankles?'

Naxi laughed out loud, the sound of it high and melodious. She was the only one still capable of laughing. Beyla and Nenya perched on the edges of their chairs, glaring; Cas and Valeska exchanged nervous looks; Agenor seemed in full agreement with Tared for once in his life.

Lyn's glance at me was an apology as she said, 'Ankles aside, we have to think about the public look of it, Em.'

'What public look?' I said, scoffing. 'I doubt we'll run into any gossiping hordes in the middle of plague land.'

'Your absence will be noticed in the Underground,' Nenya said. Her voice was as stiff as her shoulders. 'You shouldn't expect the likes of Gish and Valdora to stay quiet about that.'

'Exactly,' Lyn said, burying her hands in her red hair, 'and that will be a perfect confirmation of the Mother's version of events. Clearly the Alliance doesn't have any control over Creon after all! Or over Em, for that matter! So why should anyone trust any of our plans to … Hell, I can *hear* them say it already.'

'So what are you suggesting?' My grip on my voice was abandoning me. All those arguments and counter-arguments, magical necessity and calculated risks, and now they were going to stop me because of the one complication I hadn't thought about – the gods-damned public opinion? 'That we take a bloody chaperone with us?'

'I could come?' Naxi suggested, looking up with bouncing blonde curls.

We all blinked at her.

'That's not so odd, is it?' She sent me a dazzling smile. 'If you need demons to handle the plague, having another one around can't hurt. Creon might need to sleep every now and then. I promise I won't look at your ankles if I can help it.'

Lyn smothered a bout of nervous laughter in her palm. Creon's grin was wry but grateful, a clear sign he too had heard the words between the lines – *I won't get in the way of that affair of yours.*

'Well,' I said weakly. Time for quick decisions, before anyone else could start making suggestions – before Tared or Agenor could start making suggestions. Taking Naxi along wasn't what I'd had in mind, but it could have been much, much worse. Hell, it could have been a full company of fellow travellers. 'That sounds like a pretty sensible suggestion? Would you all agree with the plan if the three of us were to go?'

'Aren't you planning to bring any alves along?' Beyla said.

Oh, fuck.

'Not a bad point,' Nenya said, folding her arms. 'If you must venture into uncharted danger, you should be able to get out fast. And it would be good to make sure we can return there in future, if necessary.'

'Yes,' I tried, 'but—'

'I can make time,' Beyla cut in, and there was a gleam in her eyes I didn't see often – a hint of hunger at the thought of new horizons to uncover. 'As long as we confirm beforehand that the demons are indeed able to keep the plague at bay, I don't mind accompanying you.'

Which would make everything significantly more complicated – starting with hiding a secret relationship twenty-four hours a day with not a shred of privacy around. Then again, if the prize was a broken binding – if the prize was Creon's voice and the fertility of every magical female in the world ...

A few weeks at most. How hard could that be?

'Would that make you any happier?' I said to Tared, who was still looking particularly unhappy about every word spoken.

'None of this is even close to safe,' he said, and his glower at Creon left no doubt whom he blamed for all this danger. 'Wouldn't it be better if someone else went after those gods and bindings, if you insist someone has to look into the matter?'

Someone else wouldn't prioritise Creon's voice. Hell, they would prioritise everything *except* Creon's voice. 'I don't think it makes a lot of sense to send anyone else.'

He raised an eyebrow.

'I'm the only unbound mage you have,' I said, a sentence that seemed a tired cliché already. 'I'm not sure if it's possible for a bound person to break a binding. It sounds like trying to change colour with colour magic – a very bad idea. Why would you waste a risky journey on someone who may not even be able to help us?'

Agenor's muffled curse suggested my reasoning was more sound than I'd dared hope when I came up with it in the dead of night two weeks ago.

Tared started, 'But—'

'Tared,' I said, rolling my eyes. 'Weren't you of the opinion that no one should be telling a grown woman where she is and isn't allowed to go?'

He didn't smile – didn't even pretend to smile. 'I'm not allowing or forbidding you anything, but *someone* needs to think about your wellbeing here, and—'

Creon's hand snapped back to his notebook. Perfectly contained motions, every twitch of his muscles calculated, and yet the movements of his pencil over the parchment gave the impression he'd rather be drawing the same shapes in blood. *If you don't trust me to keep her safe, just say so.*

'You know what?' Lyn said hastily, because it was clear to every single soul present that Tared was about to say just that, and likely worse, too. 'This is not a decision we need to make right now. Cas, tell the elders that Agenor would like to have a word with them. Nenya, please let us know how we can help with Bakaru. Valeska, keep the nymphs as calm as you can until we know if Em has time and what we'll do about these bloody bindings. Thank you all for your input, and Em' – there was a flicker of fire in her voice that wouldn't brook a negative answer – 'could we have a word?'

CHAPTER 3

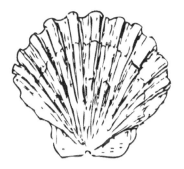

BEYLA FADED CAS, NENYA, and Valeska out for their respective diplomatic missions. Naxi threw one look at Tared, then jumped from her chair and burst into a rattling monologue on new magic and uncharted lands and how doubtlessly there were books to be read and why didn't Creon just come with her so they could look at this as demons together?

The demon in question rose from his seat with an amused quirk of his eyebrows – *as demons together*, that look said, *who in hell do you think you're fooling?*

Naxi gave him a sharp-toothed grin. 'Coming?'

With a quiet chuckle, Creon turned back to me, hesitating so briefly it wouldn't have been noticeable if not for that impossible fae grace I was used to.

If you need any help burying the bodies, he signed, nodding at Tared and Agenor, *let me know.*

I huffed a laugh. 'Will do.'

He sent Lyn a half-smile, ignored the other two entirely, and allowed Naxi to drag him out by his wrist as she chattered loudly and excitedly about a story her father's demon friends had once told her about the continent. The heavy oakwood door smothered the sound of her voice as soon as it fell shut, leaving the Wanderer's Wing soaking in a nervous bath of silence.

I turned back to the others. Lyn perched on the edge of her chair. Tared had slouched forward with his elbows on the table and his face in his hands. Agenor was peering at the rune-inscribed door through which Creon had just vanished; he didn't seem to notice Oleander venturing down into his lap and then onto what had been Beyla's seat.

'Forgive me the question,' he said before I could speak, his frown at the door deepening, 'but there isn't anything between those two, is there?'

I choked on my own breath. 'Between Creon and *Naxi?*'

Agenor blinked at me. Perhaps my voice had shot up a little too shrilly.

'I'm quite sure,' Lyn said, lips trembling in what I suspected was a hysterical giggle about to break through, 'there is nothing of the sort going on between Creon and Naxi, Agenor. Her interests lie elsewhere.'

'And even Naxi has *some* moral compass,' Tared muttered under his breath.

My heart skipped a beat.

'Tared,' Lyn hissed, laughter evaporating in the blink of an eye. 'For fuck's sake. You've voiced that opinion often enough, don't you think?'

'Well, it's hardly inaccurate,' Agenor said, still looking mildly bemused. 'But I'm reassured on Naxi's behalf, in any case.'

I didn't dare to speak. I barely dared to breathe for fear I'd find flames blazing from my lungs. Only Lyn seemed to notice, her gaze a silent plea for me to hold myself back.

On the other side of the table, Agenor blissfully continued, 'Do you want me here to discuss the bindings, or would you prefer for me to vanish?

'Don't worry about it,' Tared said sourly as he shoved back his chair, rose to his feet, and sauntered to the high windows with his hands deep in his pockets. 'I have the odd feeling we might be in agreement for once. Em—'

'You really think he'd kill me?' I managed to force out, the politest thing I could find it in myself to utter. 'After the way he saved my life at the Golden Court, you still think he'd sit by and let the plague burn me to death?'

'No.' Tared settled himself on the windowsill, the flickers of light around him intensifying in the near-daylight of the fields. 'He'll protect you adequately enough from everything else, I don't necessarily doubt that.'

Oh, hell. I glanced at Lyn, who looked tiny and torn, and forced myself to say, 'You're worried about protecting me from *him*?'

Tared shrugged. 'Someone needs to do it.'

'And you don't believe I could do it?'

He didn't respond to that.

Agenor was busying himself with the cuffs of his sleeves, his jaw harder than usual, even though the nimble motions of his fingers looked as calm as ever. His silence had the air of tacit agreement. Lyn's eyes shot back and forth between the three of us as she worried her bottom lip, looking frantically for a way out of this conversation.

Save me. From *Creon*.

I sunk back into my chair and tried to see what Tared saw – what Agenor saw. A twenty-one-year-old near-human, considering herself a friend of the male who didn't do friendship or affection, who could barely bring himself to cooperate with his closest allies when his life depended on it. A male showing them nothing but haughty arrogance, not a trace of the vulnerability I knew from him, and who appeared, for some reason, to be making an effort to charm me.

I had hoped, in these past months of tense mutual tolerance, that him being pleasant to me might slowly convince the rest of the world that he may not be all rotten at heart. Only now did I realise it may well have convinced them of something far worse: that he *was* rotten at heart and had an agenda when it came to me.

And that the presence of sensible family members was all that had kept me from throwing myself at him like the innocent young girl they assumed me to be.

It wasn't just the public opinion carving those lines of concern around Tared's lips. It was the fear that I would, unexperienced and starry-eyed, give in to Creon's ruthless games the moment we were left alone for a few days too long.

Gods help me.

'I do think,' Lyn finally said, 'that the two of you might be underestimating Em a little.'

Underestimating both my common sense and my ability to hide a full-fledged relationship from them for months – but it would be hard to convince them of the first point without revealing the latter, and telling them about my nights in Creon's bed would not improve anyone's eagerness to send us out into the wilderness alone. By the look on Agenor's face, he'd sooner drag me off to the Golden Court to separate me from the Silent Death's wiles.

'I'm touched you're all so concerned about my unspoiled innocence,' I said testily, 'but I can assure you this is nothing but a matter of strategy to me. I'm not looking for an occasion to worm my way into his bed, and it's frankly a little insulting that you—'

'No insult intended,' Tared said, resting his head against the window frame. 'Not to you, that is.'

I snorted. 'But you're convinced he must have lecherous intentions? Odd as it may seem to *some* of you, not every fae male in the world is determined to spring himself on any young woman crossing his path.'

'That,' Agenor said icily, 'is below the belt.'

Lyn sniggered, a sound containing little mercy. Tared allowed himself a quick grin but said, 'The more you try to convince me of his good intentions, the more you worry me, Em. You're not usually that dewy-eyed about people.'

'Well, fine – I'll be on guard and make sure not to get myself drawn into any cruel games with my heart. Or whatever other part of me. Happy?'

Agenor winced. 'That still leaves the matter of the rather relevant public opinion.'

'And why do I have to be responsible for the public opinion?' My voice rose; I swung a hand at Lyn, who looked far too inclined to agree with him. 'Why can't you go visit those bloody nymphs and tell them you're merely using Creon for his powers and that you wouldn't dream of letting him anywhere near a throne? Why can't the Council issue an official statement that our aim is to disband the entire empire, meaning it doesn't even *matter* to the other magical peoples who ends up ruling the fae? Why—'

'In the end,' Agenor said, closing his eyes, 'I've found war is all about symbols.'

'I'm not a *symbol*,' I snapped.

'You're an unbound mage.'

'I'm a living, breathing individual. Currently a rather furious individual.'

'I'm grateful for the warning,' he said dryly, looking up. 'Em, I know none of this is pleasant, but winning the right hearts is half of the battle, and people are going to be looking at what you do whether you want them to or not. You blinded the Mother. That's a poor start if you hoped to fade into obscurity, I'm afraid.'

Lyn nodded with a regretful plea in her eyes.

'Especially if the Mother herself seems determined to put you in the public eye,' Tared said grimly. 'Hiding you would only make it seem like we agree with her.'

I wished that didn't sound so gods-damned reasonable. 'But—'

'The unpleasant truth is we're fighting an uphill battle,' Agenor said, rubbing the bridge of his nose. 'It's hard to turn people into warriors after they've been ground down for over a century – for which I have myself to blame, I suppose – and it's even harder when they all know the odds aren't in our favour. They need *something* upon which to base their hope, and we don't have much to offer them except the pleasant surprise of a powerful unbound mage.'

'We have a couple of powerful fae lords,' I muttered, hearing the weakness the moment the words poured over my lips.

'Traitors make for poor symbols to rally behind.' Tared scoffed sourly. 'Especially traitors who were still burning children alive last year.'

'But—'

'Em.' He sucked in a breath. 'I'm not going to pretend this is fun. We all know it isn't. Hiding below the earth for a century wasn't fun either, if you want to know. Slowly going extinct at the edges of the empire hasn't been fun for anyone in the world above. Creon apparently wasn't enjoying himself either, dicing nymph queens into bite-sized pieces. Is visiting a few villages and not idolising any fae assassins in public too much of a sacrifice to ask for?'

Oh, fuck.

I parted my lips, but the words wouldn't come. At the other side of the table, Lyn looked close to tears – but she didn't disagree, and I knew she mostly wished he'd found a kinder way to put it.

Agenor was visibly wondering how I hadn't broken Tared's nose yet. Someone really should have told my poor father about the many advantages of honesty and directness.

'It's not that I don't get that,' I said and wished my voice hadn't come out so choked. There was no use in pleading. Weeks of work wouldn't mean much to them – not after centuries of worse. 'But I do think we should get rid of those bindings, and I'd hate for the public opinion to push us into choices that may make us lose the war in the end.'

Tared muttered a curse. 'You never heard me say we shouldn't get rid of the bindings.'

'But then ...'

'There might be ways to make it possible,' Lyn said, fiddling with her curls as she pulled her knees to her chest. Her high, stiff-backed chair dwarfed her little figure. 'If you wouldn't mind pretending it wasn't your idea, Em ...'

I pulled a face. 'More attention is the last thing I need. We can blame you.'

'I figured I would be a sensible candidate,' she said with a wry smile. 'We could tell the world I stumbled upon the matter and that Tared and I decided to go after it. Nobody will be suspicious about us undertaking some new reckless mission.'

Tared chuckled, but it didn't sound quite convinced.

'And then we tell the Council we need you because you're an unbound mage, we need Creon and Naxi because they're demons, and we want Beyla there because she's a wanderer and she might quietly poison Tared if we deny her the opportunity to see the continent.' She spread her arms, like a little magician whose charming assistant has once again stepped out of a box alive. 'That won't alarm anyone, will it?'

'It will take time, though,' Agenor said with a glance at Oleander, who was leisurely exploring the nooks and crannies of the room. 'Achlys and Melinoë aren't going to wait forever. Keeping those ships around the Golden Court is an expensive endeavour – we might have a month before they attack in all earnestness, but it won't be any longer, and it might be as little as a week.'

Lyn shrugged. 'We'll have to make it a short trip, then. Ten days? If we haven't found anything by that time, we'll have more urgent things to worry about.'

Ten days. I felt myself go light-headed. An entire damn continent, more land than I'd ever seen in my life – and we were supposed to find any gods in hiding within *ten days*?

'I suppose that would work,' Tared admitted with obvious aversion, 'but ...'

'But?' Lyn said brusquely.

He swore under his breath. 'You really want to do this?'

'Well, yes, unless you tell me what's *truly* bothering you.' She tilted her head at him, amber eyes sparkling with both concern and impatience. 'You're dithering. Why?'

'Do you ...' He glanced at Agenor, then groaned and swung his legs from the windowsill, turning to face her fully. 'Do you really think it's a good idea for me to let my life depend on Creon for ten full days in plague land, Lyn?'

'He wouldn't *kill* you,' I said sharply. 'He's had more than enough opportunity to do so, if he'd been planning to—'

'I'm not saying he's actively planning to kill me,' Tared cut in. 'But if he's the only thing between me and plague magic, how easy would it be for him to just ... slip?'

'Tared ...' Lyn started.

'You said that before,' Agenor said, studying Tared with narrowed green-gold eyes. 'That there would be no risk of him killing anyone else as long as he didn't kill you. Why exactly are you so convinced he wants you dead, if I may ask?'

Tared shrugged. 'Long and unpleasant story.'

'Very informative,' Agenor said, wiping an imaginary fleck of dust off his shirt. 'I'm afraid you're speaking in riddles to me. There isn't much I dare to assume when it comes to Creon, but unless I'm *terribly* mistaken, I'd swear he's quite determined to keep you alive.'

'I'm afraid you must be terribly mistaken,' Tared said coldly. 'You have no—'

'If he wanted you dead,' Agenor interrupted, his words more clipped, 'he could just have kept his voice, don't you think?'

We stared at him.

He blinked, taken aback. 'You don't know that story? Of how they bound him?'

Lyn and Tared whipped around to me as if by command, her eyes wide, his eyes narrowed, the unspoken questions on their faces oddly identical.

'He ...' I turned to Agenor, words once again abandoning me – Creon's *voice*? What in hell did his voice have to do with any of this? 'He said the Mother had him confined in alf steel because she was suspicious of his not slaughtering everyone in his path when he allegedly escaped the Alliance. And that she gave him the choice to either die or let her bind him. Is that ... is that not what happened?'

'It is what happened,' Agenor said slowly. 'Give or take a few details.'

'Could you be a little more specific?' Tared snapped.

'They questioned him.' A deep breath. 'Far longer than I thought necessary, to be honest. His story was convincing enough – he wasn't going to waste his time murdering lowly worms when he just wanted to go home and so on and so forth. The usual language. We were all surprised Achlys and Melinoë didn't set him free after a few minutes.'

I swallowed. On the other side of the table, Lyn gaped at Agenor, her eyes round as saucers.

'But they finally seemed satisfied,' he continued, sounding tired, 'and told him they would let him go ... but only after they'd disposed of their prisoners.'

Lyn's breath caught.

They were keeping us captive after the battle, she'd told me on the beach of Faewood. I stole a glance at Tared and found him frozen on the edge of the windowsill, his slender fingers clawing into his palms. *We expected her to kill us.*

'And that,' Agenor said, his deep voice a distant echo now, 'was when he broke.'

I didn't dare to breathe.

'I've seen him beg exactly once in my life. That afternoon. It was about as unnerving as every moment of that gods-damned battle put together.' He clenched his jaw, gaze resting on Lyn. 'I don't know what you did to him, but he wouldn't let them kill you – told them he didn't care where you went or what you'd do with your life, but that he couldn't stand to have you die after the way you kept him alive all those months.'

Lyn looked about to faint. 'And yet the Mother didn't kill him on the spot?'

'They asked how they would ever be able to trust him again. To which he responded that they could bind him.'

'No,' she whispered.

'They'd wanted that for decades. So they took the bait, made a bargain. The binding of his magic in exchange for' – a deep breath – 'no bodily harm or captivity for the individuals of his choosing for a year and a day after the battle. He bargained for five names.'

'Who?' Tared bit out, and it was not a question.

'Nenkhet. Anaxia. Cas. Lyn.' Agenor turned to face the window, his pursed lips something close to an apology. 'And you.'

The horror on Tared's face was mirrored in Lyn's small wail of distress.

I stared at Agenor with unseeing eyes, my thoughts spinning out of control. *Five names.* Almost all of the group that had gathered around the table mere minutes ago. The same people who'd glowered and glared at Creon and blamed him for the Mother's unflattering propaganda.

They would have been dead.

If he hadn't sacrificed his magic and his voice, hadn't given up on his plan to kill his mother right then and right there – they'd never have fought another battle at all.

Zera help me. Why hadn't he *told* me?

'So,' Agenor said, sinking against the backrest of his chair without releasing Tared from his gaze, wings flattening uncomfortably against the wood. 'Whatever occurred between the two of you, if he'd wanted to passively kill you—'

Tared vanished mid-sentence.

Lyn cried out his name a moment too late, jumping from her chair as if that would make him reappear in that empty windowsill. He stayed away. Whirling around, she flung her hands up in the air and bit out a heartfelt, '*Fuck*'.

'Ah,' Agenor said, sounding faintly amused. 'Alf honour, I suppose?'

'Bloody life debts,' Lyn snapped, glaring at the window and then at him. 'Owing Creon isn't going to soften his feelings *at* all. Inika damn us all, as if it wasn't complex enough yet – why in the world didn't Creon just tell us any of this?'

I closed my eyes as my thoughts shaped their own answers. For the same reason he didn't tell anyone about the demon powers soothing his victims' pain. The same reason he hadn't looked for any way of communicating in a hundred and thirty years – suffering in silence was vastly preferable to trying, needing, and failing.

My heart ached, a stifling, chafing pain.

'How much does it change?' Agenor was saying. 'I'm admittedly not sure how you feel about this entire plan, but as long as the Council agrees ...'

'I'll try to convince everyone,' Lyn muttered, and when I looked up, she was staring at me so apologetically I could barely stand it. 'You shouldn't expect Tared or any of the others to agree to more than ten days, though. Honestly, I don't even know if I'd agree to more than that, considering that we—'

'—have more to do,' I finished flatly. 'Yes. Do we at least have any alves who can bring us near the continent quickly, if we only have so little time?'

'Oh.' She blinked owlishly at me, then grinned, a mirthless, warmthless grin. 'Don't worry about that. The exit is above the central hall.'

'The ... what?'

'Lots of stairs, though,' she added, slipping past the table towards the door. 'I recommend finding someone with wings to fly you up. Anything else? Because if not, I should go have a word with Tared.'

'We're ...' I let out a baffled laugh. 'Good gods. We're below the continent right now?'

'Yes. Straight below Lyckfort.' She turned at the door, reaching up for the handle. 'I'll see you in a bit. Are you staying for dinner, Agenor?'

He snapped his eyes down from the ceiling, shaking his head as if he'd momentarily forgotten where we were. 'Beg your pardon?'

'Dinner,' she repeated dryly. 'Invitation.'

'Oh. I probably shouldn't. They need me at the castle.' Again he sent that wistful glance up at the ceiling, at the world above us that suddenly had a name – Lyckfort. His voice sounded oddly faint as he added, 'But keep me informed, if you will.'

'Will do,' she said. 'Later, Em.'

She slipped out without waiting for our response.

When I turned around, Agenor had slumped into his chair, rubbing his temple with unusual firmness. His smile was a watery creation, not enough by far to compensate for the brand new lines around his lips.

I wanted to go look for Creon. Wanted to ask questions and hold him and tell him he was an idiot, but also *my* idiot, and coincidentally the bravest one I'd had the honour of knowing in my life. But Creon was probably practicing demon magic with Naxi in gods-knew-what deserted corner of the Underground, and I didn't see the male supposed to be my father for more than a few hours every two weeks.

And something about Lyn's last revelation seemed to have shaken him more badly than even my mad plan to go tramping across a cursed continent in search of gods who might be dead.

'You've been there?' I said slowly, making my guess. 'In Lyckfort?'

'Yes.' He sighed and rose from his chair, either avoiding my eyes or looking for Oleander between the bookcases. 'It used to be a beautiful city.'

Used to be. There was an unbearable melancholy to those words – all the places he'd visited and never seen again during his lifetime, all the people he'd known and lost.

Something about my father's sadness left me quite defenceless. Just as all those months ago, when I'd invited him to my birthday without thinking that plan through for a second, I heard myself speak before I had fully considered the words. 'Would you like to come along?'

He stiffened. 'To the continent?'

'Seems everyone and their grandma is joining the trip anyway,' I said wryly.

He chuckled as he knelt at the nearest book aisle, glancing around for a glimpse of black scales. 'I'm afraid they can't do without me for days at the Golden Court.'

'You don't have to stay for ten days.' I stood up as well, prudently scanning the floor below my feet for snakes. 'Just to Lyckfort. I doubt anyone will make a fuss if we tell them you're there to ... help familiarise us with the terrain? How does that sound?'

'Good gods, Em,' he said, letting out a laugh. 'You're so very much your mother's daughter at times.'

Thankfully Oleander appeared at that moment; the emergence of her small head between two piles of half-rotting travellers' notebooks saved me from having to figure out an answer. By the time Agenor stood again, his snake back around his shoulders, we were both ready to pretend he'd never spoken those loaded words at all.

Your mother's daughter, even though I'd never met her in my life – but perhaps a human living among fae wouldn't be so different from a half fae living among humans.

'Are you coming to take a look at the fae quarters with me?' Agenor said.

I couldn't think of a better way to fill the time, so I followed him into the maze of Inika's quarter, which was deserted as usual. After some subtle nudging from the group around Lyn and Tared, the Council had quickly decided that the Golden Court force should be housed here if the castle had to be evacuated; not only were there hardly any phoenixes to fill the many homes, but it was farthest from the alves in Orin's quarter as well.

We made a round of the half-furnished rooms, noting where essentials were missing and whether they could be brought from the Golden Court. Within an hour and a half, we were done, finding ourselves and our handfuls of lists in the broad corridor separating Zera's quarter from Inika's quarter. Oleander was restless. I couldn't tell if it had rubbed off on Agenor or if it was his impatience that caused her fidgeting around his shoulders, but whoever was affecting whom, he didn't seem in a mood to stick around for much longer.

Back to work, as always. Back to his plans and responsibilities.

'Well,' I said, bracing myself against the unreasonable spark of disappointment. In an hour and a half of directionless chatting, he hadn't even confirmed he would come to Lyckfort. 'In that case, I suppose I'll see—'

'Good thinking,' he interrupted me, blurting it out like a murder confession, stumbling over those words for which no rules or protocols existed. Buttoned-up and stiff-shouldered, he wore his unease like an ill-fitting shirt. 'On the bindings, I mean. Really a very interesting plan ... if it works ... if you manage to find them somehow ...'

His voice drifted off, leaving a trail of unspoken yet spectacular implications behind.

'Oh,' I said, unable to come up with anything else.

He cleared his throat. 'If there's anything I can do to help out ...'

'It's barely a plan,' I muttered, suddenly painfully aware of the gaping holes in the suggestions I'd managed to present with such unfathomable confidence. The disappointment had been easy to take. This searing bolt of hopeful pride, mingled with a twinge of something close to shame, was a far greater struggle for my pounding heart to contain. 'There's so much we still need to figure out.'

'Is there?' He finally met my gaze, tilting his head ever so slightly. Not scepticism. Rather ... an invitation. 'It sounds to me like you have most of the basics in place.'

To him. To Lord Agenor himself, who planned everything and had been doing so for more than a thousand years.

I raised my chin slightly, steeling myself. 'Which parts are missing, do you feel?'

There was a flicker of approval in his eyes, or perhaps it was just relief at this safer ground below our feet. Business and strategy – that we could do, even if playing father and daughter went beyond our capabilities most of the time.

'You agree with the larger company Lyn suggested?'

'I suppose it'll make us less flexible,' I said slowly, 'but at least they're all people I trust, and it's much better than not going at all. So we can go with that group. We just need a clear destination to make up for the loss of mobility and the time constraints.'

'Yes.' He pursed his lips, and somehow he still seemed to be smiling. 'So what is your destination?'

'You assume I have one?'

This time it really was a smile, small but unmistakable. 'Am I wrong?'

I opened my mouth, then burst out laughing. 'Oh, hell. Quietly making plans was far easier when you insisted on underestimating me.'

'My heartfelt apologies for the inconvenience,' he said dryly. 'But it's hard to imagine you going to the hassle of reading Sophronia, of all people, without spending a moment's thought on who exactly you'd like to find once you arrive on the continent.'

'Of course I thought about it.' I glanced at the walls behind him – Zera's flowers and Inika's flames. How apt. 'But I'm not sure – I want to be careful. I suppose everyone down here would like to go look for their own god, and we really don't need any theological discussions when we're already pressed for time.'

He nodded slowly. 'Wise.'

'Thanks.' My cheeks were warming. Damn it. 'But ... well, Etele went mad, so I doubt she'd be of any help, even if she didn't kill Creon on the spot. And according to the alves, Orin was already a recluse before the plague. Looking for a god who doesn't want to be found sounds like a terrible idea, even though he is probably pleasant enough.'

'I always found him very pleasant company,' Agenor said, 'but yes, it could take weeks to find him even at the height of his power. I agree.'

'So that leaves Inika and Zera.'

'Yes.'

'And I ...' I hesitated. 'I haven't found any reasons to favour one over the other, really. It seems neither of them is stark mad or malicious.'

'They never were, at least.' His eyes had that gleam of distant memories, looking back into a time far before even the wildest of my imaginings. 'Inika was more impulsive and more short-tempered. That could be an advantage as well as a disadvantage. Zera was gentler, but she's less likely to get involved in anything she can't oversee. She was the last to choose sides in the War of the Gods.'

'So what would you suggest?'

He raked a hand through his hair, considering that. 'What suggestion would you prefer to get?'

I let out a laugh. 'Zera.'

'Why?'

'Because ...' I glanced over my shoulder. No one within hearing distance. 'Honestly, there's no grand strategical logic behind it. The ancestors of Cathra's humans lived in one of Zera's cities before the plague hit. I prayed to her all my life. I'd feel like a hypocrite begging for favours from anyone else.'

He gave a single, agonisingly slow nod.

'But if you think I should look for Inika instead,' I hurried to add, my words tangling up on my tongue, 'then of course—'

'I'm not thinking anything.'

Oleander hissed sceptically.

'That is ...' He grimaced at the snake. 'Fine, I'm thinking a couple of things. None of them negative. If Zera is alive, if she's still like she was a millennium ago, a personal connection is probably the best argument you can bring to her table. She is, after all, a goddess of—'

'Love,' I finished. 'And ... what's the opposite? Hate?'

'Love and grief,' he muttered, looking away. 'Although she insisted they were the same thing.'

His right hand had clenched into a fist. I couldn't help glancing down at the small black bargain mark that glistened on the inside of his wrist – a sign of life as reassuring as an executioner's axe about to drop.

'I see,' I managed.

'So.' He cleared his throat, pulling himself together with a shake of his head. 'You could aim for the temple in Zera's woods. It would be a sensible place to start looking, and it's relatively close to Lyckfort, too. If anyone gives you trouble over that decision ...' A slight tremble at the corners of his lips. 'Send them to me. I'll give my helpful and fully unbiased expert opinion.'

I snorted. 'How very fae.'

'Use it to your best advantage,' he said dryly, stepping back. 'I need to go. I'm sorry I can't be around for longer, but keep me informed if there's anything else I can do. And ... Em?'

'Yes?'

'You ...' He pressed his lips into a brief line. 'You were serious? About Lyckfort?'

I blinked. 'I'm not *that* cruel.'

'No,' he admitted wryly. 'I'm just ruined by centuries of life at the Crimson Court. Let me know when you're leaving. I'll try to be there.'

CHAPTER 4

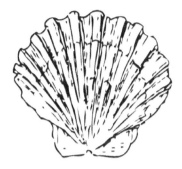

I FOUND CREON LOUNGING in one of the armchairs in the corner of his bedroom, eyes fixed on a sheet of parchment in his hand, a small frown drawing lines between his brows. Some thorny question about the movements of constellations, probably – but before I could steal a glance at his notes and confirm that suspicion, he shoved the parchment into the nearest pile of books without granting it another look.

And?

'Tared and Agenor,' I said, throwing myself into the chair by his side with a dramatic groan, 'are concerned about my unspoiled innocence and the terrible influence some savage brute like you may have on my pure and uncorrupted mind. Apparently they've gotten the idea I might be susceptible to – brace yourself – *seduction.*'

His scarred eyebrow slowly climbed to an eloquent position halfway up his forehead. *The gods know where they picked up that impossible notion.*

A bitter laugh escaped me. 'I should have followed your strategy and glared haughtily at you whenever they're around. No one seems to have considered you might be interested in anything except cruel tricks.'

Of course not. His wings flared dangerously as he sat straighter, resting his left elbow on his thigh. *Everyone knows demons don't feel love or empathy.* There was an unpleasant twitch around the corners of his lips.

'Is that even true?' I said.

For fullblood demons, yes. Halfbloods ... He shrugged. *It varies. Naxi feels very little empathy. I'm on the more troublesome side of the scale.*

The more I learned about Naxi, the more frightening she became. The more I wondered what in hell had happened between her and Thysandra, too. 'In any case, I told them I wasn't looking for a way into your bed, which I suppose is technically true.'

There was no humour to his laugh. *You didn't tell them the full story?*

'What? Gods, no.' I blinked at him. 'You don't think they'd ever let me leave with you if they had any idea, do you? Agenor would rather lock me in a tower.'

I wish him good luck, Creon signed dryly. *I think he'd lose a tower.*

I wasn't in the mood to laugh or to enjoy his faith in my abilities to ruin whatever understanding I'd managed to foster between myself and my father. 'It would still be terribly inconvenient. This is really not the moment to get delayed.'

He granted me that point with a nod and a sigh.

'So,' I said, sinking sideways into the padded softness of the chair to keep my eyes on him. 'Lyn is going to present it to the rest of the world as a plan she came up with and for which she just happens to need our magic. Which Tared didn't want to agree with, but ...'

The words dried on my tongue. *But your voice. Your binding.*

Those almond eyes of his narrowed, a question brimming in their depths as he studied the way my lips struggled for the right thing to say. He was close enough for me to distinguish every long eyelash, every stray hair escaping the silken smoothness of his locks. A breathtakingly familiar vision, and yet ...

How many more secrets still hid behind that façade – how many horrors, how many sacrifices that I would never know about?

'Agenor ...' I swallowed. 'Agenor told us why the Mother bound you.'

He stiffened for barely an eyeblink.

Then he sank back into his chair, those full, sensual lips a hard line, and signed, *With names?*

I nodded.

I see. His shoulders didn't loosen. *That explains something.*

What did it explain – had he felt Tared fade into the family home distraught and furious? I shoved that question onto the fast-growing pile of matters for later and instead said, 'Why didn't you tell any of them?'

Why would I have told them? The gestures came too fast now.

'They were convinced you ran off during the battle and never spent another thought on them! If they'd known you *did* save their lives ...'

Too little, too late. He shrugged – a stiff shrug, nothing like the usual feline grace. *There would have been no need to save them if I'd scraped myself together a few hours sooner, and they're not going to forget about that because I got sentimental and abandoned my plan to end the Mother over a handful of lives.*

'Their lives,' I pointed out.

Does it matter? I burned some of their allies alive, Em. They won't like me anyway, and I fail to see how making myself vulnerable to their opinions will improve anything.

'They could be friends,' I said feebly. 'I've found that quite an improvement, having friends.'

He hesitated, then rose, shaking his wings with a swift roll of his shoulders as he stalked to the desk on the other side of the room. Away from me. Away from my emotions as they churned against the new boundary of his mental shields, tearing at his self-control. I tucked my legs below my body to keep myself from following him; my eyes clung to his every movement as he sank down on the desk chair, drew in a deep breath, and signed, *You need to understand that I lived for three and a half centuries trusting no one but myself, Em.*

A prickle of nervousness danced up my spine. It wasn't that I'd forgotten his age. It was just that everyone else in the Underground was even older, and next to a father who'd lived for twelve centuries, next to the five-hundred-and-something years of Lyn and Tared, at times it almost seemed Crèon and I were of a similar age.

An age that was not so much expressed in numbers, but rather in how little we knew what we were doing here. No-clue-years-old.

'That's all fine and good,' I said, 'but you did figure out how to trust me.'

A grin swept over his face. *You quite forced me to.*

'So why can't I force you to trust a few more people?' I rubbed my palms over my face and added, 'It would make this trip significantly easier if you didn't have to play the invulnerable fae prince every minute of the day.'

You ... He didn't look like an invulnerable fae prince now, magic and wings and pointed ears be damned. Still that same lean, muscular body, still that gorgeous, sharp-edged face that had once made me think of him as an overly favourable portrait in the flesh – but I'd learned to see below those surface layers, and the tense lines around his lips and the erratic motions of his fingers weren't hard to read. *You really want us to go on that trip with half a household around.*

Yes. No. Maybe.

'Is there any reason *not* to take them along?' I said, throat dry.

Just the fact that you still insist on keeping secrets from them no matter how much you tell me you trust them. There was a biting exactness to his gestures. *Hiding this affair isn't going to get easier if we're forced to spend every single minute of the day with an audience. For what might be weeks.*

'Ten days at most,' I muttered, which was the weakest possible counter to the least important of his arguments. 'We should be able to hide this for ten days, shouldn't we?'

Shields or not, the piercing weight of his gaze caught me like a deer in a trap. *Because you want to or because they want you to?*

I didn't even know the answer to that question anymore – could no longer distinguish between obligations and wishes, needs and duties, in this tangle of conflicting opinions. Did they want me to? Yes, but not for the sake of hiding me, not for the sake of propriety or parental expectations. Just for the sake of winning a war, and wasn't that the main thing I strived for, too?

'I don't want to cause trouble.' I hated how that sentence echoed the first twenty years of my life. Why was I the one complicating everything again, when I'd come here to save them all? 'So much can go wrong already. If the people who know the Alliance best think I'd deter potential allies by going out with you alone, I don't want to risk that.'

Creon nodded, but there was little conviction to the gesture.

'Do you still think we should go just the two of us?'

I don't know. He averted his gaze, rubbed his forehead, and added, staring at the floor, *It's a risk whatever we do. We'll cause a stir if we sneak out together. Then again, if we go tramping around the continent with half an army ...*

I let out a laugh. 'As long as you and Tared don't kill each other, not much can go wrong.'

We'll be slower. He chuckled as he looked up – a joyless chuckle, but the light was back in his eyes. *And there is the risk, of course, that you'll throw yourself into my arms before the week is over.*

'Prick,' I said with a snort. 'You're not that irresistible.'

His wings shifted suggestively. *I seem to remember some fae party where you told yourself you could resist me perfectly well.*

And where we'd ended up fucking against a wall, dress torn and teeth bared, like animals in heat. I sucked in a cool and urgently needed breath and managed, 'I've had practice looking the other way.'

Really? His smile was of the most dangerous sort, sensuous and arrogant and wild to the core. The sight of it sank through me in disconcerting ways, lighting sparks of senseless lust on its way down. *Are you making any progress?*

'I thought we were discussing our plans,' I said hoarsely, the tone of my voice the only answer he could need.

Were, he confirmed, running his free hand through his hair in that way he damn well knew never failed to catch my attention. Strands of dark silk danced around his face, emphasising every whetted line of his features. *Astute observation.*

'We don't even have a plan yet!' But my body didn't care, the warmth between my thighs deepening at nothing but the *suggestion* of seduction. Zera help me, I was hopeless indeed. 'This is not the moment to take breaks and hope all will be well!'

There's very little we can do until Lyn has played her pieces. Somehow, the motions of his fingers told me there was in fact quite a lot we could be doing right now. *I've lived without a voice for a hundred and thirty years. I can miss its dulcet tones for a few more minutes.*

He was playing this game so damn easily – was winning it so damn easily. I grabbed the first lifeline I could think of, anything to keep my mind from fixing itself on the promise of blissful ecstasy, and managed, 'And what if *I* can't wait? What if I'm just too damn impatient to find out what your voice even sounds like?'

High and squeaky, he retorted without batting an eye, *and reminiscent of the yapping of a lady's lapdog. Does that suffice?*

I burst out laughing despite myself. 'Liar.'

You sound very confident. He leaned back in his chair, muscular legs sprawled in a way that seemed designed to draw my eye to the apex of them. *What sort of sound were you hoping for?*

'Liquid sex,' I suggested dryly.

I'm afraid it's closer to the braying of a donkey. With a lisp.

The hand I clenched over my mouth was not nearly enough to stifle the hysterical shrieks welling up in me. 'It's not!'

And how would you know? His shoulders strained deliciously as he leaned forward, resting his elbow on his thigh.

'Edored would never have stayed quiet about it if you sounded like a squeaky bagpipe!' That argument didn't seem to leave much of an impression, so I jolted up before he could strike back and added, 'And if you sounded like a braying donkey, you wouldn't even have wanted your voice back. You'd have dwelled in dramatic and mysterious silence forever while you quietly killed every single person still aware of the embarrassing truth.'

Convincing, he admitted, grin turning wry.

'I'm a very convincing sort of person, Your Highness. So, are we going to make a plan?'

Why? A single sign; it looked like a challenge.

'We'll have ten days at most,' I said quickly. If I just clung to that unpleasant new fact, he could hardly lure me into his bed before we'd figured out how we were going to handle it. 'And we'll travel more slowly with a larger group. Which means we need to have a clear idea of where we're going, and—'

You've been working without pause for weeks, he interrupted. Although he lounged in that chair, a flicker of something sharper broke through the easy seduction in his eyes – like a honed blade slicing straight through lush velvet. *Stop telling yourself the fate of the world is all in your hands. You need to breathe.*

I couldn't help glance at my hands, small and white-knuckled as I grasped the armrests harder than I'd realised. 'I'm the only unbound mage we have.'

I'm the only half demon fae prince we have. He shrugged. *Agenor is the only godsworn mage we have. Tared is ... well, one of the few alves with a brain we have, supposedly. Naxi is—*

'I know, but that's different!' I drew in an exasperated breath, gesturing wildly at the world behind his bedroom walls. 'Until we get rid of those damn bindings, no one else is going to take the Mother down and no one else is going to prioritise your voice either, so—'

Em, he interrupted, and somehow the sight of those two letters alone turned my insides to mush. *Come here.*

I clenched my fists, scowling at him. 'I don't think I should.'

He quirked up an inquiring eyebrow.

'If I sit in your lap you're going to be so stupidly seductive and ... *muscular*,' I grumbled, 'and then I'm going to accidentally touch your wings—'

Accidentally, he repeated dryly.

'—and then you're going to make that *face* and I'll be on my knees before I know it,' I stubbornly continued, 'and then we'll be fucking each other for two hours and we still won't have a plan.'

He chuckled. *I've yet to hear any negative consequences.*

'You're not helping, Creon!'

I'm absolutely helping. Just not the way you want me to.

'Sometimes I wish that well of wisdom of yours would dry up,' I ground out, gripping the armrests even more tightly. His smile was a siren's call, lethal yet irresistible like the songs that sailors heard on the

Elderburg coast at night. 'Can't you help without ruining all my plans, in that case?'

As you wish. He sat a fraction straighter, unfurling his wings. *But only if you come sit here with me.*

'No wing stroking,' I said, sending him a warning glare. 'Accidental or otherwise. And no smouldering faces either.'

Promise. Amusement twisted his lips. *Unless asked, I'll try not to appear in any way alluring or tantalising. Although it will be a considerable effort, of course.*

'Prick.' But I gave in.

He didn't seduce or tease as he pulled me into his hold, no quick kisses, no brushes of his lips over my forehead. He merely turned me around in his lap with an almost business-like motion, so that I faced the blank wall on the other side of the room, half an arm-length between us, my back towards him.

I wavered, pushing away a senseless sting of disappointment. 'What are you—'

He wrapped his hands around my upper arms. His thumbs brushed over my shoulder blades, then pressed down simultaneously, finding the exact spots where my muscles had tightened into hard, painful knots.

Agony radiated down my spine and into my arms. '*Ow!*'

His breath betrayed a chuckle as he shifted his hands half an inch and repeated the action. I let out a frayed cry, reflexively bucking away from him – but he didn't let go, keeping me in his lap as his thumbs continued to rub merciless circles over my shoulders, tracing the lines of tension until the pressure radiated into every fibre of my torso. Enough pain to leave me gasping for breath, the calloused pads of his fingers rough through my soft linen dress – but my muscles slowly surrendered to the force of his touch.

Blood flowed back into places where no blood had been in weeks. All those hours on rigid library stools ... All those times I'd fallen asleep over my books, spine twisting into unnatural shapes as I sagged onto the reading tables ...

'Point made,' I gasped through gritted teeth as he drove his fingers into a brand new section of tormented muscle, this time just above my armpits. Was it even *possible* to overstrain your armpits? 'And I could swear you're using demon powers to find where I'm hurting most, you cruel, heartless ...'

He breathed a laugh behind me and rubbed the hard zone between my neck and shoulders until I whined.

But finally the pain resided, after what felt like hours of fires igniting and fizzling out under his touch; it numbed to a dull ache at first, then turned comforting, then *pleasant*. I breathed deeper and found that my shoulders no longer stretched so painfully tight, the tension driven from my body at last.

Still he didn't stop.

This ... I closed my eyes, revelling in the deep pressure of his palms on my skin, the firm satin of his touch. This was about the moment where I should tell him I was fine and get back to work, wasn't it? I had no excuse to stall. Not if we might be leaving tomorrow, not if people might be making all the wrong plans while I was sitting here in this safe embrace of dusky faelights and autumn scents.

But his hands were warm and strong and comforting, kneading my shoulders with unfaltering intensity. And even though I couldn't see his face, couldn't see his wings, couldn't see all that stupid muscle bulging under the linen and leather of his clothes ...

His breath was growing strained behind me.

My body reacted to that sound in a twist of eagerness, razor-sharp anticipation piercing my guts. Oh. *Oh*. If his breath was hitching – if he felt my soft weight in his lap as much as I felt those hard ridges of his thighs beneath me – then surely he wouldn't restrict himself to my shoulders alone?

A tingle trailed down my body, making me suddenly and desperately aware of my untouched breasts, of the brush of my dress over my pebbling nipples.

Wouldn't he?

But his hands remained where they were, strong fingers rubbing and squeezing my neck and shoulders with a patience of centuries. I shivered, leaning closer against him, closer to his sculpted chest as it rose and sank, rose and sank, a slow cadence that made me feel drowsy and far, far too peaceful.

I was tired, I realised. A tiredness that had sunk deep into my bones, far too heavy for one night of decent sleep to chase it out again.

And why wasn't he *touching* me?

That idiot promise I'd asked for – a groan escaped my lips before I could regain control of myself. The warmth of his touch was spreading from my shoulders to my belly and lower still, hankering for more, hankering for *deeper*, and yet his hands didn't follow. Not even as I nestled tighter against him. Not even as I rubbed my bottom against his crotch and received the familiar jolt of his arousal for my answer, not even as his breath hitched against my temple.

Zera help me, I was burning.

'Creon.' It was close to a moan. There was a hypnotising cadence to his circling fingers, rubbing any sense of urgency from my bones. 'Creon ... I ...'

His hands paused on my shoulders. A wordless, signless question.

'I should ...' *Get back to the library. Get back to work.* The thoughts were still there, but hazy and unfocused – something with maps, and nothing I could care all that much about. 'I can't ...'

One warm hand slid along my neck, stroking over my jaw and chin before it settled firmly over my lips, smothering the rest of my words.

In a last flare of defiance, I bit his finger.

Wrong move. He tasted like sin, like something musky and salty I couldn't quite name – a faint echo of the taste of his seed on my tongue. I felt his laughter shake through his chest, felt the firmness of his finger probe deeper into my mouth, and the last of my defences crumbled as a blinding heat ignited at the apex of my thighs. I bit down again, harder now. Creon released my shoulder in reply, free hand slipping between my legs and yanking up my skirt with demanding strength.

His first stroke below my underwear found me drenched.

I arched towards him, my moans muffled against his hand on my mouth. My reward was a second finger sliding below my delicate un-derlinen; he effortlessly held me pinned in his lap as he drew a long, savouring line along my lips, all the way to where my slick entrance pulsed and clenched for his touch. There he waited, still like a cat in the moment before jumping – waited for me to act, to agree.

Hell take me, I didn't want him waiting. Didn't want an opportunity to make sensible choices, time to remember everything else I should have been doing. My exhausted mind craved simple and empty oblivion, a delirium that made me forget I cared about anything else in the world. If he insisted on being *courteous* ...

I tilted my head back against his shoulder, shaking his hand off my face, and murmured, 'I'll just get back to reading then, shall I?'

Before he could react, I jumped.

I didn't expect to get far, fleeing the Silent Death with trembling legs and messy skirts – and then he was even faster, a hunter as inevitable as the night itself. A flash of motion, a slap of wings, and he caught me just before I reached the door. His hands wrapped possessively around my waist, shoving me against the rune-carved wood; the weight of his body settled against my back, trapping me in a cage of warmth and power and the scent of sweet autumn. He planted his hands on either side of my shoulders. His erection pressed hungrily against my lower back, a perfect companion to his rough breath at my ear.

'I'm gathering ...' Was I moaning or laughing or sobbing? Gasps of air wrestled themselves from my lungs, my voice squeaky in that prison of smooth wood and hot muscle. 'I'm gathering that you're not in favour of reading, Your Highness?'

His rough exhale was close to a growl. I fumbled blindly for his wings, only for his fingers to lock around my wrists the next moment. He yanked my arms behind my back, pinning them in place with one hand. His other slipped between my body and the door, starting a slow descent across my belly – skimming down and down and ...

I forgot to breathe.

Down.

He stroked over that most sensitive bud so roughly I saw stars, a touch that told me I would not be reading today, that I'd be lucky if I could sit again by dinnertime. If it was a punishment, it felt like a reward. If it was a reward ...

Hell, it was a good one.

I closed my eyes as I slumped against the door. His fingers didn't allow me to catch my breath, working me in swift, heated strokes until I was too far gone to even moan. The weight of his body held me trapped between unyielding wood and the even more unyielding wall of his powerful chest; cheek pressed against the door, wrists caught in the vice of his fingers, I was a powerless prisoner to my desires.

And gods help me, he made me feel it.

His fingers were instruments of blissful torture, skimming and swirling, drawing unbearable circles around that most sensitive spot until I was sure I would shatter. I was nothing but a breathless victim at the mercy of his touch ... I was a glass about to burst, and he was the fire heating me to that coveted breaking point.

One last twist of his fingers and I disintegrated, sobbing with relief as my climax tore through me and left me boneless and brainless in his hold.

Still Creon didn't let go of me, his breath heavy in the hollow of my neck. His hand cupped my sex, cradling me, fingertips brushing over my drenched flesh until the last twitches of my release subsided. Only then did he unlock his fingers from my wrists, turn me around, and pin me like a dazed ragdoll against his chest. A breathtaking, hungry sort of triumph brimmed in his dark eyes.

Time for reading, then? he signed, and it took a long few heartbeats before I'd gathered enough of my senses to recognise it as a challenge.

'What ... what are letters?' I managed.

A dark chuckle. *Got a little distracted, cactus?*

I'd forgotten what there even was to be distracted from. The Alliance's diplomatic unbound mage and Agenor's perfectly dutiful daughter ... they were still shouting at me from some cold and rigid corner of my mind. But Creon was here, holding me, watching me with those night-drenched eyes that knew me better than anyone else in the world, and somehow his gaze seemed to slide straight past them.

I'm not your bloody audience, he'd told me in Etele's memorial.

I could crumble. I could give in and give up, surrender and be a silly, senseless little girl until the sun rose, and he'd never hold it against me.

I let go. Allowed my heart to take over, or whatever part of me was responsible for this haze of lust smouldering in my limbs, and mumbled, 'Something just occurred to me.'

Creon lifted an eyebrow, left hand drawing lazy, meandering lines along my spine.

'If I can't touch you for ten days …' I moulded my palm to his chest, unable to suppress a shiver. Ten days of playing a stranger to him. What had ever moved me to agree with that solution? 'Perhaps we should take an advance on all the times I won't be able to rip those trousers off you, don't you think?'

I would have killed to hear the laugh that broke out of him – a light transforming his face from that unnaturally beautiful murderer's façade into an expression that sparkled with life, wholly his own and so joyful I could cry. *Very damn careful now, Em.*

I breathed a chuckle and loosened the first button of his shirt, holding his gaze as the look in his eyes became a glass-edged warning. 'Or else?'

Or else, he signed, the movements of his fingers breathtakingly graceful in the smoky light of the stained glass and the faelights, *I might give up on my attempts to appear civilised, and I'll have no choice but to fuck you so hard you'll be feeling it for a full ten days at least.*

My body drew tight like a clenching fist in some nameless core just below my navel. I moved on to the next button, hands suddenly trembling, and whispered, 'Wouldn't that be a shame?'

Horrific. His smile could have driven the holiest of temple virgins to sin. *A dreadful fate, for some innocent young lady to be so corrupted that she spends days of travel just thinking about my cock.*

'In my defence,' I murmured, tearing off a button in my haste to undress him, 'that's quite a lot to think about.'

He kissed me.

It was a teasing kiss, a coaxing kiss, a kiss that promised more but kept true satisfaction just out of reach. A warning kiss, perhaps, but if it was, I didn't heed that warning – because he was not my bloody audience, and I was done making sensible choices, was done holding back and saving the world. *Ten days* – but not today.

Not tonight.

I buried my hands in his hair, drawing him closer, brushing the edges of his pointed ears until he snarled against my lips. We stumbled against the door, loud enough for incidentally passing alves to hear. For one blessed moment, I didn't care – didn't care about anything but his hot mouth on mine and his half-bared body against me and the roaring arousal that sent flurries of sparks through every spot his fingers touched.

I let go of his hair, reached behind his shoulder to find his left wing, and found the taut velvet of the upper edge on my first try.

And then he was no longer kissing but devouring, no longer warning but claiming, that first caress enough to snap the last strings reining in the monster below his skin. His hands were everywhere at once, tearing at my dress, clawing at my bottom, pressing my thighs apart. I stroked his wing again, and he nipped at my bottom lip hard enough to elicit a cry, pain and pleasure mingling in a delicious whirlpool of oblivion.

There were no chores here in this world only the two of us inhabited, no pressing expectations and obligations. Just his nails raking down my spine with exactly the right sting, just his wing under my fingertips, quivering at my every moan. Just his fingers yanking my underwear aside, thrusting into my ready wetness with all the mindless strength I needed.

Ten days.

I grabbed at his trousers as he fucked me with his fingers, kissing him, our bodies tangling up against that door in a mess of rumpled clothing and sweaty skin and hot, panting breath. Some of his buttons came loose permanently in my hurry to free his bulging erection, and I didn't care about that, either. The scorching satin of his cock in my palm was enough to obliterate the last shreds of the practical, sensible, dutiful unbound mage I'd tried to be – what need did I have for duty if I could have *him*?

We were too far gone for beds, now. Too far gone for chairs or desks. He tore off my underwear as I leaned back against the door and lifted one leg, wrapping it around his hip to give him better access to every blissfully sensitive, almost-sore spot his fingers could reach. Not enough, not even close to enough …

'Creon.' His name tasted like a vulgar plea on my tongue, as sinful as the musky fragrance of his skin. 'More.'

He curled two fingers inside of me, and if not for his other hand around my waist, my melting bones would have sent me collapsing at his feet. I wrapped both my hands around his throbbing cock, milking him at the rhythm of his thrusts until he was hard enough to hurt. His breath came in struggling gasps against my mouth, the strokes of his fingers mercilessly deep.

'*More,*' I moaned.

He slid his fingers out of me, flipped me around like a trained dancer, and dragged my hips back towards him, bending me over. Planting both hands against the door was all I could do to stay on my feet as he bunched up my skirt and buried himself inside me with a single powerful stroke, filling me so thoroughly, so perfectly, that my eyes rolled back at the impact of it.

Yes.

This.

Again he slammed into me, driving so deep it felt like he might hit my midriff, taking me until there was no room left in my body for air or thoughts or silence. Some primal part of me was crying out his name, *sobbing* his name. My nails dug into the wood under my fingers. I registered nothing of it, nothing but his rock-hard girth moving inside me, claiming me and everything I was, thrust by glorious thrust.

'Gods,' I was moaning, 'gods, *Creon,*' and then suddenly everything changed and I was lying in his arms, unsure of how I'd gotten there, unsure of anything except that he was no longer inside me and I needed him *now.* I clawed at him and found his corded shoulders taut under my fingers, movement rolling through his muscles as his wings flared out in response.

Soft linen brushed my back as he lowered me down – his bed. He'd carried me to his bed. With quick movements, he settled me in his blankets, my legs dangling over the edge of his mattress, and released me to pull my dress over my head. I breathed a curse as he stepped away from me. My body seemed naked and empty without his touch, my sight blurry with lust.

It took a moment for the shapes of his signs to come through. *Getting prickly, cactus?*

I reached for his cock, which stood straight from his torn trousers like a warrior triumphant, the dark bronze gleaming shamelessly in the dusky faelight. Creon moved out of my reach with catlike ease, shrugging his unbuttoned shirt off his torso. A faint sheen of sweat glistened on his ink-marred skin, emphasising every honed edge of his body, emphasising every movement as he slowly and meticulously stripped off his boots and trousers.

'This,' I breathed, coming up onto my elbows, 'is torture.'

He gave me a wolfish grin through the strands of long hair falling over his face, flicking his clothes aside. *My specialty.*

Fully naked, he was somehow even more magnificent than in menacing black, every inch of his body shaped for battle and glory. My mouth went dry as he closed in on me again; my legs parted all by themselves as he knelt before me, not a shred of resistance left in my limbs.

'Perhaps ...' My voice was a husky whisper. 'Perhaps I can see why Agenor is concerned about my good sense.'

His grin grew sharper. *I'm afraid Agenor knows exactly what I'm capable of.*

My fogged mind needed a moment – because my father had known Creon before the Alliance captured him, before Lyn, in a time when he'd still taken lovers and probably did so with all the lack of discretion I'd known from the Crimson Court ... And then Creon's fingers brushed over that tender bundle of nerves between my thighs, and that vague and irrelevant train of thought dissolved into the far bigger realisation that I was about to find out what he was capable of in the most immediate and pleasurable way.

His touches were so feathery as he worshipped the drenched lines of my body, nothing like the rough way he'd pinned me to the door and had his way with me. Gossamer caresses, over and over again, teasing over every sensitive spot, calling an entirely new agony from the burning fire below my skin. Far too soon, he had me pleading and writhing again, every fibre in my body chasing after that promise of bone-shattering pleasure he held just out of reach.

When he finally set me free, I was so close it took nothing but a single well-aimed pinch of his fingers. Release barrelled through me with avalanche force, leaving me shivering and gasping for breath and ...

Pleading for mercy.

Because he buried his head between my thighs before the trembles of my climax died away, dragging his tongue over the same spots he'd driven to insanity twice already.

Pleasure turned raw, a savage sensation dancing so close to pain that the lines between them blurred entirely. His lips worked my tender flesh gently, kissing and nuzzling until the last waves of my release subsided. Then somehow the next eruption was already rising from some place deeper inside me than anything I'd ever imagined – lured to the surface by the clever strokes of his tongue as he found every delicate spot all over again. A lingering kiss. A series of short little licks that had me crying out his name, until I was close, *so* close, and he circled away from that core of my pleasure, exploring the lines of my lips again ...

I informed him, or tried to inform him in between my gasps for air, that I would tragically perish on the spot if he didn't end this torment immediately.

He sheathed his tongue inside me in response, drinking deep and greedy, and I came again.

There was no breath left in my lungs. No blood in my brain. But I clung to his hard shoulders instinctively as he finally moved over me and lowered himself between my thighs, and I welcomed his first stroke into my drenched tightness with an oddly detached sensation of both delirious bliss and mortal fear. I might just die if he made me come again, might just crumble to a point beyond repair – but gods, it would be a glorious way to go.

And somehow my body wasn't yet spent. Somehow the delicious friction of his cock entering me – so much more intense now that every inch of me throbbed with the torment of these last orgasms – woke some slumbering fire in my limbs, a primal instinct that recognised his rhythm before I remembered my own name. He thrust into me, and I arched towards him. He slid back, and I set my nails into his shoulders, clawing down. He breathed out hard and drove himself back into me, faster now, and the wondrous pressure of it made my toes curl tight with anticipation ...

Again?

Again.

Our gazes locked as our bodies fused together, and I could see my own ecstasy mirrored in the gleam of his dark eyes, in the way his long lashes fluttered shut as he buried himself inside me over and over. Our breathing became a shared rhythm of panting madness. His cock stretched me impossibly wide as I met him thrust for thrust, every stroke driving me closer to a breaking point, until I could do nothing but feel, let the sensations wash over me and give in to wherever his passion was taking me.

My climax was a monster clawing free, agony and all-consuming wonder in equal amounts. I clenched around him so tightly it hurt, and he broke with me – slammed into me one last time and released a soundless growl I effortlessly read from his lips, flooding me with his seed as I convulsed through wave after wave of blinding frenzy.

All else was a blur. The world ... the war, whatever that was ... I'd forgotten whether I cared, why I would care. His body was warm and solid in my arms, and his lips against my forehead were soft like down, and when I rolled over in his embrace and kissed his shoulder, he tasted like desire and endless summer nights.

We lay tangled up in each other's arms, panting quietly, as my heart settled back into a gentler rhythm.

When I finally looked up, he lay watching me with half-lidded eyes in the smoky light of the stained glass faelights. A smile brushed over his lips as our gazes met – a small one, but my breath hitched all the same.

Enough of an advance for you? his fingers said.

Even my snort came out breathless. 'You may have to carry me across the continent.'

He laughed. I wiggled out of his hold, sat up, and rolled my shoulders, marvelling at the way they moved without aching, the way every fibre of my body had abruptly forgotten weeks of racing against time.

Creon was faster than my questions. *Learning to fly,* he signed dryly, *is a very quick lesson in all the ways one can strain back muscles.*

'That explains a lot.' I slid a hand over the lean bulges of his shoulders, then over the corded tendons around the onset of his wings, drinking in the power below his skin. When I pulled back, there were traces of blood on my fingers. 'Oh.'

He followed my gaze and let out a lazy chuckle, flinging a quick spark of blue over his shoulder to heal the cuts my nails had left. When I clambered over him to check, there was no trace of the marks I'd given him.

Blue for healing.

And I *was* going to heal him – to hell with the Mother and the plague and public opinion in my way – was going to heal all of them, was going to break those gods-damned bindings and win that gods-damned war.

I just had to figure out how.

CHAPTER 5

LYN WAS A MIRACLE worker.

When I slipped out of Creon's bedroom the next morning, the loud conversations from the living room quickly told me three things. Firstly, Lyn had managed to call the Council together over the course of the night and received permission to spend a strict maximum of ten days on the continent in search of the gods. Secondly, she and Tared had already packed their bags. And thirdly, Edored had stepped out of bed for just long enough to hear about the matter.

Quite as expected, he sounded unhappy.

Thank the bloody gods for Creon's unpleasant strategies; there was little the alf's ranting could achieve now that even Tared had decided to join this mad adventure. Nonetheless, I tiptoed into the living room with some caution, wary of alf swords and spontaneous bursts of phoenix fire.

To my relief, no one seemed on the brink of dying yet. Tared was eating his breakfast, looking grim yet composed. Next to him, Lyn sat on the edge of the table with her feet on the bench, arguing with Edored in a tone that suggested they'd been at this for a while. Naxi had burrowed into one of the plush armchairs in the corner, as had Ylfreda, who carried that look of annoyance which signalled someone had stupidly wounded themselves. Finally, Beyla had taken up her position at the far end of the table, bags by her feet and swords on her back, waiting for the rest of the company to be done with this nonsense and get on their way.

Tared was the first to notice me. He sent me a quick grin as he nodded at the seat next to him, and a small weight fell from my shoulders.

'... haven't been there for centuries!' Edored was shouting. 'You might be dragging the whole damn family into hell, Lyn sweetling, and—'

'Which is why we'll have two alves and two demons around, Edored dearest,' Lyn interrupted, her *dearest* cold enough to freeze fire, 'and why we—'

'Gods-damned *Hytherion*? You're going to let Tared's life depend on *him*?'

'Morning, Em,' Tared said dryly, ignoring his cousin's swearing with impressive equanimity as I sank down next to him. Whatever Agenor's revelations of the previous day had stirred up, the ripples had already been smoothed out with all the usual superficial nonchalance. 'You'll be glad to know you have once again managed to get the entire Underground in a frenzy.'

I huffed a laugh. 'Those are the days I live for.'

He shook his head with a faint grin as he handed me bread, cheese, and butter. On his other side, an ominous flurry of crimson sparks burst from Lyn's small figure, even though her voice remained cold and clipped.

'Why exactly did you decide to come along?' I added quietly to Tared while I cut off thin slices of cheese.

'I don't have a lot of options,' he said and gave me a sour shrug. 'Goes against my principles to lock you in your room. Goes against my principles to let you walk around plague land without adult supervision, too. So—'

I stamped on his toes. That seemed to cheer him up considerably; his curse came out with more vigour than anything he'd said so far.

'Fine!' Edored burst out in the same moment, swinging a furious gesture at the door. 'Have it your way! What time are we leaving?'

'*We?*' Lyn repeated, her young voice cracking.

'Yes?' Edored aggressively stepped back, noticing me for the first time. A quick snort was the only greeting I was given. '*Someone* needs to keep an eye on this madness, for Orin's fucking sake. When are we leaving?'

'At noon, but Edored—'

Too late – he had already stalked off, deliberately not fading to his room so he could slam every door he encountered on his way there. The living room seemed twice as large in the absence of his boisterous objections, and ten times as quiet.

'Well,' Beyla said, her eerie voice suspiciously amused. 'That makes for seven, then.'

'About that.' I cleared my throat. 'Would you mind if Agenor came along to Lyckfort? To ... you know, show us the way?'

Lyn threw me a glower, the tips of her fingers still smoking faintly. 'I take it you already invited him?'

'I'm trying to be *subtle* about this, Lyn,' I said indignantly.

She grinned mirthlessly as she jumped down from the table and rubbed her face. 'Naxi? How many people do you think you can reasonably protect from the plague magic, assuming you and Creon will both have to sleep every now and then?'

'Oh, eight will be fine,' Naxi said brightly. Only then did I notice the redness of her left cheek, as if the upper layer of her skin had been chafed off over the night; her right hand was wrapped in linen bandages, her wrist covered with some herbal salve. 'I don't think anything up to ten will give me much trouble.'

'What in hell have you been doing?' I said.

'Sneaking out into the world above,' Ylfreda said sharply before Naxi could answer, 'and trying to take on plague magic without any help or instructions. I suggest no one else follows her example. These burns are no joke.'

'Don't be such a worry-wort, Freddie,' Naxi said, fluttering invisible concerns aside with her good hand. 'I'm perfectly fine. Turns out it's fairly simple to counter that magic, once you know what you're doing – speaking of which, is Creon up already? I should demonstrate the technique to him before we leave.'

'He's usually awake around this time,' I said, tactfully circumventing the fact I had kissed him awake myself not too long ago. Her wicked grin as she danced out told me she'd heard the words between the lines clearly enough.

Ylfreda groaned as she got up, chucking some leftover bandages into her bag in the corner. 'If anyone else decides to throw themselves into any suicidal undertakings—'

'We would never,' Tared said.

She glared at him. 'You better not show up here like a piece of charcoal in ten days, Thorgedson. And for the love of the gods, make sure Edored doesn't wander off in search of any lost treasures or dragon eggs, will you?'

'I do have *some* sense in me, Freda,' he said wryly, and she huffed and faded into nothingness.

'I'll go get Agenor,' Beyla said, vanishing before anyone could reply.

Then Lyn and Tared were the only ones left, and they were both ominously silent as I chewed my bread and waited for the inevitable questions to come.

But when Lyn finally sighed and sat down, all she said was, 'Someone should probably check on Nenya before we leave. Don't want her to go see Bakaru and ... you know.'

'Will do,' Tared said, probably having heard the underlying message, too: that she wanted a word with me, either about Creon or about arcane womanly travel advice to which he was not invited. He got up with a quick smile at me, added, 'Don't start any wars before I'm back,' and dissolved into thin air in that way that had started to seem perfectly natural after a few months in an alf household.

I glanced over my shoulder to check the living room door. Edored had expertly slammed it shut; it was still closed.

'Well,' I said.

'Well.' Lyn's smile wavered as she turned towards me on the bench, folding her feet under her short body. She looked tired in that brief moment. I almost felt guilty, then reminded myself that she had her own worries about the public opinion to blame. 'Next time you want to pull a stunt like this, tell me beforehand, will you? A little more preparation would have made it much easier to handle the Council.'

'It wasn't supposed to have anything to do with the Council,' I said, a little too curtly.

She groaned. 'I know. Is Creon alright with the change of plans?'

'More or less.'

'More than I dared to hope,' she muttered, sending me a side glance. 'This is ... not his specialty, Em. People, I mean.'

'Don't worry,' I said sourly, 'he tells me that about twice a week. We'll handle it.'

She looked barely convinced but too tired to probe. 'And you?'

I shrugged. 'As long as it helps us break those damn bindings.'

Her suspicious glance told me she was questioning where my true priorities lay – but again the moment passed without further questions. She'd spent the past few hours having diplomatic conversations with Tared, fighting with Edored, and bickering with the Council, after all. I imagined she wasn't going to add another tense conversation to that list as long as our goals largely aligned.

Now all she said was, 'I'm sorry Tared and Agenor are being such ... males.'

I couldn't help a chuckle at that. 'It's alright. I'd rather have them think me a naïve young girl with an unfortunate infatuation than a victim in urgent need of saving. Or a monster, as the rest of the Underground would probably think if they knew ...'

'At some point,' Lyn said, amber eyes large and cautious, 'they'll have to find out. I'm not sure if lying about it now will help then.'

I pushed away a sting of discomfort. Too close to Creon's words, too close to something I hoped with all my heart wasn't the truth. 'I'm damn sure it won't be pleasant *now*, and no one knows what it'll be like in the future.'

'Yes, but—'

'I should start packing,' I said brusquely, swinging my feet to the other side of the bench with my breakfast still in my hand. Another admission of weakness. And hell, I *was* borrowing time without knowing how much I'd pay for it – but we had a mere ten days to comb an entire damn continent, the peace among my travel companions was already fraying, and this seemed the worst possible moment to find out how the truth of my love life would shift the balance between my allies.

'Keep your bag light,' Lyn said, shoulders sagging, although she didn't press. She really had to be exhausted. 'We'll be walking most of the time. No sense trying to get alves on horses. Beyla is taking care of the food, so keep some room for provisions – oh, and don't forget that nights are colder on the continent.'

'Right,' I said, wondering if I should ask Agenor how cold *colder* would be, exactly. 'I'll get Creon packing, too.'

She sighed and nodded, staring at her hands until I reached for the doorhandle. Only at the last moment did she snap up her head, sending her red curls scattering.

'Em?'

Her voice had that tone of a thread snapping, of hours of tossing and turning being chucked aside in favour of one desperate and impulsive decision. I dropped my hand, realising as I turned fully towards her that I may be about to discover her true reason for sending Tared off.

She looked young, suddenly – really, truly young. In all these months I'd seen her panicked and emotional and conflicted, but rarely had I seen her ... *insecure?*

'What is it?' I said carefully.

'Tell me if I'm overstepping,' she said, speaking too fast. 'I understand – I really do – no offense taken, I promise. But I've been thinking about it for so long and I just ... well, if I never ask, I—'

'*Lyn.*' I fell back against the door, crossing my arms with a joyless laugh. 'What are you talking about? If you want me to name my children after you, I must regretfully inform you I've never thought about offspring that much.'

'No!' She buried her face in her hands with a sob-like groan. 'Oh, gods help me. Just ... Would it ... would it be possible ...' She looked up, drawing in a breath. 'Would you mind if I tried to learn some of that hand language he's using? Creon, I mean?'

'Would I ... what?'

She threw me a panicked look. 'It really is fine it you—'

'Would I *mind*?' I let out a baffled laugh, taking half a step forward. 'Why for Zera's loving heart would I ever mind?'

'Well,' she said, too fast again, 'if it's just something for the two of you – your secret insider thing – I don't want to impose on anything that—'

'Lyn, it's his *voice*!' My own voice caught, as if to show solidarity with Creon's silence. 'I don't give a damn about shared secrets if he just needs to *communicate* with the world. Please learn it. Learn all of it. Force the rest of the household to get a grasp on it, too. If I need a secret way to communicate with him, I'll figure out something new, alright?'

'Oh.' She blinked, her shoulders falling at the unexpected lack of resistance. 'That ... Oh. I just thought ... You never suggested it.'

'You were keeping your distance from him,' I said, and it was a challenge not to make it sound accusatory.

'Yes,' she admitted, bitter lines around her lips. 'I was. I've decided I'm done with that, though.'

I blinked. 'Just now?'

'After what Agenor told us yesterday. His binding.' She looked away, shoulders hunched in a gesture too young for her five hundred and something years. 'It's ... Gods' sakes, Em. The day I let him out of his cell, he told me he didn't care what I had planned for him, as long as I promised I'd stick a knife through his heart if it ever looked like the Mother would get her hands on him again. And then he ... he ...'

Then he went back. Back into the hands of the High Lady who'd tortured him since he was two years old and made him believe it was an honour and a compliment. Back to the killing and the maiming, to the life he'd realised he never wanted to lead again.

I swallowed and said, 'Yes.'

'After I strung him along for months,' Lyn burst out, the words tumbling out at such speed now that I knew she'd kept them down for far too long. 'After Tared told him ... told him ...'

'Yes.'

'And of course he's an idiot! Of course he should stop playing the gods-damned invincible fae prince to the rest of the world, and of course he should have told us why he went back, should have told us how he's been using his demon powers all this time, but ...' She sucked in a breath, rubbing her face. 'He's an idiot who sacrificed so very much, and I can't keep punishing him for the mistakes he made a century ago if we were *all* acting like fools at the time, you see? So it's about time I stopped avoiding him. Especially if we'll be travelling together for the next week and a half.'

I managed a laugh. 'And despite that, Tared still agreed the two of you were going to join this journey?'

'Tared was never the one who kept me away from Creon,' she said with a slight tremble of her lips. 'Don't think that ill of him, Em. He's not one to limit anyone's freedom. If I told him I wanted to spend the night in Creon's room from now on, he'd crumble, but he wouldn't stop me. It's just ...'

'You don't want him to crumble,' I finished quietly.

'No.' She pressed her mouth into a thin line, staring at the table to avoid my gaze. 'You should keep in mind I knew Beyla before the Last Battle. Knew her when she was loud and cheerful and always up for a game. Just *thinking* about Tared going through such a change makes me—'

'Wait – the Last Battle?' I took two more steps forward and sat down again, definitively done with pretending I was about to start packing my bags. 'I'm sorry, I know that's not the point, but I thought it was Tared's brother who died?'

'She wasn't bonded to Bered,' Lyn said sadly. 'Nothing past the early stages, at least. She mourned him for a while and then fell in love with a friend of ours a few decades after Skeire happened. Byggvir. Bonded to him.'

I gaped at her, understanding suddenly what was coming with a violent, overwhelming sense of nausea. 'And then he died at the Last Battle?'

Lyn nodded, her eyes gleaming suspiciously.

'Oh, gods. I ... I had no idea.'

'She carries both their swords. Lost her own the day Skeire was attacked, so Tared gave her Sunray – Bered's sword.' She wiped her eyes with the back of one freckled hand, still not meeting my gaze. 'And she kept Icebreaker after Byggvir died, learned to fight with two blades. Training was the only thing that got her out of bed in the morning for decades.'

I tried to imagine Beyla being loud and cheerful, tried to imagine her huddled below her blankets and wishing she were dead, and didn't manage either.

'I'm sorry, Em,' Lyn muttered when I stayed silent, rubbing the tears from her eyes again. Far too many tears for the tireless little phoenix I was used to. Good gods, how long had it been since she'd last voiced these worries to anyone? 'You didn't ask for this mess. I'm just trying to say … There's a damn lot I'd do to keep Tared safe even if he isn't asking me for it.'

'But not avoiding Creon for eternity,' I said slowly.

She gave a slightly blubbering laugh. 'Even if I never wanted to shag him, he *does* mean a lot to me. So if he doesn't hate the sight of me too much, I'd be happy to find out if we could be … you know.' A strained shrug. 'Friends?'

'He doesn't hate the sight of you,' I said, because I wasn't sure what else there was to say, and this at least seemed something that had to be said.

'Oh.' She swallowed audibly. 'Good.'

We sat in silence for a while, staring at nothing, contemplating centuries of tangled history and endless misunderstandings.

'I should probably start packing,' I eventually said, and Lyn jerked from her thoughts as if I'd shaken her awake.

'Yes. Probably.'

She looked small and forlorn, her chin resting in her hands, her sad eyes aimed stubbornly at the wall behind my head. I wanted to hug her, wanted to tell her it would all turn out just fine – but I doubted a hug could solve years and years of tiptoeing around the person she loved more than anyone in the world, and with my mind on Beyla's eerie voice and shallow smiles, I didn't trust myself to provide any reassurances with even the slightest degree of conviction.

So all I said as I got up was, 'Thanks for everything, Lyn.'

'You too, Em,' she said, dabbing at her eyes. 'You too.'

It took mere minutes to pack the bare essentials for surviving a few days in unknown territory: alf steel dagger, light clothes, the fuzzy sweater Naxi had given me for my birthday. A sturdy leather water bottle, a small blanket roll. My bag still felt light then, and even though I knew it would no longer seem half as light after a full day of walking, I couldn't help glancing longingly at the small pile of books I kept on my bedside table.

Most of them were Lyn's, of course, and she would never forgive me for dragging her precious treasures into the wet, sandy world outside. But at the top of the pile were the first two books I'd owned in my lifetime, both of them birthday gifts – a richly illustrated copy of the *Encyclopaedia of Stars* that Creon had somehow gotten his hands on, and a well-thumbed, mousy brown edition of Phyron's *Treatises on Power and Privilege*. The latter, which I'd been told was an influential masterpiece of Divine Era political philosophy, would have been mind-numbingly boring if it hadn't previously belonged to Agenor and contained his and my mother's notes in the margins.

It was that smaller book for which I found myself reaching as I plopped down onto my bed, not yet entirely willing to face the rest of the household again. I opened it at a random page, which turned out to be the start of the chapter in which the acclaimed Phyron set out his thoughts on the fairness of taxation systems.

Is that a snake in your trousers, my mother had scribbled just above the chapter heading, her handwriting small and perfectly regular, *or are you just happy to see me?*

I allowed myself a few moments of hysterical giggling before I scraped myself together enough to browse on.

There was an odd comfort to it, reading her words in her own writing – as close as I had ever come to hearing her voice. She showed up on nearly every page, highlighting arguments, rebuking Agenor's half-hearted attempts to defend the Mother's policies. At times it almost seemed I could hear her behind those ink scribbles, dryly amused and yet so fiercely protective of her ideals and opinions.

Where are you? I'd whispered at the parchment more than once in the silence of my room, when not even Creon could hear me. *Why aren't you coming back?* Because it had been months since the battle at the Golden Court, months since the news of Agenor's turn against the empire had spread like wildfire over the archipelago, and still my mother had not given a sign of life.

Why?

At times, Phyron wrote, *the wishes of the individual must be secondary to the interests of the collective to which they belong.*

Allie had underlined the last words of that sentence and commented, *Note: since humanity does NOT belong to the collective whose interests are prioritised, this is a lousy argument to discredit our wish not to starve to death.*

I let out an accidental snort of approval.

A knock on the door interrupted my reading. With a sting of regret, I shoved the *Treatises* back onto the book pile; as comforting as it would have been to read my mother's notes late at night in unfamiliar lands, the small volume was too valuable to risk losing or damaging.

Creon waited for me in the corridor, hair bound back, bag over his shoulder. If he still felt any apprehension towards our travel plans, he hid it well.

Ready?

'Always,' I said, quietly enough not to be heard from the living room. Around the corner, Naxi was chattering about her first glimpse of Lyckfort, her high timbre alternating with a deep voice that sounded suspiciously like Agenor's. 'Did you hear about Edored?'

Creon shrugged. *I'm counting on you to take care of his nose if he gets too annoying.*

I laughed, came up on my toes to press the quickest kiss to his cheek, then swiftly jumped back and followed him to the living room. Edored was nowhere to be seen yet, thank the gods. Neither was Beyla, but she must have returned at some point, since it was indeed Agenor who stood discussing travel routes with Lyn and Naxi.

On the other side of the room, Nenya sat quiet and rigid in one of the armchairs, a long velvet travel coat over her shoulders and a full bag in her lap. Next to her, Tared stood frowning at some note – more Council trouble, perhaps? I decided not to ask. He looked displeased enough already.

'Oh, I would definitely aim for Zera's temple,' I heard Agenor say as I walked in behind Creon, in that pleasant yet confident tone that somehow removed all room for objection from the discussion. 'I did consider whether Inika might be helpful, too, but you should keep in mind ...'

Biting back a grin, I turned to Creon. He'd morphed into the Silent Death the moment we stepped into the room – the laughter wrinkles around his eyes gone, the truth of his thoughts hidden behind a smile like frostbite. His shoulders hadn't *tensed*, exactly, but his languid stance against the doorpost was no longer the unhurried confidence of a male perfectly at home in his surroundings. Rather, it had become that of a male who knew he could kill every single person in the room with as little as a flick of his fingers.

I lost track of what I'd been about to say for a heartbeat as every thought in my mind abruptly swirled back to the memory of those same fingers between my legs.

His smile grew too meaningful.

Thank the gods for Edored's sudden appearance the next moment, because at least his arrival was enough to protect me from whatever stupidity I might have committed in full view of the family. He barged into the room with a loud, 'Morning, Nosebreaker— Oh, Nen!'

When I whipped around, cursing the easy bait of my far too pleasant memories, the alf had already bounced towards Nenya, like a loyal dog brightening at his master's return. His earlier fury seemed forgotten. 'Didn't know you'd be coming too!'

'She's not—' Tared started without looking up from his note.

'I'll be off to Gar Temen in a moment,' Nenya stiffly interrupted, her face even paler than usual. 'Just waiting for Valdora to fade me to Rhudak.'

In the resulting silence, I heard Lyn say something about the poorly accessible terrain of Zera's woods, and wouldn't it be more practical to go looking for a goddess living near the coast?

'You're going to *Gar Temen*?' Edored repeated, and if Nenya had just called him a dishonourable coward, he couldn't have looked any more bewildered.

Tared finally folded his note into his pocket, sent Creon a glare that told me Agenor's revelations had indeed done little to placate him, and turned towards his cousin. 'Bakaru is causing trouble among the vampire kings. Someone needs to have a word with him.'

'What in hell?' By Edored's wide-eyed shock, I could have believed the reveal of Nenya's travel plans was some deadly betrayal. 'Why did no one tell me about this?'

'You were sleeping off the mead when we discussed it, arsehole,' Nenya said, but the sting in her voice was a dull one, and the stiffening of her shoulders was a weak imitation of her usual straight-backed posture. 'Didn't think you'd be terribly interested.'

'Orin's fucking eye, Nen,' Edored sputtered, kicking his bag aside as he crashed onto the nearest bench. 'I could have made you a couple of nice wooden stakes if I'd known ...'

'Wooden *stakes*?' Her voice shot up.

'What's wrong with those?' His grin was the usual raw, unrestrained one, and yet Nenya didn't roll her eyes or shake her head in exasperation for once. Quite the opposite – was that a *smile* twitching around the corners of her lips?

I *really* needed to ask Creon what in hell was going on between those two.

'You should have figured out by now that wooden stakes do very little to bring a vampire down,' Nenya said, incredulous laughter lacing her voice. 'And I'm not going to behead him, just to be clear.'

'Oh, I know,' Edored said cheerfully. 'But it would send a message if you were to slam a fucking log through the bastard's chest, wouldn't it?'

Creon breathed a chuckle beside me, to all appearances utterly unconcerned about that cold-eyed glare Tared had just aimed at him.

Nenya let out a helpless laugh and said, 'He's my giver! I don't even want to send him any—'

'You could pass on a message from me?' Edored suggested, his grin dripping with the intention of bloodshed.

'You're *terrible*.' But a hint of colour had returned to her pale cheeks, and she finally slumped into the padded linen of her seat, no longer perched on the edge as if the infamous vampire king may storm into the room any given moment. 'You're all making far too much of a fuss about this. It's only for a few days. I'll be perfectly fine.'

Both Tared and Edored looked doubtful. I bit my tongue and kept my questions down – not the moment to ask what horrors Bakaru Sefistrim was capable of, if Nenya was about to go face all of them.

Beyla returned a moment later, carrying two giant baskets of food, the contents of which were quickly divided between everyone's bags. Like Lyn, I was given an armful of lighter food: two loaves of bread, a bag of lentils, some dried apple strips. When Edored complained about the heavier packages of cheese, pumpkin, butter, and onions he'd been assigned, he was kindly reminded that no one had asked him to come along.

'But can't we just fade back and forth for—'

'We will,' Beyla interrupted, her fragile voice firm enough to shut him up. 'This won't last us a full ten days. But we have no idea how much wildlife survived the plague up there, and I'm not going to risk ending up with an empty stomach to the point where we're unable to fade.'

Edored scowled. 'But—'

With a sigh, Creon held out a scarred hand to the alf's luggage, one eyebrow raised in an expression that said, *If your delicate shoulders can't handle a few onions, I'll be happy to be a little more mature about this.*

'Oh, fuck off,' Edored grumbled, yanking the onions into his own bag. 'Do you have another pumpkin for me, Bey?'

Everything happened bewilderingly fast after that.

The last maps were consulted, the last water bottles filled, and then suddenly we were *leaving*, as if this wasn't some half-baked plan I'd thrown into their laps a day ago, as if it wasn't some mission dreamed up by a little fae brat with ulterior motives. Tared faded away first, taking Lyn and Naxi with him. Beyla threw one look at Edored, then grabbed Agenor and Creon by the wrists and vanished – aware, presumably, that Edored might feel tempted to drop the two fae males in the middle of the ocean if he got the chance.

'Bite him back,' Edored told Nenya by way of goodbye as he clasped his hand around my shoulder and faded as well.

Nenya's unconvincing smile was the last thing I saw. Then the familiar outlines of the living room distorted around us, giving way to a grim palette of black granite and the faint gleam of distant lights.

We emerged in a dark gallery of sorts, lit by nothing but a few watery flames hovering along the ceiling. To my left, a narrow staircase wound deeper into the earth, all but the first few steps shrouded in shadow. Before me, rows of sculpted arches marked the edge of this balcony, and behind that ...

Nothing.

Edored let go of me, and I slipped closer to the balustrade, ignoring the rest of the group. Glancing down, I found what I'd expected but never fully comprehended – the central hall of the Underground.

From below, I'd never figured out just how deep the city lay; the height of the hall was hard to estimate with most of its upper half concealed by shadow. Now, standing on this gallery just below the ceiling, the circle of mismatched Council seats was a doll house's interior below me, the few moving figures of alves and nymphs impossible to recognise at this distance.

I leaned over farther, squinting to make out the balconies and windows carved into the smooth walls. Behind me, Lyn sharply said, 'Em?'

'Coming!' I yelled back, unable to tear my eyes away from the abyss. Had anyone ever measured the depth? It would take a damn long rope to get all the way down there; the anchor cables of Cathra's fishing boats wouldn't do. Perhaps if Creon were to fly down slowly, he could loosen and reattach a measuring rope a couple of times?

As if he'd heard me think, he appeared beside me, resting his elbows on the dark stone with that effortless fae grace. *I suggest you try not to jump down, cactus.*

'Since you asked so politely ...' I muttered, and he chuckled. 'How deep do you think it is?'

Third of a mile, roughly? He stood a little straighter, considering the matter. *We could calculate it by dropping something.*

I blinked. 'Could we?'

Standard acceleration and all that. He had to spell the word *acceleration*; we'd never needed a sign for the concept. *Would need one of those very precise Phurian clocks, but if I chucked Edored over the edge and you measured just how long it took for him to hit the floor ...*

I burst out laughing. 'One day I'll write your biography and title it *Murder and Mathematics.*'

As long as you take care to adequately describe my godlike physique, he dryly signed, pulling me back from the edge with his left hand. His fingers were firm on my upper arm, their weight settling reassuringly into the marrow of my bones. *But let's wait until we have this trip behind us. They're waiting.*

Oh, fuck. I'd momentarily forgotten about the eyes watching us – about that cursed public opinion, about Tared and Agenor waiting for any reason to end this mission and drag me out of Creon's way. Even as I obediently turned away from the edge and tried to look chaste and innocent, the reflex to follow the magnetic pull of his fingers and jump into his embrace was painfully strong.

I pulled my arm from his grip, cursing in silence at the hungering phantom pressure his fingers left behind. Months in the privacy of silent library halls and bedrooms had lowered my guard. Time to get back into the habit of secrecy, and get there really damn quickly.

We walked on without speaking. Before us, a low tunnel led away from the dizzying depths of the hall; the others had quietly gathered at the farthest point, where the corridor ended in a low, steel-plated doorway. Three heavy bolts blocked the exit of the Underground, two keyholes between them. The heavy locks were made of alf steel, forged to resist fae magic.

A single ray of sunlight fell through the chink below the door.

Sunlight.

Behind that thick layer of wood and iron and alf steel, the continent was waiting for us – the plague was waiting for us.

It was at the sight of my companions' motionless tension – at the sight of *Edored* looking pale and nervous – that sudden talons of fear dug deep into my guts. But this was not the time to waver, not the time to turn back.

I clenched my nails into my palm to keep myself from reaching for Creon and jutted up my chin, taking care to sound like the fearless little half fae they could safely follow into hell. 'I suppose someone brought a key?'

That broke the spell. Naxi drew two keys from the pocket of her fuzzy jacket, both of them as large as Lyn's forearms, while Tared hauled the bolts aside. The door screeched open a fraction, the wail of its rusty hinges deafening in the buried silence.

A sliver of blinding sunlight fell through the chink, and I caught my first glimpse of the place where no living soul had ventured since the War of the Gods.

CHAPTER 6

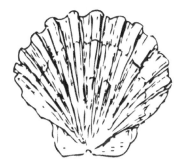

AT FIRST, I COULD distinguish nothing but outlines through the sting of the light: high facades and the broad expanse of an elegant avenue, all of it reduced to pain and whiteness under the merciless midday sun.

Edored's muffled swearing was an eloquent enough description, though.

Only several heartbeats later, blinking the last tears from my eyes, did I see what his alf eyes had already recognised even in the dazzling sunlight – a graveyard.

Lyckfort must have been a stunning city once, the jewel of Divine Age architecture that I knew from paintings and sketches in Lyn's books. But stretched out before us lay decaying ruins, the brick terrace houses crumbling, the high windows broken, the last flecks of paint on the shutters on the brink of flaking off. Weeds and vines had grown over the cobblestones, claiming the streets for themselves. They climbed over the fountains and statues, too, the marble below cracked and weathered, the faces and ornamental motifs no longer recognisable even in the clear light of day.

And everywhere, still mostly human-shaped but burned black like coal from head to toe, were the bodies.

I stared at them, bile rising in the back of my throat. The plague victims lay scattered across the street, some alone, some with child-sized companions, some surrounded by the rotting remains of bags and baskets, caught in the middle of their flight. They couldn't possibly have understood what was coming for them. They must have been surprised by the deadly magic washing over them, no time to flee their city and set off towards the sea, but even if it had been quick – and I prayed it had been quick …

These burns are no joke, Ylfreda had said.

'I've got the shields in place,' Naxi said lightly, her chipper voice jarring like a festive waltz at a funeral. 'Creon, could you try— Hell's sake, there's no need to shield half the bloody continent at once, show-off. Tone it down a little.'

After a moment of pause, Creon tilted his head, as if to ask a question.

'Still overdoing it slightly,' Naxi said with a sharp-toothed grin, 'but I suppose you'll get the hang of it. Come out, everyone. Our darling prince is keeping the plague at bay between here and Elderburg, I believe.'

With a careless chuckle, Creon followed her outside. His look around the street was devoid of all shock or aversion; nothing but shallow curiosity in his eyes as he scanned his surroundings, like an artist admiring the work of another master. Sauntering around like this, every shred of the heart I knew hidden behind an impenetrable shield, his tall form blended easily into this gruesome display of magic – nothing but yet another terror in a city that had already seen too much of them.

A sight that shouldn't make my breath catch, that shouldn't make me itch to follow him into the darkness … but gods have mercy, there was no denying the stutter of my heart.

Then I saw the unbridled hate in Tared's grey eyes, the muscle twitching at Agenor's temple, the way Edored and Beyla tightened their hands around their swords, and woke from my ill-advised swooning with a jolt. Pleasant as it might be to stand here and ogle Creon as he conquered the entire wasteland of Lyckfort with a single look, this wasn't going to convince anyone that he wasn't looking to seduce me or that I wasn't waiting to be seduced.

I shoved past a faltering Beyla and stepped onto the overgrown cobblestones.

'Em!' Agenor hissed behind me.

But no torturous magic hit me as I emerged into the sunlight and drew in my first lungful of fresh Lyckfort air. The breeze tasted oddly dusty, lacking that briny sharpness of nearby sea that I'd breathed all my life – a more tangible reminder of the strangeness of my surroundings, somehow, than even the sight of the burned corpses in the street.

I steeled my shoulders, pretending I didn't hear the muttering of the alves stepping out behind me. I was sensible and practical, I reminded myself as I followed Creon over the cobblestones. When I looked at him, I didn't see the male who'd fucked my mind inside out a mere day ago. As a dutiful saviour of the world, I just saw a weapon.

'Is the plague not giving you too much trouble?' I said, sensibly and practically.

It's surprisingly doable. He didn't look at me as he signed the words, scanning the shattered windows for any threat or movement. Only then did I realise how still the city was – no mice scurrying away between the climber vines, no birds nesting in the open windowsills. *It's like an emotional shield, except I have to push it out a little wider to include all of you. Mind if I take a look at one of those corpses?*

'Is that supposed to be a suggestion for me to stay put?' I said, not slowing down.

It was worth a try, he signed wryly.

With a snort, I followed him to the first charred body – recognisable as a torso with four limbs and a head attached, but not much more. From its shape on the mossy cobblestones, I couldn't even tell what had been the back or the front of this unlucky human.

Creon drew a dagger from his boot and knelt next to the gruesome remains without hesitation, poking the blackened, crumbling skin with the tip of his blade. Flakes of ash came loose, like the dust peeling off cinders in a smouldering fire.

'Quite thoroughly burned,' I said, unable to look away despite the bile rising once again in my throat.

But Creon shook his head, pulling his leather gloves from his pocket before he, with a quick and experienced motion, buried half of his blade into what had presumably once been a thigh. The burned, scale-like outer layer of the corpse split open with a sickening crack and revealed the untainted pink of human flesh below, the rot kept out by the hard shell of plague-charred skin.

'*Ew*,' I said.

He grinned up at me, releasing the knife to slip his gloves onto his hands. *Warned you.*

'Is there a need for this?' Agenor snapped behind me, closer than I'd expected him. Two other pairs of footsteps followed – one fast and light, one unhurried and deliberate. Lyn and Tared. 'As much as it may amuse you, the poor sods suffered enough.'

'Bit late with your sympathy, aren't you?' Tared said coldly.

'For fuck's sake, both of you,' Lyn muttered. 'Creon, what is the point of this investigation, exactly?'

He didn't rise from his kneeling position, didn't take off his gloves. Turning to me, he signed, *Trying to find out how damaging this plague magic is.*

'It only burns the outer layer,' I said slowly, ignoring the others and frowning at the cut body at his feet. 'Thoroughly – but only the outer layer. Do you think something other than skin would be enough to stop it?'

Worth investigating. He turned back to his work and quickly but meticulously peeled off a square inch of charcoal, baring the vulnerable flesh below. Grisly work, and yet I didn't manage to look away. There was something oddly hypnotising about the nimble motions of his gloved fingers, the gleam of concentration in his eyes as he examined his shred of charred skin against the sunlight.

'Please don't start chewing on it,' I said, reminded of the bankers on Ildhelm trying to decide a coin's worth.

He chuckled but followed the advice, putting the bit of skin aside to

86

flip the body around and reveal what I now realised must have been the dead human's face. The mouth and eyes had left ghastly holes in the otherwise flat surface; wherever the nose had gone, it hadn't left a trace.

'Good gods,' Agenor murmured as he emerged beside me, his jaw clenched with the distaste of a male who has always thought himself safely above the dirty work. 'Em, are you sure you want to see—'

I shrugged. 'I'd rather know what we're up against.'

Lyn and Tared joined our little circle, his face tight with cold rage, hers contorted in a frown that was equal parts disgust and fascination. Unfazed, Creon set his knife into the dead human's cheek and started carving skin away with quick, practiced turns of his wrist. Greyish white skull emerged under his blade, showing no trace of godly magic.

Tared muttered a curse, tearing his eyes away to take in the other bodies littering the street. 'I don't suppose many of them had time to get away, so close to the eruption?'

'It happened *here*?' I said, unable to suppress a shiver. No one had ever told me about Korok's death in much detail; the history books were excruciatingly vague about that fateful day, likely because most eyewitnesses had no longer been capable of reporting back.

Agenor merely nodded – a stiff, strained motion.

'Where, exactly?' Lyn said and threw a narrow-eyed glance around. 'We may want to avoid the source of the magic, if any of it is still brewing. Somewhere outside the city, wasn't it?'

'I ...' Agenor started, then faltered.

He faltered so abruptly that even Creon looked up from his skinning work, night-black eyes narrowing as they swept over my father's face. Agenor stared back at him, his expression oddly blank until a frown seeped back in.

'I'm ... not sure,' he finished, clearly hearing the oddity of that statement himself.

'You're not *sure*?' Tared repeated. The hard edge to his words left no doubt of his opinions; they might have required a new definition of the word *unfavourable*. 'You blew up an entire damn god and you're not *sure* where it—'

'I hate to remind you,' Agenor cut in, an unusual bite to his voice, 'but Korok's death was hardly the only remarkable event of that day. I remember arriving in Lyckfort for what I assumed were peace negotiations. I remember realising something had gone terribly wrong and trying to get at least *some* citizens out before everything was laid to waste. Everything in between ...' Again he paused, and again there was a glimpse of glassiness in his eyes – the look of a male grasping desperately for his memories and finding none. 'It's a blur.'

Even Lyn looked sceptical, but before any of them could speak, Creon rose, leaving the maimed corpse of his test subject behind on the cobblestones. With a last glance down, he signed, *Pretty ugly.*

'Glad you managed to confirm that through diligent examination,' I said. 'Perhaps you could double check if they're really dead, too?'

Had there been no one else around, I suspected he'd have swatted a wing at my face, then taken his revenge by kissing me until I begged for mercy. Now, under the close scrutiny of the two males who'd appointed themselves defenders of my honour, Creon allowed himself nothing but a grin drenched in indifference. *Clothes have melted into their skin. So even if it doesn't reach deep, I don't think wrapping yourself in a blanket will be enough to survive this magic.*

I pulled a face. 'Gross. Good to know, though.'

He nodded slowly. *We should look into water. There must be a reason it never reached the islands.*

'But if you and Naxi can keep it at bay anyway ...'

Want you to have options if anything goes wrong.

'Would anyone care,' Agenor said tartly, watching our conversation with narrowed eyes, 'to summarise their conclusions in a manner all of us can understand?'

I was just introducing the idea of water as a plague-stopping barrier when Edored came jogging up to us from the other side of the avenue, sword in hand, grey eyes shining with boyish excitement. 'Beyla thinks she found dragon traces!'

Melted clothes abruptly forgotten, we followed him to a narrow alleyway where Naxi stood waiting for us. Heaps of rubble barricaded the sand coating the street. It must have been a lively place full of shops once; painted wooden signs still swung gloomily from the facades, the creaking of their chains uncannily reminiscent of moaning humans. But the doors had rotted from the storefronts, the wares behind the broken windows had withered to dust, and all that remained of the former glory of the place was the occasional gleam of coins left behind.

There were fewer bodies here. No one, it seemed, had run to the barber in an attempt to save their hide.

We found Beyla clambering over the rotting balustrade of a balcony, her ash blonde braid already dusty from whatever places she'd been exploring. She jumped down as she saw us, landing like a cat in the sand and rubble ten feet down.

'There's a nest in the attic room,' she reported before anyone could ask what in hell she was doing climbing over buildings on the brink of collapse. 'About the size of a double bed, which seems large for a dragon – but then again …' She dug something from the pocket of her grey travel coat, handing it to Lyn. 'What do you make of this?'

Agenor's breath faltered next to me as the object in Lyn's fingers caught the sunlight. It was a scale – smooth and gold and about the size of my entire hand.

'Perhaps,' Tared suggested, 'it's time to get the hell out of here.'

'It was an old nest,' Beyla said, throwing him a wry smile. 'And I'm not *sure* it's a dragon's in the first place. They're practically extinct, for a start – and I don't think they're supposed to grow that big?'

'They're not.' Agenor gave the impression that he still wouldn't mind getting the hell out, old nest or not. 'The largest I ever saw was about the size of a sheep, and most were much smaller than that. This would be …' He grimaced. 'An unpleasant creature to encounter.'

'But it *does* look like a dragon's, doesn't it?'

'It is a dragon scale,' he said, rubbing his temple. 'No doubt about that. The question is—'

'It could be the plague magic,' Lyn suggested, sitting down on a nearby pile of bricks and stone-dust as she frowned at the scale. 'Like those arm-sized worms you said came crawling out of the ground where Etele's blood hit at the Golden Court. Either it kills or it results in monstrous proportions – that would fit the dual nature pretty well.'

Agenor looked even unhappier.

'So,' Edored said, brightening, 'are we going to hunt a dragon?'

Tared let out a long-suffering groan.

'I suggest we get out of the city first,' Beyla said, her wistful glance at the many unexplored windows notwithstanding. 'No use in wasting days charting this labyrinth if we have better things to do, and at least in the open field we'll see any dragons coming for us. We can always come back later.'

No one argued with that logic, although Edored grumbled under his breath until Lyn flung a handful of sparks at him.

We returned to the street we'd come from and walked west from there, past neglected parks and collapsed bridges, canals full of weeds and abandoned carts along the streets. A temple towered above the roofs, built in that familiar pentagon shape of the holy buildings I knew from home. Small offerings still lay piled up on the marble stairs, tattered ribbons fluttering on the autumn breeze.

There were even more bodies there, scattered over the pavement, their burned faces showing deep holes where their screaming mouths had been. The inhabitants of Lyckfort must have run for the protection of their gods as the magic washed over them, not knowing that the gods who'd kept them safe as long as history remembered would never help them again.

Agenor's directions grew curter and curter as we navigated the maze of destruction, until he gave up speaking entirely and just pointed wherever we needed to go, dread bleeding through his every gesture and expression. Most of the group was similarly quiet behind me. Naxi, on the other hand, drifted around in a flurry of pink-blonde curls and flapping skirts, and Creon strolled along beside me as if we were visiting a boring autumn fair, carelessly flicking a knife between his fingers.

Had just the two of us been there, his confident calm would have been comforting. Now, with the eyes of the others on our necks ...

'Perhaps,' I muttered, looking away from the burned shapes of two people clutching each other on the street, 'you should try to look a little less ... murderous.'

He slipped his knife back into the sheath at his belt, then turned to me, one eyebrow a fraction higher than the other. *A little murder never killed anyone. Does it bother you?*

'You know it doesn't.' I pulled the weight of my bag tighter on my shoulders, already grateful I hadn't given in to the temptation to bring a book. 'I'm just thinking, if you ever want them to think slightly better of you ...'

His fingers tightened so subtly I doubted even Lyn would have noticed. *I didn't survive three hundred years of torturing people to death by caring what others thought of me. They'll handle their own dislike just fine. I don't need to do it for them.*

'But—'

He shrugged, interrupting me. *Did Agenor ever tell you why he wanted to come?*

I glanced at my father, who was striding forward with the determined force of a battle ram, jaw clenched so tight it may have physically hurt. Whatever he'd hoped to find in the city he'd fled in a hurry centuries ago and never seen again, it didn't appear he'd found it between the bodies and the overgrown houses.

'He didn't,' I said under my breath. 'Why?'

He seems – Creon considered his words for a moment, fingers hanging motionlessly between signs – *shocked.*

I couldn't help a grimace. 'Some people would consider a city full of corpses quite shocking.'

He's seen worse and felt less over it, Creon signed wryly. *And he should have known exactly how bad it would be. There's no reason for him to feel surprised at the state of this place.*

Surprised? I stole another glance at Agenor, whose face was too stony to read without the help of demon magic. But his wings lay tight as stretched canvas against his back – far more tension than he'd ever show the world if he could help it.

'I have no idea,' I admitted with a twinge of nervousness. 'I could ask him later. He won't tell me when you're still around.'

Creon nodded slowly and resumed toying with his knife.

We walked in silence, endless boulevard after endless square, until finally the streets grew empty and the outer walls of the city loomed up before us. They were built from the same red brick as most of the houses, and even while they were crumbling under the force of sun and wind and the stubborn vines crawling over them, it was easy to imagine their former glory – a towering thirty feet of massive stone, the gate flanked by sculpted creatures I thought might be dragons.

Still Agenor didn't speak, and when I looked to my right, Creon didn't meet my gaze. I turned my eyes back to the world before me, catching my first glimpse of the landscape that waited beyond the desolation of the city. A tangled green wilderness, the occasional collapsed shed and farm, and beyond those ...

The mountains.

My feet caught on an uneven cobblestone as I realised what I was seeing.

Creon was just quick enough, grabbing my upper arm to keep me standing. I barely noticed. The jagged, blue-greyish shapes on the horizon appeared to stare back at me, taunting me with the distance that separated us.

The *distance.*

I'd never seen so much land in one place. It had to be days and days and days of walking, nothing but solid earth between us and those sharp-edged peaks, not even the shallowest bay to break up the endless expanse of the continent. I gaped at that unfathomable horizon, thoughts spinning to match the view with the maps I knew – with the hard and cold facts of geography. This was merely a sliver of the landmass on which we were standing. The road to the sea in the east had to be five times as long, at least – *five times* – and much more land stretched out into the south and west ...

Four lousy gods might be wandering somewhere on that massive surface I couldn't even wrap my head around, and I'd decided I wanted to find them.

In ten days.

Zera help me. Why had anyone ever agreed with this madness?

But I received no 'we told you so,' no 'time to turn back, then?' as the rest of the group passed me by. Tared looked sourly amused, Lyn concerned. Beyla sighed, a sound of long, deep yearning, and I wondered how long it would be before she'd convince Anaxia to leave for another mission across all these miles of untraveled earth.

'It used to be about three hours of walking to reach the edge of the woods,' Agenor said, words tense as if he could barely bring himself to utter them. I wondered if he'd even noticed my near-fall or Creon laying hands on me. 'I assume the paths will be in a worse state than they used to be, so it may take longer now. If you aim for— Wait, let me show you ...'

We followed him through the gate like ducklings swimming after their mother. More weed-covered fields waited for us beyond the wall. Tangles of nettles and thorns smothered every house or shed still standing, and ...

'Orin's fucking eye,' Edored sputtered next to me, freezing mid-step. 'What is *that*?'

Before us, a patch of scorched black soil disrupted the stubborn greenery, stretching half a mile in each direction.

The black earth sloped down at the centre, forming a shape that resembled the crater of a sleeping volcano. But gods help me, there were no volcanoes on the continent, were there? Had it been a wildfire, shaping this pit? A particularly disgruntled dragon? A battle during the War of the Gods?

'It's stronger here,' Naxi informed us, her melodious voice unfazed. 'The plague magic.'

'Korok,' Lyn said breathlessly.

And at once, I understood.

That crater ... A scar shaped by an eruption powerful enough to dent solid earth – by magic powerful enough to kill a creature reigning over life and death itself. Cold sweat trickled down my spine as I stared at the black crystals glistening between the ash and cinders, at the lowest point that marked the spot where a god had drawn his last breath. Where a single magical experiment gone wrong had marked the end of an era and the death of thousands upon thousands of innocent humans.

In a rare moment of unpolished candour, Agenor muttered, '*Fuck.*'

'Memory returning?' Tared said bitterly.

The silence stretched too long. Agenor's lips parted and closed once, twice, his eyes glued to the burned desolation with a gleam of bewilderment. 'I ... I don't ...'

'You don't *remember*?' Edored said, his voice so loud that I flinched. 'Weren't you here? The day the bitch killed him?'

'I was, but ...'

'Well, that must be pleasant,' Beyla muttered. 'Being able to forget things at will.'

'It's nothing like that,' Agenor snapped as he jerked around, every last piece of the buttoned-up fae lord slipping from his grip. I glanced at Creon, who stood studying him with piercing eyes, no longer so impossibly unaffected. 'I just don't remember this place in particular, but ...'

'But you were right here,' Lyn said, as if she could make it true by just speaking the words with perfect conviction. 'Every single report surviving from that day names you as one of the people who were present when she—'

'I must have been in the city,' Agenor interrupted brusquely. 'I—'

'That doesn't make *sense*, Agenor.'

He stared at her, breathing too fast. 'What else are you suggesting? Nothing about this mark looks familiar to me. Don't you think I would remember at least a *glimpse* of it?'

Something sparked in my mind as thoughts collided – a burst of insight so sudden that I didn't fully grasp what I was about to say until my lips were already moving. 'Agenor?'

'Yes?' He sounded five words away from breaking. 'What is it?'

'Didn't you say ... didn't you say she bound you by taking a memory?'

He went still – perfectly, breathlessly still.

'I beg your pardon?' Lyn said.

'The binding of his magic.' Words poured out without thought or intent; my suspicions shaped themselves, nothing but shreds of ideas until my lips forced them into glass-edged accusations. 'The Mother took a memory, didn't she?'

'No,' Agenor said hoarsely. 'That ... I see the appeal as an explanation, Em, but it can't have been this memory. They bound me long before

Korok died – long before the War of the Gods ended.'

'Are you sure?'

He blinked. 'Of course I'm sure. Why would they have waited that long to bind me?'

'Because she pulled you from the ruins of your family's home when you were a child,' I said bleakly. 'Because you were fully loyal to her, and she *knew* you were. She may have realised the bindings could have unpleasant side effects, that they could limit your magic in the wrong moments – she didn't bind Creon at first either, after all.'

'Oh, gods,' Lyn said, understanding where I was going long before I grasped the full extent myself. If the Mother hadn't bound him at first – if she'd only opted to do so *after* that first war had been fought and won ...

She must have had a reason.

'Look, this is a lovely theoretical exercise,' Tared said, and his fingers drumming against his thigh suggested more agitation than the wry tone of his voice, 'but is there any reason to assume his lordship is not just being a little selective about what he likes to remember?'

He's still very damn confused, Creon signed, his eyes shooting back and forth between Agenor and me.

'I can assure you I'm not being deliberately selective about anything, Thorgedson,' Agenor bit out. Something almost fearful sparked in his glance at Creon. 'Em, I appreciate the suggestion, but I frankly don't think it makes any sense to assume she bound me so late.'

I let out a laugh. 'Do you remember when she did bind you, then?'

His silence was the only answer I needed. Tared swore under his breath, a string of Alvish curses I hadn't heard since Edored drunkenly broke his toe at my birthday celebration.

'Is there *anything* you remember about Korok's death?' I added, holding Agenor's green-gold gaze. 'How exactly he died? How you felt when you realised what was happening? Where you went and what you said and—'

'No.' He ran a hand through his hair, leaving his dark locks sticking in all directions except their usual immaculate smoothness. 'I ... No. I thought ...' He swallowed and didn't finish that sentence.

'You thought you might remember more if you saw this place again,' I said, new pieces falling into place. 'So you did notice before. That you didn't remember.'

'Just that parts of it were blurry to me,' he said, his voice rising in what almost sounded like panic – twelve hundred years of restraint evaporating at the thought of his own mind betraying him. 'But *all* of it is a mess, even the parts I do remember – the whole day was a fucking mess. It's just that this place ...'

He inhaled slowly, unsteadily. No one else moved; only Naxi's dress fluttered ceaselessly in the corner of my sight.

'You should at the very least remember it now that you're seeing it again,' I said.

He muttered a curse. 'Yes.'

'So what if she *did* bind you after it happened?' I nodded at the scorched crater. 'Because that would explain the hole in your memory. She bound you, and this is what she took – the memory of Korok's death.'

'But why?' His deep voice was chafing against its own edges, so close to cracking I could feel it in my guts. 'Em, if she didn't bind me for five hundred years, why for the bloody gods' sakes would she suddenly—'

'She killed the god you swore to protect,' Lyn said quietly.

'What?'

'And destroyed an entire damn continent,' I added, throwing her a grateful look. She grimaced. 'Killed thousands of humans and fae in the process – you *did* care about that, yes? You said you remember trying to get them out. Your life was in danger, too. You must have cared a lot to make the effort nonetheless.'

'Em.' His bronze skin had gone grey. 'You can't be serious.'

'I'm very serious! It doesn't make sense, does it, that after all that bloodshed, you'd come home and throw the last of your morals at her feet without ever questioning what she'd done? It doesn't sound like *you.*'

'Doesn't it?' Tared said sourly.

I ignored him. 'So what if you did try to confront her afterwards? What if she realised she'd finally lost your unconditional loyalty but that you were too useful to her to die on the spot, so she bound you instead?'

Creon breathed a laugh. *Not without precedent.*

'Exactly. So she took all memories of that worst moment, dulled the horror of the rest, stifled all thoughts of insubordination you'd ever had, and declared that solution a success when you carried on just as you had before she blew Korok to pieces?'

The horror in Agenor's eyes wasn't horror, exactly. It was a yearning sort of panic – a hope that didn't dare to believe in itself.

'I did always find it surprising that the snakes stayed with you,' Naxi suddenly said, winding blonde curls around her fingers. 'Did you never wonder? I knew a godsworn nymph who betrayed Zera during the War of the Gods, and her bird familiars tried to pick her eyes out.'

Another memory found its way to the surface of my mind. 'They *are* quite touchy about people accusing you of treason, aren't they? The snakes? Coral nearly bit Tared's head off when he said something about it at the Golden Court.'

'Coral,' Tared said, 'is always on the verge of biting someone's head off.' But even he didn't sound quite convinced anymore.

'She named me Lord Protector of the empire after that war,' Agenor said, clinging to those words like they were all that kept him from shattering. 'I was aware of every single damn thing going on at the court for centuries. Why would she show me that kind of trust if I'd already betrayed her once?'

Lyn brushed a handful of curls from her face. 'Because she knew she'd broken your mind to the point where it was unlikely you'd ever turn on her again?'

Even now, there was a glimpse of bruised pride in the wide-eyed look he sent her. 'Gods and demons, Lyn, I'm not—'

Also, Creon signed, jaw suddenly tight as he met my gaze, *he wasn't aware of everything to the extent he thinks he was.*

I glanced at Agenor, who had fallen silent. 'Any examples?'

Ask him when he thinks my father died.

'Your … Oh, gods.' His father, who had nearly tortured his eight-year-old son to death, only to find his own end at the Mother's hands. Not a subject I brought up lightly, and definitely not with three alves and Lord Agenor himself around. 'Are you sure?'

Creon shrugged, and if I hadn't known better, if I hadn't seen him torture himself to insanity just to be anyone else than the male his father had been, I wouldn't have looked for anything but proud amusement behind that shrug.

'What?' Agenor snapped.

'When, according to you ...' I looked at Creon, waiting for a sign to stop me. He merely nodded, so I braced myself and blurted, 'When would you say Kertayan died?'

Agenor's eyes shot towards Creon. '*Kertayan?*'

Creon's smile was just short of patronising.

'Why in hell would that be—'

'Agenor, *when?*'

'Two months before Creon's birth,' Agenor said sharply, turning back to me, 'at the hands of a group of vampire rebels, who were promptly executed in retaliation. Could you tell me what in hell this has to do with Korok, beyond the obvious?'

'He lived until Creon was eight,' I said.

For three, four heartbeats, nothing broke the silence except Naxi's whispered, '*Oooh.*'

Lyn stared at me. Everyone else stared at Creon, who studied his nails with the bored look of an arrogant lord waiting for his subjects to stop nagging.

'You never met him, did you?' Agenor said, fear of the opposite oozing through every single word of that sentence.

Creon merely smiled at him.

'But ... How ...' I wasn't sure what had shocked the Lord Protector of the Crimson Court more: his own ignorance of these new facts or the revelation that Creon had known his father after all, a father I suspected Agenor never mentioned for his own personal reasons. The bastard had been the one to take Korok's place, after all. 'Did he survive that meeting? Kertayan?'

Now the shield of the Silent Death *had* to waver, didn't it? But Creon just shrugged, sighed, and slowly shook his head.

I *saw* the pieces of the puzzle fall into all the wrong places in the eyes around me, saw every single one of them draw exactly the wrong conclusion: that *Creon* had been the one to kill his demon parent, had perhaps even been the one to initiate the confrontation. Only Naxi looked almost elated with sudden understanding. *I don't know what made him turn away from his kind so staunchly*, she'd said months ago in Lyn's library.

Now she knew.

'Anyway,' I said, dragging the conversation back to its starting point before anyone could start asking questions no one wanted to answer, 'obviously the Mother knew about all of this. So if you didn't' – I shrugged apologetically at Agenor – 'you may not have been as privy to her secrets as she made you think.'

He looked vaguely green in the face now. His gaze wandered to the black bargain gem at the inside of his wrist, that last mark my mother had left – enough to pull him from what may have been much, much more than an indifferent blind eye.

'Well.' Even his voice sounded nauseous. 'I suppose I should get back home and look into my old notes to see if ... if anything ...'

'Yes,' I said.

'Well,' he said again.

'Let us know if you find anything relevant,' Lyn said, as usual better at finding the right words. I didn't have any words left, staring at my father's slumping wings. I just wanted to hug him, which was ridiculous, given that I'd never hugged him in my life and might give him a heart attack on top of everything else.

'I'll do that.' His attempt at business-like determination was less than successful. 'And I'll have a word with the phoenix elders, if they'll see me. I'll ...' Again his sentence drifted off, the words sucked straight into that blackened crater next to us, straight into the pit of memories he couldn't possibly reach anymore.

Not even Tared made any biting remarks this time.

'I can fade you back to the Golden Court,' Beyla said, stepping forward with a glance at Naxi. 'Please don't move that demon shield of yours anywhere until I'm back.'

Agenor grabbed her outstretched hand like a male dangling dangerously over the edge of a gaping ravine, and with a last flicker of light,
the both of them were gone.

CHAPTER 7

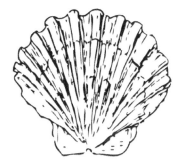

BEYLA RETURNED WITHIN MINUTES, fading safely into the shield of protection that Creon and Naxi kept up around us. The expression on her slender face was dark and hardly brightened as she shoved a handful of honey-glazed almonds into her mouth.

'And?' Tared said.

Lyn and Naxi hurried back from their quick exploration at the edge of the burned crater. Creon, who stood studying burn traces on the outer city wall, didn't even bother to turn around – but I knew he'd take note of every single word spoken behind his back, and likely remember them all long after the speakers themselves had already forgotten.

'I must admit,' Beyla said, her frail voice just audible over her chewing, 'I think he's telling the truth.'

Naxi chuckled. 'Oh, he is. About not knowing the truth, that is.'

The look the three alves exchanged was chillier than the coldest winter morning, the edge of stone in their eyes so eerily similar that, for the blink of an eye, I could have believed them brothers and sister.

'Yes,' Tared finally said. 'I do believe him, too. Which ...'

He didn't finish his sentence; there was no need to. Which meant that after blaming Agenor for centuries, after accepting an alliance of necessity only under protest and with frequent stinging remarks to compensate, they now had to consider that the Lord of the Golden Court may have been one of the few who'd tried to prevent the violence.

Honour debts and unbridled hate didn't mix well, and they all looked painfully aware of it.

'At this rate, we'll run out of fae to kill next week,' Edored grumbled, glowering at Creon's winged back. 'Anyone want to bet how long it'll take Ophion to reveal he's just some poor, misunderstood little fucker?'

Creon leisurely picked at a stem of ivy with his knife, free hand in his pocket, and ignored the conversation entirely.

'If I recall correctly,' Beyla said around her almonds, 'Ophion slaughtered his entire family long before the Mother bound him. I doubt anyone will get in your way.'

Edored looked greatly relieved.

Kinslayer, Lyn had called the Mother's lover at the Golden Court. I braced myself before asking my question, well aware the answer could hardly be a pleasant one. 'Why did he? Just for the fun of it?'

'His house resisted the Mother for a while when she was busy conquering all fae peoples,' Beyla said. 'Ophion won her favour by sending her his father's rotting head and some fingers from his mother and sisters. If we've misunderstood him so far, I don't think I wish to understand him any better.' A quick glance at Tared. 'Should we—'

A flash of azure interrupted her.

The alves whipped around as one, blades sliding from sheaths. Creon didn't turn around, but the black of his shirt had faded to a muddy brown, evidence of blue magic drawn. Before him, where he'd painstakingly removed the moss and vines from the weathered bricks, an arm's length of wall suddenly gleamed smooth and polished in the autumn sun.

And on that newly restored surface, elegant engravings had become visible under the force of his healing powers.

The shapes they formed looked just a fraction too familiar. Curls and swirls, running over the brick surface in irregular curving lines – just like the inscription that framed the doorway to Etele's Underground memorial.

Divine Tongue.

'Good gods,' Lyn breathed, darting closer as her eyes shot along the lines. 'How did you— Oh. *Oh.*' Her voice soared. 'Inika help us, but that means ...'

'Is that last word *eruzke*?' Tared said, frowning at the inscription. 'Because that's supposed to mean *brother*, isn't it?'

Creon's smile as he met my gaze carried the triumphant edge of a predator smelling blood. I dazedly stared at him, my thoughts turning over that clue three, four times before I dared to believe what I'd just heard.

Brother. In this place, in that language.

That ... that couldn't be true, could it?

'It's an epitaph,' Lyn muttered, fidgeting frantically with her curls. 'Kurrian hexameter, which would have been popular around—'

'But what does it say?' Edored interrupted loudly, and I felt a skewed sense of gratefulness that at least I wasn't the only uncivilised swine with no idea how to read these cryptic lines.

'*May you be given* ...' Lyn turned around, her eyes wide as saucers. '*May you be given more peace than you deserve, brother.*'

A ringing silence stretched out across the crater.

'Orin's eye,' Beyla said quietly.

I barely dared to believe the impossible feeling that grew in me – a surge of *hope*, pressing against my rib cage so heavily I could hardly breathe. It shouldn't have surprised me. I'd concluded the gods may still be alive weeks ago, and I'd been confident enough of that conclusion to convince the rest of the Alliance. But until this moment, there had never been *evidence* – only educated guesses and the desperate dream that someone would know how to restore a magic-bound voice.

This ...

This had nothing to do with hopes and dreams anymore.

'So they survived.' My voice had gone rough. 'If they lived long enough ... if at least one of them lived long enough to leave this here ...'

My eyes met Creon's, and whatever I'd been about to say dissolved into the red-hot burst of sparks erupting in my lower belly. His smile may have been a predator's smile on the surface, but that fervour burning below was far more than a mere hunter's drive – a gleam of longing that turned the ink black of his eyes into smouldering embers and left me incapable of breathing for two full heartbeats.

He hadn't dared to hope before.

My body grew hot, triumph mingling with a flare of frustration. Gods be damned, why did we have to make this discovery in this cursed place, surrounded by travel companions who'd surely raise some eyebrows if I were to tear off his clothes for a fitting celebration?

And how long had I stood here staring at him already?

Naxi was stifling a fit of giggles behind a bright pink sleeve. Not a good sign. I tore my gaze away from Creon, forcing myself to focus on the inscription, and managed, 'Well.' To hell with the stutter in my voice. 'That gives us something to look for, doesn't it?'

'Yes,' Tared said slowly, but there was no relief in his voice. 'So it seems.'

What had he hoped for? That after two days in this place, I would realise the folly of my plans and agree to return home and play the impeccable saviour to a bunch of frightened nymphs for the rest of the war?

Or ... I caught the steely glint in his eyes as his gaze slid towards Creon, and again my heart skipped another beat, for far more unpleasant reasons. Or was I the problem again, doing an impressively terrible job at hiding just how much the presence of an unreasonably beautiful fae murderer affected me?

'Um,' I said, clearing my throat as if that might erase my latest mistake. 'Should we get on our way, then?'

Neither of them reacted. Tared had tilted his head a fraction, studying Creon with squinted eyes as if the truth of his intentions was written in the ink under his skin. And suddenly I was nothing but a bystander in this silent war of looks and unspoken accusations, caught in the middle of Creon's menacing indifference and the glacial sheet of Tared's fury at whatever he'd found in my moment of ill-advised swooning.

Naxi was no longer giggling.

'Tared ...' Lyn started.

He didn't look away. The tension grew tangible, shimmering like heat on a summer's day – waiting for a last spark, a last nudge towards the point of eruption.

Creon raised a scarred eyebrow. An invitation, a challenge ... as if he *wanted* this mess to blow up.

Oh, damn him, damn the both of them. I lurched a single step forward, feeling like a pair of scales about to tip disastrously in one direction – gravity pulling on either side of me, wishes and demands and endless expectations. *Stop it*, I could tell Tared. *I'm madly in love with him. He's not the villain you believe he is.* But he'd think me a silly child at best and an unscrupulous flirt at worst, and with ten days to go ...

I tipped the other way.

'Are the two of you done?' There was more sting to my words than intended. I turned my back on Creon with all the disinterest I could muster and strode towards Tared, forcing him to avert his eyes. 'We should be going if we want to reach those woods before nightfall.'

'Em,' Tared said, his voice low. He didn't move. He barely moved his lips.

'What?' I said sharply, imitating that quiet, menacing tone. '*I'm* not the one who can't seem to look away from him right now, am I?'

Unsubtle, but effective enough. Surprise stiffened his features for the blink of an eye; then a sour smile broke through, accompanied by what looked like relief. 'Brat.'

'Not an idiot, though.' I gave a little scoff. 'Is it really that hard to believe I'm not going to run off with someone who'd hurt me?'

He hesitated a last moment, then sighed, nodded, and turned to Beyla, who alone had ignored the threatening eruption with what I thought was commendable disregard. 'Anything we need before we start moving?'

Beyla's answer was short and boiled down to a "no". Every fibre of me itched to hurry back to Creon as if nothing had happened and resume our conversation on divine inscriptions ... but Edored was still giving me puzzled glances, and I'd spent enough training sessions trying to surprise Tared to know he would notice.

I limited myself to a quick glance over my shoulder. Creon's dark eyes were unreadable, his face a perfect, impassive mask.

He would understand, wouldn't he?

He'd have to, I decided with a pang of annoyance; we didn't have any better options, and if he wanted to make a point of getting on Tared's nerves, he could deal with the consequences, too. So I steeled myself, ignored Lyn's look of obvious concern, and wandered off to the west of the crater, looking for the path Agenor had mentioned.

It wasn't hard to find, and the state of it did nothing to improve my already fickle mood. Thorny vines and explosions of nettles had crawled over the once-level flagstones, rendering much of the way impassable. Three hours to the woods, Agenor had said, but that had been before the woods decided to claim the roads for themselves. If we had to fight our way through this mess all the way to our destination, we'd be lucky if we arrived before sunset.

Which meant I'd be lucky if I got to speak with Creon in private before the end of the day, too.

Red magic itched under my fingertips, the colour yearning to break free from the dark linen of my practical travel dress. Perhaps we could just burn our way through the mess. The dark grey of the flagstones offered more than enough colour, and with Creon's and my powers combined, I doubted a bunch of plants would put up much of a fight. And really ... I lifted my right hand, savouring the familiar tingle of power running through my veins. If I was very honest, blowing up a few things might improve my mood significantly.

'Oh, dear,' Naxi said behind me. 'I really suggest you reconsider everything you're doing right now, Emelin.'

I jerked around, impossibly *more* in the mood to destroy something. 'Beg your pardon?'

'Oh, you know,' she said vaguely, gesturing at nothing in particular. Behind her, the others were approaching – Lyn sitting on Tared's shoulders, Edored and Beyla with drawn swords, and Creon a good ten strides behind them. 'The world is such a *place*, isn't it? Mind if I take care of these?'

It wasn't a question; she floated past me before I could reply, humming shreds of a soft, soothing melody to herself.

Around her feet, the vines untangled themselves, slithering obediently off the path like snakes slipping back into the shadows.

'Oh,' I said blankly.

She threw me a dazzling grin. 'Are you coming?'

There was little else I could do. I threw one last look over my shoulder, at the crater Korok's death had left behind, the towering walls of Lyckfort, and the temple roofs rising even higher beyond. Then I hoisted my bag higher on my shoulders and began to walk without looking back, following Naxi's little figure along the narrow path she cleared for us.

Her quiet humming was the only sound breaking the grim, determined silence of what had once been the city's farmland. Even the autumn sun couldn't lift the sense of gloom that hung over the twisted wilderness like a persistent morning fog, oozing from every burst flagstone and every gnarled branch blocking the road. There were no birdsongs or chirping crickets in this place, no signs of life but the breeze whispering through the shrubbery and the occasional stench of rot wafting past. Within minutes, we passed the first abandoned carts and wagons, the burned shapes of horses and oxen still bound to their yokes.

At least there were few human bodies – few that I could see from the path, at least. But even more so than in Lyckfort itself, the unnatural quiet of the plague-cursed landscape reminded me at every step that we were intruders here, treading paths that had not been touched by living feet for hundreds of years.

When Creon caught up with me, a tall, dark shape on the edge of my sight, the jumble of my fear and triumph and nervousness gave way to undiluted relief for a second or two.

Then I remembered the rest of the group was still walking close behind us, noticing every glancing we exchanged. I forced myself to keep looking straight ahead, at the skeletons of farm sheds peeking above the overgrown fields.

We walked and walked and walked. Creon didn't stray from my side as the landscape grew more uneven around us, the hills higher, the abandoned carts scarcer. His hands were never far from his knives, his wings always on the verge of flaring – ready for flight, ready to grab me and get us the hell out of this dead world where nothing but an invisible shield of magic lay between us and painful and inevitable death. The safest, most comfortable reassurance, except ...

Except for the coldness that lingered in Tared's eyes during our first short break, deepening whenever his gaze slid past Creon.

Except for Edored's piercing looks over his shoulder as we resumed our walking and I ended up behind him and Beyla, where he couldn't keep an eye on Creon without frequent and unsubtle turns of his head.

It was easy to ignore at first; the brambles and eerie remainders of human settlements were a welcome distraction from the daggers in the alf's glares. But by the time the sun had sunken to a hand's breadth above the jagged horizon, he was whispering urgently to Beyla, and in the lifeless silence of the continent, hissed shreds of his tirade were all too audible.

'... running after her ... can't just ... what if she ...'

What if I *what*? What if I suddenly threw myself into the Silent Death's arms after spending three months holed away in a library with him?

Except Edored might not know about that.

I didn't dare glance at Creon, whose uncannily sharp ears had to be picking up every word I was hearing and then some. Edored might not know – and the same went for Beyla, for Agenor, perhaps even for Tared. Now that I thought about it, no one except Lyn probably knew just how much time I'd spent in Creon's company – during my so-called solitary reading hours in library halls and my so-called time alone in my bedroom.

As far as most of the household was concerned, magic practice and mealtimes were the major share of my time with him. And now I was suddenly traversing half a continent by his unwavering side?

I didn't make out Beyla's quieter replies, but judging by Edored's thundering scoff, they weren't terribly effective.

For the bloody gods' sakes. I could already imagine him dashing into his friends' card rooms upon our return to the Underground, all unthinking shock and excitement. *Imagine!* he'd yell at Njalar as they emptied a bottle of honey mead together. *Ten days in Zera's woods, and she didn't take her damn eyes off the fucker for a second!*

And then Njalar's cousin Hrodmar would hear, and then Hrodmar's definitely-not-lover Anrida would know the next morning, and then she'd tell her friends Hyndla and Siguna at their weekly lunch, and Siguna would tell the head of her house, who happened to be sour-faced Valdora of Svirla. And if Valdora knew, she would doubtlessly bring it up as some offhand remark in the next Council meeting, after which *everyone* would be convinced I was just a silly little fae whore after all.

No doubt, the nymphs and phoenixes and vampires in the world above would find out soon enough – a perfect confirmation of all the Mother had been muttering in their ears, a perfect reason to give up on their rebellion before it had even started.

Edored was still whispering loudly before me.

Cold sweat stuck my backpack to my shoulders, turning my shirt clammy as we climbed what seemed like the hundredth hillslope. I needed to talk with Creon. I needed to figure out what we were going to say and do to avert these dangerous suspicions. But it wouldn't look any better if I were to break my silence of the last hours *now*, when it would be all too obvious I was reacting to the accusations rising around us …

Waiting a few more hours wouldn't do any irreparable damage, would it?

I kept my gaze stubbornly on the stark blue sky behind the top of the hill, avoiding Creon's winged silhouette in the corner of my eye.

When Edored finally stopped whispering, though, it wasn't because of my steely self-control or Beyla's soothing murmurs. We reached the top of yet another hill, one of the highest so far, which was covered in such abundant tangles of grapevines that I suspected it must have been a vineyard in some distant past. The farmhouse at the highest point still retained most of its roof, although the weight of the sprawling vines had sent part of the walls collapsing. Before and beside us, lower hills rose from the earth, the flagstone path meandering between them.

And behind them, not even a mile away, Zera's woods lay shimmering in the late afternoon sun, the deep green of the trees twinkling as if a starry sky had found a home between the leaves.

The forest stretched north and west as far as the eye could see, an endless blanket of moss green that covered hill after hill, all the way to where the first sharp mountaintops jutted into the cobalt sky. To the south ... There had to be a border there, where Etele's lands began and Zera had never wielded much power. If the trees still obeyed that ancient division of the continent, it was too far away for us to see.

Staring at the breathtaking expanse of the wood, I was overcome by a sensation I'd felt before – that tingle of insignificance that had grown in me when I'd climbed Cathra's dunes as a little girl and watched the endless ocean for hours upon hours, until I understood in the depth of my bones that no ship would ever find the end of it.

My mouth had gone dry. Once again, I'd underestimated – disastrously underestimated – just how large a single forest could be. Ten days. Hell, even if Zera was alive, we could spend a *decade* wandering through her woods and never even catch a glimpse of the goddess herself. What in hell had I been thinking, betting all I had on what had to be a losing card?

Still, no one spoke up to suggest we might as well go home and save our time for the soothing of anxious maybe-allies.

'Nightfall isn't that far away,' Beyla said, glancing at the sun with wide open eyes. 'We could keep going for an hour, probably – maybe an hour and a half – but I'm thinking ...'

'Might be better to go in by the bright light of day,' Lyn finished, pulling a face at the tranquil forest before us.

I found myself silently agreeing with her. Zera's woods were eerily beautiful from a distance, with their vibrant green and that odd way the sunlight reflected off the leaves ... but it was an ominous sort of beauty, the same way the Labyrinth had been beautiful in the depths below the Crimson Court. I imagined knotted roots slithering around my legs and arms, gnarled tree bark closing in around me, and unsuccessfully attempted to suppress a shiver.

'And we do have shelter here,' Beyla added, nodding at the half-ru- ined farmhouse. 'I wouldn't mind having a couple of walls during our first night on the continent. No idea what to expect of this place.'

'We could walk on and fade back here at sunset,' Tared said slowly. 'Then again ...'

'I could also take a look at the treeline with Naxi,' Beyla said, 'and then fade the rest of you there tomorrow morning. No need to make everyone walk more than necessary if this last part will probably be safe.'

Perhaps my feet weren't the only ones feeling like blisters on bone, because her proposal was accepted with unusual enthusiasm.

CHAPTER 8

WE LOOKED THROUGH THE deserted farmhouse and found no bodies except a handful of charred barn animals on the other side of the hill. Inside, the rooms had remained uncannily intact: the dark wooden furniture was bone dry, and some of the white-and-blue porcelain tableware had cracked, but the blankets still lay messily on the beds as if the inhabitants of the place had woken up mere hours ago.

To my relief, no one suggested using the bedrooms. But I still felt like a graverobber when Lyn lit the fire in the living room hearth and Tared found a rag to wipe most of the dust off the floor, as if the eyes of the dead farmers were following me when I installed my luggage on one of their dining chairs and pulled my sweaty boots from my feet.

Naxi and Beyla left their bags behind, then slipped out to take a quick look at Zera's domain before the sun went down. Tared set out to find a well or a brook nearby, throwing his rag into Edored's hands before he left.

'I could make dinner?' Edored suggested, scowling at the floorcloth as if it was a dead rat.

'You nearly burned down the kitchen last time you tried to boil an egg,' Lyn said impatiently. 'Just focus on the cleaning, will you?'

I threw a quick look at Creon, who lounged against the farthest wall as if he planned to stand there for the rest of the night. A better chance was unlikely to present itself. 'I can take care of the food, if Creon is willing to help?'

'Oh, of course,' Lyn said, at the same moment Edored loudly snapped, 'Why would you need his help cooking?'

'To cut the onions,' I said, rolling my eyes at him. 'Everyone knows demons never cry.'

Even Creon bit down a laugh at that – nothing but a twitch around his lips, but noticeable enough for the trained eye. A sliver of tension untangled itself in my guts, taking in that moment of vulnerability like a breath of fresh air.

As long as he was still smiling, he couldn't mind my silence all afternoon too much, could he?

Edored gave in and set himself to work, grumbling and cursing as he scrubbed the dust from the table and the cracked leather chairs at the window. There were no spiderwebs between the ceiling beams, I realised. No termite holes in the wood, either. Even the smallest pests must have died in the first waves of plague magic, freezing this deserted home in time.

Lyn trotted to the porch outside with an armful of maps to see if she could identify our exact position. It left Creon and me alone with Edored, who seemed both deeply annoyed and far too determined about his new position as our chaperone. As we unpacked the food bags and took stock, the alf followed us with suspicious eyes, muttering the occasional jab about being glad Creon was carving up parsnips rather than innocent children for once.

To my relief, Creon ignored him. One near-confrontation a day was more than enough for my nerves.

We chose our ingredients, packed up the rest again, and started slicing and dicing. Creon barely looked up from his work, only pausing every now and then to sign the quickest of instructions at me. But the longer we sat there by the fire and worked on the food together, the more his silence resembled that quiet earnestness I knew from our time at the pavilion – a dedication to our meal that seeped through even the Silent Death's uncaring mask.

A much, much more comfortable silence than the tense shield of unspoken words that had hovered between us all day.

I found a large copper cauldron we could use. We managed to secure it over the fire through some magical experimentation. Creon sautéed onions until they were *just* the right shade of golden brown and their mouth-watering smell filled the room, and I chucked in lentils and parsnips and barley at his direction, marvelling at the way even our uninspiring ingredients somehow turned into a hearty stew before my very eyes. This ruined farm in the middle of the continent was so very different from the ethereal beauty of the pavilion, and yet I felt, in a flash of déjà vu, as if we were back at the Mother's court, preparing our dinner at that birchwood kitchen table.

Working together, instinctively adjusting to each other's rhythms as we always had.

Tared returned with refilled water bottles, looking unwillingly hungry at the scents filling the house. Lyn trotted back inside minutes later and triumphantly declared she'd narrowed down our location enough to mark it on her maps, and also, why exactly were we not cooking more often at home?

Half the household would refuse every bite, Creon signed wryly.

I glanced at Lyn, who looked timid and tiny at the sight of his hand gestures, and then at Tared and Edored, who pretended not to be watching us with varying degrees of success. Behind the broken windows, the sky was slowly turning a peachy orange and pink. Naxi and Beyla would be back soon.

Did it matter? It might be better to do this with half a crowd around; at least that would send the message that none of us had anything to hide.

'Creon?' I said.

He looked up from stirring the lentil stew, eyes wary but wings lying loosely against his shoulders.

'Can we teach Lyn the basics of our signs? Might be useful seeing as we won't have too much parchment around in the woods.'

'What?' Edored said sharply.

I didn't dare to glance at Tared, who was sitting on the windowsill, soaking up the last sunrays of the day. He'd gone motionless in the corner of my eye, even that shimmer of light around him no longer as vigorous as usual.

Creon merely turned around, leaving the stew to simmer by itself. If he was at all surprised by the suggestion, his slowly raised eyebrow didn't show it.

'If it's not too much of a hassle?' Lyn's young voice was too high. 'I … I was thinking …'

She didn't finish her sentence – realising, presumably, that every single person in the room knew exactly what she had been thinking, and that any pretty lie she might utter for civility's sake would not be remembered for longer than a minute anyway.

'We could start with the alphabet?' I suggested, blithely pretending not to notice the grim tension spreading through the room. 'You'll get that memorised within an evening, at least.'

You're sure about this? Creon signed.

'Why not?'

He shrugged. *Tared might just try to cut off my fingers tomorrow.*

'Not if I'm around,' I said, which was about the only response that wouldn't immediately give away the topic of our discussion. 'And I think we can all agree it would be impractical if we get attacked by dragons tomorrow and you have to go digging for parchment.'

Whatever the two alves behind me might have been planning to say, that eminently reasonable point shut them up. Creon shrugged again, a flicker of a smile around his lips that told me he knew exactly what I was doing.

Turning to Lyn, he signed, *Take a seat.*

'That's "take a seat",' I said and stepped towards the fire to take over Creon's stirring work. He lowered himself onto the worn rug beside the hearth in the same moment, crossing his legs. 'The first sign is "take", but really, I think we use it for all vaguely related concepts, too. "Absorb" and "grab" and all of that. "Seat" is just ... seat.'

'Right,' Lyn said, climbing into one of the two leather chairs with squinted eyes. 'So it's semantically compositional, this language of yours?'

'Um,' I said.

It is, Creon signed dryly.

I pulled a face. 'Apparently it is.'

Tell her it's mostly verb-initial. That should help, too.

'You're acting like we actually came up with a grammar,' I said, turning back to our food to scrape some stubborn lentils from the bottom of the cauldron. Creon breathed a chuckle beside me. 'He says it's verb-initial, Lyn. I say you should use whatever word order your heart desires.'

'Thanks,' she said, a trace of nervous laughter in her voice. 'I see you teach languages the same way you learn them.'

I sent her a glower over my shoulder. 'Unnecessary.'

Not untrue, though, Creon signed.

I glared at him too, then quickly looked away, because if I held that smouldering gaze for a moment longer, the lights in his eyes would make me blush more than I could attribute to the heat of the flames. Something about this new development was improving his mood far more easily than I'd ever dared to dream.

It took an effort to still sound appropriately exasperated. 'Shall we get started with that bloody alphabet, or do the two of you want to wallow in your grammatical prowess a little longer?'

Lyn snorted a laugh. 'Show me the alphabet, then.'

So we did, our demonstration disrupted only by Edored, who appeared to have decided that this was the perfect moment to sharpen a sword he hadn't used all day. Tared sat motionless by the window while the sky grew pale, then dark, and we worked our way through the twenty-four alphabet signs. He never interrupted, never so much as spoke a word ... but I could feel his eyes on the back of my head at every turn, and I knew his thoughts largely followed the shrill shrieks of Edored's whetstone over the alf steel blade.

'But I feel like there should be more of a *system* to this,' Lyn complained for the fifth time, swiping a host of red curls aside in between her attempts to follow Creon's finger motions. 'Why would this be a *v*? It doesn't even look like one!'

Ask Em, Creon spelled, looking entirely too delighted to shove the blame on my shoulders. In the flickering firelight, the hint of a smile on his lips was both menacing and comforting, a challenge and a warning.

'It's not my fault I had to force you to learn this stuff,' I said, unable to suppress a laugh as I pointed my lentil-covered wooden spoon at him in mock outrage. 'If you wanted a system, perhaps you should have contributed rather than—'

Beyla and Naxi materialised from thin air mere inches away from me.

I should not have been shocked so easily. Not after months in an alf household, not when I'd known they would return around dusk. But I jolted at their mid-sentence appearance anyway, staggering a reflexive step and a half away from them before I even realised who they were and where they'd come from.

My foot caught behind the stone ridge covering the floor around the hearth.

The world toppled around me.

I reacted in another ill-advised burst of instinct, my thoughts no more than short punches of panic in those immeasurable moments. *Fire. Fall. Danger.* My wooden spoon clattered to the floor. My hand shot forward. My fingers grabbed the first surface they could find to keep me from tumbling straight into Lyn's flames –

The copper cauldron hanging over them.

For one frozen, everlasting fraction of time, nothing existed but me and the fire as we stared at each other in a tangle of limbs and blazing heat.

Then the pain hit.

Red-hot agony flared through every nerve of my palm, reducing the world to crying voices and heat and the smothering stench of burning wood. Wings slapped behind me. Hands – familiar hands – locked around my upper arms, dragging me back, dragging me to my feet. My back slammed against a wooden wall, and I barely felt it – only felt the fire searing through my hand, a raw ache so intense I nearly threw up.

Someone was shouting my name.

Someone was shouting for water.

And just like that, the pain ... dulled.

It didn't vanish, not exactly. But the mind-numbing torment that left me incapable of stringing two thoughts together softened to a nagging throb in less than the time it took to gulp in a breath, and at once I became aware of my surroundings again. Edored was cursing. Naxi was crying apologies over and over.

A hand grabbed my wrist, and strong fingers bared my throbbing palm to the cool air. Through the mist of my tears, a sea of blue lit up the room.

Blissful relief washed over me.

I slouched against the wall as the pain waned, dragging in a half-sobbing breath. The fingers holding my hand didn't let go. When I blinked and blinked again, I found Creon's sharp face mere inches from mine – hair a tousled mess, lip curled up in a silent sneer, wings blocking the view of the rest of the room. His face was several shades too pale even in the firelight, a soft sheen of sweat glimmering at his temples.

That ... that wasn't just fear, was it?

My thoughts ran seconds behind my observations. Those gritted teeth, that wild gleam in his eyes ... Not a look of concern but rather of ...

Pain?

My gaze wandered to my undamaged palm, the once-burned skin fragile and soft in the grip of his ink-scarred fingers. Only then did the realisation come through – that the worst of the pain had waned long before he healed me.

Demon magic.

My breath caught.

He seemed closer when I looked up to meet his gaze, even though he hadn't moved an inch. His scent rolled over me, that summer-sweet fragrance of honey and hazelnuts. Suddenly, his eyes were entirely his own – not the Silent Death's pools of cruel menace, not the uncaring fae prince's arrogant indifference, but simply the eyes of my lover looking straight through me, looking for hurt to soothe, for sacrifices to make.

For a moment, the world shrunk to him and me and the empty space between our lips ... Just a moment, and then I remembered who were watching us.

Another burst of panic exploded through my veins. Fuck. Three pairs of suspicious alf eyes in the room, and how long had I stood here, gaping at him like some damsel about to swoon in her rescuer's arms? Mere heartbeats, but it felt like an eternity – it would look like an eternity to Tared's eyes.

What for hell's sake was I *thinking*?

I yanked back my hand and ducked past his left wing, all but elbowing the dark velvet aside in my hurry to put a few more feet between myself and the irresistible, irrational pull of every gods-damned glorious inch of him. My heart rattled a nauseating rhythm in my throat. Creon's touch lingered on my skin with an intensity that made me want to curse out loud. Everywhere I looked were wide-eyed, startled gazes; Edorcd's hand lay around the hilt of his sword, Tared's around the nearest leather water bottle.

The stew simmered unperturbed above the fire, broth and lentils bubbling loudly in the breathless silence.

'I'm fine,' I managed, wrenching the lie over my lips. I was *not* fine. After the scene of this afternoon, after all the suspicions I'd already unwillingly fostered ... How much had I given away in this small, stupid moment of accidental intimacy? 'Good gods. Could you alves be a *little* more thoughtful about where you fade, next time I'm standing with my nose over a fire?'

'I'm so sorry, Em.' Even Beyla's frail voice sounded unusually feeble. 'I didn't realise—'

'It's alright.' I dropped into the nearest chair, not daring to look at Creon, realising only then my knees were quivering uncontrollably. I didn't want to talk about it. I just wanted them to stop thinking about what in hell had happened a moment ago. 'I'm fine. Everyone's alive. Can we have dinner, please?'

'Of course,' Lyn hastily said, but she hesitated as she slid from her chair, gaze wandering from me to where Creon must still be standing behind me. There was an unmistakable apology in her voice as she quietly added, 'Thank you.'

Oh, Zera help me. Had I even thanked him yet?

I ... I hadn't, had I?

But when I turned around in the croaking leather chair, clenching my nails into my newly healed palm, Creon didn't meet my gaze. His nod at Lyn was all uncaring boredom, all faintly amused arrogance – the look of the calculating murderer who'd saved me from the flames only because I still had a role to play in his schemes.

Behind me, Edored was pilfering antique plates from cupboards, the clattering and clanging suggestive of a horse tramping through a pottery.

'Creon?' I said.

His glance slid over me with unmistakable coolness, not even the faintest hint of a smile to break through that glacial mask. Was he just playing the game with me, keeping up the pretences for our unsympathetic audience?

Or was it rather ...

Nervousness stirred, thick and nauseating. He'd pulled me away from the fire faster than any of us could think. Had not hesitated to take that blistering pain upon his own shoulders even in the mere moments before he healed me, had preferred to suffer himself rather than let me feel a second more of that agony.

And I'd shoved him aside as a triviality, hurried away from him as if he was some horror to be avoided at all costs.

'Creon?' I whispered again.

He didn't turn to meet my gaze. Combing a hand through his hair to smoothe any rebellious strands back in place, he settled himself against the wall and watched the rest of the company gather plates and spoons and ladles with bottomless dark eyes. A cold shell of a male even to the most vigilant onlookers – even to *my* eyes.

Sickening alarm seeped into my guts, alarm he had to feel, and he still didn't look at me.

Fuck.

Fuck.

We should have talked. We should talk right this moment. But Edored fell into the chair next to me with an unusual string of curses, and Tared didn't smile even when Lyn sat down beside him with a plate of lentil stew in her lap. If I snuggled up to Creon for a cosy conversation now, they wouldn't forget. They may not stay silent. And sooner or later, the wrong people would know.

I didn't get up from my chair.

The dinner conversation slid past me entirely. There were compliments for the food Creon had cooked, demonstratively aimed only at me. Something about Zera's forest, which felt unusual according to Naxi and looked like a pretty nightmare according to Beyla. Something about our location on the map and the direction of Zera's temple deep in the woods.

I waited for all of them to finally be done, waited until they'd go to sleep so I could sneak into Creon's arms unnoticed and plead my case. But as Naxi put down her spoon, the first thing she said was a breezy, 'Mind if I take the first watch, Creon? I *hate* getting up early.'

Gods damn me, what was she doing?

Creon merely shrugged, nodded, and grabbed his bag to pull out a tightly folded blanket. Only then, as he gracefully rose to his feet, did his gaze wander back to me, not a fraction warmer than it had been before our meal.

'Anything I can help with?' I forced myself to say, which was nowhere close to what I would have said had we been alone. *I'm sorry. I love you. Can't you see I'm trying to keep the both of us safe here?*

He glanced at Tared as he raised his hand, just the quickest vigilant glimpse, yet enough to make me abruptly realise the mistake I'd made.

Lyn hadn't been the only one in the room while we blissfully chatted about hand languages, showing her the alphabet and whatever other gestures came up in the conversation. Which meant any of them could have picked up just enough to read our exchanges.

Which meant not even our signs would be private on this trip.

Apparently reaching the same conclusion, Creon returned nothing but a bland *Sleep well.*

'Thanks.' My breath had grown shallow. 'You too.'

He'd already turned away to look for a quieter spot.

CHAPTER 9

I WOKE STIFF AND sore on the creaking wooden floor of the farmhouse, the smell of dust and rot heavy in my nostrils, the thin blanket around me a woefully lacking alternative to strong arms and velvet wings.

Creon.

The memories of last night returned to me like a fist in the face, and I shot up so abruptly I nearly tore my blanket.

Watery morning sunlight filtered through the windows and the holes in the roof, bathing the living room in a deceptively peaceful glow. Edored lay sleeping next to me, arms wrapped around his backpack, leather overcoat folded into a pillow under his head. Tared and Lyn had made themselves at home in the opposite corner of the room. The distance separating their makeshift pillows suggested they'd started out with a good two feet between them, but Lyn's small body lay curled up against Tared's shoulder now, a mess of blankets and bright red curls covering most of his arm and chest.

Creon was nowhere to be seen.

I scrambled to my feet and staggered to the back of the house, rubbing the sleep from my eyes as I quickly searched the bedrooms and scullery. Most were empty. I only found Naxi sleeping in one of the small beds, sprawled out over the ancient mattress as if every inch of this house wasn't tainted by the gruesome fate of its inhabitants.

If she was sleeping but we hadn't been burned by plague magic, Creon had to be awake and near.

My guts knotted even tighter. If he hadn't waited for me to wake up and talk, did that mean he didn't *want* to talk to me?

Swallowing a curse, I tiptoed out through the back door, which hung askew on its rusty hinges and only squealed a little when I pushed it open. A panorama of wild vines and hills and mountains opened up before me, no less dizzying through the wisps of grey-white morning mist that covered the landscape in the glow of the golden morning sun. In the vibrant mess of the overgrown garden, my eyes found charred animals, a collapsed shed, and no Creon.

I made my way through the dewy grass and around the house, drawing in deep gulps of crisp morning air to soothe my anxiety. Just a few dozen steps, but it was more than enough to think of a hundred bitter reproaches he could throw into my face, to remember every cold glance he'd levelled at me last night.

My heart stopped dead in my chest for an unmeasurable moment when I stepped around the last corner and found his familiar winged silhouette on the porch.

He was sitting cross-legged against the wall, coat around his shoulders, as he scribbled some note in his lap. It took just a moment too long before he looked up, just a moment too long before he shoved parchment and pencil back into one of his many pockets.

The coldness was gone from his gaze, but this resigned, heavy weariness was an improvement only in the most technical sense of the word.

'Morning?' I whispered.

He sighed. *Morning, Em.*

No *cactus*. No smiles. Clambering towards him over the half-rotten porch boards, I felt like a beachcomber approaching a brand new shipwreck, unsure whether I'd find death or treasures inside.

'Did you get some sleep?'

His shrug was, presumably, a *no*. He'd lain awake, too, then. I recalled Naxi's quick and smooth intervention to keep us from talking last night and wondered if it had been intentional – if she'd known what was going on behind his cold façade and decided I'd better stay away from him until he'd taken a few hours to calm himself.

A nauseating shiver ran up my spine.

'I'm sorry.' My voice came out small. 'I should have handled that better.'

His hands remained motionless in his lap as he rested his head against the wall and closed his eyes. But his lips mimed, *It's alright*.

Not what I'd expected him to say. Glancing at the expressionless mask of his face, the set of his jaw too hard and the line of his lips too tense, the relief wouldn't come.

'You're not happy, though,' I managed.

Now his fingers did move, although his eyes remained closed. *Did you expect me to be happy about it?*

'No.' The conversation was slipping further from my grasp with every word I uttered. 'No, but I hoped ...'

The sentence died an unsatisfying death. But I'd hoped he'd see the necessity of it. Hoped he'd understand we couldn't let Edored run off with the explosive news of our love, hoped that he'd see it as an amusing shared secret between the two of us rather than a sacrifice that kept him awake at night.

It's alright, he repeated, signing it this time. But his wing didn't unfold to nudge me closer; no ghost of a smile touched his lips. *You don't want them to know. That's probably sensible. I can handle a few days of this.*

A few days of me acting like he was nothing to me – of me pretending I agreed with every terrible opinion the world harboured against him and every terrible opinion of himself he fostered. Zera help me, I truly should have thought this through before merrily dragging him *and* half a family of alves with me on this quest.

'I love you,' I whispered, hunching up my shoulders. 'Warn me if I'm ever enough of an idiot to make you doubt that, will you?'

He stiffened for the shortest sliver of a moment, then sagged back against the wall, wings slumping against the weathered wood. *Em—*

'Oh, there you are,' Beyla said behind me, the frail sound of her voice loud as a shout above the quiet of this dead, deserted continent. 'Breakfast?'

I jerked around. She'd appeared barefoot from the open front door, dressed in a man's shirt and leather trousers, her ash blonde hair loose and falling nearly to her waist. She was holding a generously buttered piece of braided bread; no traveller's bags, no swords.

Somehow, she looked more at home in these uncharted lands than I'd ever seen her in the safety of the Underground.

'Oh,' I forced myself to say, quelling the urge to jump up and shoo her back inside. It was bad enough that she'd found the two of us cosying up on a silent porch; I couldn't afford to make her any more suspicious. 'Yes. Thank you.'

She threw Creon a cold look, sighed when he didn't move, and sat down on my other side, tearing the bread in three parts with quick, slender fingers. I got the largest part. Creon got the smallest. When I looked to him to suggest swapping our portions, he'd turned away, examining the breathtaking scenery below our hill with the boredom of a spoiled prince who couldn't wait to return to the civilised world of balls and lavish banquets.

No chance he would accept an offer of help, no matter how small, when there were others around to see.

So I swallowed my words and nibbled on my bread, hoping Beyla would leave if she'd reassured herself I was still wearing all my clothes. To my disappointment, although not to my surprise, she didn't.

Some conversation, then. The longer I remained quiet, the more it would seem she had interrupted us in something unsavoury. So I steeled myself and muttered, 'Are you happy to be travelling again?'

A pale smile slid over her face, wistful but just a tad less shallow than most of her smiles. 'I'll never understand why so many immortals spend their centuries in the same handful of places. With all that time on our hands ...'

I pulled a face. 'Not sure if I'm the one to answer that question. For most of my life, taking a ship to the next island was a thrilling adventure.'

'The human life.' Her smile froze – reminded, perhaps, that she was the one who'd doomed me to that same life, unaware of my magic when she'd left me on Valter and Editta's doorstep. 'Are you feeling grateful for being dragged into this mess?'

A question I'd never considered before, but the answer crystallised in my thoughts with razor-sharp clarity – I *was* grateful, infinitely grateful, for even the flames that had burned my old life to the ground in that night that changed everything. Even here, farther from Cathra than I'd ever been, the idea that I might have spent the rest of my years surrounded by stifling whispers and impossible expectations made my skin crawl.

Going by the tone of Beyla's voice, though, that was not the answer she expected.

I had been cruelly dragged from my safe home into the treacherous hell of the Crimson Court, after all. If not for the Alliance intervening, I would still be living at the mercy of the Silent Death and his ruthless games.

So I chuckled, or produced a sound close enough to a chuckle, and said, 'Grateful isn't the word I'd use, really.'

Beyla breathed a laugh, then continued to eat in silence.

I tried to follow her example, but the sweet bread tasted dry and dusty with my lie lingering on my tongue – that throwaway remark which made a joke of everything the past months had meant to me. Creon's silhouette was a motionless fleck of darkness in the corner of my eye. I didn't dare to glance at him again. Gods knew what Beyla would think of another moment of unintentional intimacy.

He'd understand. He'd told me it was alright. Just a few days – we could handle a few days.

But when he rose and sauntered back into the house a couple of minutes later, he didn't look back at me – didn't even meet my eyes for the briefest of cold glances.

The company in the living room had woken up when I made my way back inside. Tared was folding blankets. Edored was scarfing down the leftovers of the lentil stew. By the window, Lyn worked her way through a melon slice the size of her head, peppering Creon with questions on how to sign this word and that word and what exactly should she make of the impractical similarities between the gestures for *table* and *landscape*?

Over his packing work, Tared followed every twitch of Creon's fingers with hawkish eyes, a cold determination on his face that suggested he might learn our hand language faster than anyone else for no reason but undiluted spite.

I loitered at the hearth for a few minutes, attempting to catch Creon's gaze and find even the smallest clue that he'd understood, that he hadn't walked away from the porch in a fit of fury. But no matter how blatantly I settled myself in the leather armchairs and leaned into his conversation with Lyn, no matter how brightly Lyn smiled at me over her breakfast, he didn't look my way even once.

For the male who always saw me, who noticed me before I could blink or open my mouth, I could only assume that was a deliberate choice.

Was it anger after all, then?

He had to just be playing the game. I repeated it to myself again and again as I finally gave up and left to pack my bags; I shouldn't be drawing any rushed conclusions from that unmistakable coldness in his last glance, or from the way he paid more attention to the dust on the floor than to my presence. He was simply doing his part to hide our relationship, as I'd asked him to …

Except that this was not what I'd asked him at all.

I was trying to hide that I loved him, yes. Was hiding that I'd spent every night of the last three months sleeping in his bed, too. But it wasn't a secret that we harboured friendly feelings for each other, was it? We'd been chatting away under Tared's watchful eye last night. There was no need to pretend we barely knew each other – so why had he decided upon this useless change in strategy all of a sudden?

I packed my luggage too fast, making a mess of my careful arrangement of clothes and food. It had to be strategy, some clever solution to a problem I hadn't even seen yet. He'd said he was alright. There really was no reason to suspect any other motives behind his deliberate disregard.

He wouldn't be doing this just to make a point, as some childish attempt to make me equally unhappy about this entire situation ... but I wished I was able to push that thought away with more conviction.

For hell's sake. Time to do the dishes and focus on anything other than Lyn's ceaseless questions on the opposite side of the room. As soon as we were back on the road, all would doubtlessly revert to the usual routine.

The others were fast, their preparation a habit of centuries. By the time I returned from the brook behind the house with a pile of clean bowls, the bags were tied, the food packed, the coats and weapons fastened. Even Naxi needed no more than five minutes after Lyn woke her up last, her cheerful reports of the previous night a sharp contrast to the tangible tension hovering in the living room.

Creon still barely glanced at me.

Just playing the game.

I had to repeat that very firmly to myself as we gathered around Beyla and he casually took her arm rather than mine.

But there was no time to ask questions, no time to kick him in the annoyingly muscular shins and tell him to stop this nonsense. The sun-streaked farmhouse blurred around us, and half a heartbeat of pulsing colours morphed into the emerald and periwinkle hues of a forest unlike any other I'd seen in my life – a sight that wiped even Creon's icy looks from my mind for a dazed heartbeat or two.

The star-flecked foliage I'd seen from the distance hadn't prepared me for *this*.

Even Edored was silent as I let go of Beyla's arm and tiptoed a few steps forwards over the flagstone path. Towards the woodline. Towards the abrupt, ruler-straight border where unremarkable vines and shrubbery became ... something else entirely.

Something as unnerving as it was beautiful.

The trees of Zera's woods were too high and too straight, towering hundreds of feet into the pale morning sky like marble pillars covered in smooth, grey bark. Hardly any sunlight filtered through the deep green canopies and the veils of mist that floated between the branches. The little of it that reached the moss- and fern-covered forest floor twinkled like starlight, reflecting off leaves and creeks in shades of silvery lavender.

The place smelled like dusk. A sultry, seductive fragrance, the scent of secrets about to be revealed.

A pretty nightmare, Beyla had called it, and that was a kind way to describe it – this world that could lure you in like a siren's song and never let you go again. And yet ...

Something about it seemed familiar.

I took another step forward.

'Em,' Tared said under his breath, the warning obvious in that single syllable.

'How old is this place?' I turned around, eyes reflexively seeking Creon. He stood two steps away from the others, his left hand on the black surface of his coat. His eyes were unreadable as they scanned the purple-grey depths of the forest. 'Because something about it reminds me ...'

He nodded before I'd finished my sentence, reading my mind even with his gaze stubbornly avoiding me.

'There's not much written about it,' Lyn said, fidgeting with her curls as she threw him a cautious look. 'The oldest sources seem to suggest the forest was already fully formed when the first human cities rose, which may mean ...'

'It was here before the gods?'

She worried her bottom lip. 'You're saying it reminds you of the Labyrinth.'

I glanced back at the silent, motionless forest, the quiet threat shimmering below every bark- and moss-covered surface. Not the same, not even remotely the same really, as the Labyrinth's gem-lit darkness deep below the Crimson Court ... but the sensation of sleeping magic was similar, of an atmosphere drenched with aeons and aeons of power.

'Let's be appropriately polite to it,' I said.

'Let's be *what?*' Edored echoed.

'Polite.' I glared at him. 'Complimentary. Generally pleasant and non-confrontational. Do you think you're capable of it?'

Edored's scowl at the forest didn't bode well. 'You're saying that as if I'm an unpleasant person, Nosebreaker.'

'For fuck's sake,' Tared muttered, exchanging a look with Lyn and Beyla. He'd heard my stories of the Labyrinth defending itself, of its long history of unexplained deaths and disappearances. If Zera's woods were at all similar ... 'Do we have to send you back home?'

That didn't sound like a terrible idea to me, if only because it would leave us with one less chaperone to glower at Creon wherever he went. But Edored scoffed something about not being an idiot and watching his words, and Beyla shrugged, a gesture that said she wasn't volunteering to chain him to his bedroom in the Underground.

'Let's just try,' Naxi said merrily. 'There's an unusual feel to it, but it doesn't seem unhappy at the moment.'

'Yet,' Lyn grumbled with a last warning look at Edored.

Want to go first, Em? Creon signed, ignoring Edored's aggrieved sputtering with deliberate cool. *You handled the Labyrinth rather easily.*

There was no sense of a compliment in his gestures, no flicker of pride. If I'd known him just a little less well, I might have believed he was simply sending me first to test the waters and take the heaviest blow of whatever magic the woods might fling at us.

He wasn't going to suggest coming with me? He *always* came with me.

'Any of us could go first,' Tared said sharply before I could make that point, his glare at Creon a knife stab. 'Why should Em be the one to take that risk, exactly?'

Oh, damn it. I could talk with Creon about whatever he was doing later; Tared's bad opinion of him would be harder to undo. Forcing a breezy laugh, I shrugged and said, 'Do you really think I would let any of you go first when you have no idea what you're dealing with?'

'Em,' Lyn said quietly. 'Please be careful.'

But I was past the point of no return now and too agitated to care. Two more steps and I stood at that invisible line between the mortal world and whatever waited in this forest, my feet still in the drab grass on this side, my eyes aimed at the ethereal twinkling and shimmering of the moss beyond.

I stepped forward.

Cool, invigorating air enveloped me as I passed that unseen barrier, a sensation like the spray of waves but without any wetness to it – the breath of something alive, something *enlivening*. The smell of the forest grew stronger, a fragrance of bursting ripe berries and blooming birchwood. But nothing moved around me, not the faintest rustle in the shrubbery.

My mouth remained dry even as I swallowed once, twice. 'Good morning?'

No reaction.

I thought of the Labyrinth slumbering deep below the earth, desperate for company, desperate for friendship. This place felt a little different, a little calmer and more dignified ... but how long had it been since it had last received guests?

Pushing away the gnawing doubt, I slowly added, 'I hope you don't mind us paying you a visit? We've read a lot about you back at home. And since obviously no one has been around this area for a while ... well, we thought it would be worth some danger to actually make the trip ourselves.'

A faint autumn breeze picked up between the branches, brushing past me, leaving tingling goosebumps over my arms and shoulders. I stifled the shiver about to run down my spine. Was that a warning? A sign of approval? Or just a breeze?

'If you'd prefer for us to leave,' I managed, and somehow my voice held steady, 'please just let us know. We won't bother you. But it really would be a shame if we couldn't see a little more of this very lovely—'

Something moved below the ferns and the moss.

My mouth snapped shut.

Behind me, his voice oddly muffled by whatever barrier separated the forest and the rest of the world, Tared was saying something, urging me to get the hell out of this place. Naxi was telling him not to be such a spoilsport. Edored was cursing. But I stood frozen in my spot, and before me ...

The shrubbery parted like arms opening wide, shaping a narrow, winding path that ran deeper into the trees.

A welcome.

The others abruptly stopped talking behind me.

I let out a breathless laugh, wishing my hands weren't shaking so ridiculously. Sentient, indeed. Did Agenor know? Or had the odder characteristics of the forest always been blamed on vague divine magic, just like the true nature of the Labyrinth had remained hidden for centuries?

'Do you mind if my friends join me here?' I said. 'We're all very excited about this trip. Lyn gathered half a library about you before we came here.' That sounded like believable enough flattery. 'There's only seven of us, so hopefully we won't be too disruptive?'

The path grew subtly broader.

'Oh.' I gave another laugh. 'Thank you so much. In that case ...'

I glanced over my shoulder, finding Creon first. He watched the forest with a cold smile around his lips, a hint of triumph in that expression.

Was he at least somewhat pleased with my approach? I couldn't tell; he was avoiding my gaze again.

'In that case,' I repeated, forcing myself to look away, to focus on Naxi's beaming grin and Edored's scowl, 'are you coming?'

Naxi practically skipped across the border, Beyla just behind her. The rest followed more slowly. Creon crossed the line with his hands in his pockets and his wings tucked in as if this was just another walk around the park – a look of harmless indifference that would have been more convincing if not for the knives gleaming at his belt and the inked scars silently reminding every onlooker of his violent past.

'Looks like you were right,' I whispered as he passed me by, and he gave me a nod that mostly said, *Obviously*, rather than, *Well done, we figured it out.*

For hell's sake.

But Lyn interrupted before I could drag him aside and demand he tell me what game he was playing. 'It's even more impressive than what we read about, isn't it, Em?' Her voice was half an octave too high. 'No wonder the humans loved it so much before the plague.'

At least someone understood the assignment. Ignoring the unanswered questions aching in my guts, I threw a look at Edored, who was still looking like someone had dropped a sharp pebble in his boot. Urgent matters first. 'Very pretty, indeed. Don't you agree, Edored?'

He huffed.

'Thought so,' I said, hoping his huff resembled agreement closely enough for the forest to accept it. 'Much more helpful than anyone told us, too. Lyn, do you think it knows where to find highlights like … like Zera's temple, for example? Because that would make it much easier to—'

Before I could finish my sentence, the winding path rearranged itself between the trees, shifting slightly northwards, like water changing its course.

'I think that's a yes,' Lyn said, sounding dazed.

'Of course it knows where to find the temple,' Naxi said brightly, patting the nearest tree with a fond smile. 'Very exciting place, this! Wish I'd come here sooner. Shall we go on our way, then?'

'But …' Edored threw a wild look around, from the newly formed path to me, and from me to Naxi, as if he hoped one of us would mercifully put an end to this ridiculous charade and invite him for beer and cards instead. 'You really want us to walk wherever the hell it tells us to walk? With no questions asked? As if some stupid forest knows—'

'Edored,' Beyla hissed.

'—what this is all about? I mean, it's just—'

A deep rumble, more sensation than sound, rolled through the earth below our feet, drowning out the rest of his sentence. Edored froze in place, eyes wide enough to reveal the white around his irises.

The unearthly thunder died away, but the memory of the sound lingered, hovering ominous in the air. I didn't dare to move. I barely dared to breathe.

'I think it's clear,' Tared said with emphatic calm, 'that this forest knows exactly what it's doing, Edored. Apologise, will you?'

'What?' Edored snapped, voice soaring.

'You insulted our host.' A nod at the trees, which had stopped rustling. 'Apologise.'

'You're joking, aren't you?' Edored's laugh was too shrill. '*I'm* not the one throwing a tantrum over some sensible questions, need I remind you? Why shouldn't this fucking forest—'

Creon was moving before I could open my mouth.

He was faster than Tared's jump forward. Faster than Lyn's sharp warning and Naxi's shriek of alarm. A slap of dark wings, a flash of black and bronze on the edge of my sight, and both he and Edored toppled over on the mossy forest floor, a tangle of limbs and wings and indignant shouts that couldn't drown out the sickening *thwack* of ...

Of a head-sized acorn slamming down in the exact spot where Edored had stood a fraction of a moment before.

'No!' Naxi cried to the tree she'd been complimenting, hurried and breathless, her voice loud enough to cover up Tared's curses. 'No, there's no need for that! He didn't mean to offend you! It's all a misunderstanding!'

Creon hauled himself and Edored upright in a single fluid motion, one scarred hand clasped over Edored's mouth with enough force that the alf turned faintly purple. The look in the Silent Death's eyes was a gathering thunderstorm, a warning that said he wouldn't mind snapping this idiot's neck and being done with him forever.

Staring at the monstrous acorn in the moss, a projectile large enough to break a skull, not even Tared appeared in the mood to object.

'We apologise *so* deeply,' Lyn stammered, her cheeks pale below her freckles as she frantically looked up at the trees again. Not a leaf stirred in reply. 'He ... he's a terrible judge of character, our cousin. He—'

'He fell from a roof as a child,' I interrupted in a flash of inspiration, throwing Edored my most imploring look as he wrestled against Creon's hold. 'Slammed his head against a stone, and he's never been the same since. It's a very sad situation, really.'

Edored wrestled even harder. Creon's arms didn't yield an inch.

'A heartbreaking accident,' Lyn agreed hastily. 'We thought he might enjoy coming on this trip because, well ...'

'It might be good for him to see a little more of the world than his nursery,' I finished, pulling a face at the forest surrounding us. 'Poor boy doesn't have that much to look forward to in his life, you see.'

'Yes, thank you, Em.' Lyn's look at me was half hysterical laughter, half wide-eyed panic. 'But if we made the wrong decision, we're more than happy to send him back home, of course. Just let us know if you'd prefer for us to get rid of him.'

For a moment, nothing moved but Edored's flailing limbs and Naxi's shaking shoulders as she desperately stifled her giggling.

Then, so swiftly I almost missed it, the earth opened up below the enormous acorn and swallowed it whole. Fresh moss grew back over the hole in half a heartbeat, as if the forest was telling us, *Fine, let's forget about it.*

For now.

Edored finally stopped squeaking objections into Creon's hand, blinking owlishly at the spot that had nearly marked his last living breath.

'Remarkably kind,' Tared said, his usual nonchalance no longer so convincing with the furious tension tightening his voice. His look at Edored was only marginally more pleasant than Creon's. 'One more word, Bragedson, and I'll personally gag you for the rest of this journey. Are we clear?'

I'd never heard him address his cousin by his father's name, and by the unusual meekness of Edored's nod, it was a rare occurrence indeed.

'Good.' Tared hesitated as he turned back to Creon, something in his steel grey eyes that was both gratitude and the absolute opposite of it. *Life debts*, Agenor had said. Knowing alves and their honour, saving Edored's life might have been an insult as much as a favour.

Creon merely raised an eyebrow.

'Thanks,' Tared said, forcing the word out like a vile accusation. 'I'll deal with him, if you don't mind.'

With the smallest shrug, Creon removed his hand and shoved Edored back onto his own feet, applying so much force that the alf nearly tumbled over. Beyla had to grab his elbow to keep him standing, hissing something when he made the mistake of opening his mouth again.

Whatever the message was, it seemed to land this time. Edored swallowed his words with nothing but a deeply affronted look at Lyn and me.

'If that's settled,' Naxi said, no longer bothering to hide her amusement, 'I think it's time to walk on?'

Deeper into this world where even the leaves might be lethal weapons, where every misstep could be a death sentence ... I looked at Creon for reassurance but found he'd turned away from me already, his hands back in his pockets as he studied the path ahead. The back of his head and wings gave no clue what he might be thinking, or how high he estimated our chances of survival.

What in hell did he think he was doing?

But I had no chance of talking with him now, and Zera was waiting for us somewhere in this pretty hell of a place. So I cleared my throat and said, 'Yes. I really can't wait to see more of the woods.'

I was telling more lies than truths today.

CHAPTER 10

Creon did not walk beside me this time. Instead, Naxi floated at my right for most of the day, chattering endlessly about the lovely autumn crocuses and the stunning white-grey trees and the breathtaking sunlight dripping over every leaf and branch.

If she was trying to distract me from Creon's more and more blatant distance, she was failing hopelessly. If she was rather the one keeping him away from me, she could piss right off as far as I was concerned.

I didn't say it out loud. Every single one of the others would notice and draw conclusions if I were to shove her aside.

We followed the narrow path deeper and deeper into the forest, winding between hills and trees and small marshes until I could no longer tell north from south. Even the sun was of no use: through the dense foliage above our heads, it was impossible to tell what direction the light came from. The longer we walked, the more I began to feel like we were moving away from reality itself, into some uncanny fever dream – an eerie little paradise that could turn against us as easily as it had agreed to let us in.

Despite myself, I had to admit I was happy to have the alves around. Without them, we'd have no way back the moment the forest decided to erase the path behind us.

Apart from Naxi's ceaseless excitement, the only sound came from Lyn, who was making use of these mindless hours to further quiz Creon on any sign she could think of. Most of her questions came too quietly for me to hear them over Naxi's rattling, but every now and then an aggravated huff – 'What do you mean, you don't have a sign for *hexameter*?' – was just loud enough.

Under any other circumstances, I might have smiled at her determination to master this new language as soon as inhumanly possible. In this place, Creon's silence more ominous than usual, alves glowering at him wherever I looked, even their innocent conversation sounded like a slow introduction to disaster.

But the hours passed without any fatalities. By the time dusk fell, we hadn't seen anything but rows and rows of trees – no signs of life, no signs of wandering deities. For all I could see from the endless path, we might have been walking in circles all day. But Beyla looked content when she finally came to a standstill in a small clearing, and Creon showed no trace of concern when I looked back to meet his gaze for the first time in hours.

He always knew north. If we'd been tricked by the forest, wouldn't he have warned us hours ago?

I'd have asked him if he didn't turn his back immediately, shrugging his bag off his shoulder with a single lazy motion that had his slender muscles bulging in ways that made my mouth go dry. Just in case Tared was keeping an eye on me, I quickly looked away, too.

'Mind if we make a little fire?' Naxi was saying in the background, speaking to the forest as if they were old friends. 'We'll keep it small and controlled, of course, but cold food is so annoyingly *cold* ...'

The earth shifted in the middle of the clearing, emptying a barren patch of sand where Lyn's flames would not be able to damage anything. I wondered how many travellers had strayed into this part of the world without understanding the true nature of the wood, and how many of them had died a violent death, never to be seen again, after they'd snapped just one twig too many.

'So,' Lyn said as she installed her fire in the designated spot and sent Creon and me an expectant look, 'are the two of you cooking again?'

Bless her little heart. I hadn't dared to suggest it myself.

But there was no comfort in the process this evening, none of the cosy companionableness that had returned between us in the farmhouse before I had unwisely thrown myself into the hearth and ruined everything. Creon was all ruthless efficiency as he picked his ingredients; his instructions came in cold, curt signs, and half of the time, he barely looked up as he delivered them. I cut my finger while chopping carrots to bite-sized chunks, and not even my sharp hiss of pain could persuade him to turn away from the piece of fresh ginger he was peeling with practiced, nimble hands.

For fuck's sake.

I drew too much blue from my sweaty travelling tunic to heal the cut, turning the skin of my finger a soft, vulnerable pink. With a muffled curse, I wiped the blood on my trousers, glanced over my shoulder to check whether the alves were still busy setting up our camp for the night, and hissed, 'Creon?'

He looked up just a fraction too slowly, as if bracing himself.

Zera help me. I shouldn't have felt nervous, talking to him. He *never* made me feel nervous. But the hint of impatience glimmering in his night-black eyes set my heart stuttering, and my sharply whispered words came out not nearly as righteously annoyed as they should have. 'What is the matter, exactly? If it's all not as fine as you said, could you just *tell* me instead of—'

'Em?' Tared said from the other side of the clearing, looking up from the maps he was studying with Beyla. 'Anything wrong?'

Your damn presence.

'Just discussing the food,' I snapped, hearing how implausible it sounded before the words left my lips. 'Nothing important.'

He glared at Creon – more out of habit than for any other reason, it seemed – and sauntered over to the fire, falling down on the other side with the map still in his hands. 'Let me know if I can help.'

It took all I had not to throw a carrot at him; had he been anyone else, I may have grabbed for my knife. Couldn't they just stop *being* here for a few damn moments? Couldn't they just give us five bloody minutes to talk?

'In case I cannot handle a handful of vegetables by myself, you mean?' I said sharply.

'For example,' he said, frustratingly unperturbed. 'What did you say about the temple, Bey?'

'The few reports I've read say it's located on a hill,' she said, walking over to our side of the clearing as if she hadn't noticed my barely suppressed murderous urges. 'So we might be able to see it from a distance. If we continue at this rate, we should catch a first glimpse tomorrow afternoon ...'

I risked a quick look at Creon. He shrugged – that damned uncaring shrug – and mouthed, *I'm fine.*

'I'm a purple rabbit,' I grumbled.

'Beg your pardon?' Tared said, looking up from the map again.

Creon did not reply to either of us. I returned to my cooking work in silence, pretending the carrots splitting around my knife were well-meaning alves and fathers who always knew better.

Within half an hour, the mishmash of ingredients somehow turned into a fragrant meal in the lightweight travel pan Beyla had brought. By the time we'd all filled our stomachs with soft, spiced carrot and bread soaked in fragrant olive oil, twilight had become early night, and the golden glow of Lyn's fire was all that kept the shadows of the forest at bay. Behind the circle of grey-white trees, the world was nothing but silhouettes and starlight, an ominous darkness that could hide hungry wolves as easily as fugitive gods.

'We'll need to keep watch,' Tared said, breaking the silence that had hovered over most of our dinner. 'Want me to stay awake with you, Naxi?'

The underlying message was clear: he was not going to spend half his night watching over us with Creon as his only waking company.

Naxi smiled broadly, as if she wasn't perfectly well aware she was the preferable alternative rather than a first choice.

'I'll take the second half of the night,' Beyla said quickly, which was another clear piece of strategic manoeuvring. For Tared's peace of mind, Lyn wasn't going to take the slot with Creon, and for considerations of family concerns and public opinions, neither was I. 'Is there anything else we need to discuss, or can I go get some sleep?'

I hadn't expected Creon to be the one to reply, but he rose without hesitation, his gestures aimed at me but perfectly visible for everyone else around the fire. *Think I'll go for a quick flight to see if I spot anything interesting.*

Now? After nightfall, and when he would have to stay awake for half of the night, too? I blinked, my annoyance briefly forgotten, and said, 'Shouldn't you sleep every now and then?'

Not particularly tired. He shrugged, wiped the moss from his thighs, and looked back at me, a flicker of a challenge in his dark eyes. *Coming along?*

Even the fire stiffened for a sliver of time.

My mind shifted from concern to understanding with a sensation strangely like emerging from ice-cold water. *Oh.* So that was the game he was playing – abduction, but of the pleasant kind this time, taking me where no unsympathetic ears could follow. Where we could talk, where I could safely figure out what game he had started playing.

Under the starry sky – arms around me, shoulders straining, wings slapping against the crisp autumn air.

Every nerve of my body drew tight at the thought, his tall silhouette in the firelight enough to send warm shivers down to the core of me. The perfect plan, except ...

Except every single member of our audience would know I'd volunteered to spend hours snuggled up tight in the Silent Death's muscular arms.

I didn't dare to look at the others. What little I caught of Edored's expression from the corner of my eye was enough of a warning.

'No, thank you,' I forced out, a careless chuckle thrown in for good measure. 'Some of us do appreciate their night's rest, you know.'

Something hardened in the lines around his lips, shutters slamming behind his eyes. But he nodded, whirled around swiftly and silently, and vanished between the trees without looking back, his footsteps inaudible on the plush moss. The shadows welcomed him like an old friend, swallowing his silhouette in the blink of an eye.

I stared at the spot where he'd disappeared for a moment too long. A faint nausea wormed its way up from my bursting stomach.

Should I have gone with him? But hell, he should have *known* I couldn't – not right before Edored's eyes, the alf who'd spread every piece of gossip like wildfire to the people we needed to win a war.

'Unexpectedly wise,' Tared said, and when I snapped around to face him, there was a wry amusement on his face that lay very close to relief. By the fire, Lyn's expression was the polar opposite, concern and annoyance warring for dominance in her hazel eyes.

Naxi was icily quiet on the edge of my sight. I decided it might be best if I just didn't look her way at all.

'Sleep, then?' Beyla said.

With nothing better to do, I followed her suggestion.

I tried to stay awake until Creon returned, just in case Beyla looked the other way every now and then during their shared vigil. But a second day of walking and worrying had exhausted me. Not even the memory of Creon's cold gaze was enough to keep my eyes from falling shut in the drowsy warmth of Lyn's fire, and sleep caught up with me within minutes.

I didn't wake up until the early morning sunlight came seeping through the emerald leaves, turning the dewy clearing into a glittering little treasure cove. The shadows between the trees were gone, giving way to a slowly rising morning mist. No wolves to be seen behind the whirling silver, and no fugitive goddesses either.

Could be better. Could be much, much worse.

Tared and Naxi were still sleeping, but the others were up and awake. Edored rinsed our bowls in the creek near the clearing, his scowl suggesting that someone had forced him with threats of smoke and hellfire. Beyla and Lyn sat hunched over their maps by the fire, discussing travel plans for the day in hushed tones. Farthest away, leaning leisurely against a tree as thick as a small house, Creon stared into nothingness, long hair loose over his shoulders, hands tucked into gloves against the morning cold. From the blank expression on his face, I couldn't tell how long he'd slept – if he'd even slept at all.

He didn't look my way until I sat up. His nod came too late and too curt – a nod acknowledging my existence and very little else.

What little calm a full night of sleep had granted me scurried back into the shadows.

I scrambled to my feet, excruciatingly aware of the eyes following me as I mumbled some unthinking greetings at no one in particular and received some equally unthinking mumbles in return. Creon didn't move, and it took all I had not to hurry towards him. Instead, I forced myself to leisurely stretch the cold from my limbs and gather my breakfast before I finally crossed the clearing to his side and sank down on the dewy grass next to him.

The two feet of air between us seemed chillier than even the most frigid of morning breezes. Creon's gaze remained firmly on the whirling mist; his wings did not budge the slightest fraction towards me.

'Did you find anything last night?' I said, hoping with all my might that Beyla and Edored would forget to pay attention if the conversation appeared practical and sensible enough.

Found the temple, he signed, and his shrug didn't betray that that single achievement was the culmination of weeks and weeks of desperate work. *Seemed deserted. Which doesn't have to mean anything, of course. I may just not be the first person Zera wants to see.*

At home I would have joked about goddesses and poor taste. Would have climbed into his lap and held him until that stiffness melted from his limbs, would have muttered jabs at him under my breath until he took the challenge, fought back, and won.

With the piercing eyes on the edge of my sight, I said, 'See your point.'
He did not react.

I tore off a piece of bread with trembling fingers, fighting the dangerous urge to blow up a few trees and sneak away in the chaos that would
doubtfully ensue. 'Creon?'

With the most minimal of sighs, he tilted his head a tenth of a turn
towards me. His gloved hands remained motionless in his lap, as expressionless as the mask of his face.

For hell's sake. I stuffed a small bite of bread into my mouth, hiding
my words behind my palm as I muttered, 'We need to talk.'

Yes. He lowered his hand with that throwaway gesture, half-hiding
his signs behind his thigh. The words followed so fast even I had trouble
following them; no alf with a poorer view and a single day of practice
would manage. *Which would be easier if you didn't insist on prioritising
Edored and his sorry opinions.*

'It has nothing to do with ...' I faltered, remembering just in time that
using names, even on a low whisper, would be a sure way of drawing
attention. 'With *that*. I'm trying to win a war here, alright?'

He raised an eyebrow. *You're not alone in that.*

'Really?' I muttered sharply. 'Shouldn't you stop provoking alves, in
that case?'

The silence fell too icily, and only then did I hear the sharp accusation
below those words, the edge of my frustration. For the blink of an eye,
his fingers hung motionless between us. Then he snapped to his feet
with a brusque shrug and strode past me the way he'd walked off last
night – all aloof disinterest, all arrogant spite.

'Creon!'

Too loud. Too desperate. Every single eye around the clearing
snapped towards me, no longer even pretending not to be watching
me.

Kneeling by his bags, Creon did not turn around.

Oh, *fuck.*

Sudden tears stung my eyes, painfully hot against the morning cold –
so I was only making things worse, now? Creating trouble even if there
hadn't been any trouble up to this point, even if he *had* been fine until

five minutes ago?

Fuck, fuck, fuck.

'What's going on?' Edored said loudly, his hand already on his sword hilt. 'Are you alright, Nosebreaker?'

He really had no right – no damn right at all – to start using that moniker now, to remind me that I was still family, that he was being an insufferable bastard only out of the purest concern for my wellbeing. I mumbled some unconvincing reassurance, focusing my gaze on the half-eaten bread in my fingers, blinking away the misty haze snaking into my sight.

Creon ignored the accusing looks of the alves with seasoned indifference. He did not grant me the sorriest excuse for a smile during the torturously long minutes of our travel preparations, either, and when we hit the road in tense, tired silence, he lingered ten strides behind me, apparently preferring Edored's company in the back of the line to mine.

A clearer message than any hand signs could have conveyed; whatever game he was playing, I'd played it wrong.

But what in hell was he trying to do, if it required treating me like a gods-damned stranger for days around people who knew damn well we were no strangers to each other?

I'm fine.

And yet ... *Did you expect me to be happy about it?*

Was that the point he was trying to make? A demonstration of just how unhappy this journey was making him, if civilised discussion wouldn't convince me to change my ways?

That ... that didn't sound like him, did it?

I shouldn't have been panicking – not until I'd talked with him, not until I knew what truly bothered him. But not panicking was easier said than done in hours and hours of walking with nothing else to do; every step was another moment to imagine all that might be wrong, all I might be ruining at this very moment by not running to him and swooning in his arms. Was that what he wanted me to do, then? Damn the opinions of the rest of the world, damn the allies we so desperately needed?

Perhaps it was. He'd always done better on his own, after all – but did he really expect me to follow him there?

And if he did, how hard could it be to just tell me? *Em, I don't think I can handle this after all* – that was a message I could work with. This ridiculous combination of reassurances and the opposite of them ... what did he want me to make of that?

By the time we crossed a clearing and caught the first glance of Zera's legendary temple, still miles away from the hill on which it was built, I was too agitated to care much about the marble spires jutting from the foliage or the sea of wild flowers growing over the arches, claiming the sanctuary for themselves. All I could see were walls. Walls meant a chance at privacy. Privacy meant a chance at honesty, or at least at explanations.

But once again the continent was larger than I'd imagined, and it took hours until we finally reached the foot of the hill, from where a rickety wooden staircase wound up the steep slope. The sun was long past its highest point by that time. My frustration had deepened to a throbbing headache, and each glance at Creon only added to the injury, his unwavering mask about as comforting as a blade to the throat.

I'd thought of him as an overly flattering portrait come to life on my arrival at the Crimson Court. He'd turned back into that gorgeous, dangerous shell – but it seemed an entirely different disguise now that I knew the male hiding below, the single damn person I loved more than anyone else in the world.

He *didn't* doubt that, did he?

The half-rotten wooden steps groaned alarmingly as we climbed the hill, splintering every now and then below a careless foot. I found myself half-wishing I would trip spectacularly and tumble down the slope; even Tared could hardly complain if Creon were to jump after me to save my neck.

But my limbs behaved annoyingly well, my body more in control of itself than it had ever been thanks to months of daily training sessions. I reached the top of the hill with sore feet and a clammy back, but otherwise unharmed.

CHAPTER 11

THE SPACE THAT OPENED up before me must once have been a lovely garden.

Bordered on three sides by towering halls and endless galleries, the temple courtyard was a tangled mess of weeds and wildflowers, roots of fruit trees breaking through the marble tiles of the paths wherever I looked. Rotting leaves clogged the intricate drainage system, and the pentagonal basin in the centre of the garden had an unhealthy green sheen of algae and gods knew what else.

Nothing about the sight suggested that anyone – goddess or mortal – had attempted to tame the chaos in the past five hundred years.

'Well,' Naxi said breezily, flinging her bag onto the ground with a gesture that said she was done walking for the day, 'I think we can safely conclude she isn't here, hmm?'

I swallowed, squashing a nonsensical sting of disappointment. I should have known better than to expect much of this place, especially after Creon's report of his first exploration. Even if she'd survived the Mother's attempt to steal her magic, why would a goddess spend her time here, in the heart of her former glory, without her priestesses or people around?

Even though ...

I halted so abruptly Edored bumped into me. 'Creon?'

He didn't avoid my gaze now; whatever lay at the heart of his cold silence, at least he wasn't risking our mission for it. I still didn't receive more than a curt raised eyebrow, though.

'There must have been people here, right?' I said slowly. 'The day Korok died?'

It was all he needed to understand where I was going. *Yes. I didn't find any bodies last night.*

I blinked. 'And you didn't mention that?'

Wrong answer, wrong tone; his responding shrug had all the wrong edges to it. *It was dark. I may have missed a few of them. And ...* He gestured at the world below the hill, a breathtaking panorama stretching all the way to the horizon. *It's just as likely that the forest buried them.*

'What was that verb?' Lyn said, squinting at his hand in fierce concentration.

Bury. He spelled it this time.

'Oh.' She released a crabby sigh of understanding. 'Of course. Like it got rid of that acorn that nearly killed Edored.'

Edored scoffed, but it didn't come out with the usual vigour. Tared shot him a look that said, *muzzle,* and his cousin abruptly shut his mouth.

'I doubt we'll find out by standing here and gaping at trees,' Beyla said, disposing of her bag as well. 'Let's take a look at the rest of the place. There may be clues. Or at least ...' She pursed her lips. 'If we don't find anything here, I don't know where else we would.'

I didn't want to think about that possibility, about having to search the entirety of this forest with seven days to go and not the faintest idea where to look. This temple alone was impressively large already – larger than my whole village on Cathra. And what sort of clue were we even looking for? Little chance that Zera had left a quick note in the kitchens with her travelling plans for the next five centuries.

'Where do we start?' Tared said, deliberately not talking to Creon, even though Creon was the only member of the company to have seen the place before.

'Creon?' Lyn said apologetically.

The wings of the building didn't seem too interesting. His gestures came slower than usual, easier to follow for onlookers with mere days of practice. *Bedrooms, dining halls, sickbay. Central part is the actual temple.*

So we piled up our bags below one of the apple trees and made our way to the open doorway on the far side of the courtyard, a towering arch decorated with such lifelike sculptures of braided twigs that I wondered if Zera had created it by changing actual wood into stone. Beyond, a spiralling structure of corridors waited for us, prayer halls and curtain-covered doorways and shadowy alcoves that seemed created for the sole purpose of playing hide and seek. Evening sunlight fell in through clever slits just below the ceiling; the air still reeked faintly of rosewood incense.

No one said much as we slowly progressed into the maze of Zera's temple, nudging open doors with the utmost caution, examining every nook and niche for whatever traces a goddess might have left. Dust whirled in the golden sunlight wherever we walked. The sound of our feet against the pale green floor tiles echoed hollowly from the ceilings, where flecks of colour betrayed the vivid frescos that must once have decorated the plaster. We passed lengthy inscriptions in Divine Tongue, rotting piles of books that made Lyn whimper, shrines where dead flowers lay scattered between the god-gifts and the half-burned candles … but not a single body and not a trace of divine life.

As if the priestesses and devoted visitors had just walked out centuries ago and never once looked over their shoulders again.

Twilight was settling over the woods when we finally reached the deepest heart of the temple, a dusky, pentagonal room, with at its centre …

A tree.

A single gnarled oak tree, growing straight from the floor, its roots stretching deep below the translucent green of the polished marble tiles. The branches reached all the way to the domed ceiling, where they curled back to fit the confines of the room; although they were heavy with leaves, no fallen twigs or blossoms lay on the floor beneath.

There were no windows, no openings to allow the sunlight inside. Still, the oak looked as healthy as any tree I'd seen in my lifetime, the foliage rustling on some non-existent breeze.

'Oh,' Naxi said breathlessly, faltering in the low doorway. 'The *forest*.'

I felt it in the same moment, that invigorating coolness that had washed over me at my first step into Zera's territory. It was a hundred times stronger here – a whisper of something ancient, something *powerful*, sliding over my skin like feather-light fingertips and stroking the magic inside me to life.

It did not feel like an invitation here.

Instead, there was a threat to the magic, a sensation like a watchdog snarling a warning.

Tared abruptly stepped back. On the other side of the doorway, Edored bit out a baffled curse, blinking at the light that flickered restlessly around his body.

'Perhaps,' Lyn said, wrinkling her nose in obvious concern, 'we should get the hell out of here.'

But now that I'd felt it, the attention of the forest lingered even as we found our way back to the courtyard, omnipresent in the dusty, rosewood-scented air. Somehow, the temple and the heart of the forest were one and the same thing – not unlike the way the Mother and Korok had built the Crimson Court straight above the centre of the Labyrinth.

Was it the magic of the forest that kept the temple from crumbling? And if it was, could it be the magic of the forest that had kept Zera alive, too?

I wanted to pull Creon aside, tell him about my theories, watch that sparkle of brand new thoughts light up his eyes as we discussed whatever secrets might be hiding within these marble walls. But with his winged back still turned firmly towards me, I barely dared to look at him – he'd become like a red-hot iron that would burn me before I even touched it.

What if I just got lost in this maze so he had an excuse to come looking for me?

Would he even care to look for me, after the last words we'd exchanged this morning? Or would he just wait for Tared and Lyn to pull me from my hiding place?

I made no attempts to get lost.

The courtyard had become an assemblage of silhouettes, the paths barely visible in the last light of day. We found our bags, then followed Lyn and the fire in her palm to the high gallery left of the temple, where Creon had discovered bedrooms and kitchens during his late night visit. The first door we entered revealed a surprisingly cosy apartment, no trace of rot or ruin except the thick layer of dust on the floor.

A quick exploration revealed five single bedrooms, each of them nearly identical with their dark wooden floors and peach-coloured clay walls. A spacious kitchen formed the heart of the house, at its centre a table that could easily fit fifteen people. There was a bathroom, too, but when I turned the tap above the bathtub, only some slimy green drops came out.

'Not lavish enough for your taste, Thenessa?' Tared said when I pulled a face, the fae title an amiable jab. Out of sheer habit, I flung a flicker of red at his head. He dodged easily, and the bathroom tiles cracked behind him.

'Could you wait until after dinner before you kill each other?' Lyn yelled from another room.

'Are we killing people?' Edored said eagerly.

For a moment, I forgot to be annoyed with them and their stupid honour as we returned to the kitchen, where the fire was already burning, flames reflecting in the copper pans and the empty glass bottles. But my eyes were drawn to Creon's motionless figure at the table before I could stop myself, and the frostiness in his expression was enough to send my mood plummeting back to rock bottom.

Surely I could find some way to pull him aside in this place, couldn't I? But if I didn't manage, if we had to continue this nerve-wracking dance for the full duration of our journey ...

It seemed an eternity ago that we'd joked and laughed and fucked in his bedroom in the Underground. However I'd disappointed him since, I didn't want to wait another eternity to find out what the consequences were.

'I'm thinking this might be a good moment for me to fade back to the Underground for news and provisions,' Beyla said, interrupting my fretful thoughts. 'Any other errands I might as well run while I'm there?'

'Oh.' Edored sounded unusually bashful as he stomped into the kitchen behind me, pulling his sword from his shoulders in that universal sign of an alf at home. 'Could you check if Nen is back from Gar Temen yet?'

I wasn't sure what was more bewildering: Edored remembering someone else's troubles, or the fact that no one in the room besides me seemed to find it at all surprising that he did. Beyla didn't even blink as she sighed and said, 'Of course.'

No one had any additional requests. She vanished without further ado, leaving the rest of us in the comforting warmth of that temple kitchen with its low wooden ceiling and its dusty rosewood smells.

Creon cooked, according to what had already become an unchallenged routine. He didn't ask for my assistance this time, though. I tried to distract myself by wiping dust from furniture and listening to Lyn, Tared, and Naxi as they exchanged theories on where a goddess could be hiding if it wasn't in her own temple. None of their ideas were very convincing, and the tones of their voices betrayed that they knew it themselves.

'But what if the plague magic doesn't harm her?' Lyn was saying for the third time in ten minutes, sounding doubtful. 'It's her own magic after all. And what if—'

'If it doesn't harm her,' Tared interrupted with a groan, 'then why has she never come forward in all these centuries?'

'Perhaps she doesn't like war? Perhaps she decided—'

Her voice stilled abruptly as a new shadow appeared between me and the fire.

I spun around, expecting to find Beyla with the provisions she'd brought. But the food baskets were nowhere to be seen, and instead ...

The greeting I'd been planning to utter froze somewhere in the back of my throat.

I'd never seen Nenya bow her head before. Had never seen her without her perfectly reddened lips or her meticulously drawn eyebrows or her elaborately braided hair, without the expression of stubborn pride that made even the grisly scars on her face look like mere annoyances. But she clung to Beyla's arm now as if that support was all that kept her knees from giving in, her black hair an unkempt mess, dark lines of earth beneath her nails. Her skin was even paler than usual, a sickly, powdery white that revealed the blue lines of every single vein in her hands and face.

She looked like hell. Had Beyla told us she was here to fulfil a last dying wish, I might have believed it.

But the alf said no such thing, made no comment on what had happened or what Nenya was doing here, miles away from any civilised company. The only explanation we received was a throwaway, 'Look who I found at home.'

'Oh, Nenya!' Lyn exclaimed before I could say anything, and although there was a hint of tightness below her superficial excitement, it was not *nearly* enough for the miserable state in which her friend had appeared. 'Finally, some decent company in this place. Take a chair. Are you staying for dinner?'

'What …' I began.

'Showing up at the right moment, really,' Edored interrupted loudly, shooting me a steel grey glare as he pulled out the chair beside him. The sight of *Edored* reproaching me for a lack of tact nearly made me drop my dust rag. 'Did Bey tell you about the temple, Nen? Pretty fun place, it seems. Pour her a glass, will you, Tared?'

'Oh, thank you,' Nenya muttered as she collapsed into the chair and Tared pressed a glass of water into her trembling hands. 'I'd love dinner. Just came home. Everything's fine.' A shivering breath, followed by an unconvincing smile at Tared. 'We won't have to worry about Bakaru anymore. He was … helpful, really.'

The way their determined smiles stiffened simultaneously at Bakaru's name told me that *helpful* was the last label the king of vampires deserved. And yet no one objected or even raised an eyebrow; only Edored contently said, 'I knew you'd manage it.'

I tried again. 'But what—'

'Em?' Lyn cut in, jumping from her chair. 'If Nenya's staying the night, we might have to revisit the bedroom arrangement. Could you help me take care of everyone's bags?'

Baffled or not, I knew an attempt at deflection when it bit me on the nose. Dumping my rag in the corner, I threw a last bewildered look at Nenya's slumping figure and obediently followed Lyn out of the room. Creon ignored me as I passed him by, blade sinking rhythmically into the onion he was slicing to shreds.

The sound followed me into the dark hallway. I shut the door behind me with too much force.

Lyn was already halfway to the farthest bedroom, and I nearly fell to my death over Edored's carelessly dropped bag as I hurried after her. A small ball of fire ignited in the palm of her hand to light my way. But she did not look back until I'd slipped into the room behind her and she'd closed the door, as if we were about to discuss the Mother's secret war plans themselves.

'Em—'

'What for the gods' sakes is going on?' I hissed, keeping my voice down even though walls and doors stood between us and the others. Her furtiveness was contagious. 'She looks like Beyla dug her out of some grave! Why are you all ignoring the state she's in?'

'She doesn't want to discuss it.' The tightness broke to the surface now, no longer buried beneath that unnatural layer of pleasant lightness. In the rusty glow of the fire, her eyes gleamed suspiciously. 'Don't stare at her like that again. Don't try to fix it. You'll only make it worse by forcing her to talk about it.'

'To talk about *what*?'

For a moment, Lyn hesitated, lips halfway to forming words. Then, with a muffled curse, she slumped down on the edge of the low bed and mumbled, 'Bakaru sucking her dry to make a point.'

I stared at her, even my nausea hitting slowly. 'He ... drank her blood?'

'Yes. Too much of it.'

'Why in hell would he do that?' My voice shot up. 'What kind of point—'

'She used to be one of his blood slaves.' Lyn spoke fast now, as if desperate to get the story over with. 'He's one of those ancient vampires who believe they'll weaken their powers by drinking from anyone but people they turned themselves. Bakaru has been the giver to a whole host of poor sods who spent their lives locked up in Gar Temen, like cattle for him to dine on.'

I swallowed a wave of bitter gall. 'That's disgusting.'

'Yes,' she said tightly. 'I've never set foot in those catacombs, but from what I've heard, it isn't pretty.'

Catacombs. The image of Nenya – proud, majestic Nenya – chained like an animal in some grisly cellar ... I stifled a shiver and managed, 'How did she get out?'

Lyn sighed. 'Edored.'

'Oh. Oh, gods.'

Her smile was joyless. 'One of his more brilliant moments of stupidity, honestly. We visited Bakaru in an attempt to make him give a damn about the war his people were losing, and Edored wandered off into places he wasn't supposed to be. Found her there. Faded back later that night, after we'd all gone home, and somehow convinced her to sneak away with him for a few hours. I think he dragged her to some nymph market.'

'*Convince* her?' I dropped down on the bed beside her. 'She needed *convincing* to get out of that place?'

'You've heard how she talks about Bakaru,' Lyn said gloomily. 'She still believes she owes him for saving her life after ... well, you've seen her face.'

'Right,' I said and decided not to ask how those wounds had come about. 'Unhelpful.'

'Yes.' She was silent for a moment, staring at her own glowing palm. 'I don't even know how often Edored went back for her. He told me it was just five times, but Tared thinks it's closer to twenty, based on ... Well, anyway, he kept pulling her out of there for just a few hours at a time and returning her to her cell, until one day she decided she'd had enough and wouldn't go back. So that's how she ended up with us.'

'But she and Edored never ...'

Lyn's long-suffering groan was enough of an answer.

'Oh, gods,' I said, wincing. 'I thought, with all his pretty nymphs ...'

'The pretty nymphs are half of the problem.' She glanced at the door, then continued in a hushed voice, 'Look, she's madly in love with him and always has been – but he's an *alf*, Em. Getting himself bonded to someone who's not ...' A grimace. 'He knows exactly what a mess that can cause. So he told her from the beginning it would never be anything, and she's stupidly proud and told him that was perfectly fine.'

I let out a laugh. 'Even though she about murders him whenever he mentions any of his bloody *friends*?'

'Yes,' Lyn said, rolling her eyes, 'clearly she's not perfectly fine, but we're talking about *Edored* here. I once joked the sky was green and he ran to Tared because he was concerned about my eyesight – so if Nenya says she's fine, he'll assume she is until she spells out the opposite for him. Which she won't, because she's far too proud to risk his rejection.'

'And no one ever thought to tell him—'

'He'd panic,' she said flatly. 'And Nenya would rather end herself than admit what she really wants. So for the past few centuries ...' She shrugged. 'He flounces into her bed every now and then, she never tells him to piss off, and then he moves on to the next fling and Tared and I spend a month putting out fires. It's all mildly ridiculous – but it's better than the Gar Temen catacombs, I suppose.'

'She ...' I swallowed. 'She really went back to that place just to tell Bakaru to stop fucking around.'

'Yes, and he was fucking around only to make the point that he still owns her.' She slid from the edge of the ancient mattress, snuffing out the fire in her palm with a snappish gesture. Only her voice pierced the abrupt darkness, young but laced with centuries of sadness. 'We may be fighting the fae these days, but don't ever believe the rest of the magical world is much kinder at heart, Em. It's wolves against wolves in the end.'

Most of the half-somethings end up here, she'd told me months ago. *The full-somethings tend to make a fuss about them.*

I didn't want to know what a vampire king obsessed with blood purity would think of a little mongrel like me.

'I'll remember that,' I said feebly.

'Good.' With a sigh, she opened the door and gestured for me to go first, back into the corridor and the faint sliver of light below the kitchen door. 'Oh, and Em?'

'Hmm?'

'Are you and Creon alright?'

My stomach gave a painful jerk. So she had noticed it, the way he kept turning his back on me? She thought it was more than just the role he was playing, too?

No confirmation had ever been so alarming. If she'd seen it too, if she'd found it unusual enough to ask the question ...

That meant it was *real*.

'Perfectly fine,' I said brusquely as I began walking back to the kitchen. Somehow, the lie seemed safer than whatever the truth was. 'Thanks.'

She sighed but didn't probe.

At the table, Edored was talking about Lyckfort and dragon scales, his voice loud and excited. Nenya was smiling when I stepped back into the firelight – a weak, watery smile, but it tugged harder at the corners of her lips with every sentence of Edored's incoherent yet pleasantly dramatic travel report. The smell of frying onions filled the kitchen. Creon didn't look up as I passed him by, didn't even halt his stirring for the blink of an eye.

Fine.

I swallowed a sting of dread at that laughable word. Tonight, then. I *had* to find a way to speak with him alone tonight. Although someone would be awake with him, of course, likely one of the alves, which meant ...

'Oh, Lyn?' Beyla said, interrupting both my thoughts and Edored's winding monologue on the burned earth we'd found outside the Lyckfort city walls. 'Agenor left a letter for you in the Underground. About the phoenixes, apparently. It's in my coat.'

'Already?' Tared said sharply.

'I know.' Beyla sagged in her chair, a wry pessimism below the thinness of her voice. 'Seems unlikely for them to agree that quickly.'

Which suggested bad news. I whirled around just in time to see Lyn pull the sealed parchment from Beyla's coat pocket. For three, four heartbeats, no sound but the sizzling of oil and onions broke the silence as her eyes shot lightning-fast along the lines.

Her gaze paused on the last words – long enough to make Tared stiffen by the table.

'Fuck,' she said.

'What does he say?' By the tone of Tared's voice, he was prepared to fade to Phurys this very moment to break a couple of phoenix noses, diplomacy be damned. 'Do they want anything from you?'

'No,' Lyn said, gaze bleakly scanning the letter again. 'No, but ... Oh, hell. Em?'

'Yes?' My voice came out higher than usual. 'What is it?'

She hesitated, then muttered another curse and handed me the letter, lips a thin line. 'Read for yourself.'

The parchment trembled in my fingers, blurring Agenor's messy writing. *Bad news*, the note started – not even a salutation to soften the blow.

Phoenix elders seem determined to trust the Mother's version of events. Very politely called me an idiot for not seeing the issue with our most dangerous weapon being fully under the Silent Death's control, etc. etc. They told me they will reconsider their decision not to join if and only if Em makes a bargain that she won't exchange a word with C. ever again.

I have no clue how to even bring this up with her. Will defer to your wisdom.

A.

I stared at the words with unseeing eyes, the firelit kitchen a haze as the full implication of my father's words sank in.

A bargain.

To stay away from Creon.

A breathless laugh fell from my lips, horror more than any other emotion. No. No, not a chance in hell. Even if we needed the support of the phoenixes – even if we needed every little bit of support we could get – surely we didn't need them *that* badly? The others would agree, wouldn't they, that even an army of fire mages couldn't be worth ...

Would they?

My breath quickened as I tried to imagine what Edored would say – what the Council would say. A hundred and thirty years of desperate resistance, a hundred and thirty years of human suffering, and was I really going to shove all of that aside and risk losing this war just because of some childish sentimentality? Because of some murderer? Clearly they'd always been right not to trust me, and ...

Fingers plucked the parchment from my hand.

'Hey!' I snapped, snapping around before I had the mind to register the crude black scars running over that offending hand. 'Will you ...'

And then I found myself chest to chest with Creon, chest to chest with a generous six feet of wings and leather and bulging muscle, and the breath caught in the back of my throat.

He merely raised an eyebrow, gracefully stepping back as quietly as he'd arrived.

'You could have just *asked*,' I managed weakly.

With a shrug, he shifted his gaze to the rumpled parchment, granting Agenor's writing no more than a slow, sceptical look. He did not meet my eyes as he lowered the note. He just turned away, wordless and careless – the way he'd turned away from me for hours and hours on end – crumpled the message between his slender fingers, tossed it into the stove with a single well-aimed gesture, and sauntered back to the pumpkin he'd been butchering.

As if the problem no longer existed with that note reduced to ashes.

And that ... that was all he was going to do? Shrug at me and ignore the catastrophic choice that had just been forced upon me, or the consequences of the decision I would make?

'What in Orin's name is all this about?' Beyla said behind me. 'What did he write, Lyn? If they're causing trouble ...'

'Em?' Tared said. 'Are you alright?'

'I ...' The room spun around me, dragging my thoughts with it. I was *not* alright. I was further from alright than I'd been in ages, our hopes and alliances crumbling because of me and me alone, and why was Creon just *standing* there scooping seeds from his gods-damned pumpkin as if he didn't feel the blood running cold in my veins?

'Not a very pleasant note, I take it?' Naxi said, sounding amused.

'Emelin?' Nenya's voice was hard through the exhaustion, her sharp-minded wariness returning. 'What is the problem?'

I couldn't tell them.

If I told them, the Council would know before the week was over – and right now, the *one* thing that would make everything worse was Valdora of Svirla trying to force my hand in a conflict where I'd rather die than give her what she wanted. But their voices were coming from all sides now, asking questions, demanding answers, and then there was Creon's silent, uncaring back ...

The door.

My eyes locked onto that last escape, and all else fell away – the need to think, to watch my words, to be the perfect unbound mage. Out. I needed *out*. The need for silence and cold air became a physical ache just beneath my skin, a hunger that moved my feet before another single thought could pass through my reeling mind – and then I was running, stumbling over bags and coats, out of the stifling warmth and into the pitch-black of the autumn night.

CHAPTER 12

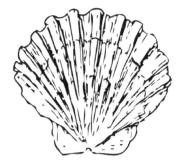

SOMEONE SHOUTED MY NAME behind me, but through the blood rushing in my ears, I couldn't tell whether it was Tared or Edored.

It didn't matter. I wasn't stopping anyway.

Stumbling past shrubbery and dead flowerbeds, tripping over roots and shattered tiles, I fought my way through the garden, towards the faint green glow that emanated from the temple gate. Branches whipped across my face. Chilly night air brushed my bare arms and legs, sending shivers down my limbs. But a few bruises and a little cold seemed a small price to pay for just a few moments to breathe without the weight of an audience on my shoulders, and my feet kept moving.

Behind me, a door slammed.

Tared's voice – unmistakably Tared, this time – snapped, 'You're not going to—'

'Tared, *let* them!' That was Lyn, sounding on the brink of tears. 'It's his business as much as hers!'

A blinding flash of blue lit up every inch of the garden for the blink of an eye.

I whipped around on the low steps to the main gate, out of breath and aching, my heart pounding in the tips of my fingers. Something had changed in the darkness before me. The shine of the firelight was gone, the doorway from which I'd fled no longer visible. In its place, just barely visible in the unearthly gleam radiating from the gate behind me ...

A wall seemed to have grown out of nowhere in the middle of the courtyard. Squinting into the night, I distinguished the shapes of stems and branches squashed together, forming a hedge-like barrier as high as the apple trees.

Blue magic.

Every plant, every tree, every last blade of grass to ever have grown in this garden, healed back to their most glorious height all at once, forming an impenetrable wall along the full length of the eastern temple wing.

Which wouldn't stop the alves for long. I backed towards the temple entrance, which was not as dark as I'd expected; the marble floor tiles glowed green in the night, shrouding the dead flowers and dusty velvet curtains in an eerie, sickly hue. Any moment, someone could fade into this corridor, and Creon had to know magic plant walls wouldn't do anything to stop them. Which rendered this dramatic show of magic entirely useless, unless ...

Unless the intention wasn't to stop them.

Unless the intention was just to hide the temple from view for a few precious moments.

The thought was still shaping itself in my mind when six feet of male magnificence burst from the darkness, sweeping me off my feet and into the air with a single powerful wingbeat.

And then all I could do was hold on to him for dear life as we surged through the temple gate three feet above the ground, into the maze and out of sight for anyone in the courtyard outside. The temple shot by in a blur: a broad side-passage, a small prayer hall ... Creon's arms were warm steel around my waist, clutching me to his chest so tightly I could barely breathe; his rough breath was the only sound accompanying the slaps of his wings as we whirled left and right and left again. Going nowhere – or perhaps just going elsewhere, any place where a pack of honourable alves wouldn't find us.

Mere corridors away, someone yelled my name.

But wings were fast, so much faster than feet or aimless fading, and we barged through the next doorway before anyone appeared around the corner. I just had time to notice pale pillows and dusty curtains and a small altar buried in flowers – a room we hadn't visited this afternoon. Then Creon landed without sound on the glowing green floor and whirled the both of us around, his left arm still locked around my waist. My dress grew a muddy brown, and another flash of blue magic lit up the room.

The narrow doorway through which we'd entered grew shut, the heavy blocks of marble sealing over the entrance without a trace.

Locking us in.

Locking them out.

The sound of Beyla's voice calling my name vanished as the last crack in the marble closed.

Creon released me so abruptly I nearly fell over. Mind spinning, I staggered back. Alone, finally ... but the relief wouldn't come, this eerie, silent place not welcoming enough, the hard lines of his face not re-assuring enough to soothe the panic burning in my veins. The others would know he'd been here with me, or at least suspect it. The rest of the world might hear. And the phoenixes ...

The air stopped dead in my throat for one perfectly silent heartbeat. The phoenixes would hold on to their demands.

'I'm not making that bargain.' The words came out jumbled and hoarse, rushing over my lips and fracturing the dusty silence. It wasn't a plea for him to agree. Rather, a plea for him to *care*. 'We'll have to find some other way to make them join the fight. Some other way to keep them happy. I'm not ... I'm not ...'

Creon stood tall and motionless before me, his eyes bottomless pools. In the pale green light, his face was all whetted shadows; the inked cut crossing his eyebrow resembled a slash of night creeping up on his eye. His fingers didn't move. His face didn't show a trace of relief. He just watched me, studying me with that dangerous stillness of a hunter who's laid his trap – waiting, it seemed, for whatever sentence I was about to utter.

The words evaporated from my lips under that gaze.

He ... he did agree, didn't he?

'Creon?' I hated the smallness of my voice. Hours and hours of deliberate silence, of his gaze avoiding me wherever I went, had sent doubt seeping into even the firmest of certainties – but whatever I'd done to displease him, surely it couldn't be *this* bad? 'You ... you don't think I should make that bargain, do you?'

He blinked – a single blink, breaking through his perfect control like a thunderclap shattering the stillness of night.

His lips said, *What?*

'I just ... If you disagree—'

What for the gods' sakes are you talking about? he cut in, the motions of his fingers sharp and rushed. In the eerie green glow of the temple, it was a challenge to read the signs – but his bewildered eyes darting over my face told a clear enough story. *I'd kill every single soul on Phurys before I let you make that bargain. Why in hell would you think—*

'I don't know what I'm thinking!' I burst out, the words echoing back at me from the low ceiling of the room. 'I don't know anything anymore! What in hell are *you* doing? Are you really so desperate to make your gods-damned point that you'd rather treat me like some stranger for days than—'

His left hand slanted over my mouth.

Endlessly familiar fingers settled on my chin and jaw, the shock of that raw force enough to put a swift end to my sentence. He stepped towards me with flaring wings – just a step, but somehow his towering silhouette swallowed half the room.

My shrieking inhalation filled my lungs with the scent of his skin. I gave up on talking – gave up on anything but my desperate attempt not to burst into tears.

He stared at me for three endless heartbeats until he finally raised his free hand. *My point?* The signs were painstakingly deliberate, every twitch meticulously measured. *What point exactly would I be making, Em?*

'That you're pissed off with me and my lies?' I managed, voice wobbling with my chin still locked between his fingers. 'That I need to change my mind about not telling the others, and that—'

And you think this is how I'd choose to convey that opinion? His signs came faster and faster – anger or confusion, I couldn't tell. *By ignoring you for days?*

'Well, apparently it is!' My words came out on a whisper, but a furious whisper sharp enough to draw blood. 'Why else would you do it? They already know you don't hate me to death, and you wouldn't tell them anything new by *looking* at me every now and then – so what's the sense in ignoring me as if I'm some disobedient child?'

He stared at me in the deafening silence for one, two heartbeats, eyes darting over my face with the full weight of his all-knowing demon senses.

Then he mouthed, *Fuck.*

'What?' Of all the things I'd expected, this was the last – the sudden understanding dawning in his widening eyes, a look of ... was it *horror?* He abruptly released my face, and I stumbled back, nearly tripping over a sturdy pillow. 'Are you suddenly realising it may not have been the kindest idea to—'

Em, his fingers interrupted, the signs brusque and snappish, *I'm not those bloody parents of yours, remember?*

My heart stilled for the shortest fraction of a moment.

Those bloody parents of mine.

And at once they were back, the memories playing out before my mind's eye – Editta's curt and unwilling replies, Valter's pointed looks over my shoulder, the two of them unable to acknowledge my existence for days because I'd been snarky to the neighbours again or worn the wrong dress again or, worst of all, nearly revealed my powers to the wrong people again ...

Like a disobedient child, indeed. Like that unwanted little creature who had never even been theirs, a heavy burden to discard as soon as the opportunity arose.

Tears suddenly burned behind my eyes, hot and shameful.

Fuck. Cactus. Hot breath brushed across my forehead as he stepped closer, signing his words at dizzying speed. *You thought I was ignoring you out of revenge? Just to spite you?*

'Why ... why else would you ...'

For hell's sake – do you have any idea what this does to me, Em? He drew in an unsteady breath, fingers stiffening for an instant. *Watching you shove me away time and time again to please Tared and his little feelings? Knowing how fucking smug he's feeling, saving yet another poor damsel from the hands of demon brood? There's a lot I can handle, but I'd rather stick a knife into my own guts than hear you declare one more time that you're not stupid enough to go near me.*

'What? But ... but you ...'

I couldn't find a way to finish that sentence; its lousy start hovered ominously in the few inches between our faces. Creon lowered his hand, but his clenched jaw and heavy breath were a clear sign we hadn't yet reached the end of this conversation.

'But you said it was fine,' I breathed, stomach turning. 'You said you understood. Why didn't you tell me ...'

I understand. I really do. Something twitched in his jaw. *But if you insist on pushing me away every time I reach out to you, don't expect me to keep reaching out. I thought that would be clear enough.*

'That ...' I stared at him, the catch in my throat growing thorny and painful. 'That's all? You weren't trying to ... to punish me?'

A scoff-like laugh fell over his lips. *You're not a gods-damned pet I'm trying to train.*

'But you're angry! You—'

Of course I am, he interrupted, the sentence ending in a sharp swing at the world outside. *At the bastards forcing you to make these decisions, who made you believe the best choice is always to forget yourself. I'm mildly annoyed with you at most, if you want to know.*

'Oh.' The world seemed to be rearranging itself before my very eyes – as if suddenly I could see through his mask again, read the quick jumps of his mind again. *Mildly annoyed.* I could handle mildly annoyed. 'But then ... then there's no problem, is there? Then we can figure out how to handle this for a few more days and ...'

His scarred eyebrow shot up. It was all that told me the calm of his signs was a lie; his perfectly still posture towering over me didn't betray his agitation in the slightest. *A few more days?*

'Ten days at most,' I mumbled, swallowing the ever-present sting of looming failure – how would we ever find Zera in that time? 'That's seven days to go. We should be able to handle that, if we actually talk it through this time.'

Yes, he signed, but somehow the gesture didn't give the impression of agreement. *And then there will be diplomatic missions and battles and endless waiting for war to happen. Armies aren't known for their abundant privacy. So if you want to hide us from the rest of the world forever ...* He grimaced. *That might be years of tiptoeing around.*

This was a conversation we'd had before. 'You're saying you want to tell them.'

No. He sighed, rubbing his eyes. *I'm saying you need to figure out at some point how much you're willing to sacrifice for the fate of the world.*

I stared at him.

My sacrifices for the fate of the world ... Hours of sleep, hundreds of lies. Losses I'd accepted without hesitation, because how could I not, when thousands of lives hung in the balance? Hell, I'd once accepted a place in the Silent Death's bed to get rid of the Mother. After that, how could I *not* go along with whatever small sacrifice the Alliance asked of me?

There is a limit, Creon helpfully added. *The demands of the phoenixes go beyond that point, it seems.*

'Yes,' I managed, 'but ...'

So where do years of secrecy fall on that scale? Is that really a price you're happy to pay?

'Don't pretend it's that easy!' My voice cracked. 'You know how much of this depends on me. If the rest of the world believes I'm some little fae whore—'

They'll hate you forever and join the Mother's side only to spite you, and all will be lost. Yes. You memorised the lesson perfectly. He scoffed. *What do you want?*

A laugh wrestled over my lips. 'To save the gods-damned world.'

Not what I asked, he signed sharply. His wings had stiffened behind his shoulders. *You know what you should want, you know what they expect you to do. Forget that. What is it you actually want?*

I swallowed. 'You.'

Clever. Try harder.

It took an effort not to punch him. What I wanted – I *knew* what I wanted. I spent long hours in training halls for it, gave up my sleep for it, suffered the endless bickering of the Council with that simple goal in mind. Deal with the Mother. Do what no one else could do, and do it fast, so at long last this weight would be lifted off my shoulders and I could ...

I could ...

I could be free to follow my own damn wishes instead.

There was no taking back that thought now that it lay there, naked and vulnerable and yet sharp enough to make my breath hitch for an everlasting heartbeat.

A jumble of images washed over me, messy but disconcertingly clear, as if my mind had simply been waiting for its cue to set them free – the beach behind the pavilion, azure water frothing over the pearly white sand. Needle and thread between my fingers, the reassuring rustle of cloth in my hands. Honey cakes and sweet dates, sunlight filtering through stained glass windows, the smells of parchment and nearby sea.

And Creon.

Smiling.

For a moment, I no longer stood in a dusky prayer hall in Zera's woods, hiding from my closest allies, looking for a goddess who may not want to be found. For a moment, I was *there*, in some world that might never even exist, a place where I woke to the smell of fresh bread and fell asleep to the sound of laughter.

But there was no trace of a smile on Creon's lips when I looked up and found him watching me with those bottomless demon eyes, studying depths of me I wasn't sure I dared face just yet. Something bitter brimmed in his gaze – something that told me he knew exactly what I was about to say.

'It doesn't even matter.' The words fell from my lips with bitter, glass-edged certainty. 'What are you suggesting – that we hand over the world to the Mother for eternity and run off into the sunset together?'

No. His left hand came up as he signed the word with his right, stroking up along the side of my neck, his slender fingers tracing the small curls behind my ear until I shivered. *Just that there's a generous grey area between trying to please every single person on our side and abandoning them to die. And that perhaps you should focus on pleasing yourself more than on pleasing a handful of phoenixes you've never met.*

'But we *need* them! If I don't manage to persuade them …'

He shrugged. *They need you, too. They'll figure that out at some point. We might just have to be a little more impolite about it.*

A shiver ran down my spine. I didn't think I wanted to know what impoliteness meant to the Silent Death, and I doubted the phoenix elders would be much happier to find out. 'Fine, but it's not just about the phoenixes. If we have to drag them into this war kicking and screaming, the family will be pissed, too, and—'

They're alves, he signed wryly. *They're always furious about something.*

'I still don't want that something to be me!' I tried to step back but found the wall closer than I'd expected, the unyielding marble cold through the linen of my dress. 'Just because you can shrug their opinions off so easily …'

Creon raised an eyebrow, waiting.

'Well,' I mumbled, suddenly defensive, 'I can't. That's all.'

Isn't it interesting, he signed slowly, *how utterly fearless you are as long as you dislike your opponents, Em? And how as soon as you start liking them, as soon as you should be able to trust them, you turn into this frightened little shadow of yourself?*

I stiffened. 'What are you trying to say?'

Just that I love your sharp edges so damn much. There was something painfully disarming about the simplicity of those signs – something vulnerable that made every retort sizzle out on my tongue. *Watching you trying to turn yourself into something soft and pliable for the rest of the world is a very special kind of torture.*

'I'm not *pliable*.' I tried to move away from the wall and ended up shoving myself into his muscular chest when he didn't budge, close enough to breathe angrily into his face. 'Just because I try not to start any wars where I don't need them ...'

You're muzzling yourself, he corrected sweetly.

'You,' I said sharply, planting a fingertip in his rock-hard chest, 'are stupidly determined to hate everyone around you for the rest of your lifetime, just so you'll never have to worry they might dislike you despite your best attempts. Do you really think you're in a position to lecture me?'

A grin flickered around the corners of his lips. *Good. That's more like it.*

'More like what?'

More like you. The darkness in his eyes had mellowed to a far more familiar smoulder, that thrown gauntlet that could have lured me from the grave just to accept the challenge. *Is this the moment to remind you I warned you against taking the alves along?*

Those same alves who might be combing Zera's temple for me while we were standing here in the emerald darkness ... but it was so dangerously easy to forget about that minor detail at the sight of the twinkle in his eyes. I scoffed, jutted up my chin. 'Are you trying to piss me off now, Your Highness?'

His smile was the most wicked of confirmations. *Is it working?*

'You know perfectly well that it's working.' Damn him, and yet ... there was something so very irresistible about this, about these fights that ended in victory no matter who won. 'Brace yourself for the force of my ire. I certainly won't be muzzling myself for *you*, at least.'

I'd take offense if you did, he signed dryly. *I like you loud and utterly undone, cactus.*

Fuck. He was too close, far too close, to sign such dangerous words to me; my skin suddenly felt feverish against the cold marble, a heat spreading all the way from some nameless part at the core of me. Thank the gods for the pale green light of this room, which would at least hide the worst of my blushing. 'We're standing in a temple, you utter heathen.'

Goddess of love. He tilted his head a fraction, pressing a single gossamer kiss to my cheek, then a second one to my cheekbone. His lips were soft as silk and trailed over my skin with the feathery gentleness of a butterfly's wings. My breath hitched when he pulled back. *Pretty sure she's seen worse.*

Scoffing was all I could do to keep my legs from melting. 'You have no right to speak. I'm pretty sure you haven't prayed to a single god in your life.'

Once, he signed, and although every flick of his fingers was drenched in languid amusement, I didn't doubt he was speaking the truth. *The hours after I first found you. I'm pretty sure I invoked a couple of gods in those moments of hoping you were indeed who I needed.*

He was so close now that I could feel the warmth of his skin against my thighs and belly, his mere presence enough to keep me paralysed where I stood. Around us, the room was perfectly quiet. The altar and pillows were unmoving witnesses, the thick marble walls unwavering guards. Shrouded in the eerie light of whatever magic the forest possessed, Creon's eyes brimmed with an intensity I could taste, three days of forced distance breaking through his impenetrable shields.

Who he needed, indeed.

'Creon ...' My voice had thinned to a cobweb whisper. 'People are looking for me. I can't ... I should ...'

He closed his eyes, rested his forehead against mine. Our noses bumped together; his breath brushed over my lips, the rhythm of his shallow exhalations too fast. One hand rested on my hip, the strength of those slender fingers a promise and a reassurance.

'Creon,' I breathed again.

He kissed me.

Warm, supple lips moulded to mine, tasting the sound of his name with slow, single-minded motions, coaxing me to let go. Coaxing me to forget about the voices still grumbling in the back of my head, something about allies, something about rumours and reputations. The looks I would get when I returned. The questions, the concerns, Edored's heated whispers ...

Perhaps I stiffened under his touch. Perhaps his demon senses noticed the flare of anxiety that made my heart clench briefly in my chest. He pulled back and cupped his hand around my chin, brushing a gentle thumb over my bottom lip – his eyes so soft, so full of worry, that once again I nearly cried.

Emelin, his lips said.

'I don't know how to handle this!' I burst out. The truth told itself, words I'd never even allowed myself to think before they broke over my tongue in that helpless whisper. 'I don't know how to save the world and save myself, too. I don't know how to make these choices. I just ... I just want to sew dresses and read books and love you, not deal with this mess of—'

I know, Em. Even his signs were caresses, gentle and reassuring. *Trust me, I've felt that weight on your shoulders. I know what it's like when the world looks at you and sees a weapon rather than a person.*

I managed a nod. I didn't trust myself to get out a single word without bursting into tears.

And you'll figure it out. Because you're my prickly little warrior, and you always figure it out in the end. He kissed my forehead, full lips lingering against my skin for one blissful moment before he pulled away. *But allow me to help you until that time. Tell me what you need. Tell me what you want.*

'I just ...' My voice cracked. 'I just want everything to be simple for once.'

His left hand trailed away from my chin and wrapped around my nape instead, leaving shivery goosebumps wherever his fingers passed. He raised his right hand between us.

Then allow me to make things simple for a little while.

Just a little while.

The others would miss me. They would ask their questions. But he was here with me, safely hidden in this sealed room, and the gods knew when I would next be able to exchange as much as a private word with him again.

I slumped against the wall in wordless surrender.

His lips were on mine the next moment, and this time there was no gentle coaxing to his kiss – this was a conqueror's victory march, a triumph to wipe out every dream of resistance. I opened my mouth to him in a primal reflex. He angled back my head to kiss me deeper in response, tongue and lips claiming the very air I breathed, swallowing my moans, smothering the last sensible thoughts attempting to rise in me. Unrelenting devotion swept over me like a tidal wave – and like an exhausted swimmer who finally ceases fighting the current, I gave in.

He could have me. Every messy, inadequate inch of me.

His shoulders were rock hard when I grabbed for him, nails meeting corded muscle below the soft linen of his shirt. I pressed myself tighter against him, and all my mind registered was his hitching breath as our bodies met – simplicity, perfect and blissful simplicity. He nibbled my bottom lip. I sucked hard on his tongue in reply, and the jolt of his cock against my lower belly set every nerve ending in my body on fire.

Zera would have to forgive me. I'd missed him too fiercely, needed this perfect and self-evident harmony too much to hold back. There was no stopping my shaking hands as they clawed for the buttons of his trousers, desperate to free every addictive inch of him; two, three buttons, and his erection lay heavy in my palm, searing hot and smooth as silk. I pumped my fist along his shaft once, and his ragged breath tightened into what should have been a moan.

That silence ... I didn't want to think about his voice either, not in this place where we should already have found our answers.

But he gave me no time to think or falter under his hands. There was an urgency to his touches, a sense of finality in every twist of his lips. He devoured me like a starving man, the way I'd devoured my winter meals on Cathra – not knowing if I'd get to sate my hunger the next day, or ever again. I rubbed my thumb over the head of his cock, finding the little slit slick already. He snarled against my lips. I half-laughed, half-moaned, and he broke our kiss to bite down sharply on my earlobe – an unmistakable punishment that sent my knees buckling in a haze of red-hot pleasure.

He caught me as I sagged against him, swept me off my feet in one easy motion, and carried me away from the cold wall, towards ...

Towards Zera's altar at the centre of the room.

Dead flowers and half-burned rosewood candles tumbled onto the floor tiles as he shoved me onto that ancient shrine. Through the blur of my arousal, it took me half a heartbeat to comprehend what was happening. Enough time for him to curl his wings around my bare knees and gently nudge them apart, enough time for him to press forward and rub his steel erection against the soaked linen of my underwear.

Only then did I gasp. 'Creon!'

His grin dazzled with unholy delight, an expression like the thrill of battle. *Are you sure you want to object, cactus?*

'It's an altar! You can't—'

He thrust his hips forward so that the full length of his cock slid along that most sensitive part of me, as if to prove me wrong. I bit down a moan, clutching the edge of the carved altar for all I was worth – telling myself against my better judgement that surely he was only joking, that surely not even a male who'd once counted himself on the level of gods could sink to *this* level of immorality.

His hand slipped between our bodies, nudging the last fragile barrier of my underlinen aside.

'You barbarian.' I breathed a light-headed laugh. 'You wouldn't dare. You ...'

The warning in his smile suggested I'd be wise not to bet any prizes of sentimental value on that claim. His index finger dipped between my slick lips, sampling the wetness pooling at my entrance, and every muscle in my body clenched around that invasive touch. I moaned – I couldn't help myself.

Why not? he mouthed and probed half an inch deeper.

'You can't fuck people on altars! You ... you ...'

My sentence dissolved into a gasp. Stringing words together was becoming harder and harder as an increasingly sizeable part of my brain decided to devote its full attention to that presence inside me instead – to the soft, tantalising friction of his finger spreading me open.

I clenched my jaw and tried to ignore the irresistible amusement tugging at his lips as I ground out, 'It's a place of worship, Creon!'

He abruptly pulled back his finger, and for one dazed moment, I thought I'd accidentally won that argument – an argument that I now realised, confronted with the brand new emptiness at my core, I desperately needed to lose. But he pushed forward before I recovered, spreading my legs wider before him, and settled the taut tip of his cock between my thighs with a single deliberate motion.

Every fibre of my body abruptly shifted its focus to that single point of skin meeting skin, to that unbearable last touch that came just before ecstasy. But he paused there – ready to conquer. Ready to claim.

Raising his hand between us, he slowly brushed a glistening finger down my cheek, filling the air with the fragrance of my pleasure. I didn't dare to breathe. Didn't dare to risk him pulling away again, to repeat whatever point I'd unwisely and unintentionally made.

He met my eyes. Smiled that heart-stopping lover's smile of his.

And signed, *Exactly.*

Then he slammed into me, and every thought evaporated from my mind at once, to be replaced by the far more immediate, far more all-encompassing sensation of *him.* I curled up to the tips of my toes, clinging to his shoulders for dear life. My body moulded to his girth at that first thrust, found his rhythm in the heartbeat it took for him to fill me to the hilt; another thrust, and we blended into one glorious cadence of cries and gasps and panting breath. Fingers tangled with hair. Nails dug into flesh. His pounding cock drove moan after moan from my lips, the sounds echoing through the low room like a sacred hymn.

A place of worship, indeed.

Ecstasy built fast and unstoppable, our union too fraught with relief and frustration to think of slowing down. Creon fucked me with quick, blunt strokes, keeping one hand on the small of my back to pin me in place. His other hand was everywhere, clawing and brushing and pinching, his skilled fingers winding me up like a coil about to snap – until there was no thought on my mind but the need for release, nothing my senses registered but the merciless force of his thrusts.

Far too soon did he lower his hand to that burning bundle of nerves between my thighs. Calloused fingers found the right spot at once, flicking over my hungering flesh as he buried himself inside me one last time.

That was all it took to set me free.

Light-headed bliss washed over me, reducing the world to nothing but his arms around me. I sagged against his muscular chest as I convulsed through my release, only partly aware of the warm seed spilling over my thigh or his frayed breath into my hair ... There was just his scent, musky and sweet. His strong pulse, pounding against his ribs. His warmth, as comforting as a fuzzy woollen blanket around my shoulders.

And for a few everlasting moments, nothing was complicated.

He was here.

I loved him.

And somehow we would figure this out. Somehow we would survive this mess. Despite those bloody phoenixes and the bloody Mother and

...

And bloody *everything*.

Anxiety seeped in too easily as my mind caught up, the sting of it numbed by the delirium of my lust but not at all painless.

The safety of this room, the warmth of his embrace ... Did they even matter? The world was still waiting for me. I had to venture out again, rumpled dress and seed-stained thighs be damned – had to deal with the watching eyes and the opinions and the expectations again, and somehow try not to drown in it.

Somehow.

'What do we do now?' I whispered into his shirt, wishing I could have held on to his gift of blissful peace for a moment longer, wishing I wasn't that frightened little coward who went straight from fucking to fearing again. The panic tightened my throat, and I wished he couldn't hear that, too. 'What ... what do I do?'

Creon raked his hand through my hair and wound the messy strands at the back of my head around his fingers. With a gentle tug, he forced me to lift my face and meet his gaze, bringing our lips mere inches from each other.

The look in his eyes ...

As if I was the universe itself, every star and galaxy in it, laid out before him in its infinite glory.

Next time you tell yourself you don't know what you want, he signed, the motions of his scarred fingers slow and deliberate in the eerie green light, *you remember this.*

This. Lightness and simplicity, love and admiration. A sense of devotion, a sense of belonging, that burned strong enough to make me forget even about saving the world for a moment.

My breath caught in the back of my throat. Wasn't it interesting how saving the world never made me forget about him in return?

'If I remember this too well,' I said hoarsely, 'I may just run off with you in two days and decide never to fight a single battle again.'

Sleep on it, Em. The joyless smile that grazed his lips didn't betray what he thought of that confession – if he'd even agree to give up on a fight for which he'd spent a hundred and thirty years torturing himself. *Figure out what your options are. And then ...* He interrupted himself, tenderly tucking a loose brown lock behind my ear. His fingers hesitated one last moment before he continued. *Then stop avoiding decisions. Stop avoiding yourself.*

CHAPTER 13

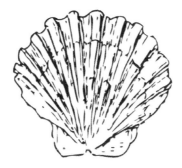

I SNUCK BACK INTO the maze of Zera's temple on my own, as presentable as I could manage, and was promptly found by an agitated Tared who wanted to know where in Orin's name I'd been hiding for the past twenty minutes.

None of your damn concern, I wanted to say.

But I knew the conclusions he'd draw from that – conclusions that wouldn't improve the relations among our travel company in the slightest. Decisions, indeed, so many choices to make, and with my mind still spinning from these few minutes of respite, I was no longer even sure what the options were.

Was I supposed to choose between love or victory?

Do you have any idea what this does to me, Em?

But Creon wasn't near enough to hear me right now, and I needed a little time to think before I gave Tared reason to valiantly murder my lover over my honour. So I hunched up my shoulders and grumbled, 'I thought it was clear I wanted some time alone?'

His shoulders loosened a fraction at the word *alone*. 'In a potentially murderous temple?'

'Well,' I said, snorting, 'my alternative was a potentially murderous forest.'

He sighed, grabbed my arm, and faded me into the smothering warmth of the kitchen I'd fled mere minutes ago. The room was deserted now; someone had finished the meal Creon had been cooking, but the plates on the table were still clean. I wasn't hungry in the slightest. Even the scent of warm spices made my stomach turn, the rush of my quick escape still far too urgent to leave room for any other bodily needs.

Tared released me and stalked to the table, scribbling down two words on a piece of scrap parchment Lyn must have left behind. Only then did he say, 'Creon didn't find you?'

'Clearly he didn't,' I said, rolling my eyes. 'If he had, you'd never have found me, because he'd have dragged me off to his hidden den of iniquity and—'

'Em.' Not the moment for fooling around, that hint of whetted steel in his level voice told me. 'I just spent half an hour fearing for your life, and I'm still not sure about the state of your sanity – so could we skip the cleverness for a bit? Where is he?'

'I have no idea!' That was true, at least; I didn't even know if he'd stayed in the temple after he opened the doorway for me again, or if he'd flown off and left it to Naxi to maintain the demon shield keeping our company safe. 'I just sat in a prayer hall for a bit and tried to make sense of the world, Tared. And could you stop treating me like an idiot, please?'

He parted his lips, then seemed to think better of it and shut his mouth again, watching me for two, three heartbeats in doubtful silence. Outside, far away, I heard what I thought might be Naxi's voice. Did even she think I had been in danger, on my own in Zera's temple, or had she simply joined the search because everyone else had?

Tared abruptly released a breath, shook his sword off his shoulders, and threw it onto the table with uncharacteristic carelessness. 'I'm worried sick about you, Em.'

My heart skipped a beat. Not what I'd expected him to say. 'How many times do I have to tell you I'm—'

'Fine?' he finished, his voice dripping with wry scepticism. 'We're walking on ground no living creature has seen in centuries, you're making grand discoveries of magical forests every other minute, and yet I haven't seen you smile in days. I may not be a demon, but you seem to forget I'm not blind, either.'

Not blind, and yet just too blind to realise the full extent of what was happening ... That *was* genuine concern in his steel grey eyes, enough of it to know that Agenor's note on the phoenixes was not the first trigger by far.

Something twisted painfully below my heart, a feeling dangerously close to guilt.

'Right,' I muttered, averting my gaze. A pressing headache was building behind my eyes, my thoughts slowly caving in under the weight of a thousand possible options. *When the world looks at you and sees a weapon* – but that was not what Tared did, was it? That was not what Lyn or Agenor did? 'Didn't realise. I'm sorry.'

He sighed. 'Do you want to talk?'

I shook my head.

'Do you want to talk with someone else?'

I managed a laugh. 'Maybe later.'

'As you wish.' There was very little relief in his voice. 'Anything else we can do for you? Food? Tea? Some noses to break?'

Gods damn him, did he have to be so ... *decent*? The world had seemed crystal clear mere minutes ago, my priorities an orderly list with Creon at the very top of them – but would the alf male before me still be offering me sacrificial noses if he had the faintest idea what I'd truly been up to in the past few minutes?

You're muzzling yourself.

Was I?

'I just want to sleep,' I managed. 'I'll be more sensible when I've had some time to think. It's just ... It's so much of everything at once.'

Had he asked more – had he asked *what* exactly was growing too big for me to handle – I might just have told him. I might have given in to that gleam of powerless worry in his eyes, the painful absence of all his usual light-hearted nonchalance, the unbearable burden of the secrets on my shoulders.

But I'd told him I didn't want to talk, and Tared being Tared, he didn't push for more.

'Take one of the single rooms.' He nodded at the dark corridor behind me, lips twisting into a mirthless smile. 'I'll go tell the rest you've been found and try to discourage Edored's plans to cheer you up with a bottle of mead. Unless you'd appreciate his company, of course?'

A chuckle found its way out, somehow. 'Thanks, but I think I could do without.'

'At least one sensible decision for tonight,' he said dryly and ruffled a hand through my hair as he strode past me, towards the open doorway and the ink-black temple night. 'Sleep well, then, little brat.'

Ironically, those words were what kept me awake for long after I'd heard the rest of the group return for their evening meal, my heart twinging with an odd sense of homesickness at the precious clamour of their voices.

I woke to dazzling sunlight, golden rays sneaking between the curtains and dancing along the terracotta walls as if to welcome me into this brand new day. From the angle of the light, it had to be far into the morning. Someone had decided to let me sleep in, my flight of last night not yet forgotten.

Last night.

Stop avoiding decisions.

Stop hurting Creon, stop hurting myself … but what was the price I'd have to pay?

I muttered a curse and sat up, shaking loose strands of hair from my face. Only then did I notice the small, linen-wrapped package on the bedside table. It smelled vaguely of cinnamon when I picked it up; I found two fresh cinnamon rolls inside, the bread still warm enough to tell me they must have been brought in straight from the Underground kitchens.

A torn piece of parchment stuck to the honey-drenched bottom of one of the rolls. I peeled it off and found a message scribbled in Creon's ever-familiar hand.

Thought I'd save you a couple before Edored ate them all. There's bread and tea in the kitchen.

On the back, it said, *P.S. You could persuade me to start praying a little more often.*

I snorted a laugh, cursing the immediate sting of warmth in my lower belly and yet unable to stop smiling as I climbed out of bed and shoved on clean clothes.

The apartment was deserted, although I heard voices outside. A full kettle hung steaming over Lyn's phoenix fire in the silent kitchen, and I miraculously found some bread Edored had not yet devoured. With a mug of mint tea in one hand and a pile of food in the other, I navigated to the temple courtyard, bracing myself for yet another morning of gruelling uncertainty.

The first thing I found was a house-high wall of plants.

In the bright light of day, the results of Creon's blue magic were fully visible – an impenetrable hedge of stalks and stems and leaves twisted together, growing from the earth like a tidal wave rising over a beach. He did not seem to have thought of bringing it down again, and after a moment of consideration, I decided that was likely the wisest decision. The forest, mild as it seemed most of the time, might have an opinion on the use of red magic against plants, even if they had been withered until the previous night.

Balancing my heap of bread, I tiptoed around the barricade and into the sunlight.

Creon lounged on a low porch, eyes closed, black wings spread slightly to soak up the warmth of the morning sun. A few dozen feet away, Beyla had settled herself in the shadow of a gnarled apple tree, stitching up a torn shirt. Nenya, Lyn, and Naxi were nowhere to be seen, but Tared and Edored were swinging swords at each other on a level patch of grass in the middle of the overgrown garden, their laughter as they exchanged jabs and insults evidence that this was a friendly training session rather than a spontaneous duel.

They were also shirtless.

I stumbled to a halt on the cracked stepping stones of my path, blinking at the two alves a little more owlishly than good manners and personal pride should have allowed me to. Somehow, having known the two of them only in a state of largely proper dress, my mind had helpfully glossed over the fact that immortal males with five hundred years of exercise behind them would likely have the physique to show for it, too.

They shared the same slender, athletic build, the honed ridges of their muscles all the more pronounced by the glow of their alf magic and the sheen of sweat that now covered their torsos. Tared's back was marked by a grisly scar crossing his entire left shoulder blade – a mark left by a weapon that must have missed his heart by mere inches. Edored, more surprisingly, sported an intricate tattoo that stretched from his left hip to his right bicep, covering most of his back. I thought it was a snake at first, and recognised only after a few moments what I should have figured out immediately – a dragon.

Of course.

It was then, generously late, that I realised I'd stood there ogling two half-naked males in public for a solid five heartbeats at least.

I tore my eyes away, hastily resuming my walk towards the rest of the company. Beyla sat bent over her needlework and did not appear particularly interested in my wandering gaze. Tared was affectionately calling his cousin a weak-handed coward, sparking a discussion that quickly evolved into a new cacophony of clashing steel. Neither of them noticed me. Creon, on the other hand …

He hadn't opened his eyes, but the corners of his lips were twitching.

Bastard.

Making decisions was easy for one brilliant instant. I changed course, too relieved to see him smile again to care what the others would think, what conclusions they'd draw. They'd seen us having breakfast together before, hadn't they? There was little to be ruined here, and that look on his face was just *begging* for some corrective measures.

Creon looked no less amused by the time I plopped down on the porch beside him, put my full mug down on the marble, and muttered, 'Wipe that grin off your face, arsehole.'

Disappointingly, although not surprisingly, that warning had the opposite effect. He opened his eyes, lips straining against a full burst of laughter now. *Having a pleasant morning, cactus?*

I glared at him as I tore off a bite of cinnamon- and honey-covered bread with my teeth. 'No idea what you're talking about.'

No? There was too much amusement in his quirking eyebrow. Of course his demon senses had picked up on the brief stutter of my sanity with perfect clarity, damn him.

'Not in the slightest,' I said, chewing indignantly.

Creon settled his wings against the wall a little more comfortably, stretching in what was both a convincing display of princely carelessness and a motion of such catlike elegance that I couldn't help but swallow my cinnamon roll a little too audibly. *Good to know. I thought for a moment you might be losing your head over the size of Edored's ...* He cleared his throat. *Dragon.*

I gave up on maintaining my straight face and slouched against the wall beside him, stifling a hysterical burst of laughter. 'Do you think he calls it that?'

He bit his lip. *I've never found myself in a position to find out.*

'Shame. Perhaps I should ask Nenya.'

If you're striving to get a pair of fangs buried in your face, he dryly signed, *that is most certainly the way to go.*

I snorted a laugh. 'Is she still here? Nenya?'

He shook his head, the twinkle in his eyes enough to remind me of last night's madness, of those scarred fingers driving all sense and sanity from my mind. *Beyla faded her back to the Underground and returned with breakfast. This entire training session is just Tared distracting Edored from his heartfelt plans to fade into Gar Temen and behead Bakaru in a fit of vengeful fury.*

'Ah.' I considered that. 'He does love her, then?'

Creon shrugged. *As much as he allows himself to love anyone.*

I pulled a face, then realised I was being just as much of a coward about my own heart and that maybe I was not in a position to pass judgement here.

On the grass, Edored was loudly listing all the bodily harm he could have inflicted in response to a small error in Tared's defensive timing. Neither of them seemed to have realised I'd gotten out of bed. Beyla, on the other hand, was throwing us watchful glances over her sewing work, the disapproval obvious in her pale blue eyes.

I suppressed the instinctive urge to shove half a foot away from Creon. What had he said? *As soon as you start liking people, as soon as you're supposed to trust them ...*

But I did trust them, didn't I?

'And where are Lyn and Naxi?' I said, because the sunlight was warm and my cinnamon roll was positively delicious and I didn't feel like spoiling my own mood with questions I couldn't answer. 'Not around to watch the show?'

Pretty sure Lyn was tempted, he signed, ignoring Beyla and her glances entirely. *Naxi pulled her along for another perusal of the temple. Said something about, I quote, "too many dicks and not enough tits for her tastes."*

I almost choked to death on my breakfast; it took a few heartbeats of coughing and laughing to retrieve the last bits of cinnamon from my lungs. When I finally looked up with tears in my eyes, Tared and Edored had paused their sparring, their jabs now interlaced with suspicious glances at Creon.

'Morning,' I said, sniffing the tears away. 'Don't mind me and my violent end, please. Didn't intend to interrupt your training.'

'You're being very damn loud, Nosebreaker,' Edored said with a scoff, easily flicking his sword around. 'Thought having a Silent Death was bad, but apparently we have a Noisy Death too, now?'

Tared took a half-hearted swing at him with his blade, not even glancing his cousin's direction to see him jump out of harm's way. 'Joining for training, Em?'

A transparent attempt to get me away from Creon if there ever was one. I exaggeratedly stuffed half of my second cinnamon roll into my mouth and said, 'I don't think anyone hauled a bunch of training sticks across half the continent just so I could spend some time stumbling over them in a temple garden.'

Tared shrugged, raking a hand through his messy blond locks. 'Edored? Could she borrow Fury for a few minutes?'

'Borrow *Fury*?' Edored echoed, his voice soaring explosively in those two words. 'Why not lend her my fucking firstborn child while you're at it, Thorgedson? You can hand over Heartfall, as far as I'm—'

'Here, Em,' Beyla interrupted, putting her needlework aside with one of those genuine but shallow smiles as she snatched the smallest of her two swords from the grass. 'You can use Sunray, if you want.'

I stared at her, speechless. Sunray. Tared's brother's sword – the sword of the first alf she'd loved, and she was putting that in *my* untrained hands?

'Unless you're too fussy for the real work, of course,' Tared said dryly, the sting obviously intended to get me moving. I blinked at him, and then at Creon, who hadn't shifted a wing as he followed the discussion with lazy, half-lidded eyes.

Choosing to accept the invitation meant going along with Tared's obvious scheming to separate us. But then again ...

Aim for his left knee, Creon signed as if he'd read my mind. *Bit of a weak spot.*

'I saw that,' Tared said, his voice cool.

Just helping with the training. Creon's smile carried more sting than I'd expected for this minor jab, and Tared's lips tightened. Not exactly a good start. But damn it, I'd never even held a real sword in my hands, and at least it seemed Creon wouldn't be terribly aggrieved if I went along with this madness.

I jumped up from the porch and hurried over to Beyla, who handed me Sunray with a quick nod. The sword was lighter than I'd expected – lighter than most of the training sticks I'd used – and glistened menacingly in the sunlight when I lifted it to study the blade. The edge was razor-sharp. It wouldn't take great force to break through skin with a weapon like this; hell, I might accidentally cut through muscle and bone if I wasn't careful.

'Well,' Edored grumbled as I made my way to the little training field. He still sounded mortally offended. 'Enough training for me. I'm going to find a brook and take a bath, if you sword-stealers don't mind.'

'I think we'll cope,' Tared said solemnly.

Edored huffed, clutching his sword as he stalked off.

I glanced at the weapon in my own hand, a weapon that must once have belonged to another alf just as passionately protective of it, and muttered, 'I'm not being terribly disrespectful by using it, am I?'

Tared sighed. 'No.'

I looked up. His smile had paled, but there was no apprehension in his grey eyes, and he did not evade my gaze like he usually did when the fate of his family came up in conversation. Was that a good sign? I decided to risk it – better to bring it up now than to find out afterwards I'd made a misstep.

'Even though ...' I swallowed. 'It's your brother's sword, isn't it?'

'Ah.' He sighed again. 'Lyn told you?'

I nodded, feeling small.

'It was Bered's, yes.' His voice only tightened a fraction at the past tense. 'But it's a damn good sword, and he would have hated for it to rot away unused. I don't mind others using it as long as it stays in the hands of family.'

Family.

My stomach knotted unexpectedly at the sound of that word. Somehow it landed not like a reassurance, but like a warning – like a reminder of how much I might lose.

A frightened little shadow.

'So,' Tared said, his voice reaching me from miles away as my thoughts turned themselves inside out without warning. 'Tilt your hand up a little when you hold it like that – you're overextending your wrist. Yes, excellent. Take position for a downward swing – watch that wrist, please.'

I followed his clues instinctively, months and months of training overriding the irrational itch of nervousness – of something I was missing, some thought chafing against my conscious mind but remaining just out of reach. What was I thinking – what had Creon said last night? *As soon as you start liking people …*

Family, indeed – and what was family but people who left when you displeased them?

My borrowed sword swept down with a satisfying *whoosh*, splitting the air as I spun around. It felt good, the steel in my hands. Better to focus on cold wrath and lethal weapons than on whatever that thought evoked in me, the memory of Cathra, of the parents who'd washed their hands of me as soon as a pretty fae prince gave them the flimsiest excuse to never look me in the eyes again.

'Not bad,' Tared was saying, and I barely heard him. 'Try that again, with a little less force. You need to stay in control of your blade.'

Control. I took another swing at some invisible target, more restrained now, my motions strangely detached from my spinning mind. I wasn't staying in control, was I? I was allowing everyone but myself to determine what sacrifices I'd make, running after my fears rather than reining them in …

Figure out what your options are.

Had I ever truly done that?

I swung my blade with unsettling precision again and again, the physical effort sharpening the turns of my thoughts. Truth or victory, I'd told myself all this time, two sharply defined possibilities with not a shred of grey in between –

But if I stopped blindly following the whispers of my fears for a moment, I had to admit not all honesty would lose me the war.

I'd still have to be careful, of course. I shouldn't tell Edored, who would immediately run to his friends to blather about my love life. But Tared wouldn't. Agenor wouldn't. Beyla and Ylfreda and Hallthor wouldn't. Most of the household was sensible enough to know a secret when they saw it, and yet …

Yet I hadn't told them.

I hadn't *dared* to tell them.

'You're back in your usual rhythm,' Tared informed me, nudging my sword aside mid-swing with his own. 'Try again. A bit of actual steel is no reason to make things too easy for yourself.'

Out of habit, I stuck out my tongue at him, avoided the reprimanding flick of his blade only by the grace of old sparring reflexes, and set to work again with gritted teeth. My biceps were starting to hurt. Thin trickles of sweat ran between my shoulder blades in the warm morning sun, sticking my dress to my back. But my thoughts stung fiercer than any physical discomfort, and there was no stopping *those* – not with every word from Tared's mouth adding to the chorus of merciless realisations.

Make things too easy for yourself.

I had, hadn't I? I'd fooled myself into believing the question was victory or love, soothed my guilty conscience with the reassuring thought that I was keeping my secrets only to save the world ... and so I had conveniently avoided the question of what would happen if the family were to find out I was not at all that innocent little half fae they'd so warmly adopted into their household. What the answer would be if the conundrum was not so much victory or love, but rather ...

Family or love?

'Focus, Em.' Tared's voice was too calm for my raging mind. That same voice that had scoffed when Agenor asked about Naxi and Creon – *Even Naxi has some moral compass ...*

We housed you for twenty years, Valter had written, and then told me never to contact him and his wife again. I'd spent five lousy months in the Underground, counting generously. What in hell would stop these alves from pushing me out again?

A frightened little shadow of myself, indeed.

And what was I supposed to do, then? If loving openly might lose me the only people who'd ever treated me as family in this world of wolves against wolves, if—

'Alright,' Tared said, interrupting his constant stream of comments and adjustments. 'I'd say that's enough for the morning, if you—'

An agonised cry tore the silence of the woods to shreds.

Screaming – shrill, unceasing screaming – echoed in threefold from the marble walls around us, making it impossible to determine the direction of danger. I whipped around, breath hitching, sore arm and frantic thoughts forgotten. The temple gates were empty. Nothing moved between the trees that surrounded the ivy-covered buildings. But beside the garden path, half-hidden behind a hawthorn bush gone rogue –

I heard my own voice cry, 'There!'

Edored.

The alf had fallen to his knees, hands frantically clawing at his skin as he howled in pain – the high-pitched, unintelligible shrieking of a male reduced to nothing but the prospect of death. What I could see of his bare torso was covered in red scrapes, or not scrapes but rather ...

Burn wounds.

Plague wounds.

My heart stood still.

Lunging forward, flinging his sword aside, Tared shouted, '*Creon!*'

Velvet wings burst past me, and I realised he had already been moving – realised that had not been an accusation in Tared's voice but rather a cry for help. Plague wounds. My thoughts moved too slowly. Edored must have walked off too far in his search for a brook, must have ended up in unprotected plague land, and faded back to the temple courtyard as soon as he realised what had happened –

Which was late.

Which was ... *too* late?

I stood paralysed in the grass, Beyla's sword powerless in my hands, as Creon grabbed Edored's shoulder and Tared grabbed the other and the bright red burn wounds grew even brighter, the sickening colour of tattered flesh. Blue magic flashed, and Edored did not stop screaming, did not stop howling incoherent pleas at whoever was holding him.

The linen of his trousers was changing in texture, turning dry and fractured before my very eyes.

'*Please.*' I'd never heard Tared's voice crack like that, half-shout, half-plea, as he grabbed Edored's wrist to restrain his wildly flailing limbs. 'There has to be something you—'

Water, Creon gestured – a single sign, so snappish I almost missed it.

Tared was already gone.

He was back in the blink of an eye, holding what looked like a tin washing-up bowl still full of soapy dishwater. Creon snatched it from his hands with inhuman speed, slamming the contents of the tub into Edored's face and chest as if the alf was a fire to be squashed.

Edored's shrieking turned into sputtering, then into quieter wailing. On his forearms, the crimson blots of burned skin were turning leathery brown and parched, deadly scabs spreading over his skin ... but where the water had hit, the advance of the plague magic seemed to have slowed.

'Let me,' Tared snapped, and Creon released Edored without a moment of hesitation. The two alves were gone the same moment, leaving an abrupt, echoing silence behind.

Perhaps half a minute had gone by since that first scream. It may have been less than that.

Only then did my trembling fingers let go of Beyla's sword; it tumbled into the grass with a dull thud, too heavy for my aching limbs to hold. Creon snapped around at the sound. There was a coldness to his gaze, to the way his eyes flicked around the courtyard and back to my face – estimating danger, estimating just how much it would cost him to pull me into his arms and fly the both of us out of this gods-damned mess.

For an unmeasurable fraction of time, I almost hoped he would.

'Where ... where did they go?' My voice came out too high and too hoarse. 'What did he ...'

Water, Creon signed again – curt, hurried gestures.

Of course. The nearest brook. The well behind the temple wing. Any body of water bigger than a little tin tub, big enough to submerge a grown alf. The pieces clicked together slowly, thoughts still wrestling to catch up with the sudden whirlwind of panic and pain.

'How did you know that would work, if blue magic couldn't heal him?'

Didn't know, he signed wryly. *Bit of an experiment.*

'Oh, gods. If that had gone wrong ...'

Something twitched at his jaw. A minimal clue – but a clue nonetheless – that told me he realised exactly what risk he'd taken, what might have happened to Edored if his theories on the sea stopping the plague had been incorrect.

More interestingly, a clue that suggested he was not entirely indifferent about it, either.

I looked over my shoulder and found Beyla still standing near her apple tree, her eyes wide with shock as she stared at the place where Tared had disappeared. In a moment of desperate genius, I blurted out, 'Should we try to fetch Lyn and Naxi? Naxi might know more about—'

'Yes,' Beyla said breathlessly, tearing her eyes away – glad for something to do, as I'd hoped. 'I'll go find them.'

I opened my mouth to thank her, but she'd already disappeared, voluntarily leaving me and Creon alone for the first time this journey. The surest clue of just how shaken she was; a shame that I was hardly in the mood to tear his shirt off him at this moment.

Clever, Creon signed.

'Not as clever as you and your theories,' I muttered, which had to be the sorriest retort I'd ever given him. 'Are you alright?'

He shrugged tersely, wings flaring a fraction with the motion. *I'm not the one who ran into a wall of divine magic.*

'No, but you look...' Distressed. Worried, even? I settled for, 'Affected.'

A dead alf wouldn't get us any closer to Zera, he signed, sticking his free hand into his pocket with what would have been convincing nonchalance if not for the short, almost unnoticeable hesitation that accompanied his words. *Not to mention the uproar the rest of the household would cause.*

Uproar. They were so damn convincing, the disparaging motions of his slender fingers, the hint of a sneer that curled around those sensual lips of his – a perfect picture of the cruel fae prince who noticed only the threat of his own plans falling to ruin. But I knew that deliberate way he flattened his wings against his shoulders. I knew the way he held my gaze just too stubbornly, his almond eyes flickering with defiance.

My heart gave a little twinge. Was this when you knew you loved someone – when you fell in love even with the lies they told themselves?

'You do care,' I said quietly.

He stiffened, hand frozen halfway to the next word.

'And you should know better than to lie to me, you idiot.' I let out a laugh. 'What am I going to do – mock you? If I need something to taunt you with, I have more than enough to say about your pathetic lack of dragon tattoos.'

A mirthless laugh escaped his lips. *Em—*

And then Tared appeared on the path between us, the soaked, battered, motionless shape of his cousin heavy in his arms, and all lies and smiles evaporated from my mind again.

Because Edored's head lolled powerlessly onto his chest, like a lifeless rag doll's head. Wet blond hair drooped like a veil around his burned face, unable to hide the crimson wounds marring his cheeks, his chin, his temple. His scab-covered arms dangled lifelessly at his sides, his eyes were half-lidded and glassy, and for one spine-chilling moment I feared, I *knew*—

'Knocked him out,' Tared said brusquely, interrupting the primal scream of my thoughts. 'He kept trying to drown me.'

My breath escaped in a burst so sudden it hurt. 'Oh, gods. He ... he's alive?'

Tared didn't reply, sinking to his knees to lower Edored into the grass with a long, shivering exhalation. His own trousers were three quarters drenched, his chest and upper arms covered in red blots and nail scratches – evidence of Edored's vehement fight as he was plunged into the water that saved him.

But the progression of the plague magic ... it appeared to have halted.

For a few instants, no sound disturbed the silence but Tared's ragged breaths and the water dripping onto the flagstone tiles. I glanced at Creon, who had gone cold and unreadable, and back at Tared, who looked like he was bracing himself for something thoroughly unpleasant – a jarring quietness after the whirlwind of their flawless cooperation of a moment ago.

I swallowed. 'Should we—'

'I suppose,' Tared sharply interrupted me, rising to his feet and scowling at Creon like a male prepared for a bareknuckle fistfight, 'I'm expected to thank you on my bare knees for this?'

I snapped my mouth shut.

That was *fury* burning in the alf's grey eyes, sharp and venomous. Where in hell was this coming from? Had Creon given the impression he expected grovelling gratitude at any moment in the past minutes – had he *ever* done any such thing?

But Creon merely raised an unimpressed eyebrow and coldly signed, *You can keep your clothes on, as far as I'm concerned.*

'Could the two of you pick literally any other moment for this nonsense?' I bit out, just in time to cut off Tared's sharp inhalation. 'Edored is still not exactly looking his best. Can we heal him with blue magic now, at least?'

Creon flicked the most careless flash of blue at Edored's marred face, the way one might toss a mouldy piece of bread in the trash. The raw burn wounds did not soften.

'Fuck,' Tared muttered.

'Naxi's wounds healed with time, didn't they?' I said nervously, remembering the burns with which the little half demon had come down after her first exploration of the continent. 'If we give it a few weeks, Ylfreda might be able to fix this, too?'

'Yes.' Tared bit out another muffled curse. 'But that does mean we're going to have to send him back home.'

I decided not to say that seemed a wise idea in any case. Creon merely threw a quick glance at Edored's contorted face and signed, *Need any assistance?*

'How very fucking selfless, Hytherion.' I'd never heard Tared this close to cracking, his voice balancing on that thin edge between snapping and shouting. What in hell was going on? Was this just the panic of Edored's near death breaking to the surface?

Creon's smile was a sprinkle of salt into a freshly carved wound. *You know me.*

'Unfortunately,' Tared bit out. 'I'd—'

'Hey!' I interrupted, my voice cracking. 'If you idiots are so gods-damned determined to make a fight out of this, could you at least do it *later*? This really isn't the moment to ...'

In a flicker of light, Beyla appeared with Lyn and Naxi by her side.

And then the courtyard was flooded with cries of horror and sobs of relief, rattled questions and panicked suggestions – enough consternation to pull the two of them apart for at least a few minutes.

But I saw the last looks they exchanged, and those did not suggest the war was over.

CHAPTER 14

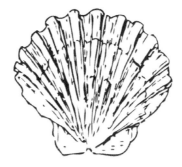

THE SMALL TEMPLE KITCHEN was painfully silent without Edored shouting poorly timed remarks at me.

We waited in tense silence for the larger part of the afternoon, barely speaking except to ask each other how long it had been since Tared had faded his cousin and Naxi to the Underground to discuss the situation with Ylfreda. Lyn furiously browsed through the piles of books she had uncovered in the temple that morning, fidgeting with her hair until she was a fuzzy little ball of bright orange at the dinner table. Creon lounged by the fire, glancing through disintegrating parchment scrolls, slender fingers unfolding text after text with an unwavering air of royal boredom. Beyla paced back and forth, throwing frustrated glances at the sun every time she passed the window, and I stared at walls and felt like an idiot.

Family or love.

Even the memory of Edored's glassy eyes and burned cheeks were not enough to squash that brand new insight, the words running through my veins like chilling poison. How had it taken me a midnight temple abduction and the unexpected honour of Tared's brother's sword to figure out that this was not just a matter of warfare and strategy?

With Edored and his loose tongue gone, I had no heroic reasons left not to tell the rest of the company they could give up on their attempts to keep me away from Creon. Hell, Lyn and Naxi already knew. All I had to do was inform Tared and Beyla of the inevitable, and life would get immeasurably easier – the part of my life, at least, that consisted of reading books in Creon's arms and kissing him awake in the mornings and sleeping wrapped in velvet wings at night.

The problem ...

How very fucking selfless, Hytherion.

Tared's voice still echoed in the back of my mind, that tone of unravelling control I'd rarely heard from him before. The other part of my life – the part filled with sword training in the sun and Alvish card games – would not become any easier at all.

I didn't think they'd lend dead alves' swords to little fae whores, either.

If only I'd been like the dramatic heroines in the tragedies Editta cried over by the fire during long winter nights – the kind that declared their everlasting love in flowery language and gave up home and hearth for whatever doom awaited them in their lovers' arms. A healthy dose of self-sacrificial tendencies would have made my choices a lot easier. But I didn't quite feel like becoming a tragedy, and as much as I intended to spend a significant portion of my life in Creon's arms ...

He'd been right when he left me behind in the Underground all those months ago, telling me I needed friends and family. I'd found that home. Made it my home, perhaps. And now he was the one threatening to come between me and the family I'd created?

The bloody irony of it.

He didn't look up from his reading on the other side of the room no matter how often I glanced his way, a small frown of concentration breaking through his princely mask, his wings spilling over the low back of his chair. My pounding heart didn't care. It didn't care I was still annoyed about his provoking Tared either, about his stubborn attempts to hold on to the heartless creature that had once lived inside him. Even Beyla's cold glances didn't soothe the painful urge to claim him for myself – to curl up in his lap and run my fingers through the silk strands of his hair, to rest my head against the perfect firmness of his shoulder and know without a shred of doubt that he was *mine*.

I did not want years of secrecy.

For the very first time, that thought rose in me not like a wish but like a certainty, a fact that sliced effortlessly through the haze of my fears.

I'd told myself I was fine sweeping him under the rug in a desperate attempt to please the rest of the world. But as I watched him from the other side of the room, watched those nimble movements of his fingers, watched the narrowing of his eyes as he contemplated his texts and the quirking of his lips as understanding dawned on him ... The mere *awareness* of him seemed to swell in me, feathery light and tingling with joy and yet substantial enough to press the breath from my lungs for a brief eternity.

A feeling I hadn't allowed myself for far, far too long.

If I shoved all fear aside for a moment, I just wanted him to be mine. I just wanted to be proudly his.

Somehow.

And if I didn't want the rest of the world to spit me out over it ...

A spark of determination took over, that same resolve that had landed me here on the continent against all odds, hunting for a lost goddess who may not want to be found. It was very damn simple, really. If I didn't want to keep secrets, and I didn't want the world to dislike the truth either ...

Clearly the truth ought to be more likeable.

Which was admittedly not the first word that came to mind as my eyes slid over Creon's quiet figure, noting the knives in his boots, the crude ink lines covering his arms and face, the ever-present air of shimmering danger he emanated. Gorgeous and brilliant and ruthless and brave, but he was not *amiable* – not a male who pleasantly talked his enemies into tolerating him.

Then again ...

I could probably do the talking. All he had to do was look like I may be right.

The thought of a plan – a *strategy* – was enough to finally calm the vehement hammering of my heart. No matter how vague and insubstantial, this was at least something to aim for, a start to regain control. I would quietly sneak away with him the moment Tared and Beyla let us. Would tell him that I was done keeping secrets and that I needed him to stop sparking small wars with our allies – to stop making himself *less* likeable to the world.

Really, all he had to do was stop pretending he was still that murderous fae torturer he loathed from the bottom of his heart himself.

How hard could that be?

Tared and Naxi returned just before dusk swept over the forest, without Edored, but with the reassuring news that he'd woken up and appeared to be as much himself as could be expected under the influence of a heavy dose of willow bark and valerian.

'Kept gabbling about dragons,' Tared said, collapsing into the nearest chair and closing his eyes as if he'd need a week of sleep to make up for the past hours. 'And he was demanding something stronger to drink by the time we left, so it doesn't seem the magic did any lasting damage to whatever brain he still had.'

Lyn let out a laugh as she jumped from her bench to make more tea. The relief was tangible even in that joyless sound. 'What did Ylfreda say?'

He opened one eye. 'Don't think I should repeat that for Em's young ears to hear.'

'Bastard,' I said.

'See?' He threw me a grin. 'You've been corrupted enough.'

I snorted, but the worst of my annoyance was already melting away.

It had likely just been the panic and fear that made him attack Creon so needlessly a few hours ago, I told myself – and could I really blame him for that? I wouldn't have been any friendlier had it been one of my family members standing on hell's doorstep.

'Ylfreda thinks the worst of the burns may scar,' Naxi added, throwing me a sharp-toothed grin as she settled herself at the dinner table, 'but most of them will probably heal. We were just in time, by the look of it.'

Beyla muttered a curse. 'Thank the gods he faded back to us immediately, then.'

And thank the gods Creon had been quick enough with his hunch about water ... but no one said it aloud in the silence that followed, and the weary lines on Tared's face suggested this may not be the moment to make that point. Creon himself had barely looked up from his reading, the pile of parchment beside his chair growing more intimidating by the minute.

Lyn rushed around to hand us all a cup of tea, glowering at Naxi when she put her mug too close to the ancient manuscripts on the table. She brought Tared a bowl of nuts to snack on after his long-distance fading. Then she pulled a fuzzy blanket out of nowhere for Naxi, filled the kettle again, and hung it back over the fire. No one offered a hand as she fidgeted around, although Beyla looked like it took an effort – but I suspected being useful was simply how Lyn dealt with danger, and making her sit down and rest would do more harm than good.

When she finally finished her hurried rounds, however, she didn't return to her own spot on the bench.

Instead, she climbed into Tared's lap without a word of warning, folded her short legs against her chest, and nestled herself tightly against him.

The light around him blazed brighter than I'd ever seen it – just a flash, like an involuntary moment of lost control. Then he slouched against his backrest, finally loosened his shoulders, and wrapped one arm around her with a sigh that seemed to come from the marrow of his bones, resting his forehead against the crown of her head.

Next to me, Beyla mumbled an apology and faded out of the room.

Bonded mates. Was it too painful for her to see the two of them like this, even thirteen decades after she'd lost the alf male whose sword she still carried? Even knowing this small moment of tenderness between Lyn and Tared was nowhere near a solution to *their* thirteen decades of indecisive tiptoeing around?

I decided not to ask that, either.

'So,' I said instead, talking mostly to Naxi because Creon wasn't looking up from his scrolls and I wasn't going to disturb Lyn and Tared, 'do we have any idea how Edored ended up walking into plague land? Or didn't he say anything about that?'

'Not a sensible word.' She cheerfully tugged her woollen blanket more tightly around her shoulders, her twinkling blue eyes evidence she knew all the questions I wasn't asking, and likely a few more of them, too. 'We asked him, but he kept shouting things about dragons. Ah, well.' A chuckle. 'We always knew he was a bit of a dum-dum.'

Not untrue, and yet ... An idea sparked. 'He's never been *this* foolish before, though.'

Creon slowly lowered his parchment.

Glancing around, I added, 'Or was he so upset about our sword-stealing that he'd reasonably forget to mind his surroundings?'

Creon cocked his head, dark eyes piercing mine, thoughts visibly whirring to find out what I was playing at. *I wouldn't say he was.*

Right answer. I barely held back a smile. 'Shouldn't we go take a look, then? Just to be sure he wasn't spooked by anything dangerous and forgot about the plague as a result?'

The miniscule twitch of his lips was the only signal he'd figured out my game. *Just to be sure* – a sensible proposal, coming from the little unbound mage trying to keep everyone safe. The fact that Beyla was currently not around to join us, and that Tared would likely not be in the mood to run after me and protect my uncorrupted innocence, was obviously entirely secondary.

'Oh,' Naxi said, a chuckle lacing her words, 'that's clever, Emelin!'

'Thanks,' I said and got up with a pointed look at the world outside. Above the treetops, the sky was turning a soft, peachy pink. 'We should probably go as soon as possible, then? I'd prefer not to walk around in the forest at night, and we'd overlook traces in the dark, anyway.'

Creon rose with the look of a spoiled fae prince forced to run after some wild toddler. *I suppose you need company?*

'Well,' I said, 'unless you want me to follow Edored's example ...'

He shrugged, sticking his hands into his pockets with perfect disinterest. Excellent. At least he wasn't provoking Tared, wasn't giving the impression he was sneaking off with me only to seduce me in dastardly fashion as soon as we were out of sight. As long as we made sure not to stay away too long – and really, how long could this conversation take ...

'May I suggest you don't venture into dangerous territory without any alves?' Tared interrupted my thoughts, sounding exhausted rather than spiteful as he looked up from Lyn's messy curls.

For fuck's sake.

'It's hardly dangerous with a demon around.' It took an effort to restrain my voice, to stick with calm, practical statements. 'We won't even be gone that long.'

'We just concluded fading out in time was what saved Edored's life,' he retorted, lifting Lyn off his lap with obvious displeasure. 'And if I have to fade another half-dead victim into Ylfreda's hands, I'll probably be cleaning out bed pans for the next five years. So unless you want to go looking for Beyla to take my place ...'

I parted my lips to tell him that seemed a better idea. Even if a confidential conversation would be equally impossible with Beyla around, at least there was slightly less risk that she'd skewer Creon on one of her swords before we had the temple behind us. But Creon brushed past me before the first word left my mouth, his movements overly measured, his dark eyes brimming with an emotion that was no longer unhurried boredom or cruel confidence at all.

Imagine trusting her to take care of herself for five whole minutes. His signs were tight and tense. *Would it kill you not to play the useless hero for once?*

It took half a heartbeat for those words to hit home – the full, venomous weight of them. 'Creon!'

He ignored me, and so did Tared, who strode towards the door with a sharp, 'It's called caring about people, Hytherion. Why don't you stay out of matters you don't understand?'

'Could the two of you behave?' Lyn snapped, a deadly shimmer of fire below her voice. 'A bit of civilisation never killed anyone.'

Tared vanished outside without a reply. Only then did Creon meet my eyes, an alarming flicker in the dark of his irises that was in no way mellowed by his joyless smile.

Still coming?

What in hell did that mean – that he'd follow Tared anyway, with or without me? What kind of madness was that? The two of them had been at each other's throats all day; wouldn't *everything* be preferable to a forest walk in the company of an alf who apparently couldn't go two minutes without insulting him today?

What had I missed?

'I think,' I said with all the calm I could gather, 'that it might be wiser if we just stay here, don't you think?'

Creon shrugged and stalked outside, with the clipped, tense stride of a male who has business to finish.

'Oh, *idiots*,' Naxi muttered, sliding down in her chair with a pained groan.

Even she was alarmed? That was bad. That was very bad. I took stock of the situation in a single faltering heartbeat, weighing my options – Beyla was still nowhere to be seen. Naxi needed to keep up the demon shield in the direct vicinity of the temple, at least as long as we weren't sure where Beyla had gone. Sending Lyn into a disagreement between Creon and Tared sounded about as helpful as throwing a bottle of oil into a raging fire, even if she was not the root of the problem this time.

Which left me.

And in all fairness, I was the one who had started this entire endeavour.

'I'll see what I can do,' I said and dashed out of the kitchen before either of them could stop me and change my mind with wiser arguments. Wiser arguments wouldn't calm anyone down, and the sound of Tared's sharp voice outside told me we'd need a lot of calming down before I could get to the more sensitive topic of my exact relationship with the target of his wrath.

It took an effort not to curse. So much for my diplomatic strategies.

They were already halfway across the courtyard by the time I flew out the door, striding in the direction Edored had gone. Sprinting after them, I was just in time to hear Tared snap something about a history of causing trouble and how he was not making the same mistake twice.

Creon's reply came in curt, meticulous signs. *Like the mistake of kicking down the people you need to win a war?*

Gods damn them both. I jumped over a last tangled flowerbed to catch up and shoved myself between the two of them with a few whole-hearted elbows into ribs – enough of an interruption to shut down the exchange of low blows for a moment. 'So.' It came out as brisk as I felt. 'Where do you two idiots think we should start looking?'

There was no amusement to Tared's half-snorted laugh, but at least he didn't resume his string of insults. 'You were the one who came up with this idea.'

An annoyingly good point, and probably not the moment to tell him I had come up with the plan only in an attempt to get five minutes alone with Creon. I nodded at the wall of grey-white trees rising from the hillslope with as much conviction as I could muster and said, 'Well, he was looking for a place to take a bath, wasn't he? So it stands to reason he'd have aimed for some brook or creek.'

There's a decent-sized pool behind the north tower, Creon signed, all uncaring boredom again. As if he'd barely noticed Tared's jabs. As if he truly didn't care. *Could take a look there.*

We walked on in icy silence, the air heavy with everything they might have told each other if not for my presence – words that must have festered for months, but why in the world were they coming to the surface *now*, when I needed their cooperation more than ever before? Did Creon truly not realise how every war he started dug us deeper into our secrets?

He had to realise that, hadn't he?

The pool emerged misty and glittery in the thick of the forest, the water so eerily still I might have believed it was a mirror embedded in the mossy earth. Nothing moved around us as we came to a standstill at the edge of the small clearing and threw a cautious look around.

No dangers to be seen, no perfect explanations for Edored's near-fatal moment of inattention.

Just a bit of a dum-dum, then.

I sucked in a breath to tell them, with more relief than I wanted to admit, that clearly I'd been overly suspicious and it was time to return to our temporary home. At least Lyn and Naxi would be around to help me tear the two of them apart if needed. There would be other opportunities to tell Creon he was being spectacularly unhelpful, and—

'Are those footprints?' Tared said sharply.

I jolted from my premature haze of relief. 'Where?'

He strode around the small body of water without an answer. Only as I hurried after him did I see what his alf eyes had noticed – the paw-shaped dents pressed into the mud on the other side of the pool, shallow but too sharp to be more than a day old.

They were enormous.

The nearest footprint was twice as long as my foot and five times as broad – a paw with three fingers at the front and one at the back, all with long enough nails to leave visible furrows in the earth. Not a bird's foot – there was an impression of pads and toes. But it couldn't be any other animal I knew either, not with that fourth toe growing back.

Oh, gods.

'Tared,' I whispered. 'Did you say ... did you say he kept gabbling about *dragons*?'

He looked up, wide grey eyes the only answer I needed.

Everything fell into place in the blink of an eye. If Edored had come here, sweaty and annoyed, and found these traces waiting for him ... Hell, of course he'd run off like a toddler in search of kittens. Who cared about plague magic and demon shields when there were dragons to be found? Dragons who must have been around recently, judging by the perfect clarity of the traces they'd left behind ...

The forest was bone-chillingly silent. I looked up and found both Creon and Tared with hands on their weapons, their eyes scanning the mist and the endless rows of pillar-like trees with the quiet watchfulness of hunters.

If this was a dragon, it had to be a giant one – mutated in size by divine magic, and who knew what that might have done to its hunting instincts? The wise decision was to get the hell out of this place and be grateful it hadn't attacked the temple yet. Only a fool would willingly go look for that sort of danger; the two males on either side of me might be powerful warriors, but they were hardly experienced dragon hunters.

And then again ... divine magic.

'Is there any chance it's connected to Zera?' I breathed. 'That we could find her through these traces?'

'If we could,' Tared said tersely, 'I'm not going to run after it right now. I suggest we return to the temple and make a plan first.'

A plan? Creon signed, raising an unimpressed eyebrow at him. *You?*

What for the gods' sakes did he think he was doing? It took all I had to keep my voice from cracking as I started, 'Could you not—'

'What's your point, Hytherion?' Tared snapped, stepping past me. 'If you're trying to call me a fool, at least don't be a coward about it for once in your life.'

'Tared!' I hissed.

Not a fool. Creon's gestures were slow, savouring every motion. The way he held Tared's gaze was a loud and clear challenge, mingled with that princely arrogance that could have inflamed a sheet of ice. *Just a little ... senseless?*

Tared drew his sword.

And then everything went so fast I had no time to think, no time to understand what for the bloody gods' sakes was happening. Even my warning cry came too late. A flash of steel sliced through the quiet dusk, a slap of wings, the merciless shriek of blade against blade. Creon retaliated while Tared's sword was still bouncing back, lashing out like a viper, the silvery flash of his knife like fluid quicksilver to my dumbfounded eyes.

Tared faded away just in time. A single lock of blond hair, fluttering down where he'd stood, was the only evidence of how close Creon's dagger had been.

Creon whirled around, some warrior's instinct warning him of the sword that was about to appear out of nowhere and take a swing at his neck. A bright burst of crimson blazed from his fingers the moment Tared reappeared, magic shrouding the clearing in a glow of destruction, and blood splattered across the mud.

Blood.

Every muscle in my body was obeying a different reflex – fight, flight, protect. My left hand grabbed for the dark linen of my dress. My right hand wouldn't come up to use the colour. The magic lay paralysed below my skin, my thoughts running five heartbeats behind – I had to stop them, but I'd hurt them, but they'd hurt each other, but they'd hurt me, but what was *happening*, but—

One infinite heartbeat of mayhem, and Tared staggered back, teeth bared, eyes wild with some primal fury I'd never seen on his face before. Red wetness glistened on the edge of his blade – blood, my mind helpfully informed my eyes, the thought as surreal as a fever dream. A long cut ran over his right upper arm, blood spilling from that wound, too. Creon ...

He'd gone perfectly, icily still, black gathering under his fingertips. Wings flaring. Muscles straining. A dark god of death – a brutal, devastating force of nature, as pliable as the advance of night itself.

His eyes were bottomless, fixed on Tared's face with the ferocity of a trapped animal facing its hunter.

'Stop.' I couldn't breathe, couldn't move. My voice was a squeaky, shivery mess, barely rising over the ominous rustling of the foliage. '*Please.*'

Neither of them seemed to hear me. Creon prowled closer, every meticulous movement shimmering with the potential of agony. Tared's fingers tightened around his sword hilt. A reflex I knew all too well – the only kind of warning he gave.

'It's as I thought, then.' Even now there was a furious triumph to his words, low and cautious as he spoke them. He didn't back away. Didn't avert his eyes from the searing intensity of Creon's gaze. 'Never mind about the pretty lies and the pretty promises. Scratch off the mask and you're still the same—'

'Tared,' I got out.

'—gods-damned—'

'*Tared*!'

His tight lips faltered one last moment, whether it was because of my shrill cry or the realisation of the madness he was about to commit. But the words came out with calm, unwavering certainty, the voice of a male who has already decided he's beyond saving.

'Demon brood.'

Creon lunged.

I heard myself cry out their names. Blades whistled through the mist, red flared, and my limbs were nowhere near understanding who to save, who to defend, who to blame, who to hurt. Creon – Creon was bleeding – but a cry of agony tore through the woods, and it was Tared whose sword tumbled into the mud with a blood-flecked hilt, Tared who stood pinned against a ghastly white tree with Creon's dagger at his throat.

A blade.

At his throat.

Time stood still for one brief eternity as that image burned itself into my mind's eye.

They had ended up almost nose to nose, lips curled and breath heavy. Creon stood motionless as a shadow, his gaze focused on the dagger between his fingers. Blood cascaded from the gaping wound at Tared's shoulder, soaking his dark green shirt and running in thick rivulets over his wrist and hand – so much blood, pulsing from his veins to the rhythm of a rattling heart. His alf light flickered around him in anxious tendrils, straining away from Creon's tall shape.

Blood welled at the tip of Creon's knife, too, as he pressed it a hair's breadth into the soft flesh of Tared's throat.

'*Creon*.' My feet finally found their motions; I staggered half a step forward, not knowing where I was going or what I was about to do. I had to get through to him – how was I going to get through to him? 'Creon, listen to me. *Please*. Let him go, or I ... I—'

Fire roared across the clearing.

It missed Tared by mere inches, surging at Creon instead, a wall of heat so violent I could feel it even six feet away. Creon leapt back with inhuman speed. The flames lashed at him one last time, then sizzled out with a furious hiss, leaving behind a handful of scorch marks in his shirt and a whirling trail of smoke ...

And Lyn.

She swept into the clearing in a flurry of sparks, tongues of fire twisting around her hands, her shoulders, the tips of her hair. Her wings burned bright behind her shoulders, shrouding her face in a glow of gold and crimson; sizzling ash and embers marked where she'd landed in the moss. Even her *eyes* flickered – truly flickered, flames dancing in what had been amber irises as long as I'd known her.

They weren't even aimed at me, those eyes ablaze with the fury of hell itself, but I flinched nonetheless.

'How *dare* you.' She spat the words at Creon as she advanced towards him, violet sparks bursting from her small figure at every word, at every step forward. 'How fucking *dare* you. Just because I didn't kill you last time I could have ...' She scoffed, and a small puff of smoke twirled from her nostrils. 'There are still *limits*, do you understand?'

Creon's lips tightened into a sneer as he signed, *At least I'm not provoking fights I can't win.*

Lyn flung a hand at him; fire crackled through the air like a whip, tearing through the linen of his shirt but leaving his skin unmarred. Bloodcurdling precision, and yet he didn't take a single step back, didn't lower his defiantly raised chin. She came to a halt two feet before him, breathing heavily, glowering up at him from roughly the height of his midriff. 'Anything else to say for yourself?'

His jaw clenched, but he didn't crack – a towering wall of furious arrogance, a male who'd rather suffer blistering hatred than the smallest defeat.

'You fucking idiot.' Her hands balled into little fists, flames licking between her freckled fingers. 'Next time you want to complain about useless heroes, try to remember who's playing the useless villain here, *Hytherion*.'

He stiffened, finally.

But Lyn had already snapped around, her wings blazing brighter as she marched to Tared's bloodied shape slouched against the tree. 'And what were *you* thinking, you—'

He grabbed her shoulder mid-sentence, almost toppling over with that movement. I blinked, and they were both gone, leaving behind blood-flecked moss, smoking footprints, and Tared's sword.

Creon didn't move.

Even the all-encompassing Underground silence had rarely been as strenuous as this moment of dazed deadlock, me staring at him and him staring at the forest, the hissing and crackling of Lyn's phoenix fire echoing in my ears. My eyes slid to the bloodied knife in his scarred fingers. The smouldering scorch marks in his shirt. The hard set of his jaw – an unspoken, unbreakable shield.

Only then did I realise what the pounding of my heart was trying to tell me.

Rage. That was undiluted *rage* searing through my veins, the taste of it bitter and metallic on my tongue. Because as much as I loved that ever-present darkness that lived inside him, his ruthless brilliance, his power and devotion ...

This had nothing to do with any of those things. This was nothing but destructive, impulsive stupidity.

'What for fuck's sake,' I whispered, my voice hollow in the creeping dusk, 'did you think you were doing, Creon?'

He made a brusque turn towards me, lips parting a fraction. A smudge of blood followed the sharp line of his cheekbone. Just above his wrist, a long, shallow cut crossed his inked scars – a painful wound, probably, but was that an excuse for that deep gash he'd carved into Tared's shoulder?

Worse – was that an excuse to blow up my last hope of a peaceful alliance?

For one last moment, I clung to the desperate hope that he'd have an explanation, a justification – that maybe these five minutes of futile violence had all been part of some carefully created plan, just the Silent Death thinking five steps ahead of everyone else. But his hand remained down as he stared at me. A hollowness grew in the dark of his eyes, the realisation of what he'd done finally welling to the surface of his rational mind.

'You could have *killed* him.' My voice grew explosively louder as the disappointment set its vicious nails into my guts. 'And don't say he started it, because you were provoking him just as much, and—'

He jerked around and walked, frantically wiping his fingers on the dark cloth of his ruined shirt.

'Oh, really?' I yelled, my stomach knotting tighter. 'That's how you want to play this game again?'

His wings swept out behind his shoulders, as if to slap my words away.

I could no longer summon the energy to run after him, to persuade and plead. I felt empty – hollow and wrung out. All I wanted was for the past ten minutes not to have happened, for him to come back and make everything easy again.

But he vanished into the darkening autumn sky with two rapid wing-beats, not looking over his shoulder even once.

With nothing better to do, I picked up Tared's sword and made my way back to the temple, my mind still unable to produce a single sensible thought through the whirlwind of numb anger. I could barely remember what sorry excuses for strategies I'd naively envisioned half an hour ago.

Morning, Tared, I imagined myself saying. *Yes, I know he almost killed you, but he's so very lovely when you're not around ...*

A mirthless laugh escaped my lips. That did sound ridiculous, didn't it?

Tared's sword was heavy as lead in my hands as I hauled it across the temple courtyard, to the apartment we'd claimed as our temporary home. Was there any way I could repair this? Hell, I didn't even know what I was supposed to repair anymore. *Senseless*, Creon had signed, and that mild taunt had been enough reason for his old enemy to draw a weapon and attack. Which was frankly absurd, unless ...

Unless there was a history to that word.

Something hardened inside me as I staggered around the majestic wall of stems and leaves and crossed the last yards to the open front door. There *had* to be a history, and whatever secrets the two of them had been keeping from the rest of the world, it was about damn time I figured out what was going on.

'... get out of here,' I heard Beyla say as I slipped into the corridor, her frail voice accompanied by the sound of brisk footsteps over the kitchen tiles. 'He's absolutely *insane*. If this is what he does to the people he calls his allies ...'

'Oh, he's definitely not insane,' Naxi said dreamily.

Beyla scoffed. 'Isn't that worse? If it's not insanity—'

Tared's heartfelt cursing interrupted her, followed by Lyn's voice. 'I told you not to move that arm, you idiot! Will you let me clean it out now?'

He was still conscious and well enough to be stubborn, then. Swallowing a sigh of relief, I threw a last glance at the closed kitchen door, quietly lowered the bloodied sword to the floor, and tiptoed farther into the house. Now I knew everyone was still alive, I could do with a quiet moment to think.

'If it's not insanity,' Beyla snapped, 'then how can you claim he's on our side? *This*' – I imagined a furious gesture at Tared's wounds – 'is not how most people treat their allies, you know?'

Naxi snorted a laugh. 'Most people don't spend days offending their allies, either.'

Days? I stumbled to a standstill, blinking at that new piece of information. The two of them had not been particularly antagonistic until this morning, had they? Of course there had always been suspicions and cold glances, but that had been going on for months, not days. Apart from that, I was pretty sure they had barely exchanged a word, let alone multiple insults, over the course of our journey.

And yet ...

A history. I must have missed *something*.

Had they spent their nights exchanging stinging remarks while I slept? That seemed unlikely; Tared had never taken the shift with Creon as far as I could recall. So what else could it be?

'Well,' Beyla said sharply, 'I don't see why Tared should bite his tongue when that fucking bastard insists on insulting him at every turn.'

'Oh, yes.' Naxi sounded like she was grinning. 'Creon started it, of course. By committing the unforgivable offense of sacrificing his voice for your life, I suppose, Thorgedson?'

What?

Oh. *Wait.*

I could not make out the words in Tared's grumbled answer, but it sounded neither like denial nor confirmation. It didn't matter. *The offense of sacrificing his voice*, and I was back in Creon's bedroom in the Underground after that conversation with Agenor, where I'd found him reading some note, looking unsurprised when I told him I knew the full story of how the Mother had bound him …

Reading a note.

What if I hadn't been the first to confront him?

I didn't allow myself another moment to think. I might not get another chance like this, the four of them all occupied with their own discussions, unaware of my presence. Holding my breath, I nudged open the door to the bedroom Tared and Edored had shared until this morning. Edored's half of the room was an impressive mess, Tared's half organised with warrior's discipline. A modest pile of clothes on the bed. A leather bag, meticulously tied shut. A grey coat hanging over the room's only chair, with peaking from its pocket …

A creased, well-thumbed snippet of parchment.

I snatched it out so fast I almost tore it in two, unfolding the note with trembling hands.

A patchwork of pencil scribbles covered the smooth surface, in two different hands – Tared's messy writing alternating with the infinitely more familiar scrawls that I knew to have come from Creon.

It's considered rude to keep a life debt hanging over someone's head, the message at the top said, written in Tared's hand. *Be so kind (if the word has any meaning to you) to just tell me what you want from me.*

I let out an abrupt breath, sinking down on the edge of Edored's bed with the parchment clutched in my trembling fingers. That had to be the note he'd sent Creon just after we'd heard the full story of the loss of his voice – the note I'd found him reading.

Creon's answer was jotted directly below.

Fae don't do life debts. You're most welcome to take your obligations and stick them wherever you feel the need to.

Followed by a series of increasingly messy scribbles ...

You may not do life debts; I still do honour.

You saved my life when I had to flee the Crimson Court. Why don't you consider the debt settled on that basis, if you must?

Em doubtlessly told you I didn't do any saving. I begrudgingly allowed her to save you, at most.

Do you <u>want</u> to be in my debt?

If principles were easy, they wouldn't need to be principles. I suppose for a male without them, that needs to be spelled out.

I sucked in a sharp breath. We must have been well on our way across the continent by the time these notes were slipped back and forth between pockets and bags. I'd *seen* them frowning at parchment every now and then, for Zera's bloody sake – would I have been able to put a stop to it if I'd realised the significance of those seemingly unrelated moments a little earlier?

Creon's next note was hardly more conciliatory.

I wasn't aware of this philosophical streak of yours. Almost as if you picked up a book or two in the last century.

Some of us tried to spend their time in a slightly more humane way since the Last Battle.

And then the longest message so far, scribbled down with obvious haste ...

The unpleasant truth is you wouldn't have survived a year of what I did to bring her down, and you know it. Rest assured, I already know it was despicable and unforgivable. Reminding me of it won't free you of your own nagging sense of insufficiency.

I winced, unable to stop reading, unable to tear my eyes away from the slow escalation unfolding on the page before my eyes. Tared's reply was short, but no less venomous for it.

Still fighting your fights with demon magic, I see.

I once tried not to, and was ungently reminded I would always be demon brood regardless. I suppose you want me to stop using the power while you retain your license to taunt me about it for eternity?

Imagine taunting being your greatest concern. Did you consider yourself the victim while you were burying desperate farmers alive, too?

No.

Hit a nerve, Hytherion?

Hardly. Just out of curiosity – has it ever occurred to you that perhaps I did change a little in the hundred and thirty years since you plucked me from that cursed bay?

Poor Em has suggested such a thing to me once or twice, yes. What is it about you that makes sensible people feel the sudden senseless need to save you?

Does Lyn know you think of her as senseless?

And there the notes ended.

CHAPTER 15

NIGHT FELL, AND STILL Creon didn't return.

I spent all of dinner in silence as the others talked around me, defending and accusing, their voices tight with tension even when they eventually agreed to wait at the temple until the next morning. Which should have been good news ... but even if Creon was back by sunrise, how on earth were we going to continue this journey with any semblance of cooperation and peace?

Tared pulled me aside after our meal to tell me I shouldn't blame myself for this mess, which was kind of him, and also useless, given how clear it was who he blamed instead. Then I wandered around the house and the courtyard for the rest of the evening, hoping for the quiet whoosh of wings but finding only rustling leaves and the murmur of my travel companions' voices around the kitchen table.

Where was he?

Anger soon gave way to worry, thick and nauseating. Should I not have exploded at him? Was he wandering around a dragon-infested forest, blaming himself for everything wrong with the world, convinced I hated him after all? After all these months, he really had to know better – but then again, why else wasn't he coming back?

Maybe he was hunting dragons. Maybe he was finding Zera on his own. Maybe he'd been wounded more severely than I'd realised and lay bleeding out under a tree somewhere right now, and I'd never see him again, and ...

I resolved to stop thinking before my thoughts could spiral any further.

But it was hard not to spiral with nothing else to focus on. Beyla was vehemently whetting her swords and didn't look in the mood for company. Lyn was a little thundercloud between her piles of books, twirls of smoke rising off her whenever Creon's name was mentioned. Tared had gone to bed to give his shoulder some rest, his wounds not healed perfectly due to my inexperience with blue magic, and Naxi slurped hot milk from a mug and giggled out loud whenever anyone glared at her.

I doubted any of them could tell me how to bridge the gaping chasm between my love and my family. If anything, they'd probably tell me there was no bridging a gap that wide.

Which meant I had to make choices, after all.

In the end, I dragged myself to bed early, unable to stand the circles of my own thoughts a moment longer. But even in that strange and ancient bedroom, while I lay staring into the dark until I no longer knew whether my eyes were open or closed, the words on that sheet of parchment kept spinning through my mind.

Does Lyn know you think of her as senseless?

Both a threat and a declaration of war. I could feel that treacherous little sentence burning in my gut until my dreams finally seeped into my fretful thoughts.

I was ... flying.

The thin old mattress had disappeared from beneath my back when I drowsily emerged into the world of the living, woken by a whisper of cold autumn air stroking up my spine. I appeared to be floating through the pitch black night, bundled tightly in my blankets and carried along by ...

Arms.

I awoke to the reality of the situation with a start. Arms. Someone was *carrying* me. Someone was smuggling me out of my safe bed in the depth of night, so quietly I had not even heard the sound of footsteps. I tried to shoot upright, tried to claw at whoever was holding me, and found I could barely move my hands, wrapped in an abundance of wool and soft linen like a swaddled child.

With a sharp inhalation, I parted my lips to cry out.

But warm breath brushed over my face before I could make a sound, smelling like ... *home*. I froze, my sleep-fogged brain unable to figure out what was happening for a moment – and then supple lips brushed over my forehead, a kiss like a lullaby. The air rushed from my lungs in an instinctive and inevitable surrender.

Creon.

Back with me.

Every muscle in my body slumped in his arms as relief surged through me. It lasted no longer than a heartbeat. Then I remembered why I'd panicked before he left, remembered Tared's blood-drenched shirt and the angry sparks burning on Lyn's skin all night, and stiffened up all over again.

'Where in hell have you been?' I hissed.

I regretted the question as soon as it left my lips; in the impenetrable dark, there was no way for him to answer it. He merely sighed, his chest rising and falling against me.

I bit my tongue as we slipped out of the door and into the temple garden, where the plant wall obscured all but the shine of silver moonlight. Only after we rounded its thorny, viney corner did the pale green glow of the temple gate become visible, as well as a small fire crackling at the edge of the courtyard, casting a fickle golden glow over the shrubbery and marble walls.

There was no other living soul to be seen. He must have returned to find only Naxi awake and sent her to bed before waking me.

Today's only bit of luck – that he'd walked into the one person not currently furious with him.

That thought was enough to rekindle the fire of my anger, no longer hindered by the fear that had held my heart hostage for most of the night. I twisted around in his arms to better see his face in the shadows and snapped, 'Maybe you should allow me to walk by myself? Then at least you'd have your hands free to tell me what you were *thinking* to wound him like that and challenge him like that and … and …'

Creon didn't let me go. Quite the opposite; his arms curled around me even tighter as he walked on towards the fire.

'And to write him those stupid letters!' My voice cracked. 'You knew exactly how hard I was trying to keep the peace all this time, and meanwhile you were throwing yourself into some useless pissing match? Without even *telling* me? What am I going to find out next – that you've secretly been chucking Lyn's books into fireplaces for months?'

He stepped over a fallen tree just beside his small fire and sank down on the weathered trunk, settling me on his thigh with painstaking care. So close to the flames, wrapped in three layers of heavy blankets, the cold of night didn't stand a chance … but the crackling flames reminded me of Lyn's rage more than anything, and no snug blanket could soften the memory of the fire lashing at his face.

'You told me to find out what I wanted,' I ground out, wrestling myself around to look him in the eyes. He didn't move, didn't raise his hand to defend himself. 'And just when I figured out I want to be able to tell them without causing an outrage, you decide to piss every single one of them off to the point there will definitely be an outrage? You managed to infuriate *Lyn*, for the bloody gods' sakes! And why? Just to let them all know you're still capable of handling a knife? Well, they know now! I hope it was fucking worth it, you … you …'

I faltered, unable to find a word that would properly express the depth of his foolishness. Still there was nothing but that dull, bone-deep weariness on his face, his wings and shoulders slumping with a rare resignation.

'Well?' I said sharply.

He rubbed his ink-marred fingers over his temple, then sighed and signed, *I'm sorry.*

I blinked at him.

You're right. He stared at the fire as he signed the words, his gestures heavy and drained. *I've been behaving like an absolute idiot, and you have all the reason in the world to be furious. I'm sorry. I really am.*

'You … What?'

He shrugged. *Maybe you should punch me in the face a couple of times. Would probably be good for both of us.*

'*Punch* you?' I bit out a baffled laugh, eyes darting over his face to find some trace of mockery in the hard lines of his features, any little clue that he was just playing a game with me. 'Is this some joke? Are you hoping I'll be so charmed by your dramatic grovelling that I'll spontaneously forget about—'

Em, he interrupted, releasing a silent groan. *Do I look like I'm joking?*

'No, but …'

He watched me – shadows in his eyes, lines around his lips – and didn't sign another word.

'No,' I mumbled again, my throat suddenly dry. There was something about the closeness of his face – about the flutter of his long lashes and the slight parting of his lips – that made it infuriatingly hard to remember why I'd been planning to shout at him for the next fifteen minutes. 'No, but you never give in this easily. Shouldn't you … you know, defend yourself a bit? Tell me it's all just as much Tared's fault, scoff a little about alves and their tempers, remind me you don't need them anyway and you don't have any reason to muzzle yourself because of their opinion?'

His grimace told me that last remark had hit home. *Would it help if I did?*

'No,' I said and rolled my eyes, 'of course it wouldn't, but helpfulness has hardly been a critical factor in your decisions today, has it, Your Highness?'

A wry smile flitted around the corners of his lips. *Are you sure you don't want to punch me?*

'You *are* joking!'

I'm not. The amusement slid off his face. *You're just so absurdly beautiful when you're angry and telling me to do better. It's your eyes, I think. Could swear they get greener whenever you're glowering at me.*

I glowered at him a little harder.

Em ...

'I am not susceptible to clever seduction right now, Creon,' I tersely informed him, well aware that there would have been no need to say it if it had been entirely true. 'You're not going to talk your way out of nearly killing my friends by complimenting my eyes, especially because you know very well they are ditchwater-coloured at best. And even if you could ... well ...'

I faltered, no longer sure where I'd been going with that sentence.

Another ghost of a smile brushed over his lips – a tired, mirthless smile, and yet it strangely reminded me of that glorious true laugh of his, of the way his amusement broke out of him when he chased me around his bedroom because I'd stolen his breakfast or when he tickled me until I was pleading. An expression as comforting as a warm bath, but a little more daring, a little more reckless – an expression like the drowsy excitement of one glass of wine too many.

I parted my lips. Some sort of syllable came out – not a word I could recognise, and certainly not a sentence in any shape or form.

His smile broadened a fraction as he repeated, *And even if I could?*

'I'm going to punch you,' I managed.

Please do, he signed.

I flung my arms around his neck and crashed my mouth into his instead.

It was easier to kiss him angrily than to keep my head clear, and kissing angrily was a far more satisfying way to make my point than reiterating my grievances. His lips were warm. Warm and firm and sinfully ravenous as they parted to receive me, welcoming my fear and fury, inviting the graze of my teeth and the sting of my nails.

In a flare of vexation, I nipped at his bottom lip.

He didn't retaliate. His kiss only turned more patient, more soothing, his hand trailing down my nape with gossamer gentleness. I tangled my fingers in the soft silk of his hair in response and yanked him closer, met the slow probing of his tongue in a last attempt to find the fight I so desperately needed in that heated touch.

He pulled back.

I tore myself away from him, breathing heavily, lips wet and sensitive. My heart was a beating drum behind my ribcage. 'You *bastard.*'

Me? His expression remained suspiciously grave, but a smile gleamed in his dark eyes – a very dangerous smile. *Do I need to be even more apologetic?*

'No!' I swatted a hand at him, barely suppressing the urge to set my teeth in his pointed ears by way of revenge. 'That's the last thing I need, you absolute monster! How am I supposed to stay angry when you won't even fight back?'

He raised an eyebrow. *I didn't realise you intended to stay angry forever.*

'It's easier than most other emotions,' I grumbled.

Ah. He considered that. *I could carve up a few more alves to infuriate you again?*

'For the bloody gods' sakes, Creon.'

I suppose that's a no? he signed wryly.

I allowed myself a joyless laugh and slumped against his shoulder, huddling deeper between my blankets. Somehow, I didn't even feel like punching him anymore. The anger had leaked out of me, the violent need to take revenge for every minute I'd wasted worrying today; in its place, I found a hollow, ice-cold desperation, a sense of fighting against an unrelenting rising tide.

I just wanted to curl up in his arms and forget about this mess we had created. I just wanted him to mend the world for me again.

'I need your help,' I whispered.

He waited wordlessly, his fingers playing with the loose strands of my hair as I stared at the small fire and tried to gather my thoughts. The world was silent around us, the garden so dark – as if nothing even existed anymore except the two of us, safe in our little cocoon of light, safe in each other's arms.

'I think I want to tell them.' It was miraculous how easily those words fell from my lips after a full day of agonising about the very same thing. 'You were right, last night. These are not secrets we can keep for much longer. But if we're going to tell them ...'

His fingers stilled in my hair.

'I need you to stop being an idiot,' I blurted out, my breath quickening. 'I need you stop acting like you're the damn king of hell himself – you don't need to become the best of friends with them, but if you could just be a *little* more yourself when they're around—'

He sighed, interrupting me. *Myself?*

'Yes.' I snorted and sat straighter on his thigh. 'The person you are with me. You know, rather than the murderous bastard who might casually kill his allies between lunch and teatime if they annoy him.'

I wouldn't go so far as to say that murderous bastard isn't truly me, he signed, and whatever trace of a smile had lingered on his face surrendered to the wryness that now tightened around his lips. *Half of the time that version of me seems significantly more real than whatever I am with you.*

My mouth slapped shut.

He frowned, those midnight eyes of his fixing on my face. *Wrong thing to say?*

'Yes,' I said briskly and hunched up my shoulders. 'Don't pretend that whatever you are with me is some pretty fever dream to escape your contented life of murdering and maiming, Your Highness. Or that being an utter prick to the rest of the world is somehow the noble and honest thing to do.'

I've been that utter prick for centuries. He averted his gaze, lips parting in some agitated reflex. *I'm fine like this. Don't expect me to let go of the only—*

'You did let go of it with me.'

You're not the rest of the world.

'But you're not even trying with them!' There was a raw edge to my voice – not accusation but simple, bitter despair. 'You just decided they hate you all anyway and that you might as well keep giving them reasons to! And it's really not very fair to blame me for wanting to keep these secrets while *you're* the one who's making the truth so bloody hard for everyone else to stomach, don't you see that?'

His wings shifted restlessly. *It's not as if they'd hate me any less if I suddenly made a habit of smiling.*

'If you never try ...'

Em. His jaw clenched. *I sewed one of their friends' lips shut a few years ago. Then slit his throat. That's not the sort of thing you forget because of a pretty face and a few friendly pats on the back.*

'But the poor sod never felt it,' I managed. *Sewed his lips shut* – those same fingers dancing through the night before me, jabbing needle and thread through vulnerable flesh ... I suppressed a cold shiver. 'You took his pain. They need to realise—'

They do, he interrupted sharply. *And then what? I caused them grief all the same. If I'd burned Cathra – burned your friends and family and everyone you knew alive – would you ever have forgiven me? Even if you knew they never felt a thing?*

I clenched my teeth, not willing to lie, but too damn stubborn to speak the truth.

You make something of me that I've never been before, Em. He signed the words at dizzying speed, as if he'd lose his thoughts forever if they didn't make it into the world within the next five heartbeats. *But the only reason I can be who I am with you is that every single time I've made myself vulnerable to you, every single time you found a weak spot, you chose to do no harm. You should understand—*

'That's not true,' I blurted, barely realising I'd interrupted him. 'I hated you to bits, and don't pretend I was pleasant about it. I ... I made you blow up the pavilion by comparing you to the Mother. How is that doing no harm?'

He shrugged. *You apologised.*

I stared at him. It took a moment for the memory to return – after I'd returned from my ill-advised trip to Faewood that afternoon, on our way to lunch with the Mother ... I *had* apologised. And he'd shrugged it off and ignored me, as he'd shrugged off everything I said in those first days ...

But maybe I should have known there had been more to that bland reaction.

People don't apologise to me, he added flatly, as if he'd read my mind.

They never do. I can tell you the exact number of times it's happened in my life, and you were the second one.

I decided not to ask the obvious question; the answer would doubtlessly be Lyn. 'Fine, but—'

You figured out I cared about this stupid voice of mine. His signs were hurried and jumbled. *Most people would have used that against me. You should have, too, but what did you do? Taught me your bloody hand language, even though you despised me. Do you have the faintest idea how wildly confusing that was?*

I managed a laugh at the memory. 'You once said that's when you started wanting me. In that letter you wrote me at the court.'

Yes. He drew in an unsteady breath. *And for a while I thought it was because you were so gods-damned beautiful when you stood there staring me down, or because you were so ridiculously fearless – but looking back, I don't think it had anything to do with that. It was just that you found a wound and decided not to deal another blow to it.*

Basic decency, I wanted to say; surely that was not enough to set me apart from the rest of the world? Fine, he may have been raised at a court where weakness was death and vulnerability an invitation to do harm, but the Alliance was not like that. These were decent people, or at least ...

My mind faltered.

Or at least they were decent to *me*.

And then the point shaped itself, crystal clear in all its deadly simplicity: because others had found wounds, too. Tared had found one. And rather than leaving it be, rather than making one mistake and apologising ...

Demon brood.

Understanding slowly turned my gut to ice.

'So we're just running in circles here?' I said, swallowing something bitter. 'Tared is not going to stop taking stabs at bleeding wounds because you're still behaving like the bastard who came between Lyn and him, and you're not going to stop behaving like that bastard because he'd make use of your newfound vulnerability to actually hurt you?'

Creon shrugged, but a darkness had settled over him, as grim as the lines of ink marring his arms and fingers. *Suppose that summarises it, yes.*

'Oh, *fuck*.'

I warned you, Em. His knuckles turned pale as he clenched and un-clenched his fingers. *I do make things harder. If you want a lover everyone likes, I understand. I'm just not that person.*

'Don't say that.' My voice shot up.

You can't—

'Do *not* say that, Creon Hytherion.' I slapped his hand aside, so vio-lently I almost slid off his lap. *Not that person.* The cold was climbing through me, advancing from my knotted stomach to my lungs, en-veloping my ribcage like a corset pulled tight. 'You are *my* person. Don't underestimate me and how much I want—'

I wouldn't dare underestimate you, he interrupted with a wry grimace. *The opposite. I consider you fully capable of working yourself to death at-tempting to keep me and also please everyone else, and I'd rather stop you before that happens.*

'So what would you have me do?' I said shrilly. 'They have no idea who you are when you're with me. If we tell them now, they'll either think I've lost my mind or that I'm some heartless flirt who chooses pleasure over morals, and ...'

The stutter of my breath would not let me finish that sentence. In some cold, deep abyss of my mind, it seemed I'd never stopped staring at Valter's letter, those obnoxiously elegant letters shaping their sick-ening words on the page. *We housed you for twenty years ...*

Do not come after us. Do not write to us.

My heart squeezed again.

Em. Creon's left hand slid around my waist and rested on my hip, that gentle but resolute touch enough to pull me back into the starry night outside Zera's temple. *People will be unhappy whatever you do. You're still trying to deny that, and so far the first victim of it is your sanity.*

I let out a blubbery laugh. 'And you think it would make me happier if we lost the war because of me? Or if Tared kicked me out of his home and—'

Creon's eyebrow shot up. *He wouldn't.*

'Damn lot of trust in someone you don't trust,' I grumbled.

He's one of the people I trust most in the world, he signed with a sour grimace, *as long as it comes to Lyn's wellbeing or your safety. I don't trust him with me, that's all.*

'And yet ...' I rubbed the back of my hand over my eyes, a useless attempt to press back the dull headache emerging behind my forehead. Love and hate. Trust and distrust. The two clear paths that lay before me had become uneven trails twisting through dense woodland, their destination unknown, their direction invisible. 'Yet you want him to know I'm sleeping in your bed at night? Isn't that the greatest vulnerability of all?'

His lips parted – that little involuntary sign of distress, a reflex so deeply ingrained that even a hundred and thirty years of silence had not been able to erase it. No hand gesture followed this time. Only an emphatic blink and a blank look that slowly grew into a shallow frown.

'It is,' I concluded wryly.

I suppose ... He didn't finish that sentence.

'So why do you want them to know, exactly?' I trailed my fingertip over his chest, hard ridge after hard ridge, each muscle tense to the point of bursting. 'Is it really just because keeping secrets is impractical? Because this insufferable charade of yours is pretty damn impractical, too, but that doesn't seem to have convinced you to put an end to it yet.'

He averted his face. *No.*

I waited, toying with his linen shirt, pretending not to notice his wings shuddering behind his shoulders.

I suppose I'm somewhat proud of the person I am with you. He still didn't look at me. *It's the only version of me I've liked in a long time. Having to hide that ...*

'That version of you that actually knows how to be vulnerable,' I said sourly. 'Interesting.'

He gave a soundless chuckle. *I feel like you're talking me into a corner here.*

'It's a corner of your own making. I'm just telling you you're not making sense.' I let go of his shirt and pulled my blankets around me, then nestled myself against his bulging shoulder once more. 'You can't merrily insist you need to stay all glowers and sneers to keep Tared from being mean, then in the same breath claim you desperately need the world to know what a cuddly little sweetheart you actually are.'

Creon swatted his wing at me over his shoulder, and I ducked away, unable to hold in my laughter. He pulled me back against his chest without wasting a moment, hooking an arm around my waist to keep me in my place.

'See?' I muttered, burying my face into his shoulder.

His chuckle vibrated through him, although not very convincingly. When I looked up, the corners of his lips had already sagged back down, and that small crease had grown back between his brows.

'Creon?' I whispered.

Maybe you're right. His throat bobbed. *Maybe I do want to be ... this. Maybe it's just ...* He lowered his face into my hair, inhaled deeply as if only the scent of me would give him the courage to sign whatever words were hesitating on the tips of his fingers.

I wrapped my fingers around his left hand on my waist. 'Just?'

You're the only weakness I have that he would never try to hurt, he signed with staggering gestures.

Oh.

A way out of that never-ending circle, an eye for an eye for an eye for an eye ... A chill ran up my spine, half fright and half relief. If he *wanted* to no longer be the soulless monster whose mere name woke children screaming in cold sweat at night, if somewhere deep inside he *was* looking for a way out of the prison of his own reputation ...

Then could I really deny him that?

You don't have to tell them, Em. There was so much sadness in his eyes, a starless night that hadn't seen the light of the sun in centuries. Such infinite self-restraint in the small smile he forced to his lips, and even that steely composure was wavering. *I'd rather keep a thousand secrets than cause you hurt. But ...*

'But if the choice were yours,' I said hoarsely, 'you would tell them.'

His nod was small, barely distinguishable from an involuntary twitch in the dim firelight.

And why shouldn't the choice be his, too? I glanced over my shoulder, at the eastern temple wing that stretched out along the garden, the barrier of tightly entwined plants that rose before it. They weren't just *my* friends and allies. He was forced to deal with them just as much, and if the truth would make this company pushed upon him any more bearable ...

Why should my fear and discomfort be the only factor of relevance? It was so damn easy to assume he would handle it somehow, the male who always handled everything somehow – but clearly he didn't *want* to handle this.

Ignoring that was choosing a side, too, and not the side I wished to choose.

'Tared ...' I swallowed. 'Even if he doesn't kick me out of the house, he might be unhappy for a while when he finds out.'

When. Not *if.* I heard it the moment it passed my lips, and the brief stiffening of Creon's wings told me I was not the only one.

He might sulk a bit, yes.

'So maybe this is not the place to tell him.' I gestured at the dark courtyard. 'There's no avoiding each other here. I don't want to deal with both time pressure and grumbling alves if we're forced together for the rest of our journey.'

Creon sighed, but nodded.

'So for the coming week ...' I pursed my lips. 'Could you stop attacking? Just shrug and walk away if he's being a prick. Pretend you didn't hear him. Chat back about the weather, if you must. Just act like he's a five-year-old trying to start shit, and ...'

A smile quirked his lips. *Not sure if you want to know what I'd do with five-year-olds trying to start shit, Em.*

I rolled my eyes. 'Try not to skin him alive.'

I've been making that effort for a while.

'Keep doing that,' I said, swatting at him. 'Six more days at most. And tell Lyn you're sorry for upsetting her, which you are, even if you don't give a damn about the state of Tared's shoulder.'

He looked like he was about to object, but miraculously swallowed his protest.

'Alright. That should get us through the rest of this trip.' I drew in a deep breath. 'And then when we're back in the Underground – when we can just camp in some vacant house in Inika's Quarter until the alves figure out how not to kill you ...'

My chest tightened again – that familiar flare of panic, warning me that the fragile life I'd built for myself might come tumbling down any moment. And yet I managed to keep breathing this time. Because things would change, and I might hate the changes – but if even *Creon* didn't think the Skeire family would chew me out and never exchange a word with me again, then who was I to doubt that?

And choices had to be made.

I felt it in the marrow of my bones for the first time, the violent scene of the afternoon a frightening demonstration of the alternative. Trying to walk all paths at once was a recipe for disaster, a guarantee of end-less misunderstandings leading to bloody escalations. My alternatives were either telling the truth or giving up on any public encounters with Creon for months or years to come, and that ...

Hell, was that even a choice?

'When we're back in the Underground,' I repeated, and my voice only croaked a little as the words spilled out of me, 'I'll tell them.'

CHAPTER 16

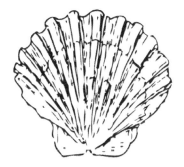

I DIDN'T REMEMBER FALLING asleep in his arms; the memories of his embrace and his lips against my forehead mingled seamlessly with my feverish dreams. But when I woke, the crackled ceiling of my bedroom had replaced the starry continent sky, and instead of the spiced smell of autumn and warm honey, the pervasive mustiness of dust and stale water now filled my nostrils.

And shouting.

Someone was shouting.

Lyn? I scrambled out of bed with enough speed to strain an ankle, processing the shreds of my observations only slowly. That *was* Lyn's voice, although there was no making out the words with walls and doors separating us; all I could identify was that clipped tone of exhausted patience, a tone I instinctually connected to Edored. But Edored was no longer at the temple – my heart squeezed at the memory of his burn wounds – and for anyone else to bring Lyn to that level of exasperation ...

Something had to be very wrong.

I yanked my dress over my head, stepped into my boots, and stumbled out into the corridor, ignoring the mess of hair around my shoulders. Now I heard Tared too, sounding thoroughly displeased. The third voice, interrupting the two of them every other heartbeat ...

That *was* Edored.

For one bewildering moment, I was convinced the previous day had been a dream: my training with Sunray, Edored's ill-conceived dragon hunt, the knife Creon had pressed to Tared's throat. Then I staggered around the corner and found Edored lounging against the kitchen counter with thick layers of greenish salves on his face and a generous number of bandages covering his arms, and came to the even more disconcerting conclusion it had all been real.

And he was back.

'You're not some sapling of ninety winters!' Lyn cried out as I faltered in the doorway. 'How hard would it have been to *warn* us before you ran off after those bloody traces, you slug-brained—'

'Let's not insult slugs here,' Tared said reasonably, throwing me a quick grin over his cup of morning tea. 'They've done nothing to deserve that.'

'And what is Ylfreda thinking, allowing you out of bed at all in this state!' Lyn spat, ignoring Tared entirely as she stomped back and forth between the table and the stove. 'You should be sleeping and resting, not—'

'First of all,' Edored said, looking hurt, 'I'm a grown male who can decide for himself whether he should be in bed, Lyn darling.'

'Debatable,' Tared mumbled.

Lyn just snorted. Quite to my relief, there were no tendrils of smoke this time, although she did still look more inflammable than usual.

'Second of all,' Edored continued in the same wounded tone, 'I have a message for you, which is why—'

'Oh, you're back!' Naxi said behind me, dancing into the kitchen in loose pink morning robes I suspected she'd nicked from some temple wardrobe. 'I was wondering what all the fuss was about. How exciting!

How very stupid! Are you here to hunt dragons?'

Lyn threw her a deadly glower and grumbled, 'Don't even *think* about it.'

'Morning, Naxi,' Edored said cheerfully, only now noticing me. 'And morning, Noisy Death. Didn't mean to wake you. Thought these two would be a little more understanding about—'

'You were nearly *dead*!' Lyn burst out.

'Don't die that easily.' He grinned so broadly the burn wounds contorted to grisly scabs. 'Ill weeds and all that. Now can I pass on my message, Lyn poppet, or were you planning to shout at me until those poor nymphs are dead and six feet under?'

The kitchen cooled to a wintry quiet within the blink of an eye.

'See?' Edored said contently, looking around our small, frozen circle. 'Now I've got your—'

'Nymphs,' Tared interrupted, a steely bite to his voice, 'are *dying*?'

'Well, not yet, but—'

'And you waited ten minutes to tell us that?'

'Don't blame me!' An offended scoff. 'You were the one who started telling me to go back to bed before I could get a word—'

'Edored, what's going *on*?'

'Really not very fair,' Edored was still grumbling, 'to pretend I'm the idiot here when you didn't even ask— *Ouch!*'

He abruptly fell quiet, curling up against the cupboards with a kitten-like mewl.

Plague wounds? A spontaneous foot cramp? But it wasn't his burned arms he was reaching for. Instead, his fingers had flown to the sharp line of his jaw, as if it had locked shut by itself.

Confused, I started, 'Are you—'

'Who?' Naxi bit out, interrupting me with her fierce blue eyes aimed at Edored and her small hands balled into fists. 'Who are dying?'

Only then did I understand – demon magic, the venom of it reflected in the gleam of her pearly white teeth. *Nymphs*. As little as she flaunted that part of her heritage ... that was still her kind out there, threatened by whatever danger Edored had merrily forgotten to mention.

'Tolya.' He blurted out the word like a murder confession, shrinking as far away from her as the countertop would let him. 'Fae. Threatening to burn the entire— *Ow!*'

'When?' she bit out. There was nothing melodious left in her voice; she'd gone cold and razor-sharp in her bright pink robes. 'And *why?*'

Edored whimpered again.

'Naxi,' Tared said calmly, rising from his bench with the caution of a male approaching a terrified animal. The glance he exchanged with Lyn didn't escape me; that single look seemed to contain hours of careful deliberation. 'You've made your point. Let him go. Torture is not going to speed this up.'

'But he—'

'Naxi, the *rules.*'

She staggered back as if he'd slapped her in the face. Edored slumped against the counter with a squeal of relief, and at once Naxi's sharp-toothed menace was gone, that wild gleam of urgency in her blue eyes. 'Oh.' She breathed the word like a sleepwalker waking up to find a corpse at her feet. 'Oh, fuck. I'm sorry ... I'm so sorry ... I—'

'Edored?' Tared said sharply. 'When and why?'

'Soon.' It came out breathless. 'Later today, they think. The Mother says she'll spare them if they tell her where the Alliance is hiding, but—'

'But they don't know,' Lyn finished. She'd gone pale as a sheet below her freckles. 'Except the rest of the world will hear the tale and that threat and think the Tolyi *did* know – that they died because they chose to support us.'

Naxi uttered a high, wailing sound. Tared stoically said, 'Clever.'

'It's rather stupid, isn't it?' Edored said, wildly looking back and forth between the two of them. 'The poor girls have no idea! Why is she threatening them if they'll never be able to—'

'She isn't threatening them,' Tared said with another vigilant glance at Naxi. 'She's killing them and threatening the rest of the world with their example. Which is going to shrink the numbers of our allies significantly, I suppose.'

'Some of them may see through it.' Lyn didn't sound particularly hopeful. 'It's not the first time she's played that game, after all, and—'

Naxi let out another quiet whine.

Not the first time. I glanced at Naxi, suspicions sparking at the sight of the tears gleaming in those bright blue eyes. She had mentioned her demon father every now and then. Her mother, on the other hand, or any family members on that side ...

Not a word. Not the quietest whisper about them.

'Is there anything we can do to stop them?' I whispered.

'Go there, I suppose,' Tared said grimly. 'Put a few swords in their way. The Alliance showing up to help would shift the narrative, at least, even if we can't save the entire island.'

Go there – which meant leaving the continent. Which meant giving up on this mission, or at least pausing it. Lyn gave me the quickest apologetic glance before she turned back to Edored and said, 'Is anyone at home preparing to help out?'

'Thorir is gathering people,' Edored said, pulling a face that suggested he hadn't been invited and wasn't happy about it.

'Enough of them?'

Edored gave a helpless shrug.

'That's probably a no,' Lyn muttered, plopping down on the edge of the lowest stool in the room. 'Fuck. Alright, Edored sweetling—'

'You can't send me back home!' he sputtered. 'You need more people!'

She threw him a blistering glower.

It took a few more garbled objections and a couple of pointed remarks from Tared, but in the end he faded back to the sickbay he'd never have left if not for the urgent need for a messenger able to reach Zera's temple. Naxi didn't speak until he finally vanished, although the wafer-thin line of her lips was evidence of the effort it took.

'Em?' Lyn cut in before anyone could get out another word. 'Go find Beyla and Creon, will you?'

Creon. Even though she hadn't seen him since unleashing a firestorm at him the day before, even though the fact that we hadn't turned to charcoal while Naxi slept was the only reason they knew he was still around. If he was invited, this was not going to be a friendly discussion among trusted allies.

Rather, a council of war.

I threw one glance at Naxi's chalk-coloured face and decided to ask my questions later.

Beyla was surprisingly easy to find, scurrying around the periphery of the temple where she was looking for more dragon traces. It took half a sentence of explanation for her to fade back into our temporary home. Creon found me five minutes later, landing in the flowerbeds beside me with soundless fae grace just as I was beginning to wonder if I'd have to search all of the temple for him.

Tared is allowing you to leave home on your own these days? he signed wryly as he tucked in his wings and raked his flight-ruffled hair back in place.

'The Mother is threatening to attack the nymphs on Tolya,' I said, not in the mood to laugh. 'We're gathering to make a plan.'

His amusement evaporated. Only then did I recall why the name of the island had sounded so familiar to me – Valeska had mentioned it the day before our departure, the place where Creon had sliced a nymph queen to pieces a few decades ago.

Another complication everyone but me must have been aware of. But his only reaction was a curt, *How long do we have?*

'Not long.'

He nodded and swept around, following me to the temple home.

Naxi's shrill voice reached us before we'd stepped through the front door, half tirade, half plea. 'But we *do* need more people, and if Thorir can't get them …'

I turned to Creon to ask if he knew more about the nymphs she called her family, but he was already striding through the kitchen door ahead of me, hands in his pockets and face an unreadable mask. The conversation on the other side of the wall abruptly dried up at his entrance, leaving a silence broken only by Naxi's rapid breathing.

'Ah,' Lyn said coolly as I hurried after him. 'I see you've been found.'

At least she wasn't giving off smoke anymore, sitting on the edge of the dinner table with her legs dangling over the edge. But Tared stood beside her with that edge of steel in his eyes, and Beyla's hand had wandered to Sunray's hilt, an unmistakable warning.

Creon merely shrugged and signed, *Plans?*

No apologies, but at least there were no stinging remarks either.

Perhaps he had listened last night. I quietly relaxed my right hand but didn't take my left from my black dress yet: in a conversation where every other word could be a declaration of war, I needed to be ready to draw red at anyone who dared to unsheathe a weapon.

'They *need* our help,' Naxi blurted before anyone could respond. Her voice was an octave too high. 'Even if you don't care that much about their lives, the rest of the archipelago will be looking at—'

'We know, Naxi.' I wasn't sure how much of the tightness in Lyn's voice was a consequence of the news Edored had brought and how much of it had to do with Creon's presence and the memory of his blade against Tared's throat. 'The problem is ...'

'We might not be done in a day,' Tared grimly finished. 'Yes.'

The consequences of that point hung meaningful and ominous in the air for a moment.

Ten days at most, we had said when we left; any longer, and we would be wasting valuable time that we needed to prepare for war. But war had caught up with us long before that self-imposed limit, and if we left now to face it ...

Would we ever have time to come back?

One battle could spark another, and another, and another. For all we knew, we'd leave the serene silence of Zera's temple and step straight into years of warfare, day after day of nothing but survival, the secret of the bindings forever beyond our reach.

And with them, Creon's voice.

'We could split up,' Lyn said slowly, her eyes shooting around the circle of clenched jaws and hunched shoulders. 'If there's still any chance we'll find Zera, Em and Creon could stay here while the rest of us—'

'No!' Naxi burst out, jolting up her head so that her blonde and pink curls cascaded over her back and shoulders. Her eyes latched onto Creon's motionless silhouette. 'No, please! We need your magic! We need every bit of magic we can get!'

Pretty sure most Tolyi would rather die than allow me on their island ever again, Creon signed, to all appearances entirely unmoved by both her despair and the memory of the nymph queen who'd died under his knife. *You won't win any hearts by bringing me along.*

'I don't give a damn about winning hearts!' She staggered two steps towards him, wringing her hands like a desperate fisherman's wife staring out over an empty sea. 'Please. *Please*. You can't let this happen again. You can't ...'

She fell quiet, staring up at him with wide-open eyes, breathing in little squeaks; I all but expected her to cling to his leg if he refused. Creon didn't even blink as he shifted his gaze to the other side of the room.

Tared merely raised an eyebrow back at him, as if none of last day's ugly scene had happened at all. 'We can't afford to lose Tolya.' *And if the price is pissing off a few nymphs*, his undertone said, *or if I have to stand the sight of your face for a few more hours, so be it.*

I braced myself for Creon's reaction, for the jab that would have followed any other day. But he shrugged and turned back to me without a word, the slight tilt of his head an elaborate question.

What did I think?

Was I going to fight with the others, or would I stay here to continue our search?

And at once the heavy burden of choices was back, pressing on my shoulders with the weight of the world itself. *What do you want?* Creon would listen to whatever my preferences were. If I went to fight, he would never let me go alone. If I decided to stay here and look for Zera until we'd found her or eliminated every last clue, he would likely be happy enough not to confront an island full of nymphs who despised him.

But if we stayed, the others might lose whatever battle was waiting for them. The Tolya nymphs might die, or at least see some of their sacred trees destroyed.

And the rest of the world would know the Alliance hadn't done everything to protect them.

So we had to go. *Clearly* we had to go. But if we left the continent now, there would always be reasons not to return, every other mission more urgent than a doomed attempt to find a goddess no one had heard from since her presumed death some five centuries ago. And that would be the end of months of work – that would be the end of my promises.

My gut turned cold. Why were they all looking at me as if I, the clueless-years-old little unbound mage, should be the one to solve this conundrum?

Because I had been the one to start this madness, my thoughts helpfully reminded me. Because it would just be plain impolite for them to tell me this was where we gave up, even if it was the only conclusion I could reasonably reach. Were they just waiting for me to say that part out loud so we could all move on to the more important matter of saving lives?

Was I going to say that part out loud? I didn't have a choice, did I?

You're still trying to please everyone ...

For fuck's sake. I couldn't think here, with their expectant eyes on my face, with Naxi's almost-tears glittering on the edge of my sight. My mind filled itself with the need for silence and solitude, the almost physical itch to *run*.

'Would you all mind ...' It took an effort not to snap the words, or worse, not to say a single thing and just sprint off. 'Could I take ten minutes to think? Do we have that time?'

Naxi looked like she was about to tell me no, but Lyn said, 'Of course. Just be careful.'

As if I'd hurl myself down the hillslope just to avoid making a choice ... and then again, the forest and its deadly quietness seemed unusually attractive as I fled the apartment, unsure of where to go and even more unsure of what to think. At least if I died a tragic death by giant acorn, no one could blame me for losing a war.

I gave myself a mental kick in the shins and set a course for the temple gate instead.

The building was a blur around me, useless altar after useless altar, empty room after empty room. It was madness, wasn't it, to think that we may still find Zera after all these centuries? Lyn had looked through every book she'd saved from the rubble. We had searched every room twice, maybe more often. There were living dragons in the woods, fine, but there was no strong reason to assume they were linked to Zera, and even if they were ... what sort of fools would we be to run after creatures of that size drenched with divine magic? They might kill us before we found anything.

So I should make the wiser choice and save the lives that still *could* be saved, focus on those innocent nymphs instead of some idle dream. Creon had sacrificed worse to win this war. I knew he wouldn't blame me for giving up on his voice.

I would blame myself, though.

I wasn't even thinking anymore. I was just fleeing and falling to pieces.

Why did it have to happen to me, this life of bad options and worse alternatives, of trying so hard and never hard enough? I just needed someone to tell me how it worked, saving the world. Needed someone to take my hand, the way Editta had sat me down by the fire all those winters ago and shown me how to sew – pins here and fingers there and all will be well. Where did the pins and needles go when there were lives at stake? Where was my practice rag, a world I could safely ruin a few times before I got the hang of this job?

Where were the adults, if even the twelve-hundred-year-olds around me had no clue what to make of life?

My boots slapped against the floor faster and faster, the hollow sound echoing at me from the pillars and the alcoves. I had to be near the centre of the temple by now, and still I wasn't any closer to finding an answer, to figuring out what role I was to play in this war for freedom. How long had I been gone now? Five minutes? Ten?

I should return to the others and start packing my bags. It truly was the only sensible thing to do. But I rounded the next corner, and before me …

Low and broad, the door to the heart of Zera's temple.

Only then did it occur to me that my feet had known exactly where to go.

The magic of the forest was tangible here, a cool presence against my skin, enveloping me like shrouds of morning mist. It didn't feel particularly hostile now, and I tiptoed forward until I stood on the threshold of that pentagonal room. The gnarled tree looked as healthy as two days before, growing straight from the smooth marble in a room where no sunlight had ever reached it.

I did not turn back this time. If we were leaving before the hour was over, what did I have to lose?

Nothing stopped me as I took my first step into the room, sucking the delicate smell of verbena and cherry blossoms deep into my lungs.

It was a fragrance I knew. A whiff of it had lingered in the temple ruins on Cathra, too, that abandoned complex at the centre of the island where only the children still visited to play. Where I'd spent so many hours hiding in the bushes and laying traps for wild birds, sure that if I just stalked Zera's grounds long enough, one of them would be that coveted white dove carrying her blessing.

I'd tried so hard. Even then, long before I understood the side glares Editta's friends would send me, I'd tried so very hard.

It was the scent that broke me, somehow, that intangible reminder of the girl I'd been, the girl I'd wanted to be. The first tears came leaking from my eyes at my next inhalation, and then there was no stopping the rest of them; I sagged onto the floor in an eruption of sobs, further from being a saviour of the world than ever before. I'd just wanted to get back his voice. Just that one thing for the male who had already sacrificed so much, and I'd have to give up even that for the greater good and whatever hopeful symbol the world had found in me?

I curled up against the wall, knees to chest and face between them, and found myself praying for the first time since I'd given up on those bloody birds.

Hear me, gentle lady of our hearts – the words welled in me so easily, ingrained in a part of my consciousness too old to forget. I mouthed them into the smothering warmth of my own skin, even the quiet shapes of the syllables a comfort. *Saviour of the broken, finder of the lost, embrace me in my hardships ...*

I lifted my head, wavering. No goddess magically appeared between the blossoming branches to find and save me.

'Please,' I whispered, forcing the word from my clenching throat. 'Tell me what I need to do. If you're still anywhere – if you're wanting to be found ... Give me a sign. Anything at all. Because I need your help, but I can't keep running after some impossible dream if I have to sacrifice other lives for it, and ...'

My voice caught. I wiped my cheek with a wrinkled patch of skirt and drew in a blubbering breath, only to be defeated by that smell of my youth again.

'People are dying,' I managed. '*Your* people are dying, and I don't know if I'm supposed to give up on you and go save them, or—'

Or if I should stay true to my promises, I'd wanted to say – but a loud crack interrupted me.

A raw, tearing sound, as if the wall itself was splitting in two behind my back. Yet when I snapped around, the marble was untouched, and there was no sign of damage to the dome over my head, either. I jumped to my feet as the desperate cracking continued, ready to run and hide under the nearest sturdy altar while the temple collapsed around me ...

And then I saw the tree.

The rough, gnarled bark ... it was *stretching*.

I froze, gaping at the stirring of the bulky trunk. Branches shuddered. Leaves and blossoms rained to the floor. And the wood itself was *moving*, as if something had woken up below the bark, something shifting and fighting violently in an attempt to escape its prison.

Should I ... help it? Or was unleashing red magic in the heart of Zera's forest the worst idea I'd had so far?

Before I could come to a decision, the trunk split open with a last, thundering bang.

I flinched, expecting splinters and falling rubble and perhaps some newborn monster or two. But not a branch dropped to the floor as the tree gaped wider, revealing a hollow behind the bark and wood. Or not a hollow, but ...

A forest.

As if I was looking out a window, the familiar landscape of Zera's wood became visible through the hole in the tree: straight white trees and purple-gold sunlight, the silence broken only by the cheerful gurgling of a brook. Small tendrils of mist floated from that peaceful scenery into the temple room, like siren's songs luring me in, inviting me to take my first steps on the path that had opened up for me.

It took a few moments before I became aware of my own sensible mind again.

A *path*. I staggered forward, my heart rattling in every fibre of my body. The landscape behind the newly opened portal looked like any other part of the wood to me, but surely her temple would not answer my plea by sending me into deserted plague land? If it wanted, it could just have ignored me. Since it hadn't ... since it *had* responded ...

Was she there, somewhere between those trees?

I should turn back and find Creon before I took a single step, of course. There was no sense in diving into this hole on my own. But the gate had opened for me, and the gods knew how long it would stay that way. For all I knew, I'd return to find the tree whole again, my only chance gone.

And wouldn't that be worse than a bit of danger?

Holding my breath, I leaned into the hollow of the trunk. On either side of me, rows and rows of trees stretched out as far as the eye could see. When I looked down, I found a broad creek running through the moss, knee-deep and clear as glass.

Water. That meant I'd be protected against plague magic.

In a flare of courage – or perhaps stupidity – I kicked off my boots, picked them up, and stepped through the gap, into the frigid creek.

The sting of cold told me it was real, as real as the rest of the forest around me. When I glanced behind me, the temple room was gone. I only found another gnarled oak on the water bank, its bark shifting back into place over the nubs and stumps that marred the stem.

Fuck.

I turned back around, breath quickening. There were no landmarks I recognised, no hill or temple spires as far as the eye could see. Which was not very far, with the rustling canopy hiding most of the sky from where I stood – but even if the temple lay just behind the farthest line of trees I could see, the unpleasant conclusion was that I had not the faintest idea where I was, where I should go, or what in the bloody world I was doing here.

'Fuck.' I said it out loud this time.

The trees rustled reproachfully around me.

I glanced down at my bare feet in the creek, then at the plague-in-fested banks that would surely mean certain and immediate death by divine magic, and decided that the only sensible way forward was through the water. The temple heart must have sent me here for a reason – I just had to cling to that assumption, for lack of anything else to cling to. As long as I did not panic, all would be well.

Not a very reassuring thought, given how fervently the whirl of my thoughts was scratching against the bonds of panic, but for a moment or two, it was enough. I started walking.

The water was cold. Within a minute of wading, I no longer felt my toes; another minute, and the soles of my feet had become numb to the touch as well. I stubbornly refused to think about that problem.

Keep moving. Don't panic.

I followed the brook around a low hill, ducking to evade the lowest branches. Past a mess of man-high shrubbery, and ...

And into a *lake*.

I stumbled to a halt in the frosty water, blinking at the landscape that opened up before me. The creek fed into a lake the size of a small town, so crystal clear that I could see the orange and silver flashes of fish below the water. At the centre, a small island rose from the mirror-like surface. No white trees grew from that small patch of earth; its shores were besieged by weeping willows and thorny hedges instead, looking about as welcoming as a glass-spiked wall.

But behind that first row of vegetation, a thin trail of smoke rose towards the bright blue morning sky.

Smoke.

Life.

I splashed forward with more vigour now, ignoring the water spraying up to my knee-length skirt. All I saw was that thin column of smoke, evidence of fire, evidence of habitation. And really, how many people could reasonably survive here, in this plague hell at the heart of a murderous forest?

The lake wasn't deep. By the time I reached the island, boots in my hand, my dress was soaked to my hip, the bodice still mostly dry. Now I only had to find a hole in those mean-looking hedges so I'd be able to climb on land and—

A growl rumbled through the forest behind me, deep and mighty as thunder.

I snapped around so fast I nearly fell and went under. A flash of gold moved between the trees at the shore, and then I blinked again and that shadowy silhouette grew into ...

Into a *monster.*

I barely felt myself stumble backwards, never mind the soft sand and sharp stones below my feet.

Here it was, then, the dragon for which Edored had nearly given his life – as tall as an average house on Cathra, its serpentine body so long that I couldn't see the end of it between the trees. My eyes registered fangs, claws, knife-edged spikes along the spine. Its scales were far brighter than the old one we'd found in the deserted nest in Lyckfort: on this living body, they shimmered with fire, a rich gold that appeared to move restlessly below the polished surface.

The dragon's eyes – amber-coloured and unnervingly knowing – burned too, and they were fixed on me.

My lungs gave up on me. The air fled my body in a single powerless sigh, and I couldn't quite blame it for getting the hell out. I staggered another step back, found cold earth in the small of my back, and stayed there, caught between thorns and the unearthly creature slowly slinking up to me from the shadows of the wood.

The dragon did not release my gaze as it leisurely lowered its first paw into the shallow water. A few sparks burst from its long, narrow snout as it growled again, more quietly now.

'I'm not here to cause trouble,' I squeaked, grasping for support in the wet earth and grass. 'No need to eat me ... I'm just—'

The dragon yawned. Three rows of small sharp teeth blinked white and deadly in that giant beak, drool dripping over its leathery lips.

Zera help me.

'Of course,' a voice I didn't know said behind me, sounding wistfully amused. 'This way, please, Emelin.'

CHAPTER 17

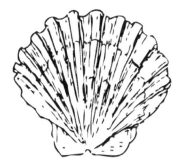

THIS TIME, I DID lose my balance.

My feet tangled up as I spun around, and only some brand new battle reflex saved me from submerging entirely; I caught myself somewhere mid-fall, drenched to the chest as I stumbled upright.

Behind me, the impenetrable wall of thorns had parted without a whisper. And there, in the misty morning light ...

A small woman in muddy homespun clothes and knee-high leather boots stood between the weeping willows, a small rake in one hand and a bulging hessian bag by her feet. Her long, grey hair lay loosely over her shoulders, slightly tangled and sandy. A fine web of wrinkles covered her tanned face and hands, and her long fingers were bony, the way my fingers had looked after the longest, hungriest winters of my youth.

She did not look like a goddess. If anything, she resembled Miss Ariel-la from my village on Cathra, who went to visit her sister on Orthune once a year and returned with sweets for all the island's children, even me.

But I'd never seen this woman before, and she'd called me by my name.

I stared at her. I couldn't quite come up with anything else to do.

'You should come out of the water.' Only then did I realise I didn't know the language she spoke – didn't know the sounds that spilled from her lips – and yet I understood the meaning of her words effortlessly, as if somewhere on the way to my ears they slipped into a disguise more familiar to me. 'It's chilly around this time of year. You'll catch a cold if you stay there too long.'

A cold. I parted my lips in the desperate – and idle – hope that some fragment of civilised language would return to me at the hint of that familiar motion. A *cold*. I had just travelled through a tree, a giant dragon was standing behind me, and I was being warned against *colds* by ...

By ...

My mind refused to think the thought, as if such foolish hopefulness would be enough to shatter the mirage before my eyes.

'Well, dear?' The ... woman ... stepped back, smiling with a softness that spread like a balm over my cold, sore skin. 'You're usually quicker than this.'

Shivers started running down my spine, colder than the water gathering around my waist. 'You ... you know me?'

'Of course I do,' she said, clucking her tongue with the gentle impatience of an old nurse. 'You've been talking to me all your life. Did you think I wasn't listening?'

I opened my mouth and found that I had once again run out of words.

'It seems you did,' Zera concluded, now with a spark of amusement to her voice. 'Well, this is a pleasant surprise, then. Or an unpleasant one, perhaps. My apologies for not sending you that bird, but I do not like to make promises I can't be sure I'll keep. Are you coming out of the lake, now?'

'I ...'

I lost track of that sentence one word in, my mind crowded by a thousand other points vying for attention. If she knew every thought I'd ever devoted to her, she knew my every desperate attempt not to fall madly in love with Creon. She knew every failure, too. She ...

Did she know he'd fucked me on her altar only one night ago?

Thank the gods for the cold water embracing me, because I might have blushed if not for—

'Oh, you're most welcome,' Zera said dryly. 'What were you planning to blush about – that temple business? Don't worry about it. If I had to smite every couple to have a go at it in my sanctuaries, I would never have a free minute in my life. Glad you had a good time, at least.'

'Is it your intention to make me drown myself?' I said, and my teeth clattered a little as if to lend strength to the suggestion.

She chuckled. 'I see you take after your father and his dramatics. Do tell him I'm proud of him when you see him again, before I forget. That's a lovely little spine he has located after all this time.'

I imagined Agenor's face if I were to pass on that dubious compliment, then imagined Creon, whose lips would not stop trembling for hours if he heard the story. And then I thought of him and the others, waiting for me in that warm kitchen temple, and the flicker of warmth that had seared through me at the thought of his amusement cooled down again.

'Um,' I said and glanced over my shoulder. The dragon lingered in the same place, peering at me with eyes that seemed to be counting the seconds to its next meal. 'Speaking of the others – my friends have no idea where I've gone. Would it ... um ... would you mind terribly if I went back to let them know I found you before I—'

'I would not *mind*, necessarily,' Zera said, her smile dwindling. 'The forest might, though.'

I blinked at her.

'It's the forest that keeps me alive and hidden, these days. It's the forest that allowed you to find me. If you return to the temple ...' She gave half a shrug, her chapped lips tightening. 'You might not manage to convince it a second time. It does not play by simple immortal rules.'

'You ... you can't tell it to let me come back, either?'

'My dear,' she said, looking amused again, 'a flower does not argue with the earth that nourishes it.'

I swallowed and dared another glimpse at the dragon. Behind it, the forest waited with perfect stillness, uncaring and unaffected.

Creon should be able to read my emotions, I realised. He had been able to reach me while he was at the Golden Court and I was in the Underground, and considering that we were still in the same forest, the temple could hardly be that far away. So even if he was concerned, he could confirm I was safe and unharmed. He might even figure out what had happened.

And we *needed* this chance.

Biting down the last sliver of doubt, I put my boots on the grassy banks and climbed out of the water, dripping like a drowned stray cat.

'That's more like it,' Zera said, bending over to pick up the large hessian sack. Every inch of her fragile frame seemed to protest the weight as she hauled it off the grass; her voice strained as she added, 'Just follow me, then.'

'Should I help you carry that?' I cautiously suggested, tiptoeing after her as she staggered away with her burden. She was shorter than me, for the bloody gods' sake – well, perhaps not for her own sake. I resolved to stop using that phrase. 'It looks heavy.'

She gave a laugh. 'Thank you, dear, but you couldn't carry it. It is quite heavy, indeed.'

'What's in it?'

'Oh, the grief of the world.' From her twinkling eyes as she glanced over her shoulder, I almost thought she was joking. 'But if you insist on being helpful ...' She untied a smaller bag I hadn't noticed from her belt and waited for me to catch up, then held it out to me. 'You can carry this. Don't drop it, though.'

This purse was made of fine linen, and it was so light it almost floated from my palm. I stared at it for a moment and slowly said, 'Love and grief, isn't it?'

'So you can be quick, after all,' she said lightly.

I decided not to ask what would happen if I dropped the bag filled with the world's love, and followed her as if treading on brittle ice, along the trail of flattened grass, between the apple and cherry trees that covered this side of the island. Zera walked ahead of me in the direction of her smoking fire, her bony shoulders twisting painfully with every step.

A small wooden cottage appeared between the trees, surrounded by a rich food garden, large bushes of herbs, and a host of blooming flowers. There were chickens, a good dozen of them, scratching peacefully around the house. The smell of verbena and cherry blossom wafted over me, mingled with a scent of burning wood that made me abruptly aware of my ice-cold limbs.

It looked like home. Truly, it looked more like home than home had ever done.

Zera was now positively limping, dragging her bag of grief to the low front door with laboured, uneven steps. But her voice was crisp and clear as she said, 'Come in, dear. Warm yourself. I will find you something to wear.'

Disobeying a goddess – even if she had lost most of her powers, and even if she appeared closer to a friendly grandmother than a deity – was likely not the best of ideas. I ducked dutifully through the doorway and stepped into a small room, all dark wood and floral embroidery. A fire burned in the hearth, and my skin breathed a sigh of relief.

Zera installed her bag in a corner, vanished to the back room, and returned within a minute carrying a simple tunic dress made of the same homespun cloth as her shirt and trousers. I was too dazed to object by that time. I just undressed and dressed again, hanging my wet clothes over a chair to dry, while Zera politely looked the other way and pulled a bottle of wine and sachets of spices from shelves and drawers.

'Please don't make a fuss for me,' I said nervously, having made myself somewhat decent. 'I really don't want to eat all your food.'

'The forest gives me plenty,' she said and waved at the pillows strewn around the fireplace. 'Let me spoil my first human visitor in centuries a little – well, half human.' A chuckle. 'The dragons are sweethearts, but as conversation partners, they leave much to be desired.'

I thought of those three rows of dripping teeth and suppressed a shiver that had nothing to do with my cold limbs. Installing myself in the pillows, I said, 'I thought dragons were Inika's animals.'

'Oh, they are.' She gave me a small smile as she pulled out a rather wrinkled orange and began cutting off slices. 'Sizzle travels between us to deliver notes. The other surviving dragon is with her, at the coast.'

Somehow it made me feel better to know she had at least had some company through the centuries, or at least more than the deluge of prayers and invocations that must be flooding her every moment of the day. 'So Inika is alive, too.'

'Yes. So is Orin.'

The silence at the end of that sentence was too pronounced. There was one goddess left that she hadn't accounted for – the same goddess who had gone insane with anger towards the end of her era, the same goddess whose cursed blood could kill a hundred warriors with a few drops.

I waited as Zera stuffed the orange slices into a small cauldron, added a handful of spices, and poured in half a bottle of wine. Only as she bent over to attach the mixture above the fire did she say, her voice flat, 'We are unsure about Etele.'

'Did you ...' I hesitated, not sure if making suggestions would be presumptuous or altogether ridiculous. 'Did you go look for her?'

'I did.' A mirthless smile at her bony, old hands. 'As you can see.'

'What do you—'

'We did not just lose our powers that day.' She let out a small groan as she sank down in the pillows on the other side of the fire, her face contorting into a grimace. 'Our immortality left us, too. Or at least, we started aging – I presume it is possible we are still immortal, but frankly, I wouldn't want to ruin my knees any more than I already did these past centuries.'

A baffled laugh, or a sorry excuse for it, fell from my lips. 'Then how are you still here?'

'The forest.' She shrugged, as if it was the most self-evident explanation in the world. 'Time doesn't pass here like it passes in the rest of the world. I did leave the forest for a few years in between in some hopeful attempt to find out what had happened to everyone, and you can see what it did to me.'

'Oh, gods.' My mouth had gone dry. 'I mean – hell, this is hard. I'm so sorry. Perhaps ... perhaps I could go look for Etele? After all of this is over?'

'An admirable attempt to once again solve all the troubles of the world by yourself,' Zera said, crossing her legs. They were bony below her trousers – strong but sinewy, worn down by the passing of the years. 'You do take after your mother. I'm glad to see it.'

A flush of warmth rose to my face, having nothing to do with the crackling flames. 'Do you have any idea where she is? My mother?'

'I'm afraid I don't,' Zera said slowly. 'She doesn't speak much to me these days – really, I'm afraid she has quite given up on gods in general.'

Not what I'd come here for, and yet, I couldn't suppress a twinge of disappointment. 'I see.'

'But you may have questions where I can be of more help.' She rose with another pained grimace, pulled her sleeves over her hands, and lifted the now steaming kettle of spiced wine from above the flames. 'Surely you did not decide to risk certain death and more of such nonsense just to ask me about your mother?'

I managed a smile. 'No.'

'As I thought,' she said, pulling two earthen mugs from her dark wooden cupboards. 'So what is it, then, Emelin of Agenor's house?'

'I ... I wanted to ask about the bindings.' After all that time I'd spent reading up on the damn things, I really should have been able to come up with a more eloquent introduction – some sweeping and convincing monologue rather than this timid stammering. 'I want to figure out how to break them, but we don't know enough to have any idea of how they work. So I thought – I hoped – that you would be able to tell me more about them.'

She finished pouring the wine without answering, her wizened face expressionless.

'Do you ...' Now, suddenly close to the impossible goal I'd fought for, the question felt lethally dangerous on my lips. 'Do you know how to break them?'

The silence was a frail, delicate thing, and somehow the thud of the kettle as Zera lowered it to the floor couldn't break it. Her lips visibly hesitated a last moment before she quietly said, 'Yes.'

My heart launched into my throat. 'You *know*?'

'I'm a goddess, Emelin.' A joyless smile briefly curled her lips. 'What use would I be if I didn't know things?'

'Can you teach me?' I blurted out, vaguely registering that my fingers had clenched painfully tight around a handful of wool. 'Or tell me how to—'

'No.'

She spoke the word softly, gently. But it was a *no* nonetheless, and there was no doubt in that single treacherous syllable.

I stiffened in the pillows, breath catching for an everlasting moment. 'No?'

'I wish you'd come to me with any other question, Emelin.' She averted her eyes – weary, worn eyes, even below the kindness. 'I would be so very glad to be of use to you. But I cannot help you break the bindings.'

'Why ... why not?' I felt like I was slipping, gaping at her – like this little cottage was built on quicksand, and every word either of us spoke was another inch deeper into the mire of hopeless defeat. 'I mean, if you can't ... but since you said you know ...'

Zera hesitated for the briefest moment, then said, 'It requires magic you don't have.'

'Divine magic,' I mumbled.

She nodded.

'That ... that means she's godsworn, too, doesn't it? The Mother?'

'Yes.' A flash of bitterness swept over her features. 'In all the wrong ways, I'm afraid.'

I pulled up my knees, unsure how far I could probe. 'Do you mean ... your brother ...'

'Korok,' Zera said flatly, 'was an idiot. I loved him, but he was a starry-eyed idiot, and he gave her far more power than he ever should have.'

That, at least, we could agree on.

'We had an agreement,' she continued, her voice softer now. 'We decided to never teach any race the magic of another, and then the blustering fool went forth and gave her blood magic in addition to the colour magic she already had. The same blood magic she used to kill him in the end, to be exact.'

A shiver ran up my spine at the memory of that stark black crater just outside Lyckfort. 'So it's blood magic? The bindings?'

'Oh, no.' She did not look glad to continue. 'Just the ritual that killed Korok. The bindings are a form of ... let us say, advanced colour magic.'

I blinked. 'Like I have?'

'Not exactly.'

'But ... but almost?' A dazed laugh escaped me. 'Close enough that you could teach me how to break them?'

She merely sighed and handed me my mug of spiced wine, then took her place opposite me again. Her eyes remained aimed at the floor, her white-grey hair a long and slightly muddy veil around her face.

No answer. Nothing but that defeated, meaningful sigh.

'You *could*,' I concluded breathlessly.

'I'm not sure,' she said quietly, still not looking up. 'I truly don't know, Emelin. I lost much of my power. I may still be able to draw out those abilities in you if I try to swear you to me, but it's equally possible that even that is far beyond my capacities now.'

'But couldn't you ... try?'

'No.' Her bony fingers clutched tight around her mug. 'I'm afraid I can't.'

It took an effort – a heavy, physical effort – not to throw myself at her feet and beg. How could she not even *try*? If she had heard the pleas of the unlucky humans suffering under the Mother's reign, if she'd lost her *brother* to the bitch's scheming of all people ... how could she possibly sit here, resigned and restrained, and just accept the unlucky fate of the world?

'I don't understand,' I breathed. The smell of warm wine and cloves clogged my throat, stealing the air from my lungs. 'Why can't you ...'

'The magic you need to destroy bindings,' Zera said softly, 'is the same magic that would enable you to *create* them.'

Only the chickens still clucked cosily in the silence that fell; inside the house, the world appeared to have frozen as understanding hit me.

Create bindings.

Me?

'And you do not *want* to teach me that.' It seemed the words were spoken by someone else entirely, someone fully in control of herself – someone whose heart wasn't pounding with the overwhelming sense of loss that washed over me. All the risks we'd taken, all the work we had done ... and this was where I'd lose my last hope of ever hearing Creon speak? 'You don't want anyone to have that power ever again.'

A cramped smile flitted across her weather-beaten face. 'I've seen the mistake made once too often already.'

'I'm not the Mother,' I said, my voice hollow.

'Achlys and Melinoë weren't always the Mother, either.'

'No,' I managed, 'but ...'

'They had such *lovely* ideas, Emelin.' The bitterness in her voice made me flinch. 'End all wars. Peace and prosperity forever. Korok loved it so much, hung on to every empty word they spoke – and I think they truly believed it, those days. I think they were truly the saviours of the world in their own minds.'

That frosty pale, doll-faced creature, with her porcelain laughs and her cruel games ... I shivered. 'So then what changed?'

'Her son died. Her first son, that is.'

The story Creon had told me in the pavilion, all those months ago; somehow I'd managed to forget most of it. A son, indeed, half fae and half god, killed by humans.

An ill-conceived plan that subsequently sparked the War of the Gods.

'Why did they kill him?' I said hoarsely. 'Creon's version of the story said they were jealous that Korok no longer spent any time in his own cities, but ...'

'Yes,' Zera said with a small scoff, 'I imagine that is the story Achlys and Melinoë prefer to tell.'

'So what happened?'

'The fool ignored his people.' Her face twisted into a sneer of what was *almost* anger – but it lacked the sting of true fury, ending up a violent sadness instead. 'Spent all his time dallying around the courts with his newfound fae family and forgot to keep an eye on the humans he'd left behind. Morhall was starving. There were riots all over his territory. We couldn't do much on his lands, and he laughed off every request to come back and take care of the chaos. Finally, he sent the boy to look into the matter.'

I realised I was holding my breath.

'The little prick took after his mother,' Zera said slowly. 'He was only supposed to report back and leave the rest of it to Korok. Instead, he decided to solve the issues himself by killing an innocent family member of every rioter he encountered. A disincentive, I suppose.'

A bitter laugh escaped me. 'Death isn't a disincentive to people who are already dying.'

'So it turned out.' She took a small sip of hot wine, as if to gather courage. 'There were still a good number of godsworn human mages in Korok's lands around that time. Banding together, they were powerful enough to defeat him. But the battle escalated, as battles do ...'

'And he died,' I finished.

'Yes. And suddenly world peace no longer mattered as much to Achlys and Melinoë – not while they were looking for heads to put on stakes.'

The Mother. No other names had been relevant to her anymore, no memory of the individuals with hopes and dreams she'd been. Nothing but an empty shell of revenge – nothing but a mother's rage.

'Do you understand, Emelin?' Zera's voice was quiet, but it seeped into my very skin with its unsettling weight. 'I don't doubt your good intentions, dear. I know you wouldn't hesitate to swear you'd never create a binding yourself, that you truly believe you'd never attempt to find new and malicious ways to use the magic. But neither of us knows how you might be hurt in the future – and I know that as soon as Achlys and Melinoë were hurt, nothing mattered to them except their own pain and suffering.'

'You truly hate her,' I said hoarsely.

'I don't hate.' She took another sip of wine. 'But I learn.'

I raised my mug to my lips with trembling hands and forced a few drops of the warm drink over my lips. If any divine magic lingered in this wine, it wasn't enough to slow my heartbeat. *I learn* – and she wouldn't be fooled a second time. Not even with the fate of the world on the line. Not even as war stirred on the islands, defeat looming around every corner.

Pleading wouldn't change her mind. Pleading was what a mage hungry for power would do, a mage who might turn that treacherous magic against the world at the slightest provocation.

Would I ever choose that road?

I steeled my heart against the twinge of doubt, lowered my wine, and said, 'So you'd rather leave things as bad as they are? Because the alternative is risking worse?'

Zera sighed. 'I suppose that summarises it.'

She'd been the last to choose sides in the War of the Gods, Agenor had said, the last to conclude there was no other choice but to fight. I should have heeded that warning. Should have known I wouldn't find her brooding for revenge in her forest, ready to launch into battle at the first opportunity.

I'd be damned if I gave up that quickly, though.

'If you won't give anyone else the power to break the bindings ...' My mind was spinning at breakneck speed. 'Would you be able to do it yourself?'

'I doubt it,' she said, a mirthless smile spreading over her lips, 'and no, I'm not coming with you to try. If I'm left with a mortal lifespan, I don't have much time left, and the world needs me for the little things I'm still capable of doing. Carrying some grief. Sending some blessings. What little magic remains in me.'

Wasn't that choosing a side, too? I bit my tongue.

'Yes,' she added, reading my expression correctly, 'perhaps I've given up, indeed. And perhaps you should be glad of it. You know the weight of choices, and they become heavier with power. Are you sure you want to burden yourself that way?'

Her voice was so gentle, and yet it hit me with the force of a sledgehammer – those gods-damned choices, again. Paralysing me, adding the weight of all those lives to every small decision ... The world would expect more from a binding-breaking mage than from an unbound one. It would be even more disappointed with the fallible little cactus hugger it got instead.

Then again ...

Who else would do it?

'I need to take a look at the pumpkins,' Zera interrupted my thoughts, rising to her feet with the smallest groan. 'They've become the target of an army of slugs, it seems. Join me if you have any other questions.'

'I'll ...' I gestured weakly at my wine. 'I'll finish this and come find you.'

A meagre excuse for the moment of silence I needed, but she smiled, took up her bag of grief again, and staggered out of the door, leaving me behind in that small living room smelling of warm wine and resin-soaked wood.

I put down my mug and lay back in the pillows with a carefully curated yet heartfelt series of curses.

None of this made sense.

Only that thought felt solid to my wavering mind as I stared at the dark wood ceiling and the bushels of dried flowers that hung from the beams with unseeing eyes. One way or another, the universe had to be making an utter fool out of me, and I'd completely missed the joke. Was this really where my mission was going to end? I'd found the goddess I needed despite all sensible predictions, and then she'd kindly yet resolutely turned me down?

Because I might just turn into a second Mother if she were to help me?

I drew in a deep breath, held it, released it, the calming rhythm Tared had taught me. His voice echoed in my ears, imperturbable and wryly amused – *How many times do I have to tell you a clear mind is everything in the thick of a fight?*

Right.

Time to think.

I sat up straight again, forcing my breath to keep that slow, steady pace. Methodical, meticulous thinking, now. If Zera was afraid I might ruin the world even more than the Mother had already done ...

Was there any chance she was right?

What would I do if someone were to snap Creon's neck tomorrow?

Every muscle in my body tensed up at that thought alone. I forced myself to stay calm. Slow breaths, rational thoughts; I couldn't allow sentimentality to cloud my senses here. If Creon died tomorrow ... I'd take bloody revenge, probably. Find whoever was responsible. Kill the Mother out of nothing but the purest spite, save the world in his memory.

But would I go on to eradicate every single soul to ever have served the Mother? Would I sacrifice Lyn and Tared and everyone else I knew just for the sake of retribution, the way the Mother had gladly sacrificed Korok to destroy everyone who had condoned the murder of her son?

The problem, Zera had said, was that Achlys and Melinoë didn't care about anyone's grief but their own. And that was not me. That was fundamentally not me, because Creon had told me I'd rather drive myself to insanity than hurt anyone else. There may be darkness inside me – but I'd let her escape, that violet-eyed fae female at the Golden Court, despite knowing how she might hurt us.

I was *not* the evil I was fighting.

My hands had stopped trembling when I picked up my wine again and cautiously took another sip, savouring the wry sting of its flavour on my tongue. Believing myself helped. I doubted I had it in me to lie for power, to persuade Zera through smooth yet empty promises – but I could tell my truth.

Which was that I was frightened. But determined.

The weight of choices would be there. But I'd made my choice to stop hiding Creon, too. So perhaps I could learn to handle that, strengthen my heart the way I'd grown muscles to fight; perhaps I could slowly learn to carry a heavier burden. And this might be training in itself – the choice between easy cowardice and power with responsibility.

I drank more wine. The tang of sourness oddly sharpened my thoughts, lent unexpected clarity to the sun-streaked world I saw through the small windows.

It would take time to convince a goddess after centuries of fears. The others might be looking for me in the meantime, might think I'd run off and hid myself to avoid the battle on Tolya. But our bargain mark would tell Creon I was alive, and as long as he could read my feelings ...

I closed my eyes and allowed myself to feel deeply triumphant for the first time – to realise to the marrow of my bones that I had found a goddess, that I'd been *right*, that I was sitting here and rewriting the history of the world as we knew it. And because he felt emotions stronger when they were aimed at him, I called up the memory of his quiet smiles and reassurances, of every single time he'd told me I wasn't mad to hold hope, every single time he'd promised me it would all be well.

You were right, too.

That should do.

I poured the last splash of wine down my throat and jumped to my bare feet, limbs buzzing with the prospect of work to do. Out of the door and down the garden path I trotted, nearly stumbling over a fat chicken without any sense of self-preservation.

Zera knelt between a handful of cart-sized pumpkins. She broke off the quiet melody she was humming as I approached, looking up from her weeding work with twinkling eyes.

'Once again,' she said dryly, 'you seem to have found me.'

I came to a standstill beside her with half a laugh, too agitated to feel the sting of pebbles beneath my bare soles. 'I'm going to try to change your mind.'

'I know, dear.' She sighed, but there was nothing but compassion in the pale green of her eyes. 'I know.'

CHAPTER 18

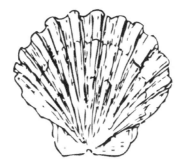

THE DOVES ARRIVED AS evening fell.

I was sitting in the open doorway, gobbling up a plate of mashed potatoes and grilled chestnuts dripping with herb oil, when the loud flapping of wings broke the peaceful silence. Zera, who had eaten perhaps a third of the serving she'd given me, was already back in the garden, dragging her unwieldy bag with her wherever she went.

She looked up just in time to watch them soar down from the peach- and purple-flecked sky – three chubby birds, cooing excitedly as they landed in the grass.

I forgot for a moment how hungry I was.

The doves only vaguely resembled the grubby brown specimens that lived on the islands of my youth, the birds that had filled my waking dreams for months until I finally gave up on that blessing I was chasing. These were larger than the scrawny birds I knew – not as monstrous as Sizzle the dragon, but large enough to prove they too had been subjected to a generous dose of divine magic. Their sounds were sweet and low, nothing like the shrill cooing of the doves I was used to.

And they were white. A flawless, snowy white, not a speck of dirt staining their feathers.

A full day of weeding and relocating slugs may have left me ravenous, but not ravenous enough to prioritise dinner over more myths come to life. I shoved my plate aside, jumped to my feet, and hurried over to where Zera was tickling the largest bird in the back of its neck.

'So they're *real*?'

The doves looked affronted.

'Of course they're real,' Zera said, turning to face me with a chuckle. 'And so are the blessings, before you ask. As I said, I'm not *entirely* useless even without my powers.'

I ran a hand through my hair, which was a little sticky with sand and sweat. I would have to take a bath in the lake soon, if Sizzle didn't try to eat me. 'How do you bless people if you no longer have your powers?'

'Oh, I let the recipients do the work for me,' she said dryly.

'What?'

'The blessings were never more than a confirmation. The doves don't change anything. They just tell the people they visit they're on the right track to happiness.' The corners of her lips quirked up into a conspiratorial smile. 'Interestingly, that is usually the only thing they need to stay on that track for the rest of their lives.'

I blinked at the largest dove, which glared back at me as if I was an idiot. 'That ... that sounds like cheating, somehow.'

'Goddesses don't cheat,' Zera said lightly. 'They just change the rules.'

I huffed a laugh. 'So there's little sense in asking you to send my friends a few doves to fix their messy love lives, then?'

'Your friends?' She sounded genuinely surprised as she rose to her feet.

'No need to sound so shocked about me having friends,' I said sourly.

She laughed. 'Not at all, dear. But most visitors I've had over the centuries asked for their own blessings, not for help for others. You caught me by surprise, that's all.'

'Oh.' I hunched up my shoulders, not sure what to make of that. Was it a good thing, surprising her? 'It's just ... they are the ones who spent the past few centuries making life harder for themselves. I have Creon. I'll be fine.'

Zera did not reply for a few moments as she staggered over to the grain chest against the outer wall of her cottage, dragging her bag along. The doves followed at her ankles, cooing and bobbing their heads, ruffling their snow-white wings with the content air of birds who have completed their mission.

The goddess opened the chest, scooped out a handful of grain, and scattered it on the ground for the birds to eat. Only then, shooing a few curious chickens away with her free hand, did she slowly say, 'Be careful about that, Emelin. It's easy to claim eternity, but much harder to actually live it.'

I stared at her, thoughts grinding to a halt for a nauseating moment. She did not look up at me, her gaze focused on her hessian bag as she struggled towards me through the falling dusk.

Easy to claim eternity. What was she suggesting – that I may need those blessings after all? That Creon's devotion may not go as deep as I believed? That I might lose him if I wasn't careful enough?

Suggestions I'd have laughed at from any other source – but she was a *goddess*.

'What ... what do you mean?' Goosebumps pebbled my arms as the chill of dusk found an unexpected ally in the cold gripping my guts. 'He *does* love me.'

'Yes, of course he does, dear.'

I knew that tone. Editta had used it to reassure me on those cold winter nights when I was too hungry to fall asleep – to promise me there would still be food tomorrow, to remind me that spring would return soon. True words, most of the time ... but people *had* died during those winters.

'But?' I managed.

'But love doesn't like to be taken for granted,' Zera said quietly, lowering her bag to the ground as she halted and lifted her gaze to meet mine. She was slightly out of breath. 'Don't take his devotion as a given.

Even the deepest well isn't bottomless.'

The warning in her voice lingered in the misty air even as she continued her staggered path towards her front door. I stepped aside to let her through, a reflex that was all limbs and no thought. My mind was sliding back to a dark temple room, to scarred fingers moving in the dark – *Do you have any idea what this does to me, Em?*

But I was solving that problem, wasn't I? I'd listened to his opinions and followed his preferences, hadn't I?

This time, at least.

There was no squashing that thought once it appeared, bright like quicksilver and just as deadly.

It couldn't have been the last time. Not in a world that hated him and needed me. Not in a world where we both had too many roles to play, where choosing the role of his lover may cost me lives I didn't want to sacrifice.

'Zera?' I spoke without thinking, whirling around to follow her into the house. The woods were darkening quickly, and in contrast, the warm glow of the fire was blinding. 'Zera, how in hell am I supposed to choose between people I love?'

'You love yourself first,' she said without a moment of hesitation, settling her bag back into its usual corner. Without that impossible weight in her hands, even her words sounded lighter. 'And then you see who celebrates that and who tries to stop you.'

I swallowed. 'You make it sound like it's easy.'

'One day, it will be.' She looked back at me, tired eyes twinkling. 'The trick is not to make too many stupid choices until that time.'

'That really helps,' I said sourly.

Her laughter was lively and melodious, joyful like a bird's song. 'Of course, dear. Answering questions is what I'm here for.'

In that warm room, surrounded by dried herbs and dark wood, it was easy to take the risk. 'So how do I break a binding?'

She laughed again. 'I *may* just have written down the secret and left the note on the bottom shelf of that cabinet over there.'

That was too easy. I shut the front door behind me, gave her a suspicious look that she answered with an innocent smile, and tiptoed over to the cabinet to open the heavy wooden door she'd indicated. Quite as I had feared, the bottom shelf did not contain any written notes with world-shaking revelations. Instead, I found a mustard-coloured woollen blanket and two linen sheets, smelling faintly of cloves and wormwood.

'I suppose,' I said, pulling a face at her over my shoulder, 'that this is your way of sending me to bed?'

It was impossible to be annoyed by the laughter wrinkles that deepened around her eyes. 'You've had a long day, dear.'

Which was true, and I should have been exhausted. But I lay awake for hours in the abundant pillows by the fireplace, thinking about Creon, thinking about bindings and dying gods and the Mother's hopes of eternal peace, before I finally sank away into feverish sleep and dreamt I was building a bone throne in my old bedroom on Cathra.

I woke up late the next morning, and still no one had shown up looking for me.

I pondered that fact as I untangled myself from the blankets, raked my fingers through my hair to tame the fuzziest locks, and clambered from the pillows. The bag of grief was gone from its spot beside the door, which suggested Zera was already up and moving. When I glanced outside, the doves were nowhere to be seen; they likely had flown off again, looking for new fortunate souls to be tricked into blessedness.

The world was turning as it always turned, and yet no one appeared to be terribly concerned about my disappearance. Creon had not reached out to me with demon magic, at least. And wouldn't Zera have told me if they were desperately combing the forest right now, or if Sizzle the dragon had chased my friends away from their attempts to rescue me?

I snuck out the front door, still rubbing the sleep from my eyes. Had my message of heartfelt triumph been convincing enough to make them leave me alone? Or worse ...

Had my message never reached Creon? Did the forest block his demon magic to protect Zera from the outside world?

A cold fist clenched around my heart. Hell, for all I knew, he'd spent the last night hanging on by the last threads of his sanity, fearing for my life at every heartbeat, while I was sleeping the sleep of the innocent on a goddess's cottage floor. I half-ran, half-stumbled around the garden, tripping over chickens, the grass cold and dewy under my bare feet – where was that bloody goddess when you needed her?

'Here, dear,' Zera said behind me, her gentle voice laced with amusement.

I snapped around and found her on a little stool behind a man-high bush of blackberries, her hessian bag on one side, a bucket full of fruit on the other. Her wrinkled hands were stained with purple juice, and so were her lips. She didn't look like a goddess. She looked like a mischievous child sneaking away from work to indulge in autumn fruits, except she was a few millennia too old to play that part.

'Breakfast?' she dryly added.

'Yes. I mean, thanks.' I dragged myself towards her, pulled a plump blackberry from the nearest thorny branch, and stuck it in my mouth. It was juicy enough to drown in. 'Do you have any idea where Creon and the others are?'

'Hmm.' She dropped a handful of berries into the bucket. 'They're fine.'

That was about as reassuring as Tared telling me I wasn't to blame for his troubles with Creon. I plucked another blackberry, stuffed it into my cheek, and said, 'Are they looking for me?'

'Oh, not exactly.' She looked entirely unbothered by the statement. 'It's hard for me to tell you where they are right now. But you can trust they won't be particularly worried.'

Which did not make sense, a full night after I'd disappeared – but doubting her too openly seemed impolite. I sank down in the damp earth beside her and began pulling berries off branches more systematically, sticking half of them straight into my mouth and dropping the rest into her bucket.

'Why can't you tell where they are at this moment?' I finally said, having discarded several brusquer alternatives.

'It's the "this moment" that gives me trouble.' She smiled that young smile at me. 'Time is not linear in the forest, and around this island in particular. Our moment is not the same as their moment.'

Which explained how the forest was able to extend her lifespan, but created several other questions, too. I swallowed a berry and slowly said, 'What even is the forest?'

Zera chuckled. 'What is sunlight?'

'Um.' I glanced up at the straight blue sky, squinting. 'The ... light ... of the sun, I suppose?'

Her weathered face was so very gentle, her eyes so deeply compassionate – but there was a decidedly devilish edge to the smile that trembled around her lips. 'A great philosopher was lost on you, Emelin.'

'Hey!' I burst out laughing, realising only at the very last moment that I probably shouldn't throw berries at goddesses – even if they were goddesses making me the target of their amiable ribbing. 'No need to stoop below the belt, Your Divinity. What you're trying to say is that the forest just ... is?'

'I'm confirming my suspicion that you think best when annoyed,' she said, sticking a blackberry into her mouth with nimble fingers. For a moment, she oddly reminded me of a content squirrel munching on its nuts, and every flicker of annoyance melted away again. 'But, yes. The forest was here before I came to be. It may have had something to do with that happy occasion, but I couldn't tell you for sure.'

'Are Orin's mountains the same?'

'Not the same at all,' she said slowly, 'but similar in some ways, yes. They certainly have a soul and have kept him alive since Korok's death. Inika's underwater caves, too, before you ask.'

Underwater caves. We had been wise to target the forest in our search, after all; I wasn't *that* much of a swimmer. 'And the Labyrinth is one of those places, too? The one below the Crimson Court, I mean?'

She heaved a sigh. 'The poor Labyrinth.'

No elaboration followed. For a few minutes, we focused on our plucking work against the comfortable background noise of rustling grass and clucking chickens and the occasional splash of water in the distance.

I finally worked up the courage to say, 'If the woods are linked to you, and the mountains to Orin, and the caves to Inika ... is the Labyrinth in any way linked to Etele and her colour magic?'

'Yes,' Zera said softly.

'But she wasn't hiding in the Labyrinth the way you are in your sentient places.'

'No.'

'And yet ...' I hesitated. Could I probe this far? 'Yet you aren't sure whether she's still alive.'

'The Labyrinth is not the only one of its kind,' Zera said, so composed that I may have believed her stoic if not for the way she avoided my gaze. 'Although it is by far the sweetest. There are other caves on the continent. She may be hiding there, for all we know.'

'But you never found her,' I guessed cautiously.

'No.'

By the tone of her voice, it was time to let go of this particular subject. I swallowed my questions and a few more blackberries, until I was sure I'd be brewing berry liquor in my stomach if I ate a single bite more. The bucket was overflowing by that time, and still the branches were heavy with fruit.

'If you could carry our harvest, dear?' Zera said, rising with a small groan. 'I'll take the grief.'

I obediently hauled the bucket of blackberries from the grass and waited for her to drag the bulging bag of the world's grief with her, back to the cottage. Her thin arms trembled violently by the time we arrived, stringy muscles clenching and unclenching under her tanned skin.

She lowered her burden with a sigh that was almost a sob, then seemed to remember my presence behind her and forced her pale lips into a deeply unconvincing smile. 'There's bread inside, if you'd like some more to eat.'

It seemed almost obscene, scarfing down her food while she was running herself ragged dragging that bag around. I put down the bucket beside the front door, wiped my sticky hands on my lower arms, and said, 'May I ask why you need to take the world's grief with you all the time? Isn't it safe inside the house?'

She gave me a tired smile, brushing her long grey locks from her face with purple-stained fingers. 'It would be safe, yes. But the farther I'm away from it, the more of its weight lands on the shoulders of the rest of the world.'

I parted my lips, thought better of the remark I'd been about to utter, and instead said, 'So now it's on your shoulders instead?'

'These shoulders are better equipped to deal with it,' she said, glancing at her bony hands. 'Admittedly, it was easier before I lost most of my powers, but the poor souls out there... They have enough to suffer without my help.'

What could I say to that? I knew the hollow faces of hunger, the tears of the mothers who'd lost yet another child to the claws of winter, the ever-present fear of the Mother's rule looming over the islands. Knew Valter's thin-lipped worry and Editta's quiet sobs at night. Too many of them were ground down already. One more blow might break them like dry twigs.

'Is there any way for you to get your powers back?' I said helplessly. 'If someone were to reverse the plague, for example, would that ...'

I didn't finish my sentence. A small grin had grown on her face, not the gentle goddess's grin, but the amusement of the tough, wiry creature who'd built up this quiet life from the rubble of the world she'd reigned. 'Did you have anyone in mind for that task, Emelin?'

I blinked, then let out a mirthless chuckle. 'That wasn't intended as some indirect question about the bindings.'

'I know.' She gestured for me to leave the bucket where it stood and follow her inside. As she dragged the bag of grief over the threshold of her home, she added, 'And yet, if I gave you the opportunity to go after the plague, you would.'

'It's not that I *want* to do it,' I said, not sure why I suddenly sounded defensive. Had it even been an attack? 'I don't want the bloody power to deal with those bindings, either. It's just that I want it to happen, and so far no one else has stepped up.'

There was a sadness in her smile – not so much scepticism but rather a wistful wish that she'd be able to believe me. 'And why do you want it to happen, dear?'

'Because ... Well ...'

I faltered, realising just in time that I ought to be more careful before blurting out answers. This was not the moment for quick ripostes. This was the moment to weigh every word on my lips as if my very life depended on it.

Because it just might.

The cosy autumn air chilled to a sensation like hoarfrost. Why did I want it to happen? Because the world was suffering – that was the easy answer. Because I'd lived in the reality of the Mother's empire, and because I couldn't let gods knew how many more generations endure that existence of hunger and fear of death.

Was that all?

There was no lying to a goddess. I should probably not be lying to myself, either.

If I didn't kill the Mother, if I didn't disband the empire ... My body tensed, and it wasn't the image of empty grain sheds and hollow-eyed children that filled my mind. Instead ...

You embarrass me, Emelin.

'I suppose ...' My voice croaked a little at the familiar sting, every fibre of me wincing as that verbal slap in the face hit me for what had to be the hundredth time. 'I suppose I want to prove I'm good enough to do it.'

'Yes,' Zera said and sighed. 'Of course.'

I sank down on the nearest stool, resting my elbows on my thighs and my chin in my hands. 'Is there anything I'm overlooking?'

'That depends.' Zera cocked her head a fraction, studying me. Her eyes were full of questions. 'Some people are drawn by the prospect of glory, no matter how noble their intentions appear at the surface. They'll save the world to be a saviour, not for the wellbeing of the people in it.'

'Like Achlys and Melinoë?'

A scoff-like laugh escaped her. 'My dear, they sit on a throne of bones. No one who doesn't secretly revel in their power would make such choices in life.'

'They're not terribly secretive about it either, these days,' I said sourly. 'Do you happen to know why that bloody throne is so important to her? We thought it may be a weak spot because she's so protective of it, but we haven't exactly figured out how it could hurt her.'

Zera raised a thin eyebrow. 'I'm not aware of any hidden powers it might have. As far as I know, it's simply one of the pretty toys Korok made her.'

Had Creon been wrong, then? I pushed that thought away to mull over later. 'And you think I might just end up with the same sort of pretty accessories if history takes a wrong turn somewhere?'

'I don't know, Emelin. I no longer know how to know. And that scares me.'

'For what it's worth,' I said weakly, 'I don't think I'm exactly looking for glory. It sounds like yet another burden to bear, honestly.'

'Hmm.' She looked away, unsmiling.

Not good enough. I felt it in my gut, the sharp-toothed gnaw of failure. Whatever I should have said, whatever I might have done to persuade her ... this wasn't it.

'Is there anything I can say?' I hated how desperate those words came out. One day in this place, and I was already begging? 'I know I can't predict the future, but ...'

But is there really no promise you can trust? The unspoken words filled the small room with an empty weight, a stupid, unthinking plea for which only one response was possible.

Zera's thin fingers tensed, but she turned without an answer, her shoulders slightly bent even without the burden of the world's grief in her hands. 'Come, dear.' Her voice, low and resigned as it was, didn't waver. 'It's time to bake some blackberry tarts.'

And that was all we said on the bindings that day.

I woke at sunrise on the third day and found the bag still by the bedroom door.

Curiosity got the better of me. I scrambled out of my nest of pillows and blankets, tiptoed to that closed door, and listened sharply for signs of life – no creaking of floorboards to be heard, no shred of hummed melodies or even audible breaths. Either Zera was very quiet, or she was still fast asleep. Likely the latter.

I decided to risk it.

The bag looked heavy – like the full bags of flour on Cathra that even the miller's bull-necked son could only lift with an abundance of groaning and growling. I studied it for a moment, estimating my chances. Even if I wasn't able to pick it up, I should at least be able to shift it a little, shouldn't I?

Cautiously, I wrapped my fingers around the knot at the top of the bag and gave a gentle yank. The rough cloth didn't give way – not even the tiniest fraction of an inch.

I glanced at the door, which was still closed, and pulled a little harder.

Nothing. I might as well have tried to drag a towering cliff somewhere. The bag wasn't just heavy, it appeared to have taken root where it sat, a colossal weight so immovable that I wasn't sure how it hadn't cracked through the floorboards yet. I gritted my teeth, locked another hand around the rough hessian cloth, and gave another sharp yank, with more conviction now.

The bag didn't budge.

Just as I was flexing my fingers for another attempt, the sound of a footstep in the next room told me Zera had woken up. I shot away from the grief of the world, grabbed a blackberry tart from the kitchen counter, and had already shoved two big bites into my mouth by the time the goddess emerged from the narrow door to the backroom.

'Morning, dear.' She looked suspiciously amused as she casually grabbed the bag and dragged it with her to the kitchen side of the room.

'Sleep well?'

'Pretty decent,' I said, trying not to stare at those bony arms pulling the weight of half a mountain along. 'You?'

Her smile waned a fraction. 'Oh, the usual.'

Which wasn't too great. I stuffed the rest of my blackberry tart into my mouth at once; perhaps it was better if I just didn't talk until my brain had been granted some time to wake up.

We spent the entire morning fixing a leak in the cottage's hay roof, ate porridge with warm apple and raisins for lunch, and gathered chicken eggs in the afternoon. When darkness fell, I taught Zera my best technique for darning socks, and we stitched up holes by the fire until we were both drowsy with warmth and exhaustion.

I asked questions as we worked and as we ate and as we sat by the fire and didn't do anything else, and received answers to only those I didn't care about. No, she still couldn't tell me about the bindings. No, she couldn't tell me where the others were. No, she couldn't tell me how to kill the Mother.

And still no one showed up to look for me. Still no demon messages arrived, not the slightest reassurance Creon was indeed alright as Zera insisted.

I snuck outside after she had gone to bed, unable to find the peace of mind to lie down and sleep. The night sky was brilliantly clear. My eyes traced the shapes and patterns I knew, the constellations Creon had drawn for me twinkling down in pinpricks of silvery light. There was Istia, the Star-ship with its recognisable sails ... Alyra, the mythical proud eagle who flew too fast and found herself stuck behind the firmament ... Kothro, the Slumberer, infamous for its flickering star ...

I blinked a sudden wetness from my eyes. Creon had spent several sheets of parchment on his attempts to explain the matter of the flickering star to me, in a burst of mathematical delight that had rendered his signs close to unreadable and sent his wings trembling excitedly. Something to do with breaking light and angles and fractures. I'd failed to fully grasp the theory.

Right now, I realised, clutching my arms around myself, I'd give my life to watch the stars with him and feel like an idiot as he patiently explained the essential properties of ellipsoids to me for the fifth time.

'Where are you?' I breathed at the black- and purple-flecked night sky, my breath creating little clouds in the chilly air. 'I need your help.'

No sweep of velvet wings eclipsed the light of the stars.

Minutes went by, me peering at the darkness in the silence of the sleeping forest, before I realised I was looking at the wrong sky.

They were constellations I knew, stars I knew. But we were in the last days of wine month, and Istia was not supposed to appear until the last frost of mud month came around. The flickering star of Kothro was a harbinger of thaw, not of approaching winter. I was looking at a spring sky during the cold fringes of autumn – a notion so ridiculous I wouldn't have believed it if I hadn't spent hours browsing through the *Encyclopaedia of Stars* to memorise each of the signs above me.

Were we outside of time entirely? Outside of even the seasons that governed life in the rest of our world?

I crawled into bed feeling unfulfilled and hopeless, unsure what powers I was toying with, and even more unsure how I'd ever come out of the game victorious.

The morning of the fourth day brought more clarity of mind, combined with a flare of some much-needed annoyance. Zera had been right: I really thought best when I was irritated.

I'd been on this bloody island for three full days now, and although that had taught me a thing or two about the gods, the prehistory of my world, and the hidden shadows of my own motivations, I'd achieved exactly none of the things I'd come for. Creon's voice was still as much out of reach as it had ever been. The Mother was no closer to being defeated. If I considered the matter objectively for a moment, I was progressing absolutely abysmally, with little outlook of improvement. I'd have been more useful with the nymphs on Tolya; at least there I could have left a decent impression on the rest of the world.

So something had to happen. Either I had to get some work done, or I'd have to leave.

Leaving sounded far too much like giving up for my taste, so I climbed from my makeshift bed with renewed determination to prove I was nothing like the Mother and her violent ambitions. There was a compost pile badly in need of turning behind the house – I had noticed while we were looking for eggs the previous day. Surely Achlys and Melinoë would never stoop to shovelling chicken shit and rotting fruit?

A good hour of sweaty labour and rotting apple peels later, I came to the conclusion that perhaps there were things I had in common with the High Lady of all fae, such as a deep-felt wish to never lay eyes upon another compost pile again.

Taking a quick bath in the crystal-clear lake around the small island was not the relaxing endeavour I'd hoped for either, due to the presence of a giant dragon watching me suspiciously from the other shore. I splattered out of the water as soon as I'd scrubbed the last mud stains from my skin, slipped into the loose shirt and trousers Zera had lent me, and went to look for the goddess, hoping at the very least the effort had not been entirely in vain.

That was an idle hope, again.

For another long afternoon, my every question on the bindings was gently but resolutely shoved aside. We discussed Bakaru Sefistrim – 'an unpleasant relic of a bygone age' – and the state of Agenor's magic – unbound until Korok's death, Zera confirmed – but never the questions I had come to ask, never the answers I'd have killed for.

'See,' the goddess said mildly when I grumbled something to that effect, 'that may be the entire problem. For all your good intentions, there *is* a darkness inside you, dear.'

'There's darkness inside you too,' I said. 'You just told me Bakaru should be dead.'

'Not in those words,' she said, although her chuckle suggested agreement.

I huffed a laugh. 'I'm pretty sure you were thinking it. What's the difference?'

'The difference,' she retorted without hesitation, 'is that my darkness is kept in check by empathy. It's hard to mercilessly destroy people you understand, even when you do not agree with them.'

The last to choose sides in the war. Had she understood the Mother's fight, even if she decided to resist it in the end?

Did I understand?

I'd thought I did. But I'd explained myself to Zera time and time again, and she still believed I was missing something – a *goddess* still believed I was missing something. So maybe I was. Maybe I was utterly, laughably wrong about myself; maybe my desperate attempts to keep everyone happy would easily lose the fight to my sharp edges; maybe it was better for everyone in the world if I ceased my attempts to become a second Mother right this minute.

And if that were the case, I would go home, of course.

But how in hell was I supposed to know?

I watched Zera limp through the garden as she tended to her food – her bony frame about to snap under the weight of a world she could no longer save. Reining in the darkness. Keeping the peace.

Understanding.

The insight struck with lightning force, coming out of nowhere and yet so painfully self-evident I should have seen it days ago. Of course I hadn't been able to move that bloody bag. Not with the way I'd gone about it – out of curiosity, trying to make a point. But none of this was about being right or wrong. It was about keeping the world safe, about protecting the last bit of hope we could find.

If I truly only wanted to know on which side of the line I fell, rather than to show anyone what I could or couldn't do ...

Maybe it was time for one last attempt.

CHAPTER 19

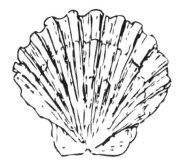

I WAITED A FULL hour after Zera had gone to bed, sitting on the doorstep of her small cottage, staring at the spring constellations, thinking of Creon. I wondered where he was and what he was thinking. Wondered if he missed me, wondered what he'd say of the idiocy I was about to attempt, and decided he'd probably enjoy himself tremendously if he had any idea – a thought that cheered me up far better than the prospect of likely failure.

It was the image of his smile in my mind's eye that eventually moved me to get up and make my way back into the cottage, where the last glowing embers in the fireplace still provided a little light. I lit a single candle, just to be sure the room wouldn't go all dark, then tiptoed back to that damn bag in the corner by the bedroom door, which looked deceptively unremarkable.

I sat down before it, breathing slowly to keep my rattling heart in check, and gently placed my palm against the rough cloth.

Understanding.

How else would one carry the grief of others?

I closed my eyes and thought of Creon – not the dangerously seductive, painfully brilliant side of him, but the part he hid like a shameful secret, the loss and the loneliness and the overwhelming guilt. Thought of Agenor, of his fears as the years passed and my mother was still nowhere to be found. Thought of the tears leaking from Lyn's eyes, thought of Tared and the light blazing around him—

And the bag's grief rolled over me.

It wasn't mine, and yet it was. Somehow it felt *familiar*, the anguish blooming from the marrow of my own bones and oozing into every fibre of my being; I learned to distinguish a dozen shades of sorrow in that first heartbeat, the gnawing cold of guilt and the suffocating weight of lingering heartbreak, the bitter taste of what could have been, the never-ending spirals of self-reproach. The shadows of Creon's soul were part of mine, suddenly, a tangle of blood-drenched memories. The years of Agenor's life pressed down on my shoulders, the awareness of the world he'd lost and would never see again. I recognised the bruises on Lyn's overburdened heart, the scalding flares of Tared's bonded love, the yearning emptiness where their life together should have been.

And under my palm, the rough cloth gave way just a fraction.

Nothing more than a hint of softness where unyielding steel had been, but it was *movement*, and the breath caught in the back of my throat as I pressed my fingers deeper. I hadn't expected even that much yet. This was the easy part – the people I loved and understood already.

How in hell did Zera empathise with people she wanted dead?

The softness under my fingers turned rigid again. Damn it. Perhaps that was not the place to start. I drew in a deep breath and thought of Valdora of Svirla, the sour-faced, thin-lipped alf female who seemed to have made it her life's mission to object to every single word I spoke on the Council floor. An adversary I didn't want to see dead by any means – I just wanted her to shut the hell up every now and then.

But if I stopped being offended and tried to understand ... She was the head of a large house, overseeing several dozen alves whose safety depended on her decisions. She'd lived to see a proud, independent family reduced to underground rebels, had survived centuries of warfare and the hell of the Last Battle, and now some stubborn twenty-one-year-old was telling her how to save the world?

I recognised her particular flavour of sadness the moment it unfolded within me, as if my flicker of empathy was the only invitation it needed – the aching absence of a father she'd lost, the burden of a house she felt she could never do justice to, a worry for the future that kept her awake at night.

Oh, hell. I swore to the bag before me I'd never snap at her again.

It shifted another fraction.

Encouraged, I thought of Thysandra – cold, stoic Thysandra with her almost unwavering loyalty to the fae empire and the Mother. Had she ever known anything other than the intrigue and backstabbing of the Crimson Court? Wasn't it quite understandable, really, that she'd ended up clinging to anything stable in that environment, even if the most stable thing happened to be a murderous High Lady terrorising the world?

And there it was, rising in me with a timidity bordering on fright – Thysandra's quiet pain of always remaining overlooked and undervalued, of fighting for every word of appreciation. It was *my* pain now, memories mingling with magic, and again the bag moved when I pressed against it, shoving perhaps half an inch over the smooth wooden floorboards.

Ophion. I pressed away the sting of cold loathing at the image of that slick smile and those vicious green eyes – loathing was too easy. Sure, he may be a violent bastard, but then again ... *Kinslayer*. Would any creature, no matter how ambitious, really slaughter his entire family and not waste another feeling on it? Or might the cocky arrogance be some stubborn attempt to convince not just the rest of the world, but also himself that the sacrifice had been worth it?

That thought was all it took.

Ophion's grief didn't rise timidly. It pierced through me like a blade to the heart and brought a tidal wave of agony in its wake, the wounds of dozens, if not hundreds of other fae I'd wanted dead. Hurt took over, a tangle of spine-chilling images. I was the blade cutting my own father's throat. I was the cries of a dying child. I was the fearful glance over my shoulder, I was the odd smell of the wine an enemy handed me, I was the straight-faced lie that framed the innocent ... My own body ceased to exist. I became the fears of a conniving court, the forced smiles and the desperate kills and the bone-crunching *loneliness* of that life in the service of death.

But I understood. Hell take me, I understood.

There was no stopping the flood anymore, all that suffering I couldn't help but relate to. My arms wrapped around Zera's bag, and the bag moved, not enough for me to lift it, but enough to let it rest against my shoulder – enough to make me brace for what was to come. Because if I could understand Ophion, I could understand the Mother. I could understand that ice-cold rage at the death of her first son and her fury at every cursed soul standing between her and bloody revenge ...

Her hollow grief joined the cacophony of emotion, a blinding misery that eclipsed everything but the need to lash out and cause more hurt, more suffering to compensate.

My heart hurt. My spine hurt. My face was wet with tears. I tried to stand, and the bag almost gave way, yet resisted that last tug off the floor ... that last bit of weight. The last people I truly didn't wish to understand.

But I *had* to.

I dug deeper.

And then I was Valter and Editta, too, and my own memories turned inside out as suddenly I saw my childhood through their eyes. I felt the fear squeezing Valter's chest as he shouted at me for losing control of my powers again. I felt Editta's raw grief at her miracle child turning into yet another threat, felt the powerless coldness seeping into her words, felt her avoid the child's teary eyes rather than lose composure at the sight of the little problem she couldn't afford to love.

Something fragile shattered inside me.

I didn't want to understand. Didn't want to give them an excuse for a single cold word, for a single silent hour, for the panic that still slumbered in my veins. But their fears spoke for them, and as I tried to rise again ...

Zera's bag came loose from the floorboards.

A weight I couldn't carry but carried all the same, reducing me to a tiny fleck of dust in a cold, dark, aching void. Breathing had become painful, every gulp of air like biting acid. My arms had gone numb. My knees shook so violently that they rattled against each other. But I *stood*, I held the grief of the world clutched against my chest, and I did not succumb to the endless barrage of hurt battering my heart. I stood, I stood, I *stood*, I ...

'Emelin,' a voice said behind me.

My eyes were closed. I hadn't realised. I tried to force them open and could no longer identify the muscles I needed for the motion, could no longer gather the strength. Cold grief rained down on me, death and hunger, destruction and heartbreak. I *stood*, but the gods knew on whose feet; I no longer felt mine.

My body was a hollow shell. The world still suffered.

'Emelin.' It was so very calm, that voice. Like a lullaby. Like a perfectly made bed whispering at me to lie down. 'That's enough. You carried enough. Let go of it.'

Let go?

My arms. I had to loosen my arms.

Somewhere, somehow, a few of my muscles relaxed. Not the right ones. The floor hit me, or maybe I hit the floor – my knees had buckled. I curled around the bag, breathing in little gasps now. Dying. People were dying. And mourning, and screaming, and ...

Calloused fingers wrapped around my wrists, pried my arms away from the rough cloth. The gentle voice drifted back into my ears, more quietly now. It murmured soothing words I didn't understand, hummed a melody I didn't know ... but the screaming in my head stilled, and I became aware of my own body again. Clammy skin. The friction of clothes. A brand new bruise on my hip.

The bag was gone, and so was the pain.

'Sleep.' The word reverberated through my depleted mind, every sound in that strange divine language infused with unyielding power. A last stubborn core of my mind tried to resist its call, but my thoughts folded in whether I wanted them to or not, surrendered to the blissful prospect of silence and weightlessness. 'Sleep, Emelin.'

I gave up on struggling.

And slept.

Sunlight brushed over my eyelids.

I stirred against something soft – a pillow, I deduced, that was a pillow below my heavy head. A soft down comforter had been draped over my body, tucked in tight on either side of me. The smell of ginger drifted into my nostrils, strong and spiced, tickling me awake.

Every inch of my body felt stretched thin, worn down, run over – a powerless exhaustion, as if I'd swum underwater for too long and been pulled to the surface *just* in time not to drown.

I tried to speak and found my mouth parched as desert sand. A pathetic moan was the only sound that escaped my lips.

But beside me someone chuckled, and a vaguely familiar voice said, 'Good morning, dear.'

Zera.

My brain abruptly reconnected voice to name. I shot up in the pillows, or tried to; my elbows slipped in the soft blankets, muscles lacking the strength to support my weight. The world was a patchwork of dazzling shapes when I forced open my eyes. Sunlight slanted in through a narrow window, flooding the light wood of the walls and the bed in which I lay. There was a closet, a woollen carpet, a night stand on which a cup of ginger tea stood steaming.

And in the chair beside the bed sat a goddess in a long white nightgown, a blanket over her shoulders and her hair bound in a messy grey braid.

Memories returned, rolling over me like an avalanche. The bag. The grief. The voice pulling me from the pits of that unbearable understanding when I had no longer been able to do so. Most disconcerting of all, lingering like a lead ingot in my chest, the realisation of what I'd felt and would never be able to un-feel: the fragile, flawed humanity of every single soul I'd wanted dead.

I stared at Zera, who blithely lowered her own cup of tea and said, 'I was starting to fear you wouldn't wake up until nightfall.'

'I ...' I made another attempt to sit up, a little more successfully this time, as the last pieces fell into place. 'I woke you up.'

'I was woken by a rather sudden moment of blissful quiet,' she corrected me, and although her lips curled into a smile, her eyes didn't join in her amusement. 'For which you should be grateful. If I hadn't pulled you out when I did, you might have been dead a few moments later.'

I blinked at her.

'As I said,' she added, with not the slightest hint of triumphant *I told you so*, 'it's a rather heavy weight.'

'Dead,' I repeated, thoughts still catching up. As if I may have misunderstood her. The sound of the word didn't make any more sense on my own lips.

'Yes, dear.' Again that cheerless smile. 'A monumentally stupid idea, if I may put it like that. Although, I should of course have warned you. If I'd had the slightest suspicion you may actually be able to lift the cursed thing ...'

Her voice drifted off. This time not even the most minimal of smiles followed.

'I ... I just wanted to test myself,' I said hoarsely, words tumbling over my lips. 'I wasn't trying to make a point – wasn't trying to prove you wrong – I just wanted to know if I should give up. I didn't mean—'

'I know, Emelin. I know.' She sighed and nodded at the cup of tea on the nightstand. 'Drink something. Take a few deep breaths. You've had enough excitement for one morning.'

I hauled myself up, shoulders against the headboard of her bed, and cautiously lifted the heavy earthen mug into my lap. The tea was scorching hot; I didn't dare to let more than some tiny sips over my lips.

'Stupidity aside,' Zera finally said, staring at the window with unseeing eyes, 'I'm glad you didn't give up.'

I nearly spilled the mug of tea over myself. 'What?'

'Well.' There was something forced about the unwavering lightness of her voice. 'If you had, I may have spent five more centuries seeing everything and everyone through the lens of my fears, and that would have been a shame, wouldn't it?'

I stared at her.

'And I know you weren't trying to prove me wrong. You wouldn't have been able to lift the bag in that case.' She bent over to set her tea on the floor, then rose from her chair and strolled to the window with short, restrained steps. 'But you *did* prove me wrong, dear. There's such a thing as being too cautious, and I'd crossed that line. I'm glad you were stubborn enough to make me see that.'

Glad?

Glad?

I no longer felt my worn-out limbs, too busy trying to follow Zera's words and barely managing. This was going too fast. I'd committed the stupidity of the century. I could have been dead, and yet ...

'What?' I said again.

'Lifting that bag requires unusual empathic abilities,' Zera said, turning to settle herself on the sun-streaked windowsill and resting her head against the glass. 'And a good dose of self-sacrificing tendencies. Neither of which Achlys and Melinoë ever showed in great amounts, in case that wasn't yet abundantly clear.'

Was she ... was she making an offer here? Was she saying I'd *convinced* her? I tried to come up with something sensible to say in the silence that fell, failed miserably, and settled for the ever-versatile, 'Oh'.

Zera closed her eyes, and for a single moment, she looked her unfathomable age – her body thin and fragile below the loose linen of her nightgown, her shoulders sagging with a weight I'd never understood so well. But when she looked up, there was a sharpness to her gaze I hadn't seen before, something that lay fixed on its goal like a well-aimed arrow.

'So.' That single word seemed to hang suspended in mid-air, like a world about to crash and smash into smithereens. 'Do you still want to know about the bindings?'

It shouldn't have been a question, and yet it was, posed with too much gravity to be taken as innocent teasing or an invitation to excitement. Did I want to know? Of course I damn well wanted to know – I hadn't survived dragons and forest tempers for nothing at all ...

But Zera knew that, too. And she was still asking me.

I retreated, hesitating with lips already parted to blurt out my answer. A few hours ago, that same unthinking disregard of a goddess's warnings had brought me to the brink of death. If Zera thought it necessary to ask the question now, despite all reasons to take the answer for granted, perhaps I would be wise to think for a moment.

'Why would I have changed my mind?' I said carefully.

She merely raised an eyebrow, gaze flicking to the spot behind the door where the bag doubtlessly waited.

Right.

Because of choices. Because of what I'd felt. Because this new knowledge, just like new power, would make my life harder, and it hadn't quite been a walk in the park so far. My fingers tightened around my mug as my thoughts swerved off, away from the bindings and towards that memory that lay heavy and inescapable in my chest –

Valter and Editta.

The thought of them alone awoke the memory of their fear and grief, the sensations no longer as overwhelming without the bag in my arms, but vicious enough even as echoes.

'My adoptive parents ...' I hesitated, awkwardly putting my mug aside. They could hardly be a subject Zera wanted to discuss, and yet my thoughts latched onto it with overwhelming fierceness, pushing even the matter of the bindings aside. 'They had their reasons, didn't they?'

Zera sighed, turning her head to stare outside. 'Yes.'

'They were frightened.' I wasn't sure if I liked it, that newfound insight that wasn't just rational understanding but *experience*, an explanation so vivid it became a justification. Could I still be a victim if they were hardly perpetrators? 'They ... they didn't mean to do any harm.'

'No.' She sat still as a statue except for the restless motions of her bony fingers plucking at her long grey braid. 'But that doesn't make them harmless, of course.'

I shut my mouth and swallowed audibly.

'Here is something you need to understand,' she continued softly, looking back at me. Her eyes were pools of eternity, dark with knowledge far beyond my imagination. 'Something quite essential to make sense of the world once you've seen it like this. Just because people have reasons doesn't mean they're right. Reasons are easy to come by. It's wisdom that creates the true challenge.'

'Like the Mother,' I said hoarsely. 'Who has reasons, but ...'

'But chose the wrong path nonetheless. Yes.' A joyless chuckle. 'Once someone ends up casting her living children aside in her hunger to avenge the dead ones, you can be rather sure she's beyond saving.'

Creon. My throat squeezed violently and unexpectedly. 'Yes.'

'And similarly, you don't need to excuse Valter and Editta for their choices simply because you understand *why* they made them.' She tucked her brown woollen blanket tighter around her shoulders. 'They were out of their depth, of course, and I feel for them. But they still chose the wrong solutions, and you suffered for it. Empathy and anger are allowed to exist side by side.'

'Yes,' I said again, because I wasn't sure what else to say. My chest was tightening, as if to work against the relief that welled in me. 'Thank you.'

'You are very welcome,' she said, her slow exhalation close to a sigh. 'But that understanding won't make the path forward easy, dear. You will still be hurting people you may truly not want to hurt.'

And the more power, the more hurt I could inflict ... I was slowly getting dizzy. How much did I trust myself – enough to make those decisions?

Then again ...

'If I don't have that power,' I said, and my voice came out unexpectedly clear, 'is there another way we could ever break the bindings? Will the magic be reversed if we kill the Mother?'

'I don't know.' Her mirthless smile betrayed that she knew the conclusions I'd draw, hated them, and still couldn't bring herself to lie to me. 'I'm not an expert on binding magic. The basic facts are all I know.'

Which meant this might be our only chance to break them – to restore the fertility of every magical female around the archipelago, to get Agenor's memories back, to hear Creon's voice. The dizziness waned. Doubt solidified into steely resolve, into the only conclusion I could draw: those were not prices I was willing to pay.

What it would cost me ... I would find out, and if I was unlucky, I'd find out soon. But the gods-damned bindings had to go, and here lay the way to break them.

So I said, 'Teach me. Please.'

And with a last, tight-lipped sigh, Zera nodded.

CHAPTER 20

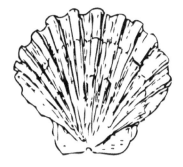

EVEN THE CHICKENS WERE restless when we strode out into the garden, my knees shaky despite the five slices of bread I'd munched down after dragging myself from the blankets of Zera's bed. The bag of grief lay safely in the goddess's bony hands again. Even so, my senses seemed to have been sharpened, as if the world had grown brighter, louder, *harsher* around me: the sunlight was a dagger to my eyes, the fragrance of cherry blossoms a smothering perfume, the rustling of trees a rumbling thunderclap. I was wearing my own comfortable dress again, and the grass brushing past my bare lower legs seemed rough like cat's tongues.

As if my entire being was a freshly healed wound, sensitive to the gentlest prodding.

Zera walked before me, closer to nervousness than I'd ever seen her before. 'I'm not sure it will work,' she told me for the fifth time as she led me through the low arches of the willow trees, towards a side of the island I hadn't yet visited. 'I haven't tried anything like this since I lost my powers. Honestly, I'd say it was impossible if not for ...'

She faltered, gripping the bag tighter as if it threatened to slip from her fingers. I reflexively took half a step forward to help, then realised what I was doing and dropped my hands with an ice-cold shudder.

You could have been dead. If I could barely handle sunlight, this wasn't the moment to lay another finger on that bag.

'... if not for Korok and his idiocy,' Zera stubbornly continued while she staggered on, talking over her unwilling moment of fragility. 'He managed to teach Achlys and Melinoë this magic even though he never had any colour magic himself. So perhaps it doesn't matter if I have any magic at all. As long as I'm still capable of waking those powers in you ...'

That sentence remained unfinished. Out of breath, she dragged the bag around the last bend of our narrow path, then lowered it into the grass with a heartfelt sigh.

'Well.' A tinge of relief to her voice. 'There we go.'

I followed her, treading with utmost care so as not to bruise my toes against my boots, which felt rigid and rough to my oversensitive skin. Around the bend ...

I thought it was a small arbour at first, then realised the intricate roof over the little clearing was nothing but willow branches braided together. They created a small, leafy dome, a shield to protect what grew below – a single blooming plant, rising from the centre of the open space.

Its bulb-shaped flowers were a crystalline azure, five petals curled protectively around a vulnerable heart. It was only when I snuck closer that I saw the veins glittering in the blue. They were finer than cobwebs, but unmistakably gold – an eerie, pulsing gold I recognised in the blink of an eye.

I'd seen it before in a pentagonal basin, sending strange flickers of light over the mosaic walls of Etele's Underground memorial.

My gaze dropped to the roots of the plant. The earth around it seemed strangely dry, but small beads of gold stuck to the lowest leaves and stem, like dried, cracking paint.

'Blood?' It came out breathless. 'You've been watering it with your *blood*?'

'It's a helpful way to concentrate what little power I have left,' Zera said, a touch of amusement to her low voice. 'And on this specific occasion, a more pleasant method to swear you in. But do tell me if you prefer to drink it straight from my veins. Korok always claimed the magic was more effective that way.'

I blinked, not sure which of the several disconcerting thoughts sparking in my mind deserved most priority on the way to my lips. 'You ... you need to drink divine blood to be godsworn?'

'Mm-hmm.' She did not look disturbed in the slightest.

'Hell.' I glanced at the plant and grimaced. 'You're saying Agenor drank Korok's blood.'

'It would hardly be the most ridiculous thing he's done in his life,' Zera said dryly, smoothing her linen tunic over her angular hips. 'Although he'll doubtlessly tell you it was a most dignified and honourable ceremony. If you could step aside, dear? Thank you.'

I stumbled out of the way, and she knelt beside the plant and gently pulled one of the plump blue flowers from its stem. It unfolded at that, revealing a white- and gold-flecked heart in Zera's palm.

'Last time I saw divine blood', I said and swallowed, 'it blew up half an army.'

Zera's chuckle was joyless. 'I didn't curse these flowers, if that is your concern. Our blood is not inherently malicious.'

I eyed the petals suspiciously as she plucked them from the heart. They didn't *look* malicious, admittedly, and nothing exploded ... but the merciless destruction caused by just that little vial of Etele's blood was hard to block from my mind's eye completely.

Zera turned to me, pretending not to notice my wariness, and pressed two of the petals in my palm. 'Eat them.'

'Just ...' My heart leapt around my chest like a goat kid seeing a meadow for the first time. 'Just like this?'

She nodded. I gave the delicate petals a last glance, told myself it was better than sucking blood straight from her veins, and stuffed them into my mouth without further ado. They tasted oddly sweet – not metallic like blood at all – a honey-like flavour that bloomed in my mouth as I chewed and brought an unexpected warmth along, like the heat of heavily spiced food. The petals tingled down my throat when I swallowed, drawing a slow line to my stomach.

The warmth trickled into my limbs, spreading through me in a rosy blush. My knees stopped trembling. My heartbeat slowed. The sunlight and the rustling leaves mellowed, slipped back into their roles as background noise rather than a constant assault on my vulnerable senses.

'Good,' Zera said softly. 'At least my blood still does what it needs to do.'

I looked up and stiffened.

Gone were the kind green eyes and the tanned face, the fragile frame and the bony limbs. The creature before me was five solid feet of whirling power – still human-shaped, but there was nothing human about the dizzying play of light that made up her physique now, a storm of magic only barely contained by mortal skin and bones. If this was what she was *without* her power of old …

My throat turned dry, and still I couldn't tear my eyes away from her. The true meaning of divinity – of magic that could tear worlds apart and minds that understood the secrets of the universe itself – had not fully dawned on me until that moment.

'Ah, yes.' Even her voice sounded different, low and deep like howling wind. The amusement was still there, however, a touch of humanity. 'I'd forgotten about that part. It'll wear off. Best sit down, dear – this may lead to some dizziness.'

I needed no further urging, plopping to the ground in breathless obedience. Zera sank down beside me and held out the blazing fleck of light that was her hand to me; her flickering fingers gestured for me to take it.

'Um,' I said, studying the unearthly matter of her body with some suspicion. 'Is that safe?'

Her laughter vibrated the very air around me. 'I'm not the one who nearly killed you last time.'

An annoyingly good point. I wrapped my fingers around hers, finding her light-drenched shape more solid than expected. She squeezed down with the firm reassurance I'd come to know from her, and for a moment, the silhouette of materialised power before me seemed a little less intimidating.

'Very well.' If she was still tense, her voice did a stellar job of hiding it. 'Now I need you to listen closely and repeat what I'm saying. Not the words that you understand. The words I'm *speaking*. Is that clear?'

I swallowed but nodded, chest tightening. That odd divine language underlying the words I'd easily interpreted from the very first time I heard it … it took an effort to dig below that comprehensible surface and identify the alien sounds she was truly pronouncing, The sight of my own small hand caught in those fingers of divine light made me feel a little faint – which did nothing to improve my faith in my own reciting abilities.

'Good,' Zera said, except she didn't say *good* at all. She said *ikaz*, and once I'd deciphered that true sound of the word, I could no longer figure out how I'd ever understood it as *good*. 'Then repeat after me …'

She went through the oath slowly, two, three words at a time, allowing my lips the time to find their way around the strangeness of her language. Coming from me, the sounds were utterly meaningless to my ears. My only sense of what I was saying came from Zera, from the shreds of meaning I caught between my intent listening. Loyalty. Service. Lifelong. Bargain.

Magic.

My tongue almost twisted at that particular word. But I forced it over my lips, and the warm blush on my skin abruptly drew inwards, solidifying into a brewing little core of something … *new* just below my midriff.

Was it working?

The final words seemed to take an eternity; I could barely muster up the self-restraint to sit still and repeat the rest of Zera's oath. The moment she released my hand, my fingers flew to my chest, prodding that brand new sensation of warmth just below the lowest ribs. It felt new, and yet it was a part of me I recognised, something that had always slumbered just below my skin yet escaped my notice.

'You can feel it,' Zera said, sounding breathless.

'I ... I think so?' When I looked up, she had taken on her human form again, not nearly so grandmother-like anymore now that I knew what lay beneath. 'What am I supposed to feel, exactly?'

'Power.' She jumped up more easily than ever before, nodding for me to follow. 'Come. Let's try.'

I couldn't get to my feet fast enough, and still she was faster, rushing off with the bag of grief as if her very life depended on it. As I hurried after her, she added, 'The fae interpretation of colour magic is rather limited, you see.'

It took a physical effort to steer my brain back to magic theory after the whirlwind of developments it had already been forced to process. 'In what way?'

'It's all about hue. Etele's magic was not strictly limited to colour, but rather the broader concept of light and surfaces and the external appearances that we see. Once ...' She interrupted herself as the bag got stuck behind a rogue root; the gnarled wood slithered obediently back into the earth when she glared at it. 'Once you start looking beyond the obvious powers of hue, far more interesting possibilities arise.'

'I see,' I said, which was a hopeful statement at best and an outright lie at worst. Every minute of this day sucked me deeper and deeper into a swamp of bewilderment. 'Do you, um, have a concrete example of—'

'Light reflections.' She'd never interrupted me with such urgent agitation. 'Of course, colour is just light reflection, too, in the end ...'

'Of course,' I said weakly.

'... but so is texture and shine and all of those other factors. Which brings us to the ones Etele never taught most members of your people. Smoothness for mind. Softness for movement. Iridescence for magic.'

'Wait.' Only now did my brain slowly come around to the point she was making. 'You're saying there are *more* colours. Different colours. Things that aren't colours, but ...'

'You could probably call it surface magic rather than colour magic,' Zera said without turning around, 'and then consider colour just one of the many surface properties that you can draw power from. Does that clear things up?'

It did – marginally so, but an improvement nonetheless. I glanced at the world around me, the willow trees and the cottage appearing at the end of the path, drenched in colours I had learned to instinctively take stock of wherever I went.

Just the reflection of light.

Like the sunlight dazzling on dewy leaves. Its soft glow on flower petals. The shadowy grooves of tree bark. I blinked and blinked again as my vision shifted, gaze latching on to sights I had never given much consideration before.

Softness for movement.

Like the Mother, who had moved heavy iron chains with her magic, that night she hung Creon by his wings in the bone hall. I stumbled to a halt as understanding rose into my mind with a sensation close to nausea.

'Those pillows.' My voice had gone rough. 'That mass of velvet and silk she's sitting on – she used *that* to draw magic? The ... the soft gleam of the light on their surface?'

'Very good, Emelin. Very good.' Zera finally lowered her bag at the fence of her garden and turned around, panting lightly. 'Soft surfaces with a diffuse light reflection make it possible to create movement. Or the opposite – it's an application of that same magic that binds human servants to the island, restricting their movement.'

'But— *Oh.*' Light flickered around me, and my thoughts appeared to do the same, jumping from memory to memory faster than I could follow. '*Iridescence for magic*, you said. Is that what she uses to bind people, then? The surface of ... of things like pearls and feathers and opal and ...'

'Yes,' she said slowly. 'That is part of it.'

'And the other part?'

She sighed. 'Smoothness for mind. Mirroring surfaces like steel and polished wood are sources of mind magic, and you need that, too. Bindings take effect when magic is wielded with the *intention* to do harm – that's where the mind comes in.'

My breath escaped in a dazed laugh. 'Good gods.'

'Yes, you're very welcome.' There was a wry edge to her grin. 'Let's see if we can get you to move something. I should have a velvet hair scarf somewhere I haven't touched in centuries – knew it would come in handy one day.'

Velvet. *Softness for movement.* The words sung through my mind like a brand new lullaby as I stumbled after her to the cottage, still desperately struggling to make sense of every new crumb of information. I had to memorise this – had to remember every single word she spoke, because who else would tell me once I left this place?

The hair scarf – an antique piece of wine-red velvet – was located at the bottom of a blanket chest. I could have tried with other fabrics as well, Zera explained as she put it in my hands, but the more reflective, the better, and why make this first attempt harder than necessary?

A good question; it seemed a rather intimidating task already.

I stared at the scarf, at the soft gleam of daylight reflecting off the folds of the velvet, and felt my mind wander back to those first days at the Crimson Court and all the hours I'd spent blowing stones apart before I figured out how to keep my powers in check. This time I didn't even have Creon's guidance to help me. It was me against this slip of fabric, and so far, the slip of fabric appeared to have the advantage.

Really, that sounded rather pathetic.

I kicked myself into motion and strode towards the window, where the velvet caught as much sunlight as possible. *Softness.* Colour magic was all about imagining colours, about vividly seeing the hue and saturation I needed, and setting it free. So could I do the same here? Could I isolate just the texture, that soft, velvety gleam, and make it do my bidding – make it *move*?

I closed my eyes. Thought of Miss Matilda's workshop, swatches of velvet and finely woven wool, the fleecy surfaces under my fingers. Thought of the downy softness of young chicks, the fuzzy buds of grey willows, the plush gleam of moss.

A familiar tingle awoke under the fingers of my left hand.

I let the magic flow without thinking, clinging to that impression of softness as I stretched out my right hand at the first object that came to mind. Movement. *Movement.* If I could just release whatever power was sleeping under my touch, could just take that soft reflection of light and make it *mine*—

Magic seared through me.

And with a bang that made me cower and shriek out loud, something slammed through the window, sending the chickens outside clucking hysterically as they fled.

My eyes flew open. The glass had shattered. Shards lay scattered in a semi-circle on the grass outside, perfectly centred around the projectile that had caused all the havoc – a heavy earthen mug, the same mug that had contained my morning tea, that had stood peacefully on the dinner table until mere moments ago.

And now it was outside.

I glanced down at the scarf in my hand, which had gone oddly ... *plain*. It still had the same wine-red colour, but without any of that plush, velvety texture to it; instead, the fabric had gone flat like the most expressionless sheet of empty parchment.

'It works.' The conclusion fell from my lips before my mind had fully wrapped itself around it. 'It ... it actually works.'

Zera didn't reply. When I whirled around to her spot by the hearth, she sat studying the broken window with damp green eyes, her lips trembling in what might be a smile as easily as a desperate attempt to hold back tears.

'Look at that,' she quietly said, looking up to meet my gaze. 'Seems I'm not yet entirely useless, after all.'

'You're not *useless*.' I flung the ruined scarf aside and fell into the nearest chair. 'You're carrying all that bloody grief. You're sending the doves.'

She sighed and averted her eyes. 'Yes.'

'And this ... You changed *everything*.' I nodded at my hands, unable to suppress a breathless laugh. 'If I can break the bindings, she's lost her best advantage. We might actually *win*. Get rid of her and of the empire and ... and ...'

Only at that moment did the triumph hit me, no less glorious for being a trifle tardy. I *could* face the bitch now, not just as Emelin the little unbound mage, but as Emelin the little godsworn mage – a true threat, rather than merely the only pesky enemy she hadn't rendered harmless yet. Hell, I might just *survive* this war.

Another laugh found its way to my lips, and then suddenly I was standing again, unable to resist the burst of energy that spread like wildfire through my limbs. I just had to practise. I just had to figure out those bloody bindings. *Mind and magic* – where should I start?

'Yes,' Zera said, and something close to a smile returned to her eyes. 'You may actually win.'

'Are we sure I can do mind magic, too, if I can do movement?' I bounced two steps to the door, laid my hand against my blue dress, and flashed a good dose of azure at the broken window. It repaired itself almost flawlessly; only a few cracks in the glass reminded us of where it had shattered. 'I could try. Well, maybe I shouldn't experiment on you, before I blow up your mind by accident, but—'

'You will not be possessing my chickens, dear,' Zera said dryly, following me into the garden. 'I draw the line there. Find a few victims of your own, if you wish to experiment – and for all that is holy, start small. Blowing up a few memories is more than enough in most cases.'

'You're ...' I wheeled around, blinking against the sunlight. 'You're not going to teach me that?'

'Me?' She gave a small chuckle. 'Dear, I know about as much about fae magic as you know about astrology. I can point and name things, but don't ask me to understand how any of it works. You'll need others for that.'

The rush of victory paled. *Others* – which meant that I had to leave.

As obviously I would have to do sooner or later. Hell, as I *wanted* to do while I wasn't even sure whether my friends were safe and not worrying their hearts out. But leaving meant I had to leave Zera here, too, in this little cottage for the rest of eternity, miles and miles away from every other living heart in the world – that I had to leave the comfortable safety of this island, this little patch of the world where I didn't have to worry about allies and opinions and the Mother's ugly propaganda.

'Right,' I said blankly.

She sighed and stepped between the rows of carrots, bending over to pull a few of them from the soil. 'Let's make lunch.'

There was no elaboration, but we both knew what the weight of her words meant: that it would be the last one.

We ate toasted bread and grilled carrots drenched in parsley oil, hardly speaking in between bites. My mind spun. The world dazzled me with its flecks of light and textures, all that new information to keep track of, all these new gifts to figure out. It would be alright, I told myself; Creon would be able to help me. So would Agenor. Lyn would be delighted from an academic point of view and doubtlessly find me a handful of books on Etele's powers, and Tared would look amused and tell me I still wasn't allowed to use magic during training sessions, and ...

A smile had crept up on my lips without me noticing. I ate the rest of my lunch faster.

After four days of talking, I had no questions left to ask. There wasn't even anything to pack; I had arrived carrying nothing but my boots in my hands. Once I'd recovered the mug I'd launched through the window and rinsed our plates, nothing was left except the comfortable silence of a finished conversation, of a door about to be closed again.

'I'll walk you to the water,' Zera said, the bag of grief already back in her hands.

I tried to imprint every single glimpse on my mind's eye as we made our way over the small island, the swaying willows and the lingering fragrance of sweet blossoms. There might not be a second chance to remember. I could try to come back, of course, could make pretty promises about visiting again after the war had ended ... but if the forest may not even let me, what was the sense of it?

Zera had to know, and yet that calm smile didn't waver when we reached the crystal lake. She merely hugged me, warned me a last time not to get myself into trouble, and turned to the forest without waiting for a reply.

'Would you mind sending Emelin back to the temple, dear?'

The towering white trees groaned and croaked a little, but on the other side of the lake, a gnarled oak split open like the tree in the temple had done. As the crack gaped wider and wider, I distinguished marble walls in the space beyond, and the blossom-covered floor tiles of the room from which I'd left four nights ago.

Four nights – when the others had been preparing to leave in mere minutes.

Anxiety gripped me by the throat, colder than even the water when I lowered myself into the lake and began wading to the other side. The temple room behind the portal looked unchanged. No one had left a message, as far as I could see. There was no sign anyone had even entered it to look for me.

My pulse sped to a dizzying rhythm. How much time had passed, exactly?

'Good luck, Emelin,' Zera said behind me, her voice eerily quiet, like fading wisps of mist. 'Make good choices.'

Easier said than done. But when I turned to respond, standing thigh-deep in the frigid water, the island and its goddess were gone, and only a burbling creek was left where the wide expanse of the lake had been.

CHAPTER 21

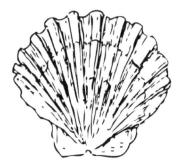

I DID NOT BURN to death the moment I clambered through the portal and landed in an inelegant sprawl of limbs on the marble floor.

Which meant someone was still protecting the temple complex against the plague.

Breath hitching, I scrambled to my feet and made for the low doorway of the room. The gallery beyond looked as it had done four days ago; the heavy curtains still hung before their niches, the doors to the prayer rooms were still closed. Dust whirled in the light falling through the roof slits – light that came pouring in from the east, I realised with a start. I may have left Zera's island at midday, but this part of the world still lived in the early morning.

Early morning ... of what day?

I slipped my boots back onto my wet feet and started running.

The temple around me was the same temple we'd searched for days, the place where Edored had nearly died, where Creon had scooped me up and flown off with me to fuck me on a sacred altar. A temple I *knew*, and yet nothing looked the same anymore as I sprinted through the maze of corridors, breath ragged in my throat. Just four nights. But in four nights I'd learned of gods and blessings and carried the grief of the world in my arms, and this deserted place had changed from a mystery into the most comprehensible part of our journey.

As if I'd stepped into a strange fever dream and awoken as a different person – godsworn, barely alive, and years older.

Finally, I reached the wide outer gate of the complex and stormed into the courtyard behind, my heart so high in my throat I could have gagged on it. This was the moment where I would discover they'd all left without me, gone to fight their war on Tolya when I didn't return. Or I'd find them in a state of utter frenzy after four sleepless nights, and they'd be furious with me for ruining their alliance with the nymphs. Or they'd have blamed each other for my disappearance, and I'd find them with bloodied knives and swords. Or ...

'Oh, Em!' Lyn's voice exclaimed. 'There you are!'

I slipped to a standstill on the overgrown tile path, blinking the blinding morning sunlight from my eyes.

And there they were.

The five of them scurryied around the courtyard like busy bees – gathering bags, burning waste, consulting maps, and whatever else one did to prepare for departure. Naxi looked sick with nervousness. Tared, Lyn, and Beyla looked grimly determined. Creon ...

He'd raised his head when Lyn cried out my name, kneeling next to the bag he'd been tying shut. My gaze locked onto his, and for an everlasting moment, I saw nothing but those inscrutable dark eyes, nothing but the male I'd imagined frightened and desperate with worry for four days – looking perfectly tantalising and casually invincible as always, not a spark of relief in his look.

As if he hadn't missed me for a heartbeat.

I stared at him, feeling like a sleepwalker waking up in entirely the wrong spot, at entirely the wrong moment.

He hadn't missed me?

Four days. Four nights. I *had* been gone all that time, and yet ...

'Em?' Lyn said, a whiff of concern to her voice now. 'Are you alright?'

Creon slowly rose to his feet, eyes narrowing on my face as his demon senses became aware of my raging bewilderment. On the edges of my sight, I could see the others turning towards me, bags and maps lowering to the ground, and still I didn't manage to pull my gaze away from him – from the unhurried looseness of his muscular shoulders, the nonchalant curve of his wings. From the flawless, gorgeous *wrongness* of it.

Four nights.

It *had* been four nights, hadn't it?

'How long ...' I staggered two measly steps forward, then thought better of it. The earth was swaying beneath my feet. 'How long have I been gone for you?'

Lyn blinked at me as if I'd started speaking Faerie. 'What?'

'How long?' My voice cracked. 'Since I walked into the temple – how much time—'

'Some twenty minutes.' Lyn glanced at Tared, who shrugged with a slightly helpless grimace, as if to say he didn't have anything more sensible to add, either. 'What is it, Em? And where did you get yourself that wet, if—'

My knees buckled.

Creon shot forward before Lyn cried out her warning. Two slapping wingbeats and his calloused fingers wrapped around my elbow, hauling me upright before I could collapse completely – warm, strong fingers, a touch that radiated through my skin and into the marrow of my bones.

A touch I'd missed like hell during all those sleepless nights, and yet ... twenty minutes. Like a fever dream. As if I'd fallen asleep below that tree and spun myself a story of goddesses and dragons, of spring skies and doves.

But my dress was still wet from the creek. The aftertaste of carrots and parsley lingered on my tongue. And my magic ...

My magic.

Reflexively, I grabbed for Creon's wing, barely registering the way he stiffened as the fingers of my left hand brushed over that sensitive velvet surface. *Softness for movement.* I may have gone mad, but magic didn't lie. If I had made that oath, if I had moved that mug, shouldn't I be able to repeat the trick?

Power tingled up my fingers. I swung my right hand without thought, aiming for the nearest bag that lay beside the path.

With a dull thud, the bag bounced ten feet away from me, then tumbled sideways into the grass.

Deafening silence greeted me.

'It's a different sort of colour,' I breathed. My tongue seemed to move all on its own; the words poured out without rhyme or reason as my mind finally caved in. 'It's all about surfaces – it's all about light – but she wouldn't tell me at first. For four days. But the sky was all wrong, because time isn't linear in the forest, and—'

Creon swept me into his arms without waiting for that scrambled sentence to end, striding to the side of the courtyard. The musky scent of his body rolled over me, and every last word abruptly dried up as my body recognised the unspoken reassurance of his hold – *you're safe. I'm here. I'll die before I let anyone hurt you.*

I slumped against his chest. I could no longer think of anything else to do.

'Bey?' Tared was saying, his voice too business-like for my crumbling mind. 'Could you and Naxi go take a look on Tolya? We'll follow as soon as possible. Let us know if the situation gets urgent.'

I didn't hear a confirmation from either of them, but by the time Creon lowered me down onto the temple's marble porch, they were both gone. I stammered an apology, or maybe another attempt at explanation. The words turned to meaningless mush on my lips.

Em. Creon knelt before me, dark eyes scanning my face with that razor-sharp focus of a soldier about to face battle. *Breathe.*

I gulped in a lungful of air, and another one. My chest hurt like hellfire. More than anything, I wanted to crawl into his arms and bury my face in his chest until I could wrap my mind around these mad games of space and time ... but Lyn came trotting towards us with eyes that were making powerful attempts to escape their sockets, and Tared followed close behind, a leather travelling flask in his hand.

He did not look happy.

Alarm flared through me, and Creon's hand stiffened halfway to my knee. His wings shifted slightly, hiding his signs from the audience behind him. *Cactus* ...

The exhausted look in his eyes said enough – was this really the moment to worry about the opinions of angry alves?

'We talked about this,' I managed on a choked whisper. Five nights ago – an eternity ago – and yet for him it had to be mere hours. 'Not here. Not now. Please.'

A shadow seemed to cross his face, but he nodded, folding in his wing again. If not for the small twitch at his sharp jaw, I may have thought him in full agreement. Now that minuscule hint cracking through his polished shield of indifference told me an entirely different story – that it took every little bit of self-restraint not to jump up and pull me back into his embrace, where we both knew I wanted to be.

Perhaps I had underestimated just how much he despised this, having to be some stone-hearted murderer when what I needed was the opposite. Zera's voice drifted back into my mind – *Love doesn't like to be taken for granted* ...

Is that what I'm doing? I almost blurted out, the words aching on my lips now that he was suddenly right before me again, every inch the male I loved. *Taking you for granted? Testing your devotion too much with these stupid fears of mine?* But I was going to tell Tared, I really was. Just not when he was looking like this, thoughts of blades sharpening his every glance at Creon, not when it may be minutes until we were dragged into battle.

This wasn't the moment for even more ill-timed doubts. Once this mission was over and we could return to the Underground, there would be more time to talk.

So I swallowed my questions and said, 'I'm fine,' which was a lie, but at least a constructive one. My smile at Lyn felt weak and watery; she didn't look reassured in the slightest. 'Just ... just a lot to take in at once.'

'Here,' Tared said, chucking the leather flask into my lap before he sank down on the porch beside me. 'Might help. Unless you didn't eat anything for those four days, in which case honey mead may not be the best place to start.'

I managed a chuckle and pulled the cork from the bottle. The pungent smell of liquor made my eyes tear up, and my small sip scorched its way down my throat like a mouthful of burning oil. But my shoulders relaxed even as my stomach objected, and some of the whirlwind in my mind died down at the shock of that vile, fiery taste.

I handed the flask back to him and buried my face in my hands, trying to figure out where to start. *I nearly died. I drank a goddess's blood. I saw your deepest fears and hurts – of each and every one of you.*

Maybe not there.

'Should we conclude that you found her, Em?' Lyn said, her voice too high. 'Zera?'

'It was the tree at the heart of the temple.' I didn't lift my head from my palms. Stringing four days of memories into comprehensible sentences was enough of a challenge already. 'It split open – became a portal to her. The forest is hiding her, you see, keeping her alive even though she lost her magic, so ...'

'And what was the thing about time?'

It took three jumbled attempts to clarify the thing about time, and several more cautious questions to pull the rest of the story from me – the refusals, the bag, the godsworn magic. I didn't tell them about the doves. Didn't bring up any of what Zera had taught me about my own motivations, about my parents and their mistakes, about choosing between people you love. The only person who would hear that part of the story was Creon – but later, when the battles had been fought and everyone else had vanished.

'So you can ... bind people?' Lyn finally concluded, and there was a caution to her young voice that made my heart squeeze in unpleasant ways. Zera hadn't been the only one who disliked the power in any hands, even in mine.

'Technically,' I muttered.

'Good gods.' She rubbed a stubborn curl from her eyes and repeated, more breathlessly now, 'Good gods.'

'Well,' Tared said, with a chuckle that couldn't conceal the slight feebleness below the word, 'it's more or less what we were aiming for, isn't it?'

More or less – except that none of them had known, or even suspected, that it would take magic this powerful to stand a chance of destroying the Mother's bindings. I glanced at Creon, who had barely signed a single word so far – afraid, for a moment, that even his expression would suddenly reveal that unwilling edge of caution.

But the smile with which he studied me, sitting cross-legged in the grass, rather glowed with ... *pride*?

'What are you thinking?' I said weakly.

He shrugged, smile quirking into an unburdened expression of satisfaction. *Wondering if you'd beat me in a duel.*

Even my doubts faltered in surprise. 'What?'

'Is your invincible track record really the point of importance here, Hytherion?' Tared snapped – some of that sharpness probably thanks to his own defeat at Creon's hands, which had to be a fresh wound of the previous day for him. 'We're dealing with powers none of us have ever dealt with before here, and—'

I spent centuries dealing with powers no one has dealt with before, Creon interrupted him with a shrug. *You're both worrying about the wrong things. If a damn goddess trusted Em with this magic, then why exactly are you doubting that decision? Even I'm not that much of a heathen.*

A snort-like laugh escaped me. Signs aimed at the other two, but I knew they'd been meant for me just as much – *stop doubting yourself.*

It worked ridiculously well.

'And the right thing to worry about,' Tared said, acid in his voice, 'is, according to you, whether you'll get your fun duelling godsworn mages?'

No. Creon's smile was like a dagger, ready to slice through skin and muscle. *The real question is if we're going to keep those nymphs on Tolya alive. Or if we'll ever get ourselves deep enough into the Crimson Court to throw the Mother off her throne. Which is going to be significantly easier if the most powerful mage on our side isn't bound, if I need to remind you.*

Which made sense – enough sense to make even Tared grumble a few words of unwilling agreement – and yet I doubted whether the greater good was the first thing on Creon's mind here. There had been too much wicked amusement in his smile at the thought of me besting him. Centuries of dealing with unmatched powers ... and now who knew what I might be able to do?

And just like that, apprehension turned to excitement, the dark road ahead suddenly a realm of unexplored possibilities. Damn him and his demon eyes; he'd managed it again.

'I'm nowhere near winning any battles,' I said, straightening my shoulders as I turned to face the other two. Time for a little diplomacy. 'Or binding or unbinding anyone, for that matter. I've barely figured out how to move something, and I've never tried to use the other two types of magic, because Zera wouldn't let me possess her chickens. So ...'

Tared chuckled – a joyless chuckle, but enough for the circumstances. 'Disappointing.'

'Oh, don't worry, Em,' Lyn said, waving some invisible concerns aside with a brave attempt at a smile. Thank the gods. 'Of course we'll help you figure it out. It's just ...'

Just that I was now wielding the same powers that had taken her freedom, her fertility, and her friends' lives. I grimaced and said, 'I know.'

'Yes.' She groaned a sigh, running her chubby fingers through her wild red curls. 'Hell take us all, and I thought this morning couldn't get any wilder. So what do we do now? Do you think you can manage Tolya in this state?'

A question that would be easier to handle if I had the faintest idea of what was waiting for us – a few innocent skirmishes or a full-blown battle of the sort we'd barely survived at the Golden Court? I glanced at Creon, who raised an eyebrow in return, the question obvious in that one little gesture.

What did I want?

'Are you coming?' I said slowly.

His scarred fingers tensed a fraction. *Depends how much we can afford to anger the nymphs.*

'I prefer their anger over their deaths,' Tared said. It was no longer just curtness in his voice, that cold distaste that had brewed there for months. This was outright lust for murder, kept in check only by the thinnest veneer of civilisation and self-restraint. 'Your pretty face may lose us Tolya, but if they survive, at least we still have a chance to mobilise the rest of the world. So if it's not too far beneath your station ...'

'Tared,' Lyn grumbled, gaze shooting between the two of them.

I braced myself for Creon's explosive reaction, but it didn't come – nothing but a look of mild pity at Tared and a resigned shrug at me. *Looks like I'll be there.*

I drew in a deep breath, granting myself a glance at the temple wings around us, the forest stretching towards the horizon below the hill. We were done here. *I* was done. And as hard as it was to wrap my head around that thought ... Would Zera really want me to loiter for another week while an island full of innocent nymphs was about to be slaughtered?

'Give me a moment to see if I can get that magic under control,' I said weakly, gesturing at the fallen bag. 'An hour, maybe? Then I'll come with you.'

'Alright.' Lyn jumped up, all breathless agitation. 'We can wait a little, if Beyla is keeping an eye on things. Tared, I want to go take a look at that tree – coming with me?'

He looked like he was about to object – something about Creon, doubtlessly, and about my fragile state and that fae bastard laying hands on me once too often already this morning. But Lyn scowled – *don't start that shit again,* that look said – and he got to his feet with nothing but a muffled curse and a nod.

I watched the two of them walk off in silence, Tared's strides long and tense, Lyn jumping over every loose branch and rock. Creon moved only when they'd both disappeared through the broad temple gate, offering me his left hand as he gracefully rose to his feet.

'I take it you apologised to Lyn?' I said, wrapping my fingers around his.

He grimaced but nodded as he pulled me to my feet.

'What did she say?'

That she'd tie my wings in a knot if I ever tried something similar again, he signed wryly, *but that she'd probably forgive me for your sake this time.*

I managed a laugh. 'Tell her she'd have to get in line.'

Already did. His lips trembled. *I'll behave, Em. No more stupid letters. Can't start pissing off godsworn mages, after all.*

The spark of amusement in his eyes was unmistakable, but something far more profound brimmed beneath that emotion – another glimpse of almost reverent satisfaction, as if *I* was the goddess at the heart of this story. My lips faltered halfway to the retort I'd been planning to utter, words sputtering out on my tongue under that gaze.

He released my hand to slip his fingers around my waist instead. Golden warmth radiated through me, a perfect comfort, a smouldering temptation. I swallowed, threw a look at the empty temple gate, and breathed, 'What if Tared—'

Tared, his lips said, *can go fuck himself.*

'But if he fades back and—'

Creon hooked his left arm around my waist, pulled me flush against him, cupped my cheek with his free hand. His thumb drew a gentle line along the curve of my bottom lip, and the air abruptly eddied from my lungs, taking the last of my feeble objections with it. Gods help me, the way his lips parted in a slow invitation ...

Lyn knew what she was doing, didn't she? She wouldn't send Tared back to the courtyard within a minute?

'I missed you,' I heard myself whisper, tilting my head back, bringing my lips inches away from his. 'Missed you so damn much.'

A small smile quirked his lips as he slid his hand around my nape. *Missed you too, Em.*

I let out a breathless laugh. 'Wasn't it less than half an hour for you?'

So? he mouthed, and kissed me.

His lips were warm and perfectly soft, enveloping mine with a certainty that made me forget about wars and petty squabbles for a long, blissful heartbeat. His fingers dug into the back of my neck, nudging me to surrender. His hand in the small of my back lowered along my spine, clawing into my bottom. I moaned, and his wings shuddered behind his shoulders.

Welcome back, that kiss said. And *I'm proud of you.* And *I'm in awe of you.* And – clearest of all in his twinkling eyes when he finally broke away – *That duel is going to happen soon.*

That duel that I might not even lose.

I breathed a laugh, resting both my hands against his muscular chest to steady myself. 'You're really not intimidated at all, are you?'

You're a hypocrite, cactus, he dryly signed, letting go of my neck. *Don't pretend you've ever been terribly intimidated by me.*

'Well …' I bit my lip, considering that unexpected argument. 'You were somewhat frightening at times. At the start.'

He raised an eyebrow. *You mean those days when you couldn't look at me without wanting to jump into my trousers?*

'You weren't supposed to notice that,' I said, sniffing haughtily, 'and I never said it wasn't a rather alluring sort of frightening.'

He chuckled. *There's your answer.*

I blinked at him. He pressed a last kiss to my forehead, then gently pulled my hands from his chest and stepped back, nodding for me to follow.

'You didn't just call *me* an alluring sort of frightening, did you?' I said, flouncing after him as he made his way back to the pile of bags at the centre of the temple garden.

Why not? He grinned at me. *I've rarely been so out of my depth as when you started demanding I get better at that thing called communication. Utterly terrifying. Made me want to lick you until you were screaming. What sort of softness do you think that movement magic of yours requires?*

'What sort of …' My voice had gone raw and husky; it took a physical effort to drag my thoughts away from the image his signs conjured up, bronze muscles and black wings between my thighs. 'Softness?'

His smile was impressively innocent. *Thought you wanted to practice your new magic?*

Oh. Softness. Movement. Nymphs in danger and divine powers to master. I sucked in a deep breath, a hopeless attempt to soothe the fire in my lower belly, and grumbled, 'Bastard.'

That shouldn't be news to you, he signed, looking far too content with himself. *Are we practicing your magic or not?*

I flung a blast of red at him, just for the hell of it. He avoided it with a lightning-quick turn, his shoulders shaking with laughter.

'Zera said ...' I rubbed my eyes, trying to reproduce the goddess's exact words. 'She said it's actually all about light reflections – because colours are really just reflections of light, apparently?'

The Thremian school will be happy to hear, Creon signed dryly. *They've been arguing that point for centuries.*

'There are arguments about this?'

Of course. Does an object change in colour if you put it under a red light? Philosophers have come close to bloody murder over that question. He grinned at my face. *Please continue.*

I shook my head, concluding not for the first time that I'd rather drown myself than ever end up a philosopher's apprentice. 'She said textures also cause different sorts of light reflections, which is why Etele could draw magic from that, too. So there's smoothness ...'

Which mirrors light, he finished, nodding as if that made perfect sense. *And softness should be surfaces with a more diffuse reflection, then?*

'I hate that you make it look self-evident,' I said, 'but yes. She said surfaces work better the more reflective they are.'

So velvet, which has an obvious gleam, works better than wool, which does not?

'Suppose so.' I pulled a face. 'We'll have to find out.'

Fascinating. Last time I'd seen him this enthralled by a theoretical question, it had been that damned blinking star of Kothro. *Let's try—Wait ...*

Yellow light blazed around me before I could blink. When I glanced down, my simple linen dress had changed into black velvet, falling loosely to my knees.

'This is a terrible model for velvet,' I said, pulling a face at him. 'You're making me look like a shiny bag of turnips. What should I try to move? I suggest something that isn't likely to hurt anyone or break anything.'

He sank down beside his own bag, pulled out a tightly folded coat, and chucked it onto the path before me. *Go ahead, my lovely turnip.*

I tried to magically fling his coat at his face.

My first attempt was an utter failure. The tightly woven cloth fluttered like a dying bird on the ground but didn't shift even the smallest inch closer to where Creon was sitting. Perhaps, I admitted, I should have taken a moment longer to see the soft gleam of my dress in my mind's eye, the way I instinctively imagined colours whenever I drew.

On my second attempt, the coat shot past Creon and ended up tangled in the branches of the plants that still obscured half of the eastern wall.

Typical, Creon signed, looking delighted.

I yanked the coat from the towering hedge and dropped it onto his head, then tried to change my dress back from that strange flat texture of drained softness to lush velvet. The black cloth should have provided plenty of colour, yet no matter how much yellow I swung at it, the texture of my dress wouldn't change.

'Creon?'

He was raking his long hair back into place, still chuckling lightly. *Yes?*

'What did you do to change my dress to velvet, exactly?'

With a minimal flick of his fingers, he swung another burst of yellow magic at me. The dress went back to unblemished velvet at once.

'That ...' I blinked at it. 'That's what I tried to do. Do you ... do you think it's like not being able to change colour?'

You mean you're no longer able to change texture with yellow magic now that texture has also become a source of magic for you?

'Because magic can't affect its own source,' I said blankly, repeating what he'd told me months ago. 'And you don't have texture magic, so it's no problem for you ... But that means we can produce almost infinite magic as long as we're together, doesn't it?'

So you'll have to spend more time with me? he signed dryly. *Such a shame.*

I magically yanked the coat from his hands – my best attempt yet.

Lyn and Tared returned after fifteen minutes of magical experimentation, announced a good thirty seconds in advance by Lyn's cheerful chatting echoing through the temple halls. If we'd been in a state of rumpled undress, we'd probably have had time to make ourselves decent before the two of them finally emerged from the high open gate. But as it happened, I was busy dragging Creon's ruined coat from a puddle of muddy water at the moment of their arrival; no effort was needed to make the scene look utterly unerotic.

Even Tared looked a fraction reassured at the sign of my progress – sufficient proof that we'd spent most of our unchaperoned time in a properly educative manner.

Lyn beamed at me as she hurried towards me and brightly said, 'We found you something, Em!'

'A goddess?' I suggested wryly.

She chuckled, pulling something from her loose trousers that looked far too sharp in the hands of a seven-year-old. It was a long, curved dagger, the blade a strange, black-veined steel, the hilt inlaid with gems and mother-of-pearl. 'A god-gift from one of the altars. Thought it might come in handy.'

In case I needed more weapons for Tolya? The point reached me only after a moment of owlish blinking – mother-of-pearl. *Iridescence for magic.*

'Oh!' I whirled around. 'Creon?'

Planning to bind me on the spot? The brightest of his laughter had melted off his face at Tared's arrival, but there was enough of it left in the twinkle of his eyes.

'Bold of you to presume I'd need it to beat you,' I said with a snort, and this time he did actually laugh. Tared looked mildly confused. 'No, I was thinking ... Iridescence fuels magic that affects magic, yes? Would it be possible to block the attacks of others with it?'

Probably. He shrugged. *The Mother is able to do it, at least. I'm just not fully sure how – she never told anyone about the details of her divine powers.*

I glanced at the dagger in my hand. 'Would she have had access to an iridescent surface on those occasions?'

A wry smile grew around his lips. *I'm suspecting there might be more to her favourite pearl necklace than I always assumed.*

'Oh, fuck,' Lyn said breathlessly. 'That enormous, ugly thing she was wearing after the Last Battle? When she bound us?'

Creon nodded.

She blew out her cheeks, looking slightly sick. 'If we'd known we only had to get those pearls away from her ...'

He shrugged. *I know.*

Of course that whirlwind mind of his had already identified a thousand occasions where he might have saved the world by just yanking a few velvet pillows from his mother's reach. I saw the grim tightening of his lips, heard Tared's muffled curse, and quickly said, 'Should I make an attempt, then?'

Creon raised an amused eyebrow. *At binding me?*

'I was just hoping to block a bit of your red, but if you insist you'd rather lose all your magic ...'

He huffed a silent laugh and pulled one of his own daggers from his boot. As he threw it five yards away into the earth, he signed, *I'll try to hit it. Stop me.*

The blade was forged of alf steel, which meant he wouldn't damage it even if I failed to divert the magic – clever, I had to admit, but a mild blow to my confidence, too.

'Alright.' I sucked in a deep breath, clutching my fingers tighter around the temple dagger. *Iridescence.* Bubbles of soap, the pearls I'd stitched onto Miss Matilda's dresses, the light reflecting off the dark walls of the Underground ... The familiar tingle of magic trickled up my arm, and I nodded. 'I'm ready.'

Creon raised his hand more slowly than usual, allowing me just a moment longer to prepare. Then he unleashed his magic, and so did I – two flashes of light that met inches away from the alf steel blade and sprung apart with an audible sizzle and a blinding flash.

His burst of red deflected and slammed into the garden tile next to the knife, digging a deep crack into the flagstone.

I dropped my dagger with a ragged cry of triumph.

Could have been worse, Creon dryly signed.

I burst out laughing. 'It actually works!'

Of course it does. The look in his eyes was not nearly so unconcerned as his signs – that gleam of unending possibilities again, of a power that may just turn our world upside down. *Again?*

I glanced down at the dagger. The mother-of-pearl layer had gone a boring greyish white; only at very specific angles did the light still reflect in faint rainbows. I might be able to pull one more attempt from it, but even that could be a challenge.

'Let's get the movement magic right first,' I said, grabbing his soaked coat again. 'There's only so many new skills I can figure out in a day.'

So we practiced another five, ten, fifteen times, experimenting with the force of my magic and with the weight of whatever objects I moved, until I finally began to get some sense of what this new power of mine could do. It was like stumbling around with sleeping limbs, an utter lack of control over my own body – a sensation I'd quickly forgotten after those first disorienting days of lessons at the Crimson Court.

Unsubtle, Creon signed as I launched a woollen blanket roll into a nearby tree for the third time. *You'll learn to climb trees before you learn to handle this magic if you continue like this.*

'You,' I said, sending him an impolite gesture, 'will very quickly learn to keep your arrogant mouth shut if you continue like this.'

His grin turned positively villainous. *Threatening me now, Thenessa?*

'Not at all.' I yanked the blanket down from the branches. 'Just encouraging you to make better choices in life.'

He chuckled and changed my dress back to soft velvet once again. *Which has never been my greatest strength, admittedly.*

Sitting in the sun by the temple walls, Tared no longer even pretended he was paying attention to the sword he was supposedly sharpening. Instead, he observed Creon and me with ever-increasing confusion as we swung coats back and forth, his frown deepening with every playful jab and every honest chuckle.

Hell, even *I* barely dared to believe the number of smiles escaping Creon's mask in those sun-streaked minutes. For someone who'd only ever seen the cold, arrogant fae murderer, it had to look like a whole new person had risen from my lover's bed this morning.

I shouldn't be hoping so soon ... but for Creon, it had been mere hours since we'd sat by that fire and talked. Had he actually listened when I'd told him it was his own behaviour that made me so desperate to keep our secrets? If he'd understood and decided to change his own ways at least a little ...

I was still pondering the consequences when Beyla appeared out of nowhere in the sprawling garden, one sword in her hand, the other still on her back.

'Fae seem to be preparing.' She snapped the words at no one in particular, although they came out vaguely in my direction. 'If you still want to save our arses, don't wait too long. Nymphs are in hysterics. We're on the south side of the island.'

Tared and Creon had jumped up at her first appearance, ready to ask questions. But she was gone before anyone could utter a word, back to the nymphs and their hysterics, leaving nothing but ringing alarm in her wake.

CHAPTER 22

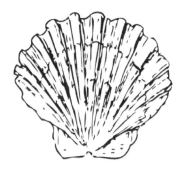

THE ISLE OF TOLYA looked like a dream.

When the blur of Tared's fading dissolved and the world took clear shape around us again, we stood on a pearly white beach, bordered by a dense forest. Vines hung from the trees like festive garlands, with bright blue and red flowers blooming between the vibrant green. The beach itself was strewn with pastel-coloured shells, glinting at me wherever I looked, and on our other side, the water gently lapped the shore, bright turquoise darkening to a nearly violet indigo where the ocean deepened.

But there, on the horizon, where deep blue sea met the puffy autumn clouds ...

I knew those slender vessels, the stilted wooden wings along the hulls, the sunlight reflecting off the bronze plates on the bow. They'd shown up on Cathra twice a year to take our harvests and leave fear and hunger in exchange – fae ships, looming like predators about to strike.

My throat went dry. I could see two of them from this side of the island. Doubtlessly there were more of them around the bends of the narrow beach, half a dozen if we were unlucky.

'Fuckers,' Lyn grumbled next to me, scowling at the distant shapes in a way that suggested she'd gladly burn a few cracks into the hulls.

Creon had gone icily still while we hastily grabbed our bags, and there was not a trace of a smile left in his expression as he let go of my arm and turned to Tared. *Can you make out the symbol on the sails?*

I could barely make out the sails themselves, but Tared shrugged and said, 'Looks like a sun of sorts.'

Iorgas, Creon spelled, pursing his lips. *Always a pleasure.*

The name sparked a vague memory. 'Was he the one who had an unregistered halfblood child and was forced to kill all his children?'

'The same one,' Tared said grimly. 'Don't suppose he's gotten any more pleasant over it.'

Creon's mirthless chuckle spoke volumes, but he turned his back on the fleet without wasting another word on Iorgas and his unlucky offspring. With an absent nod at the forest, he signed, *Think it's better if I don't show up uninvited.*

Lyn muttered a curse but trudged to the woodline and bent over to whisper something to a twisting strand of ivy. A gentle breeze picked up, and the rustling of the foliage grew louder, then swiftly died away in the distance, deeper into the woods.

We didn't need to wait long.

Without warning, the curtains of tangled vines were swept aside and a small female strode out onto the beach, followed by a cacophony of vehement hisses and anxious squeals from the shrubbery behind her. She was dark-skinned and red-haired, dressed in sparkling chiffon that hid very little of her lithe body from view. Two curved horns rose from the wild cascade of her hair, and her nails curled into dark claws of the same smooth black material – nails that looked more than ready to scratch a few eyes out if we made the mistake of stepping within reach.

Her eyes were an unnerving, pupil-less green, the irises sparkling like minerals. They fixed upon us with searing intensity as she came to a standstill and jutted up her chin, her thin lips curling back to reveal small shark's teeth.

'What for the goddess's sake is this?' she snapped in fluent Alvish, although with a thick, melodious accent. 'Decided to speed up our impending death a little, Phiramelyndra? Or is this piece of filth the *help* that our little demon traitor swore you'd send here to save our hides?'

'Offended three people in two sentences,' Tared said, sticking his hands into his pockets with a joyless grin at her. 'I'm impressed.'

'And don't even get me started on *your* bloody people, Thorgedson,' she spat, ignoring his remark entirely. 'If not for all this senseless shouting about rebellion, none of us would be dying now – could you not have thought of that before this useless attempt to rescue what can't be rescued?'

He sighed. 'Helenka ...'

'And *you*.' She whirled around to Creon, her emerald eyes blazing brighter. 'Here to see what'll be yours once you steal that fucking crown? You may have convinced these desperate fools of your noble intentions, but—'

'*Helenka*,' Tared interrupted.

'He's not setting a foot on my lands.' She was trembling from head to toe, but she held Creon's gaze without flinching and didn't back down even as the chorus of fearful laments behind her swelled to a shrill pitch – the clearest proof I'd ever seen that fear and cowardice were different things. 'And neither is his little whore. Get rid of them and I *might*—'

'They might save your people's lives,' Tared said sharply. His jaw had clenched at the *little whore*; if I hadn't felt so guilty for lying to him, I would have appreciated the coolness in his voice. 'Think of them before you burn any bridges. Please.'

Helenka scoffed, tossing her red-golden hair over her thin shoulders. 'It doesn't even matter anymore, Thorgedson. Even if they manage to ward off that fleet, the fight will destroy our trees and soil. The island is about to turn into a graveyard regardless. You're too late. Admit it.'

Nymph trees – as close as family members and revered as holy life. I tried to imagine Iorgas and his men making landfall here, red magic flashing everywhere ... Even though I hadn't noticed Helenka's individual grief when I lifted Zera's bag, even though it was guesswork to figure out what was going on in her mind, it took me very little effort to understand her fears at this particular moment. If she was who I thought she was, Creon had killed her predecessor. All she knew about me was what the Mother's envoys had told her. And her forest – the forest that formed the heart and soul of her people – was about to be irreparably maimed.

No sense in arguing against that. There was too much hurt here for arguing. The only way to solve that ...

I barely heard Tared's agitated reply as my gaze swerved back to the indigo horizon, to the spine-chilling shapes of the ships that lay waiting for destruction.

'We could move the battle,' I said quietly.

Helenka and Tared didn't hear me, engrossed in their heated discussion. But Lyn spun around to face me, and Creon raised a scarred eyebrow – the first sign of human emotion he'd shown since our arrival on the island.

'They want me, don't they?' The plan shaped itself as I spoke. 'And Creon, I presume. More than they want to kill a bunch of nymphs they only picked as an arbitrary example anyway. If they were to see us fly by ... Don't you think the main force of their army would go after us instead of attacking the island?'

I didn't need to elaborate. There was something delightfully ominous to the smile that curled around Creon's lips, a glimmer of that ruthless, dangerous intent that always lingered just below the surface of him. *Interesting thought. They probably would.*

'Don't be ridiculous,' Lyn hissed, throwing him a furious glare. 'You've barely recovered from your time with Zera, Em. You're in no state to take on an entire army.'

'I do have some new magic to help me out, though.' I glanced at the sand around my boots. The pastel blue shells were all covered in smooth mother-of-pearl on the inside, a perfect iridescent surface. 'Excellent motivation to develop a steep learning curve.'

Creon's smile broadened to a grin of wicked bloodlust; I suspected he may have burst out laughing if not for Helenka's presence. *Your father is going to kill me, cactus.*

'What is that last sign?' Lyn said, narrowing her eyes at his fingers.

'Long story,' I said hastily, because the glint of amusement in Creon's eyes suggested he was about to make some outrageous claims I didn't want ending up anywhere near Tared. 'Look, I know it's a risk, but it might solve the problem, yes? It's only ...'

The two of us against a full army? Creon finished helpfully.

I pulled a face. 'Yes?'

The way he bit back his laughter could have sent me swooning into his arms. *Yes, that sounds pretty doable.*

'Oh, for fuck's sake,' Lyn burst out, loud enough for Tared and Helenka to finally pause their sharp discussion of lives and principles. 'Don't be idiots. This would be an extraordinarily bad moment to lose you, Em.'

'Beg your pardon?' Tared said.

'She wants to use herself as bait,' Lyn snapped. 'We really can't take that risk! I know it's an unpleasant situation, but sending an entire fae fleet after our only ... our only unbound mage ...'

Unbound. Not *godsworn.* The small hesitation in her tirade told me enough: that she didn't dare trust Helenka with that information yet.

Tared's glare at Creon told me the blame for this madness had already been allotted. 'Yes. That sounds rather reckless.'

'Less reckless for me than for anyone else,' I said briskly.

He turned to me with a look in his grey eyes that I knew all too well – the same look of tired resignation he'd given me when he told me he'd come along rather than stop me from venturing onto the continent. He wasn't going to chain me to the trees. He just wasn't going to be happy about it, either. 'And I suppose that plan would be executed by you and our princeling here?'

Princeling. I ignored that sting. 'Consider it from the bright side – I doubt he'll have time to ogle my ankles while we're slapping the fae off ourselves.'

Lyn may still have been furious with Creon, but she huffed a laugh at that. Tared just gave me another mildly exhausted look.

'And what's the alternative?' I added, shrugging at him. 'Do you want him to fly *you* to those ships instead? I doubt Iorgas and his men would shove aside their mission just to catch you, even if there were no other objections to that plan.'

By the flash of pure horror on Tared's face, there were indeed objections to that plan, the first of which was the fact he'd have to spend a full flight cosied up in Creon's arms. 'Couldn't he go on his own? I suppose the Mother wants to get her hands on him almost as much as she's looking for you.'

Glad to see so much faith in me, Creon signed, *but my magic is still bound. I doubt I'd survive.*

'And wouldn't that be a fucking shame?' Tared muttered.

'*Tared*,' Lyn snapped.

I risked a glance at Helenka, who had frozen where she stood, eyes still menacingly bright but shoulders sagging. For the first time, her desperate fury seemed to be wavering. In its place had arrived something far more vulnerable – something that might become a flicker of hope if we were very damn lucky.

We hadn't lost her alliance, that single glance told me – not yet. But we were close, and now that a solution had been mentioned that could save her trees and people, we'd alienate her once and for all by weaselling our way out of it.

I glanced at Creon, who smiled and pulled a strap of leather from his pocket to pointedly bind back his hair.

'Does anyone have any better ideas, then?' I said, making my decision in the blink of an eye.

'Inika have mercy,' Lyn muttered under her breath, which was more than enough of a reply. 'Do you at least have a *plan*, if you insist on going through with this madness?'

I didn't, or at least not in the sharply drawn, meticulously scheduled way I supposed she was looking for; my thoughts hadn't jumped much farther than a vague idea to swiftly work out the applications of iridescent magic and somehow nullify all magic my opponents would try to use.

'I suppose we could start with one ship.' I fell to my knees in the sand, shook my travelling bag from my shoulders, and began gathering shells. 'Do we have the time to take them on one by one?'

'If we're very lucky, yes,' Helenka said sharply, breaking her silence, 'and what in the world are you doing with those shells, girl?'

'Preparing.' I gathered my loot into a little pile and looked up at Creon, who'd just tucked the last loose strands into his bun. 'How many fae do you expect per ship?'

Forty or so. He looked not at all deterred by that number. *So one crew should be manageable. If our dear alf friends could arrange a little distraction in the meantime, so the others don't all attack us at once ...*

'Can't say I'd be glad to,' Tared said grimly, 'but will do.'

'Greatly appreciated,' I quickly said, just in case Creon was planning to be more unpleasant in his reply. 'Alright, then we'll take care of one ship first and see what we can do with the others after that is done. If anyone tries to attack the island in the meantime, I'll make sure to show my face and hopefully lure them away again. Is everybody happy with that?'

Happy, it turned out, was too ambitious a term; by the looks on their faces, they quite regretted bringing me here in the first place. But Tared nodded, Lyn muttered an unwilling confirmation, and even Helenka looked slightly less inclined to set those claw-like nails into my eyes.

The nymphs hiding in the forest behind her had gone dead quiet, or maybe they'd fled the sight of the smile lingering on Creon's lips – that strangely seductive smile of bloodlust that was entirely the Silent Death's. Gone was the laughing, teasing creature of a few minutes ago. The air around him had gone sharp with anticipation, an energy like the pressure of lightning about to strike.

Hell, I'd missed him. I'd missed *this* – the intoxicating thrill of diving headfirst into danger and doing it well, of dancing right along that exhilarating edge between recklessness and brilliance. Which did sound like madness, admittedly, and then again ...

Even if I was untrained, the fae fleet wasn't prepared for godsworn magic. I would have the Silent Death himself by my side. And as long as Creon thought we'd survive the endeavour, who was I to doubt him?

'Time to get to work, then?' I said, rising, and it took an effort to suppress the heady grin that bubbled up in me.

Helenka was already moving back to the forest, never taking her watchful eyes off Creon's tall figure until she reached the wall of flowering vines. Tared took two steps after her, then turned back to Creon one last time and hissed, 'If anything happens to her, I might just kill you, Hytherion.'

Creon looked faintly amused. *If anything happens to her, I'm afraid you'll be too late for the honour.*

Tared's cold glance suggested he didn't have much faith in that promise, but he restricted himself to a tight-lipped nod and a curt, 'Stay safe, Em.'

'Idiots,' Lyn muttered, sounding close to tears as she tottered after him and Helenka.

Then all three of them were gone, swallowed by the dense greenery of the nymph trees, and we were left alone on an apparently empty beach, nothing but two miles of indigo sea left between us and the warships on the horizon.

Creon turned towards me, and I knew from the look in his eyes that there would be no fleeing for our targets – that I'd unleashed the predator slumbering under his skin, and that nothing but the taste of blood would rein him in again.

'I'm going to need one of your coats,' I said.

His gaze flicked down to the small heap of shells at my feet. *Pockets?*

'Yes. As many as you can get.'

The coat he pulled from the bottom of his bag reached to halfway down my thigh, inches above the hem of my dress; it was black and tightly-woven and had pockets *everywhere*. I tucked the ammunition I'd gathered into one of them, then scurried around the beach to collect even more, selecting only the shells with an unblemished layer of mother-of-pearl on the inside.

Creon stood in the surf while I made my rounds, an obsidian silhouette against the background of blue sky and woolly white clouds – turning his knife around and around between his scarred fingers, watching the ships with that cold, calculating gaze of looming death. When I finally joined him, my pockets were so full of shells that my shadow showed odd bulges on every side of my silhouette and I couldn't take a single step without hearing the faint tinkling of chalk against chalk.

'What are you thinking?' I muttered, keeping half a wingspan between our bodies just in case anyone was watching us. I'd be disappointed in Helenka if she hadn't left any spies between the trees.

He finally tore his gaze away from his targets, knife stilling in his left hand. *Don't think we should start by sinking them.* His gestures were swift, the way he signed when his fingers had trouble keeping up with his spinning mind. *It would leave us without a place to stand, and fighting in flight is a challenge when you're severely outnumbered.*

'Right,' I said, biting my cheek. 'Too many dimensions to get surrounded.'

A grin slid over his face. *Yes.*

'So what do we do? Land on the deck, get rid of the crew, and *then* cut a hole in the bottom?'

Sounds like a plan. He knelt and slid his knife into his boot, where two others were already cleverly hidden in their sheaths; three more hung at his belt, and I knew his sleeves contained a blade or two as well. *How much faith do you have in your iridescent magic?*

'Faith is too big a word,' I said wryly, 'but I'll probably get the hang of it if I need to.'

Probably. He did not look at all disconcerted; if anything, that was a deadly sort of amusement gleaming in his eyes. *Are we ready, then?*

I wasn't ready, of course. This entire plan was nothing but a desperate leap of faith. My magic was a gamble. Once again, I was doing this only because *someone* had to do it, and no pile of pastel shells could change the fact that every single soul on that ship would be vying to kill me from the moment they saw my face.

But I'd been there before, and the Golden Court had taught me none of that mattered much as long as I could pretend I was fully prepared for the madness.

'Ready,' I said, and it felt almost true.

With the smallest smile, Creon held out a hand to me. Perhaps I jumped into his arms a little too enthusiastically; a gasp or two rose from the foliage.

Nymph spies, indeed.

But Creon's wings swept out wide, the solid earth sank away beneath us, and we soared into the open skies, leaving Tolya and its watching eyes behind.

It had been ages since we'd flown together. I'd forgotten how that particular combination of fright and excitement felt, the perfect safety of his arms contrasting sharply with the sensation of my stomach slamming into my throat at every sudden descent. We soared just over the surface of the waves, the wind whipping through my hair and carrying that briny tang of the sea I knew so well – towards the first of those ships that looked almost equally familiar, and far less comforting.

I'd learned to recognise them as omens of death before I could speak in full sentences. There was a grim kind of justice to it now, sneaking up on them with magic brimming under my fingertips.

We were close enough to hear the billowing of the sails when the first cry of warning rose from the ship.

Two winged silhouettes launched from the deck a moment later, surging towards us with blades gleaming in their hands. The same bastards collecting human tributes, I reminded myself at the flash of doubt that rose with the memory of Zera's bag, the kind of fae who would happily burn down an innocent nymph isle to make the Mother's points ... Reasons didn't make them harmless. My fingers wrapped themselves around Creon's dark sleeve, hungry for red. Just a few more seconds. Just a few feet closer ...

I knew the exact moment they recognised the male carrying me. In a flash, their triumphant approach faltered, their swords sagged – and my magic bloomed bright and crimson in the air between us, cutting a clean slash through the wing of the nearest fae warrior.

He plunged towards the sea, his cry of pain smothered immediately by the icy water.

His companion got a single shout of alarm over his lips. Then Creon's wings slapped against the air behind me and we shot forward; I fired my next bolt of red the same moment. The second fae went down, shrieking all the way until he hit the waves with a painful-sounding splash.

'They may just realise something's wrong, now,' I said, peering at the ship while I flexed and unflexed my fingers.

Creon chuckled against the crown of my head, his wingbeats accelerating. We tore through the open skies so fast I could barely breathe against the wind slamming into my face; the muscles of his shoulders rolled in the rhythm of his flight, every inch of his body straining with pent-up tension. Closer and closer to the copper-plated ship we soared, close enough now to distinguish the sun symbol Tared had already noticed, close enough to make out the ropes and the lines and the handful of fae sprinting around the deck in sudden alarm ...

A voice shouted, '*Hytherion!*'

'They've noticed,' I concluded dryly.

Creon laughed again and dove at the ship. Red magic flashed towards us. He whirled aside with a lightning-quick slap of his wings, avoiding the attack without slowing down; again a burst of scarlet lit up the sky, and with the speed and grace of a trained dancer, he darted out of its way. More fae were pouring onto the deck now, more voices shouting for help. A handful of them came flying towards us, their barely contained bloodlust visible even from dozens of feet away.

I swallowed a sting of fear and fired three quick, sharp attacks at the easy target of their wings. Two avoided my magic. One went down, still flinging red at us as he fell. Creon spun away from another bolt of destructive magic, and this time the flash of light only barely missed us.

His arm under my knees didn't budge, but the one he'd curled around my torso shifted so his fingers could tap against one of my bulging pockets. Shells tinkled in reply.

'Alright,' I whispered breathlessly, grabbing for the smooth mother-of-pearl. 'I'll try.'

He kissed the crown of my head, then shot towards the boat again, straight through the swarm of armed fae separating us from the safety of the deck. Red blazed around us and I swung wildly, an instinctive reflex of *please don't let me die* rather than any deliberate application of the magic I pulled from the shells under my fingers.

Beams of ruby red exploded into sparks. We flew through a firestorm of destruction, magic dwindling and sizzling out around us. The flickers of red left pinpricks of pain on my face and hands before they died away – not enough to draw blood, but enough to know I could have gone about this better. Did I need more iridescence? But no, explosions had always been a sign of too much power ... Perhaps I'd be wiser to hold back a little?

I barely had time to finish the thought before the next attack lit up the air around us. I drew on instinct, this strange new power just familiar enough to cling to reflexes I'd ingrained deep into my bones for months. Not the brightly lit iridescence I'd drawn before, with rainbows blooming everywhere in the surface, but a softer, milder sort, like the dark feathers of starlings ...

Again my magic collided mid-air with the aggressive flare of red, and this time there was no explosion. Instead, with nothing but the quietest sizzle, the colour just ... vanished.

As if it had been swallowed by alf steel, never to be seen again.

Wingbeats faltered in surprised on the edge of my sight, someone cried out in confusion, and Creon broke through their ranks before they regained their composure. We slammed against the deck with so much force it was a miracle the wood didn't crack beneath us. In a flash, I was back on my feet, two fresh shells in my left hand. Steel gleamed in the corner of my eyes, and I knew Creon had already drawn his knives as he whirled around to shield my back.

The loud gurgle behind me was clear enough evidence he'd found his first victim.

No time to think about that, about the fight that was going on behind me. A bulky fae female plunged from the sky with a drawn blade in each hand, and my mind stuttered in a surge of panic. Red – I should use red – except she'd collapse right on top of me if I killed her, or drop right next to me and restrict my movements when I needed my agility most of all ...

I grabbed the hem of my velvet dress and blasted a mindless thought of movement at her.

The magic hit her right below the midriff like an invisible giant's fist. She doubled over with an audible *oomph* as she slammed ten feet back, her flailing arms and knives colliding with two comrades' wings before she clattered gracelessly to the deck. One of the males she'd hit went down, too, landing wing-first into another's sword as he lost control over his flight for just a moment too long.

Not bad at all. I spun away to avoid a sword swinging towards me, a physical reflex so deeply established by Tared's training sessions it required no more thinking than walking, and fired some habitual red at every throat within reach. Two attacks bit back at me, and again I jumped aside, avoiding one while meeting the other with a flash of iridescent magic. Too strong – the flare of red burst apart into a thousand scarlet sparks.

Then again ...

Those pinpricks of destruction didn't hit me this time. I'd caught the attack close to the fae male who'd fired it, and he and his neighbours were the ones crying out in shock as their own power rained down on them. What if I could streamline that effect a little – would that take more force than I'd used this time or less of it?

Without warning, Creon's arm locked around my waist and whirled me aside, out of the way of a fae warrior crashing in from behind me. He released me before I could blink, driving a blade into my attacker's guts and flinging the twitching body into another female's arms to slow down her frantic approach.

I got a breathless, mindless laugh over my lips as I found my balance again and realigned with my own circle of attackers. Red lit up the edge of my sight. In an instinctive experiment, I blocked the attack with as much iridescent magic as I could pull out of a single shell, and a spray of sparks burst forth, spreading wide enough for the strongest of them to reach my hands and face. They tickled rather than hurt. Not what I was aiming for – the force of the magic got watered down too much this way.

Less power, then.

My next attempt was weaker, just a fraction more than the magic I used to nullify their attacks entirely. It intercepted a ray of bright red in mid-air and deflected the colour the way a mirror would deflect a flash of light, changing its direction and sending the magic two foot past me instead.

The cry behind me betrayed that someone had not been prepared for an attack from that side.

I risked the quickest glance over my shoulder and found a bald fae male furiously wiping blood from his eyes as it gushed from a deep cut in his forehead. Creon was already lunging forward to finish him. As I averted my eyes and jumped away to avoid another attack, the confused cries of the bleeding fae male abruptly stilled behind me.

More and more motionless bodies sprawled over the deck around us as we fought; pools of blood turned the wood slippery and bright red. I nearly stumbled over a snapped leg with the next burst of magic I deflected. The iridescence still did what it had to do, though, and the flash of crimson flung itself back into the left eye of the fae female who'd fired it, taking her out without as much as a squeak.

If I very carefully controlled the strength of my blocks, I learned with my next few attempts, I could even determine at what angle I redirected the magic – could wield the attacks of others as weapons of my own, taking down fae from the direction they expected it least. Five, ten more of our opponents went down as I scattered their red around me like a particularly deadly mirror. Behind me, Creon's knives tore wing after wing from the sky with uncanny efficiency, piling twitching bodies at his feet.

There were some fifteen of them left when they started shouting about retreating.

We managed to bring down a handful more as the last survivors fled. In the end, seven battered members of the ship's crew found their way to safety and soared in the direction of the next fae ship, bleeding and shouting frenzied warnings at each other. Creon and I were left behind on a blood-streaked deck, filthy and out of breath, surrounded by dropped weapons and handfuls of oddly dull shells.

One ship down. Gods knew how many more of them to go.

I drew in my first deep breath in what felt like hours, feeling the swaying of the ship for the first time, hearing the deep roll of the sea that my senses had stubbornly blocked from my perception as long as I had better things to worry about. Next to me, Creon was coldly and systematically checking bodies, slitting throats whenever our victims did not look dead enough for his taste.

My stomach rolled. Repulsion – another unwelcome guest I had managed to ignore in the mayhem of the past few minutes. They'd have done the same to the nymphs, I reminded myself, and to any human isle too if they'd been given the order … but that reminder didn't do anything to erase the memory of Zera's bag, of every individual's desperate struggle to stay alive in the cruel games of the Crimson Court.

And this was how they ended up. Graceless bags of meat in pools of blood.

Creon must have noticed the twinge of my heart, because he looked over his shoulder as he rose from the body of a female with snapped wings and a half-severed head. His eyes – rock-hard with focus during the fight – had softened. Easily avoiding the limbs and weapons, he made his way towards me, wiping his fingers on his dark trousers.

'I'm fine,' I whispered. My throat was squeezing shut. 'Don't worry. Just a little unease about—'

Without waiting for me to finish that sentence, he slipped his arm around my shoulders and pulled me into a fierce, breathless hug.

He smelled of blood, of safety. I instinctively clutched my arms around him, burying my face in the firm warmth of his chest; his free hand cradled the back of my head and pressed me even tighter into his embrace. A whisper of velvet told me he'd wrapped his wings around me, too, creating the perfect shelter, a little cocoon in which no one was desperately and fruitlessly hanging on to their last heartbeats.

'I'm fine,' I breathed again, not sure who I was trying to convince, 'I'm fine, I'm …'

Creon's hands didn't falter. I gave up on whispering lies into his shirt and squeezed my eyes shut, wishing that simple gesture would be enough to stop seeing.

His fingers played through my hair, slow and gentle. An eternity seemed to pass before he finally let go of me, stepped half a step back, and signed, *No need to lie, cactus. You shouldn't be.*

Right.

Because I wasn't like him, and he'd begged me not to become like him, either – because it wasn't weakness, disliking the look of a pool of blood around my boots. I sucked in a shuddery breath, swallowed the next apology that had been on its way to my lips, and muttered, 'No.'

Good. In the bright light of the midday sun, his smile was still joyless as frost. *Want to return to the island?*

I glanced at Tolya – a lush line of emerald on the horizon. If we returned now, we would have allies to help us with the next fight. I might avoid most of the throat-slitting and blood-shedding that was about to follow, might have older and more experienced friends by my side to take care of the unpleasant parts.

But we'd also lure a vengeful fleet after us.

I shuddered at the thought of Helenka's reaction. 'We can't do that, can we?'

Creon shrugged. *We can do whatever the hell we like.*

'But they'll be unhappy.'

His unimpressed eyebrow told me exactly what he thought of that argument.

'Let me think.' I stepped back, away from him, forcing myself to breathe evenly despite the wide-open eyes staring up at me from ghastly pale faces. 'What do you think the survivors will do now? Warn the other ships and come at us with the full force of the remaining army?'

Not the full force, probably. He nodded at the west side of the island; only now did I notice the flames rising from a ship anchored there. *But as many as they can spare, yes.*

Lyn. I found myself smiling despite the carnage around us. 'Tell me more about Iorgas and his fleet.'

Pack of bastards, Creon signed, understanding the silent question behind that request instantly. *That unregistered daughter of Iorgas wasn't some act of defiance against the Mother, in case you were wondering. Just him forcing himself upon a human woman and then drunkenly forgetting about it until she and her magicking child were betrayed by the rest of their village.*

A cold shiver ran down my spine. 'Did he do anything to save them when the Mother found out about them?'

Creon just scoffed.

'Right.' I glanced at the undignified bodies around us, my stomach settling a little at the thought of that dead child – a little girl whose fate oddly mirrored mine, an ominous glimpse of what could have become of me if not for Valter and Editta's ungentle yet effective secrecy. 'How about the rest of his fleet?'

He glanced at the burning ship as he considered that. *Didn't know every individual member well. But the Sun Fleet has always been known as one of her more vicious divisions, and no one was ever forced to join it as far as I'm aware. More than enough volunteers.*

Fae warriors hungry to claw their way up the ranks, to buy their place in the Mother's court with the blood of innocents. A reason I understood, a motivation I'd felt like it was my own for a few nigh-lethal moments.

But that didn't make it right.

'Chose the wrong path,' I muttered, remembering Zera and her words as she sat on that sun-streaked windowsill. An explanation, not a justification. 'Alright.'

Creon narrowed his eyes. *Zera's bag?*

I nodded.

He sighed, and I wondered for an instant how often he had faced the same dilemma – reading the fear and pain of his opponents even while he was killing them. A question for later. At the south-east side of Tolya, the nearest ship was swarming with activity visible even from where we stood, and I didn't suppose it would take those reinforcements long to come our way.

If we still wanted to leave ...

But if we left, the nymphs would bear the brunt of their anger.

I rubbed my thumb over the bargain mark on the inside of my wrist, a quiet reassurance even with Creon right by my side. Choices I didn't want to make. People I didn't want to hurt. Zera had warned me, and yet I'd accepted this power, or worse, *asked* for it.

Somehow, that thought made the choice easier.

'Let's stay here,' I said, my voice uncannily firm. 'People are going to die whatever we do. And if we have to be responsible for bloody slaughter anyway, I'd rather have the victims be our enemies.'

Creon's nod was terse, almost curt. But his calloused fingers found mine, a short squeeze before he strode off to continue his round among the corpses, and I knew by the tightness of his wings that the gesture hid something not nearly as blank and uncaring.

Always the solitary murderer, always the devil to blame.

This time ... If we had to be responsible for bloody slaughter anyway, at least there'd be two of us.

CHAPTER 23

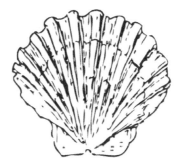

WE WERE STILL GATHERING weapons and clearing the deck when the surviving fae rose from their ships, gathering in a long, triangular formation between us and the shores of Tolya.

Against the stark blue sky, the remainder of Iorgas's army resembled a swarm of crows flocking towards the smell of death – every single one of them dressed in black, their weapons reflecting the bright sunlight. No sound of their approach reached us yet, distant as we were. The creaking and groaning of our ship grew twice as loud to my ears in that unreal, ominous silence, and as I threw the last sword onto the small heap I'd built by the mast, it took an effort not to flinch at the obnoxiously loud clattering of steel against steel.

Creon, of course, didn't move. He leaned against the taffrail where he'd just chucked the last corpse overboard, watching the steady approach of Iorgas and his warriors with nothing but the faintest smile on his lips. An invitation of the most menacing sort, reminding me faintly of a spider spinning a pretty, glittery web for its prey.

'How many of them would you guess there are?' I muttered as I positioned myself beside him, planting my elbows on the polished wood of the railing.

He cocked his head. *A little over a hundred.*

'Fuck,' I said.

Creon chuckled.

It wasn't even fear, the sharp-toothed emotion in my lower belly – not exactly. Rather ... I rubbed my eyes and added, 'How in hell did I become the sort of person taking on fifty fae at once?'

I've been told once or twice I'm a horrible influence, Creon dryly signed.

I laughed despite myself. He straightened, tucked a long, fluttering lock at his temple behind his pointed ear, and casually flicked a spark of yellow magic at my dress. The soft surface I'd used to shove some dead fae into the sea restored itself, turning my dress back into a lush, if terribly unflattering, velvet.

'Alright.' I straightened my back as well, not daring to look away from the approaching force. They were close enough now for us to hear the shouts of their commanders and the whooshing slaps of their wings against the briny sea air. Was that as close as Zera's temple wall had been when I threw my blanket into it with soft magic? No, that had been a slightly shorter distance. 'I'm ready.'

Creon just smiled – a smile that said, *You always are.*

I swallowed something dry and painful. I'd damn well prove him right.

Closer and closer our attackers flew – an impenetrable wall of wings and blades, near enough for us to distinguish their faces, to recognise gritted jaws and furious eyes. Pulse thumping in my throat, I waited. *Just* a little closer ...

This was still too far for most magic attacks. The distance would water down the force of my red, and most of them would not even wield enough power to reach this far. But a sharp edge of steel would do as much damage as a burst of red magic could, and we had blades in abundance after our scavenging of the past minutes.

I could see their knuckles now, tensed white around the hilts of their weapons.

With a quick step back, I turned towards my first pile of blades, lowered my left hand to my plush dress, and let the magic flow through me. A sound like a whiplash cracked through the air. My carefully sorted swords and knives launched themselves from the deck with no regard for flesh or gravity, flinging themselves at the tightly-knit formation of fae with a force that turned my dress into bland, flat cloth. Voices cried out in pain and surprise, blood splattered in the corners of my sight, and Creon's magic flashed over me, restoring the soft black velvet once again.

I didn't give our opponents time to realise what in hell had happened before I flung the next armful of weapons at them.

A few dark shapes tumbled into the waves when I dared to glance their way. Most of them were luckier, and the first blasts of blue magic were already restoring some of the damage I'd done ... But their advance had slowed, and their neat formation had scattered as fae ducked away and dove after injured friends. Only a handful of individuals had not yet realised this was the moment to slow down, and before they could turn around and join the rest of the group again, Creon's red flashed, cutting through their wings like a hot knife through butter.

Their screams as they went down did not seem to boost the morale among their friends. At the most vulnerable ends of the line, fae hesitated with the shock of small predators who'd abruptly figured out they weren't at the top of the food chain at all.

I gave them my most witless smile, that giggle-adjacent expression that had worked so well to placate the Mother.

The fae closest to me swerved another few feet back.

Creon casually cut a few others from the air, then turned a quarter turn towards me as fae dashed back and their commanders bellowed loud orders to restore the formation. *Em?*

'What is it?' My heart was a loud drum in my ears. I barely dared to look at his signs, gaze clinging to the army as it hurried back in line, ready to wash over us once again.

My magic is giving me trouble for some of them. Guessing it's the ones she likes most.

He didn't need to elaborate. The Mother's preferences – strong enough for the death of some of these fae to cause her indirect harm and invoke the bindings, even here, miles and miles away from her throne. We'd predicted it, and yet I felt like cursing at the confirmation.

'Which of them do you expect will be problematic?' I muttered, scanning their lines with watchful eyes.

Purple wings at the back. Blond one with the absurd helmet. The one who's shouting – that's Iorgas. He paused for a moment, then added with hurried gestures, *Can handle the rest.*

'Alright.' I flexed my fingers, marking the three fae he'd indicated. 'I'll take care of them.'

Creon's smile as he turned away was a thing of dazzling, dangerous beauty, the smile of a wild animal about to be unleashed. I would have shivered, but my body was strung too tight with the anticipation of battle, and all that escaped me was a breathless chuckle.

A mere fifty feet away, Iorgas – white-haired, red-winged, and armed to the teeth – hollered commands to attack.

Time for the next surprise, then.

Creon's magic slashed a cruel red line through the air, and I saw fae warriors flinch and duck even as they surged forward to strike. The force of destruction wasn't aimed at them, though. Instead, it cut cleanly through the ropes that held the mainsail with its sun emblem attached to the largest mast, sending feet and feet of heavy, waxed linen tumbling down.

I was already drawing my soft magic again.

The sail was swept aside as if drawn by a heavy gust of wind, straight at the centre of the attacking fae formation. Their screams couldn't stop it as it fluttered towards them like a murderous butterfly; their bursts of red left no more than a few tears behind. None of it stopped the cloth from folding around seven or eight of them as I abruptly surrendered it to gravity.

Sucking the last bit of softness from my dress, I gave the sail a firm tug down. It dragged at least a dozen fae with it on its unnaturally swift plunge into the ocean, their screams muted by linen and the flailing of limbs and wings beneath it, until the entire wrapped package of warriors hit the ice-cold waves and nothing but desperate splashing gave away their presence.

Some of them might make their way out from under that sail, but for now, they'd have better things to do than attack.

Yellow flashed as Creon restored my velvet dress without even glancing my way. Then the first of Iorgas's people came within mage distance, and only a quick grab at my pockets full of shells saved me from the colours lighting up every corner of my sight.

There was no time left for clever strategies. Fae surrounded us like hungry vultures, their wings obscuring the sky above and around me. Everywhere I looked were swords and knives and surges of red, and my thoughts stilled as physical reflexes took over, numbing even the cold touch of my fear.

One mistake away from death, I could do nothing but fight.

My mind narrowed to that one instinct – *survive*. Wielding a rainbow of death, I no longer saw anything but weapons and targets, heard nothing but the whooshes of steel and the splintering of wood, smelled nothing but fear and blood. Red light burst from my right hand, cutting through skin and wing. Iridescence, nullifying an attack inches from my face. Red. Iridescence. The occasional flicker of blue to heal a cut I barely felt in my upper arm, and more red … There was an addictive simplicity to this, staying alive and nothing else. I swung my magic like I breathed, instinctive and unthinking, driven by nothing but the need to keep my heart beating another second, another minute.

A small pile of shells grew around my feet as I blocked the attacks of our opponents time and time again. Behind me, Creon's alf steel knives did the same, catching bursts of light from the air with unimaginable speed and grace. We found each other's rhythms as we always did, left and right and left again, turning back and forth over the blood-stained wood … Transforming this unlucky ship into the world's bloodiest ballroom, the cries and screams of battle into the most gruesome of dancing tunes.

In the corner of my eye, something purple whisked past.

I snapped around, avoiding a ray of red in that same movement and reflecting another into its wielder's face with a well-aimed bit of iridescence. There, another glimpse in the madness – the purple wings of the fae female Creon had pointed out for me, attempting to sneak up on him from behind the throng of bleeding bodies.

Of course he'd already noticed her. The quick flick of his right hand in her direction didn't escape me, a gesture as if to release his magic at her. But no flash of red followed – the bindings blocking his power, just as he'd predicted.

A knife whistled just past me from behind, slammed into the mast beside me, and remained there, trembling with the force of its speed. Purple Wings moved at the same moment, flinging a bright blaze of red forward. Creon avoided the attack by quickly whirling aside, but she was too damn close – and soon, far too soon, she would realise he *couldn't* hurt her.

Hell. I didn't want that realisation to take root for any of them.

I'll take care of them, I'd said. Time to get a little more serious about that promise. Slipping over the bloodied wood, dodging and counter-ing at every step, I made my way to where she half-hid behind a smaller mast, seemingly unbothered by the dead and dying bodies littering the deck. Her stunning pale face split open in a grin when she noticed my approach, the look of a hungry cat spotting its first mouse of the day.

The question was, of course, which of us was the mouse.

I fired a ruby-red bolt of magic at her, and she laughed out loud as she whirled away, slender limbs moving with that perfect fae grace that made me feel like a stumbling child. Another fae female diving at me distracted me for the shortest moment. As I jumped aside, Purple Wings flung out her wings, fluttered just out of my reach, and crooned, 'Coming to play, Emelin?'

Gods help me, no wonder the Mother liked her. This female had ex-actly the same honey-sweet way of speaking, singing her threats with a porcelain doll's smile – a memory that brought my heated blood to a full boil. But she wouldn't be goading me without reason, and the only reason I could see ...

She was trying to lure me away from Creon. Without each other to shield our backs, we'd be ten times more vulnerable.

Gritting my teeth, I inched a few small steps forward, mindlessly flinging a full shell's worth of iridescence into a flash of red to my right. The magic flew apart into vermillion sparks, and fae shrunk back, crying out in surprise. Purple Wings faltered, too, hesitating for just a heartbeat – but enough to shrink the distance between us by perhaps half a foot.

I risked using the last softness in my dress on her.

Was this new magic even visible to others the way colours were? She didn't attempt to dodge, and my experimental attack caught the outer edge of her left wing and yanked her towards me like a puppet on a string.

For the first time, there was real terror in her scream – a frayed echo of the fears I'd felt with Zera's bag in my arms. I flinched, the red I'd planned to draw at her staggering halfway up my arm. Wrong choices, wrong path ... but exchanging even a word with her had been a mistake, had made her far too human through the rage and hate.

Magic bit me in the shoulder from behind, sharp and vicious. *Fuck.* I shouldn't have hesitated. Shouldn't have shown weakness. Like a dance that couldn't be resumed once your feet had tangled up, my rhythm had broken; I was flailing in frantic panic rather than instinct. More red, and the fierce flare in my left thigh told me I hadn't been fast enough as I jumped aside. Wings slapped, announcing the arrival of yet another opponent, and Purple Wings was already rising from the deck, blood streaking her pale arms and cheek ...

A knife split the air just beside my ear, burying itself three inches deep into the soft skin below the fae female's jaw.

Creon.

I dragged in a breath, not daring to turn towards him even for the briefest thanks. For fuck's sake. I'd been planning to take care of these three bastards, hadn't I? And now Purple Wings had ended up with Creon's knife in her throat anyway, my moment of weakness nearly the end of both of us – as if I needed coddling after all.

Fury did what fear hadn't managed. Two brisk attacks ridded me of my next opponent, and just like that I'd found my footing again, Creon at my back and magic itching under my fingertips. Damn them, and damn their hidden hurts. I had lives to save here. Two binding-protected fae left to handle, and this time I *was* going to handle them.

The blond male with the pompous, lion-shaped helmet wasn't hard to spot. With that clump of gold around his head, I'd have noticed him a mile off. Making my way towards him would leave Creon's back vulnerable, of course, but that wasn't to say I couldn't move anything *else* his way ...

My dress had gone dull, not a glimmer of softness left. But Creon was mere steps behind me, methodically cutting fae to pieces, and his wings lay smooth and velvety against his shoulders.

I struck my red at the small mast before me as hard as I could, then jumped back and planted my palm against the tight, velvety membrane of those wings. Again I drew soft magic for movement. No more than a little nudge was needed to push the towering length of wood just where I wanted it to fall. Silly Helmet's attempt to avoid the weight was timed to objects obeying the laws of gravity, not to objects dropping down with magical speed; he was just a fraction too slow, wood crashing into wing and flesh with blood-curdling precision.

Pinned between mast and deck, he had no way to flee me, no way to dodge my attacks. I blew another fae out of my way and risked two steps forward, just enough to bring Silly Helmet within reach of my magic. Someone moved in the corner of my eye. An issue for the next second; I decided in the shortest fraction of a heartbeat that my magic could fend off that attack. First I had to get rid of this bastard before he healed himself back to fighting shape with the blue still contained in his green-brown shirt.

Red cracked from my fingertips, stilling Silly Helmet's wretched screams at once.

In the same moment, something smacked against my back.

Everything happened far, far too fast. I was still parting my lips to scream, was still trying not to topple over, when a hand clasped over my mouth, pressing a cold, sharp weight into my bare cheek. Another arm locked around my waist, pressing me roughly against an unfamiliar body. A single slap of wings, and my feet came away from the slippery deck, into the open sky.

Fuck.

Fuck.

I reacted reflexively, clawed my nails into that tanned arm around my waist, and drew as much red from my dress as I could. But the familiar tingle of magic didn't come – as if I was trying to suck the colour out of a white sheet of paper.

Only then did my mind fully register that cold sting against my cheek.

Alf steel? I forgot to breathe for a moment as my abductor dragged me higher into the sky, as much as breathing was even possible with that stranger's arm pressing my guts into my ribcage. I hung magicless and unarmed in an enemy's grasp, dozens of feet above the deck, soaring around a tattered sail and out of Creon's sight, and red wings slammed behind me, carrying me farther and farther.

Red wings.

Iorgas.

Blinding panic twisted through me. Even when Creon came after us, his binding would stop him from harming my abductor. At least I wasn't dead yet, at least Iorgas could use as little magic as I could with that alf steel trinket pressed against his fingers. But all he needed was a knife and a free hand ...

Think. I had to *think*. Wind whistled around us, Iorgas's ragged breaths and the stench of his sweat filling my mind. I tried to twist and squirm out of his hold, and in reply, he tightened his grip on my waist so violently that I nearly threw up. Black spots danced on the edge of my sight as his hand on my mouth and nose clenched tighter.

I tried to bite his finger, to no avail.

'Little bitch.' He growled the words, his lips a hair's breadth from my ear. Goosebumps rose around my spine – a cold, paralysed shiver. 'Calm down, or I'll—'

I jerked my head back before he could finish that threat, slamming the back of my skull into his nose.

Bone cracked. Iorgas roared a curse. His left hand let go of my face, let go of the alf steel, and I blew every bit of red I could find into his right arm before he recovered, digging a deep cut through his skin. A desperate half-turn, half-squiggle did the rest of the job. I slid from his arms, away from his body ...

Into the empty air.

Only one thought reverberated through my mind as I hung weight-lessly in the air for an endless sliver of time – *You'd better be there to catch me, Creon.*

And then I crashed into the frigid ocean with a smack that drove every last breath of air from my body, and I stopped thinking entirely.

The water was cold – cold enough to chill me to the bone in that first instant. I barely managed to shriek in half a breath before the first wave swept over me and drowned me in a world of darkness and pressure, the salty water enveloping me as if determined to keep me submerged forever. After the mayhem of the fight and the roaring of the sea, the silence underwater was deafening – a silence that made me wonder, for one numb moment, whether maybe I was already dead.

Stop that, some last voice of reason chided. *Swim, you idiot!*

My legs kicked frantically, and I came up, gasping in the salt-flecked air. *Swim* – but the ship was two hundred feet away at least, and already the freezing cold was paralysing my limbs and lungs. Creon, I reminded myself, Creon would come and look for me ... But he was nowhere to be seen, and if he flew this way now, how would he even find my tiny head between the man-high waves and the bodies of fae drifting around the hull?

Red flickered over me.

I wasn't fast enough to grab for shells, to figure out if any of the shells in Creon's coat pockets had even survived the fall. Flailing in the water, I had no time to dodge either. Instead, in some last and thoughtless reflex, my left arm flew up, catching the force of what would have been a straight hit to the face.

Skin split open from wrist to elbow, and the salt of the sea sprayed undiluted agony into the wound.

I would have screamed if my mouth hadn't filled itself with ocean water the moment I parted my lips.

Fuck, fuck, *fuck.*

Above me, Iorgas was already preparing for another attack. I dove back below the surface, deciding in a split second that I preferred another moment of cold suffocation over a blast of red to the eye. The icy water at least dulled the sting of the wound as I fumbled for my pockets with my right hand, trying to find the sharp outlines of my shells with numb fingertips. I found perhaps three of them, the rest washed out by my fall and the force of the current.

Three was not enough.

Zera help me. I didn't want to go back up into the world above, where Iorgas was waiting for me, ready to strike the moment I showed my face. But my lungs were bursting. My skin was slowly turning to ice. If I didn't come up now, I might never come up again.

Pressing a shell into my left palm, I kicked myself back to the surface. The water broke around me, and I spat out a mouthful of brine, raising my hand to defend myself.

No red flash followed.

Instead, I was welcomed by the thundering of the waves and the screams of dying fae and the squeaking of ... a bird?

It took me a moment to blink the salt from my eyes, wrestling to stay above the water. Iorgas still hovered over me with those crimson wings spread wide and the lower half of his face streaked with blood. But rather than diving at me, rather than showering me with red, he was entirely occupied slapping away a tiny white-grey ball of feathers that darted around his head, clawing at his eyes and ears, squeaking like a bag of mice at every flutter of its little wings.

That *was* a bird.

Zera.

My breathless laugh was smothered by another wave, and I nearly went down again. Didn't matter now. Iorgas was cursing in furious exasperation, and that didn't matter, either. With renewed vigour, I began to swim, splashing closer to the ship. Creon had to be there, somewhere. That was all I had to worry about now – find him, draw his attention.

There.

From behind a mast tumbling over, his dark silhouette shot up from the fae ship like a lightning bolt called back into the heavens, a sweep of black against the stark blue. I tried to call out his name, but my voice had shrunken to a husky whisper, and I barely heard myself over the roar of the waves. Gods damn it, I hadn't survived to this point to be defeated by some unwilling vocal chords, and if *I* couldn't make the sound I needed ...

I turned around. Iorgas was making clear attempts to follow me, but failing hopelessly with the small, fluffy bird still pecking at his face in unrelenting bloodlust.

Pressing my numb left hand to my dress, I swung a wild flash of red at him.

My shivering hands and the turbulent waves did make it harder to aim, and I hit him on the hip rather than the intended weak spot of his wings. But his roar of frustration came out no less loud for it, and the grey bird shot forward in that single moment of distraction, digging its little claws into Iorgas's left eye.

This time the bastard's howl was far louder, and hoarse with pain.

Creon changed course.

And then all I had to do was hold up my arm as he dove towards me, one hand stretched out as if he could drag me out of the water by the sheer force of his will. His strong fingers closed around my wrist the next moment. With one powerful motion, he pulled me up and into his arms – impossibly warm arms, wrapping around my soaked, shivering body like the safest of blankets, pressing me against his chest as if he'd never let me go.

Em, his lips said, and again, *Em*, and then a few words I couldn't make out. I didn't need to. The wild look in his eyes told me enough – that I was not the only one who had died seven deaths in the last minute alone.

'I'm fine,' I garbled, hooking my arms and legs around him, digging my nails into his shoulders in a desperate attempt to convince my body it was true. 'Iorgas tried to kill me – alf steel – we need to—'

The little bird squeaked behind me, the sound shrill and urgent. I turned my head to find Iorgas chasing after it. Blood poured from his left eye, and red magic flashed wildly as he attempted to aim with only half of his vision.

In a reflex, I pressed a hand to my formerly velvet dress and let loose

348

all the magic I could find, vaguely wondering if I could stop him moving completely.

Iorgas did not freeze. But he abruptly dropped both his arms, his body went limp mid-wingbeat, and when I caught a brief glimpse of his good eye, his gaze was oddly empty, like a sailor who's been hit by the boom a few too many times. More than that one glance we didn't get. With a jarring, almost serene grace, the Mother's commander folded in his wings and slid from the sky like a leaf whirling down, dropping into the sea without another sound.

He didn't even try to swim.

Only then did I realise that my dress was no longer velvet. After all the magic I'd already drawn from it, there was nothing soft about it left, nothing I might draw for movement. Soaked with seawater, though, the nameless cloth was strangely shiny, enough to mirror glimpses of blue from the sky overhead.

Smoothness for mind.

I hadn't stopped him from moving. I'd stopped him from *thinking*.

'Oh,' I said numbly.

Even Creon's chuckle was laced with bewilderment. But he swerved around in mid-air without another glance at Iorgas's wine-red wings drifting on the indigo ocean surface, pressed a kiss to the crown of my head, and carried me back to the ravaged ship from which I'd been abducted mere minutes ago with slow, steady wingbeats.

CHAPTER 24

VERY LITTLE WAS LEFT of the Mother's proud Sun fleet. Even though Creon flew me directly to the undamaged bow of the ship, from where the remaining sails obscured most of the carnage, the passing glimpses of severed limbs and torn wings didn't allow for any illusions about the fate of our opponents. The ship's bronze figurehead – a flying lion roaring triumphantly at the waves below – looked like a wry joke in comparison.

We landed on the forecastle deck in silence. Creon grabbed my arm as soon as he'd set me back on my feet, healed the cut left by Iorgas's magic, then checked every other limb for wounds twice. Only after he'd finished that quick but thorough investigation did he throw a tight-lipped glance at the ocean and sign, *Did he touch you?*

My stomach turned as the human woman and her unregistered child returned to my thoughts. 'Not like that.'

Creon's nod was slow, ominous, and nothing even close to reassuring.

'He had alf steel.' I peeled off the wet coat from my body and sank down on the rough wood of the deck, knees suddenly no longer able to support my weight. The world was oddly silent around us, the sunlight soothing as a hot bath for my icy skin. 'Must have figured out it would be the only way to stop me. I broke his nose when he tried to fly off with me.'

That elicited a joyless chuckle from him. *Proud of you.*

My heart gave a little jump, then pounded on, still prepared for danger and fight. Wiping salty strands of hair from my face, I nodded at the rest of the ship and muttered, 'They're all dead?'

Yes. His blood-streaked face could have been hewn from stone. *Turns out I could get more unpleasant than I thought.*

I swallowed. 'When you realised I'd disappeared?'

They were trying to stop me from going after you, he signed curtly, the small twitch at his jaw a menacing indication of the fate that had befallen those unwise fae. *So I made haste. The last few of them fled when their numbers were down to a dozen or so. Didn't bother to go after them.*

Which meant the Mother would likely hear about our little stunt before the day was over. I suppressed a curse and nodded, trying not to think about what the bitch might do as soon as she heard I had been back above the earth. Threaten more islands for my location, perhaps. Tell more people not to trust a powerless fae puppet in her son's hands. Whatever she decided, I doubted I'd have time for a few weeks off.

Gods, I needed a few weeks off.

Creon sank down next to me, so gracefully not even the swaying wooden boards creaked under his muscular weight. Tucking in his wings, he unbound his hair, then began loosening his torn shirt with nimble fingers. The skin below was marred by a macabre spider web of old inked scars and brand new cuts, none of them deep or dangerous, but plenty of them looking painful.

I abruptly forgot about vacations. 'Do you need help?'

He sighed, shrugged, and continued to strip off his clothes with the heaviness of a battle-weary warrior taking off his armour.

Of course he did not need my assistance. He'd dealt with worse, and done it often enough to make this a matter of unpleasant routine at most. I gave myself a mental kick and corrected, 'Do you *want* help, then?'

A flicker of surprise broke through that stony battle composure. Flinging his shirt aside, he signed, *You're exhausted.*

'So are you.'

Yes, but …

He faltered there, fingers stiffening between the two of us. Our gazes met, our bodies less than a foot apart, and in that one quiet moment, the full course of this discussion unfolded between us: I'd argue he deserved a little care as much as I did, he'd counter that he had more experience with these things, I'd object that I wasn't going to gain that experience by being pampered by pretty fae princes. At which point he'd smirk and ask if I was trying to flatter him, and I'd just climb into his lap, damn the blood on his trousers and my own soaked dress.

He dropped his hand without finishing his signs, grimacing in surrender.

'At least you learn,' I said and scrambled up to straddle his thighs. He was tense as a coiled spring beneath me, muscles straining against my cold skin – a sensation that made me abruptly aware of just how long it had been since I'd been so close to him. His chest burned hot under my touch, his bronze skin slick with sweat. As I cautiously brushed along a shallow cut just below his right shoulder, I quickly added, 'I don't need a lot of blue for these, do I?'

Less than you think you need. His lips quirked into an exhausted smile, eyes following the cautious movements of my fingers. *As usual.*

I chuckled and drew a soft, eggshell blue from my formerly black, currently drab green dress. The cut grew shut under my touch, leaving no scars behind but turning overly smooth and oddly pale – quite like the skin of a newborn child.

'Right,' I said, pulling a face. 'Less than that.'

Creon's smile had a little more life to it this time. *Just a tad less.*

I used too little magic on my second attempt and only just closed the next gash, the outlines of the injury still clearly visible even though my magic had stopped the bleeding. The third time, I got it right.

From there on, I quietly worked my way over his torso, sparking blue wherever my fingers went, following the taut ridges of his muscles from wound to wound until his age-old scars were the only blemishes cutting through the smooth bronze.

When I looked up, he hadn't taken his eyes off me, watching me with wistful wonder – as if I was no more real than a bubble of soap, bound to burst and vanish any moment.

Warmth flushed through me, hotter than the blissful warmth of the sun caressing my skin, and with it came the renewed awareness of his rock-hard thighs beneath me. Just a few inches and I'd have that sculpted chest under my lips. It was so damn tempting to follow that magnetic pull towards him, to grant myself that moment of simple desire, drive away the cold in my limbs and my blood-drenched memories ...

But Creon didn't move – not the slightest twitch in my direction.

'What are you thinking?' I breathed.

I'm realising that I barely looked over my shoulder during this fight. His signs were stiff and hesitant, as if his fingers weren't quite sure yet what to make of his thoughts. *It's ... surreal. Battling alongside someone I can actually trust with my life.*

An entirely different warmth joined the seductive glow simmering in my lower belly. I swallowed and managed, 'Even though I got myself dragged off halfway through?'

He shrugged. *You fought your way out of that.*

'I nearly drowned.'

You wouldn't have if you hadn't expected me to come for you.

That gave me pause. I wouldn't have. If no one had been around to help me, I wouldn't have dreamed of flinging myself into the sea – it would have been certain suicide, an even faster path to death than whatever awaited me in Iorgas's arms. And yet I hadn't even waited for the confirmation Creon was coming after us, that he would indeed be there to pull me out.

A strange thrill ran down my spine. 'I ... I don't think I looked over my shoulder, either.'

No. His lips curled into half a smile. *I know.*

The moment lingered, a silence broken by nothing but the slapping of tattered sails. Creon was watching me – eyes alert but wings slowly tucking in, shoulders loosening, thighs melting into the deck beneath me. Small signs of safety, but coming from the male who hadn't been truly safe in his lifetime, they were far, far more than that.

'I remember thinking of you as a one-man army,' I said slowly, quietly. 'When we first met. But we're quite past that, aren't we?'

Even below the unnatural grace of his movements, the tightness that slid across his lips was unmistakable – an expression that I could only describe as the very opposite of a threatening burst of laughter. *You have no idea how much I want to be past that.*

'A two-man army it is, then.' I smoothed a hand over his chest, letting my fingers trace the contours of his muscles, and found myself releasing an unexpected chuckle. 'Really, it's about time someone protected you, too. I think I'm going to have your back until you've become spoiled and lazy and forgotten how to draw a knife.'

This time it *was* laughter tightening his lips. *Ambitious as always.*

'Has that ever stopped me?'

No. He wrapped his left hand around my waist – delightfully warm fingers, nudging me as close as I could get while his right still moved between us. *I might still try to object, though.*

I cocked my head, raising an eyebrow at him. 'Bad form, fighting against your own comrade in arms.'

The opposite, cactus, he signed, head tilting ever so slightly in the opposite direction – a gesture that was somehow, unmistakably, an invitation. *I'm finding those are my favourite fights by far.*

Oh, hell. My heartbeat quickened at that stormy look in his eyes, pumping a heady anticipation through my veins. A feeling I really shouldn't allow here, on this ship that had become a floating graveyard … But he was alive. I was alive. And as soon as we returned to Tolya, the watching eyes might not leave us alone for days and days to come.

I leaned forward ever so slightly, inch by inch, until our foreheads bumped together, noses brushing past each other but never truly meeting. Creon moved back in perfect harmony with me, keeping our lips just one breath apart as he lowered himself onto the deck with agonising slowness.

'Are they?' I murmured. 'Because I should probably get started with spoiling you, then.'

A chuckle stroked my lips. His wings flattened out on either side of us as he came to rest on his back, stretches of rich dark velvet over the weathered wood; his head was last to settle against the deck, his face framed by ruffled strands of hair, his eyes burning wild and untamed.

I hovered above him for one still moment, drinking in every single detail of his inhuman beauty – his long lashes, the sharp edges of his jaw, the way his lips curved ever so slightly in that irresistible smirk. His eyes sang a siren's song, luring me closer, daring me to start this most joyful of battles.

'I'm yours,' I whispered.

His fingers gripped the back of my neck in response, pulling me into a kiss of searing intensity. His lips were soft yet demanding, tender yet devastating, returning that claim more eloquently than the sweetest of words ever could – captivating me with nothing but desire as he pinned me to his chest. I kissed him back with equal fervour, wrapped my hands around his jaw, tangled my fingers in his dark hair. His wings swept up, embracing us both. And just like that, days of separation shrunk to insignificant moments, all those hours of missing and long-ing and worrying reduced to a faint echo in my memory ... He was here. He was *mine*. We'd take on the whole damn world if we had to, and who was going to stop us as long as we were together?

I moaned as his possessive kiss deepened, and again as he clawed at my dress with a growled breath, tugging at that last barrier separating our bodies. His other hand skimmed over the small of my back, tracing circles over my bottom and thighs before slipping beneath my soaked skirt. My skin had gone feverishly hot under his touches. My legs spread themselves for him as his fingers squeezed and kneaded their way up along the inside of my thighs, torturously slow on their way to that little spot that burned for him like hellfire.

I licked over his bottom lip. He nipped mine in retaliation, breathing a rough chuckle as I gasped.

In that same moment, his fingers finally slid below my underwear.

He found me slick and ready, drunk on the bliss of this brief escape. I grabbed for the bulge of his cock as he probed half an inch into me, and felt his straining length twitch in my palm as I moaned his name – a sensation so intoxicating that I failed to register, for one or two heartbeats, the impatient squeaking that suddenly broke through the backdrop of creaking sails and groaning ropes.

A familiar sort of squeaking, no less.

I froze, one hand gripping Creon's crotch, one hand pressing into his bare chest. He'd gone equally still beneath me. His fingers lingered unmoving between my thighs, but he slowly lowered his wings back to the deck like a dark flower unfolding its petals, welcoming the warm sunlight and the briny sea breeze and that persistent, high-pitched sound.

Zera's miniscule bird perched on the taffrail of the ship, chirping as if it was about to claw out our eyes next.

Burning lust turned to clammy shame in less than the time it took to blink. I yanked my hands away from their incriminating wandering and shot upright in a reflexive and somewhat half-hearted attempt to tug my dress back in place. Creon's hand between my thighs quite spoiled the effect. The little bird abruptly shut its little beak, however, puffing out its chest as it peered at me with impatient beady eyes.

If you have time for this frivolous nonsense, that look said, *shouldn't I be a little higher on the list of your priorities?*

'Oh,' I said sheepishly, unwilling to acknowledge I had entirely forgotten about my little helper in the bewilderment of Iorgas's death. 'You're ... you're still here?'

I hadn't known until that moment that birds were capable of scowling, but this little specimen managed it, her wings twitching in annoyance as she hopped from one foot to the other. Her piercing look vaguely reminded me of—

Wait. *Her?*

A strange certainty swept over me as I stared at her, a realisation that came out of nowhere and yet settled into my bones as if it was the result of days of deliberation. For some reason, I was absolutely sure she was female, this fluffy bird barely the size of my hand. It didn't matter that nothing about her snow-white chest or her grey-and brown-flecked neck spoke of gender to me. In the blink of an eye, I *knew* her – knew her fierce pride at defeating a foe, her palpable annoyance at my dallying with some boring fae male instead of offering her my well-deserved gratitude.

'Right,' I said, clambering off Creon's lap as the last of that delirious arousal ebbed from my body. My feet were unsteady on the rocking deck. 'Um. That was discourteous of me, and I apologize. You were very brave. And fearsome. I owe you my life, and if there's anything I can do to pay the debt, please let me know.'

She cocked her head, considering that offer. Some kind of falcon, I determined in that moment of silence – but she had to be the smallest falcon I'd seen in my life.

And why did I feel this unsettling, almost violent instinct to scoop her up from the rail and tuck her close against my chest, like a child to be protected? Was Zera trying to tell me something?

But that didn't make sense – none of this made sense. I *had* asked for Zera's help in that moment underwater, but if she'd sent this bird here from the continent, it would have taken far longer than half a minute for her to reach me. So what in hell was going on?

The little falcon continued to glare at me as if she was waiting for something.

'I ...' I turned to Creon for support and found him sitting on the deck, muscular arms wrapped around his knees. To my bewilderment, he was grinning broadly, his mirth wrinkling the bronze skin around his eyes. 'What am I missing?'

He shrugged. *You're godsworn.*

Godsworn.

Like Agenor.

And his snakes.

I felt my eyes widen as I whirled back to the bird, who let out an excited squeak, as if to congratulate me on finally figuring it out.

'You're ... you're here to *stay*.' The words tumbled over my lips. What had Agenor said about the snakes? Hundreds of years. Gods help me. 'With me? You're ...'

She huffed, ruffling her feathers in apparent offense.

'You're here to gracefully tolerate my existence, I mean?' I corrected myself blankly, and she looked significantly happier at that.

Behind me, Creon breathed a chuckle.

I turned again and helplessly whispered, 'Doesn't she need a name?'

You're supposed to name her. He rose to his feet with a slight flutter of his wings, studying the small creature with unmistakable amusement. *And that's all you need to do, as far as I know. Clearly she has already claimed you.*

I once again blinked at the bird, who beamed back at me expectantly.

'I ... I see.' That was optimism bordering on untruth. I needed to have a good word with Agenor about this brand new family tradition of swearing ourselves to gods – hell knew what else I might be unprepared for. 'Of course. I'll try to come up with something, then. What ... what is the plan?'

Perhaps we should return to Tolya, Creon dryly suggested. *Not sure if our new family member would be happy if we resumed our activities before her very eyes.*

Something told me the tiny falcon would object loudly and violently if we made the mistake of testing that theory. I grimaced and said, 'Let's not risk it. I'd like to keep your naughty bits undamaged, if possible.'

Wise. He paused to pick up his shirt from the deck. *Don't think you'll find a better replacement anywhere.*

I sucked the last bit of red from my dress just to fling it at him. He whirled away in a burst of laughter, chest still shaking as he pulled his shirt over his wings and shoulders.

'Alright,' I said, suppressing my grin as I turned back to the yet to-be-named bird – gods help me, how did one name a bird? 'We're going back to the nymph isle over there. They don't yet know I'm godsworn, so maybe it would be wise if you were to hide yourself for a bit while we try to—'

My newfound familiar interrupted me with a furious squeak, fluffing up her downy feathers until she oddly resembled a ball of yarn on legs.

I think that's a no, Creon offered.

'For fuck's sake,' I said, glaring at her and then at him. 'Listen, the nymphs—'

Are Zera's patron people, he signed with a shrug. *They might grant a sworn mage a few more favours than a treasonous fae puppet.*

'But Lyn didn't tell Helenka.'

It's not her secret to tell. Did you expect her to go around boasting about your powers?

That was a perspective I had not considered yet. 'Not particularly, but ...'

It's a pretty convincing argument you've got here, really. He raked a free hand through his long locks, thinking for a moment. *No one in his right mind would argue that Zera supports my bid for the empire's throne. So the fact that she swore you in regardless ... Well, as soon as you're ready to spread that news, it may turn some heads.*

As soon as I was ready. I glanced at my bird familiar, who was slowly shrinking back to her usual size, then at the distant green shores of Tolya. *Ready*, as usual, was too optimistic a word – but my newfound powers had claimed me in any case. Wouldn't it be best to just confidently and wholeheartedly claim them back?

I threw a last doubtful look at the feathery little monster on the taffrail. She fluttered up with a joyful squeak, and somehow it was that sound of unbridled excitement that gave me the last nudge I needed.

'Fine.' I would be ready when I needed to be. 'Let's go upset a few more nymphs, in that case.'

CHAPTER 25

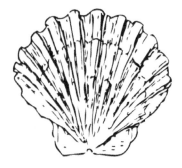

THE LITTLE BIRD PROTESTED loudly when Creon scooped me into his arms, and she did not calm down until I patiently explained that those fluffy wings of hers would never be able to hold my weight. Even then, she scowled at Creon from her spot on the wooden rail, squeaking aggressively when he swept out his dark wings and launched the two of us into the air with a powerful slap or two.

As he soared towards the waiting shores of Tolya, she shot past us at twice his speed, then darted around in mid-air and waited for us to catch up. *See?* her triumphant chirping seemed to tell us. *Not so fast now with those big wings of yours, are you?*

It was pure blasphemy for Creon's laughter to come out silently; it *needed* its sound, damn it, that burst of amusement that shook his whole body and turned the gorgeous mask of his face into a far more gorgeous mirror of the soul below. Before I could tell him to ignore the challenge, his wingbeats accelerated. We shot forward so fast that the wind stilled every cry I might have uttered, and my little falcon squeaked in outrage and surged forward with even more vehement flapping of her wings.

Just like that, her name hit me.

It emerged in my mind with absolute certainty, just as the understanding of her thoughts had done before. Of course. Of *course*. Sucking in a lungful of briny sea air, I lifted my head from Creon's taut shoulder and yelled, 'Alyra?'

She pivoted mid-wingbeat, frozen in surprise for just a moment. Then, with a joyful yelp, she raced back to us, whirled one full circle around us with such vigour that she nearly flew face-first into Creon's left wing, and darted off again, still twittering ecstatically as she fluttered farther towards Tolya.

Well.

That was a yes, I supposed.

Only then, when I was sure we would not be hit by a feisty, feathery projectile any moment, did I dare to look up at Creon. He met my gaze with quiet, shining eyes. A look of approval on the surface, but something far more meaningful than that lingering just below ... *Alyra*, the Eagle, a spring constellation named after the proud mythical bird who flew too fast and found herself stuck between the stars with no way back home.

'I've been reading your book,' I said, as if that explanation was still needed.

A hint of a smile played at the corners of his mouth – a smile that abruptly reminded me why I'd been about to kiss him senseless mere minutes ago. It took a stern reminder of the rapidly diminishing distance to the watching eyes of Tolya to stop myself from revisiting that plan immediately.

We flew on, Alyra dancing ahead of us. With every wingbeat, the shoreline of the island came closer, the waters of the many bays and coves sparkling in a thousand shades of turquoise and aquamarine. At the sight of those pristine white beaches and the verdant trees beyond, it was hard not to feel like a rumpled mess; my dress stuck damp and stiff to my skin, and my hair was a tangle of rough strands sticky with salt. Then again, what would Helenka expect – that I'd rise from a desperate battle looking like Miss Matilda's finest clients, ready for court?

Creon seemed to know exactly where to go, a small bay at the south side of the island. As we descended towards the shore, his wingspan cast a deep shadow over the rippling waves. Alyra skipped ahead of us, and a few birdsongs answered her call from behind the treeline – but no other living soul showed up to greet us, or even just to chase us away.

As soon as we touched down on the beach, Creon put me on my feet and stepped away from me. He'd gone cold again, no trace of lust or laughter remaining in the haughty lines of his face, a stranger to the lingering yearning below my skin. Which I should have expected, of course ... And yet I had to press away a sting of disappointment, the stark contrast to the male I knew and loved almost physically painful.

Soon. I sucked in a breath as I repeated that promise to myself – I'd tell them soon. This was just not the moment.

Scraping myself together, I kicked off my soaked boots and wriggled my toes in the soft, sun-baked sand. 'I suppose they'll come to us if they feel the need to?'

Creon nodded slowly, scanning the woods. *I can sense a few of them near, but they're waiting for something. Doubt we'll make them happy by walking in without invitation.*

'My thoughts exactly,' I said and grimaced. 'Let's just wait, then. Alyra, how about we get you a nice seat on my shoulder in the meantime?'

She seemed particularly excited about that suggestion, which I suspected was for a large part due to the fact that I had not offered Creon a cosy shoulder patch to settle on.

My yellow magic turned out to work just fine as long as I didn't try to make changes in surface texture. With a few quick experiments, I managed to create a thicker, sturdier layer of fabric on the shoulder of my dress, where Alyra could perch without piercing my skin with her tiny claws. She practised her balance in that new spot for about three whole heartbeats before shooting off again to explore a bunch of brightly coloured flowers.

We waited in silence after that. Puffy clouds slid by in the bright blue sky. The surf crashed into the pearly beach again and again. Creon sauntered back and forth over the stretch of sand, absently twirling a knife between his fingers, and I stared at the foliage and prayed someone would show up before nightfall.

No matter how quiet the island, I didn't hear Helenka approach until the moment she strode out from the veil of dangling vines and flowers.

The queen of Tolya gave the impression she was no longer quite sure how to deal with us and had decided civil hostility would be her safest bet. She marched onto the beach with her chin up high and her lips pressed into the displeased scowl of a lady who has spotted a hair in her food but is too polite to mention it to her hosts; her red hair had been tamed into smooth waves, but her hands with their curved, black nails were still clenched with suppressed rage. Her emerald eyes flitted from Creon's bloodied figure to my salt-stained dress, finally coming to rest on my face.

'Well?' she said coldly.

I should probably have curtsied, or something to that effect. I was too tired and too fed up to care. Straightening my spine, I smiled and said, 'I'm happy to report the Sun fleet will no longer be an issue.'

She stared at me for a solid five heartbeats. I stared back, unblinking and unflinching. I'd faced an entire damn army, for the gods' sakes; I'd be damned if I let a single nymph queen – horned and clawed as she may be – get under my skin.

'I see,' she finally said, in that low, melodious voice. 'And why, exactly, did you return to this island despite my obvious request never to show your faces here again?'

Because she wasn't my sovereign and her requests meant about as much to me as a bag of dry earth. I decided to diplomatically swallow that point.

'My friends are still on Tolya,' I said instead, emphasising the word *friends*, just in case she was planning to tell me Lyn and Tared didn't care where I went next. 'We're exhausted and in dire need of a bed, and I hoped endangering our own lives in order to save those of your people might be reason to reconsider your suspicions.'

She huffed, eyes flicking briefly towards Creon as if to assess a threat. 'I've seen more fae trickery than you've seen sunrises in your life, girl. Who is to tell me the Silent Death wasn't in on the scheme with his brothers from the start? That all of this wasn't simply a ruse to fool us into trusting you and your—'

With a shriek like metal grating against metal, something white-grey and feathery plummeted from the sky.

'Alyra, no!' I lunged forward, realising just too late what was happening. If not for Helenka's quick reflexes, she may have ended up with a falcon beak embedded in the back of her skull. The nymph queen whirled aside in a blur of dark skin and lacy fabrics, and Alyra changed course just in time to avoid crashing into the sand, still squeaking furiously as she surged back up into the sky.

'*Alyra*,' I repeated breathlessly. 'Stop that. She's not an enemy. We're just having a civil disagreement— No, *don't.*'

The falcon's look of hurt pride uncannily resembled Edored's expression whenever his well-intended offers of bloody murder weren't taken seriously, but at least she seemed to give up on her determined intention to draw blood. I held out my arm to her, and she landed grumpily on my shoulder, still fluffy with anger.

From the corner of my eye, I noticed Creon slowly releasing his black shirt. I didn't want to think about who he'd have targeted if he'd been forced to intervene – Alyra and her aggression or Helenka and her doubtlessly impressive nymph magic.

'Apologies,' I managed to grind out, turning back to Helenka with my heart still hammering in my throat. No sense thinking about what could have happened. 'Won't happen again. Remind me – what were you saying?'

Two steps away from the first trees, the queen of Tolya had gone silent.

The fury had melted from her face. Her claw-like hands had fallen to her sides. Only her strange, pupil-less eyes moved, shooting from Alyra to me and back to Alyra, growing wider with every turn. She didn't appear to have heard me. Really, she didn't appear to have taken note of anything but the ease with which my familiar had settled on my shoulder and stayed there.

'That ... that's impossible,' she finally breathed, her dazed laugh not as confident as her words. Her voice had abruptly gone husky. 'What did you do to that poor bird, girl? What ungodly magic did you use to make it—'

Alyra let out an indignant screech.

'You're talking about my familiar, I presume?' I politely suggested.

On the edge of my sight, Creon bit back an unexpected grin.

Helenka didn't even notice, gaping at me with emerald eyes that grew impossibly wider. 'You are ... how old?'

Not old enough to have lived and met Zera before the War of the Gods ended. We both knew that was the true answer she was looking for, but I bit my tongue and restrained myself to a less pedantic, 'Twenty-one summers.'

'The gods ...' She visibly swallowed. 'They've been dead all your life.'

I braced myself. 'Zera is alive.'

Helenka was trembling now, shaking like a leaf; her gaze wouldn't stop darting back and forth between Alyra and me, taking stock of the facts she knew. A familiar. My mysterious magic that her spies must have told her about. Only one explanation possible, but it was an explanation that made a lie out of five hundred years of a godless existence, and would she be able to accept that in the little time we had?

'She's lost most of her power,' I continued, my voice steadier than my fluttering pulse. This was not the moment to give her the opportunity to gather her thoughts and decide the miracle was just another filthy fae trick, after all. 'She's living in her woods on the continent, where she is mostly protected from the plague. But she is alive, she still hears your prayers.'

Helenka drew in a rough, shivery breath. 'You found her.'

'Yes.'

'She ...' Again she glanced at Alyra. 'She made you ... *Vedra*.'

I didn't know the word, but her voice had dropped to a breathless, almost reverent whisper that made questions redundant. 'Yes.'

A string of syllables fell over her lips – curses or prayers, I couldn't tell. Her hands shook as she gestured at the woodline behind her; she didn't follow the direction of her gestures with her eyes, as if even now, even after the battle, even after Alyra, she did not dare to trust the choice she was making.

'No servant of Zera is denied sanctuary on my island.' There was a desperate quality to her voice. 'Walk on, fae girl. Your friends are waiting for you.'

I did not move. 'And Creon?'

Even through the breathless shock, the repulsion was evident as daylight on her face, and this time she spoke without a shred of doubt. 'The beast murdered a queen of Tolya. Unless he's willing to kill me, too, he's not setting a single foot on my grounds.'

Well. That was a clear enough statement.

And that ... that would be it, wouldn't it? I saw the next few seconds play out before me while I turned to meet Creon's gaze, exhaustion and defeat heavy on my shoulders – he'd shrug that uncaring shrug he'd perfected over the course of centuries, that gesture that said, *it's not my loss that you refuse to acknowledge the glory and perfection of my existence.* He'd smile that beautiful, bone-chilling smile that was somehow a death threat and a promise at once. And then he'd vanish and either take me with him or leave me to deal with the wiles of our maybe-allies – because it was better than vulnerability. Because the Silent Death, nightmare in the flesh, didn't plead or haggle for access. Because ...

Creon cocked his head just a fraction, gaze wandering to me like a compass needle finding its true north. And with quick, nimble fingers, he signed, *Offer her a bargain for truth.*

Surprise wiped the concept of language from my mind for a good two seconds.

A bargain. For truth – *his* truth. Which meant ... Which meant he was going to *try*? And risk rejection and failure? The notion seemed so utterly impossible that I found myself blinking owlishly at him in the midday sun, forgetting for a moment to be the godsworn mage who knew exactly what she was doing.

'Are ... are you sure?'

A grin slid over his face, gorgeous like a summer's day and yet hiding a spark of understanding below that inhuman façade. *As long as you have my back.*

Good gods.

My laugh was a weak, unconvincing attempt. He'd listened, then, not just today but that night by the fire, too – my secrets, but his inability to make the truth just a little more palatable. And his answer ... a bargain for the truth, for a little crack in that impenetrable shield of the Silent Death's disguise.

I could have cried.

But a shaken nymph queen was watching me, and the future of our alliance might hinge on the very words I was about to speak. So I merely faced her and said, 'He offers you a bargain for the truth. Whatever questions you have about his motivations and ambitions.'

She blinked – thrown off-balance as much as I had been, as if the abrupt revelation of Zera's survival had not been enough. 'A bargain for *truth*?'

'Yes.'

'In return for what?' The disbelief in her voice was tangible. She'd dealt with fae before, knew the blades and poisons that could hide below their bargains ... and a bargain for truth was a damn powerful thing. Could I blame her for not believing the Silent Death would offer her a look straight into his mind without any hidden intentions?

Creon merely nodded at the forest behind her, not even granting the matter any signs. Access to the island.

Helenka's laugh was a tad too shrill. 'That very much depends on your answers, Hytherion. I might reconsider my stance after hearing what you have to say, and that's the most I'll bargain for.'

A meagre promise, but Creon nodded without hesitation, agreeing to a deal so unbalanced it would have reeked of desperation from any other fae.

Helenka wetted her lips, the lack of resistance only strengthening the suspicion in her eyes. Once again, it didn't take any divine powers to understand. It had been mere months ago that I'd found myself in her position, forced to trust a heartless fae murderer despite every instinct screaming at me to run and save myself. As far as she knew, Creon had to be playing a game – because he and his kind *always* were. But I didn't appear to be the witless little fae whore the Mother's envoys had told her about either, and it was Creon who had just saved her people and her trees ... so what did she have left to trust, now?

Bargain magic. That, at least, offered a hope of certainty.

I knew she'd made her decision the moment her hand came up – just a few inches, but a clear enough motion towards Creon's quiet silhouette. The look of disbelief lingered in her eyes as she said, 'How many questions do I get?'

Creon shrugged, holding up five fingers.

'Make it ten.' There was a reckless glint of greed in her eyes, like a child prodding a chained animal in some suicidal attempt to figure out when it would bite. But Creon merely quirked up an amused eyebrow and added three fingers of his other hand.

Eight. Giving in to her demands without any objection would be too suspicious, likely.

'Eight will do.' She took the smallest step forward, and then another one, until she reached him in the surf, her bare feet searching for stability in the wet sand. The claw-like hand she reached out to him looked small against his scarred fingers. 'Answer my eight questions truthfully and with no attempts to deceive me in either writing or gesturing, and I will *consider* allowing you access to this island. And if I decide not to, you will leave without further objection or damage done to any of the souls under my protection.'

He merely nodded.

Blinding light erupted from between their fingers. When the bargain magic settled an eternity later, a bright blue mark had appeared on the insides of their wrists, contrasting sharply with the violent red of the mark Creon shared with me.

'Good.' Helenka sounded on the brink of fainting. 'My first question. Do you want to rule the empire yourself?'

Creon shook his head as he knelt gracefully before her, a black, bloodied shape against the pastel colours of her island. Drawn with quick strokes in the wet sand, letters appeared under his finger – *Would rather die.*

Helenka's eyes widened, but her voice didn't give way. 'Are you loyal to the Mother?'

Not since Last Battle.

'Then why did you come here and kill Zoya?'

Creon sighed, wiping his writing with two quick sweeps of his hand. And there the words appeared, as if this wasn't a secret he'd held onto so stubbornly amidst even the closest of our allies, as if these weren't powers he'd have cut from his own flesh had he been able to ...

No one else in my place would have taken her pain.

We stared at that sentence together, Helenka and I, speechless for entirely different reasons.

'Her ... her pain.' The nymph queen looked up at me, a flicker of help-lessness in her eyes – as if she was considering, for just one moment, begging me to intervene and reveal that all of this was just the fae joke of the decade. 'Do you mean ... with your demon powers?'

Creon nodded, no trace of aversion on his hard face. We were at four questions, now. Was he keeping count like I was? Was Helenka even keeping count? I wasn't sure if she'd realised that last sentence had been a question, too.

'Do you mean ...' Her hands had balled into fists, but they shook. 'Does that mean she didn't feel any of your torture and that you ... that *you* felt the pain instead?'

Again, Creon nodded. It wasn't a nod that betrayed anything of the grey-faced mess he'd been that night at the pavilion, or the similar mess he must have been after slowly cutting himself to pieces through the poor nymph he'd been sent to kill, but Helenka let out a small wail regardless.

'Is that something you've done before?' she whispered. 'With other victims?'

Everyone. The word gleamed bitter and meaningful in the sand. *Since Last Battle.*

For five, ten heartbeats, Helenka gaped at those letters. She didn't move, didn't even seem to be breathing – but behind her, the trees and vines rustled in the breeze like restless children, betraying the spinning of her thoughts. *Everyone.* She wasn't stupid, the queen of Tolya; she, too, knew exactly how many lives had ended at his hands, in how many torturous ways.

She may hate him like death itself, but even so, she could recognise a sacrifice when she saw one.

'How many ... No, wait.' She jerked up her head, red-golden curls scattering around her horns and face as she met my gaze. 'How many questions do I have left?'

Asked of me, not him, so it wouldn't count as a question in itself. Clever. 'Six so far.'

'Two left,' she muttered, rubbing a claw over her delicate face. 'Goddess help me. My seventh question, then. The fae ambassador who cut down our trees, twenty years ago, who died the same day as Zoya – did you kill her, too?'

Creon nodded, then added in the sand, *All I could do to protect you.*

Helenka let out a high, nervous laugh. A last glance over her shoulder, as if to check her trees were still there and undamaged, then she blurted out, 'What is Emelin Vedra to you?'

My heart stood still.

But Creon moved without hesitation, and the letters formed under his fingers as swiftly as any of his previous answers. *I'd die to keep her safe.*

He hadn't bargained for the full and complete truth, I realised only then – just for truth. And this *was* an answer, perhaps the easiest of them all.

Helenka sighed, and I couldn't tell if it was relief or disappointment. Had she hoped for more scandalous details? Or feared that the situation would be worse?

All she said was, 'Thank you.'

Creon rose to his feet, wings shifting a fraction against his back as he readjusted his posture. His face was unreadable. No impatience. No triumph. Just a blank invitation for her judgement, for her to fulfil her part of the bargain.

Helenka stared at the azure gemstone lodged in her dark skin, fingers prodding the mirror-smooth surface of the mark. Her hands trembled, but the line of her lips was firm, a sign of decisions made. 'One night.' Her voice had recovered that old edge of authority. 'You will be allowed to rest here and make plans. Then you will leave and never return to this island. Is that clear?'

There was a tinge of arrogance to Creon's smile, but it was not the sort of arrogance I usually saw in his dealings with the rest of the world. The Silent Death's smile was a condescension to whomever received it, a soundless reminder that it was by the mercy of his ink-black heart that he hadn't yet killed every worm crawling around his feet. The look he now exchanged with Helenka, on the other hand ...

A gesture from ruler to ruler. *I see your power,* it said. *I respect it.*

Helenka straightened her back so that the tips of her horns almost reached to the height of his shoulders. Her gaze shot back to me and Alyra, and for one sliver of a moment, I saw the bewilderment in her eyes, the weight of the world-shocking revelations that had rained down upon her in these past few minutes.

She recovered within the blink of an eye, though.

'And you may stay as long as you wish, Emelin Vedra.' She swept around, her flimsy chemise fluttering about her small body as she strode over the beach and towards the woods. 'Follow me, then.'

CHAPTER 26

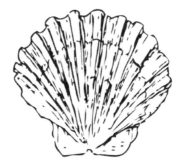

WE MAY JUST HAVE spent the past week wandering through another forest, but the differences between Tolya and Zera's woods couldn't possibly have been greater.

The place we'd left behind had been quiet and dignified and utterly devoid of life – as close to a graveyard as a living forest could be. The nymph forest we entered now, on the other hand, was as vibrantly alive as the creatures inhabiting it. As we followed Helenka along the winding path between the tangled vines and branches, movement broke through the dazzling shades of greens, blues, and violets wherever I looked. Mice and birds skittered between the leaves, butterflies broke from their flowers, and sometimes a storm of nervous cries and giggles betrayed that a flock of nymphs was unsuccessfully hiding in the foliage.

Curious as they seemed to be, they never showed their faces, darting away time and time again to avoid our gazes. At first I assumed it was because of Creon, who sauntered along next to me with blood streaking his sharp cheekbones and his sleeves rolled up to reveal the ink marks in his skin. Even without those mementos of battle, it would have been hard to overlook the raw force of his power in this place, where the colours were bright like gemstones and brimmed with the potential of magic. Of course the nymphs were frightened. Of course they were wondering why their queen was now leading him into their forest if she had staunchly refused him access until mere minutes ago.

But the first bit of comprehensible speech I caught from the hushed voices hiding behind a large, pink-flowered bush was *my* name.

And suddenly their thinly veiled hysteria took on an entirely different meaning.

Because it wasn't just Creon strutting through their forest covered in blood and teeming with a power they could barely grasp. It was me, too – an unfamiliar face with godsworn magic and a tiny falcon on her shoulder, emerging victorious from a scuffle with an entire damn fleet. To these people, I was no longer little Emelin, clueless unbound mage. I was a force to be reckoned with.

And while part of me felt like shrinking and insisting they were vastly overestimating me, there was something oddly addictive about the realisation, too – about being a match to the predator beside me, rather than the hapless victim the world liked to make of me.

The whispers accompanied us as we progressed deeper into the woods, a razor-edged sound that contrasted sharply with the peaceful hum of the wind and the occasional trickling of water. Helenka never spoke, no matter how obvious the hisses from the foliage grew. We passed clearings full of flowers, where the air was heavy with the sweetness of honeysuckle and roses; crystal-clear ponds, where the mist smelled of moss and damp soil; thickets of trees heavy with fruit, perfumed with the fragrance of ripe berries and honey. Wherever we went, I caught no sign of towns or other organised habitations – not even the loneliest house or shed.

We had been walking for maybe ten minutes when a very different sound broke through the constant harmony of whispering voices and rustling leaves.

Screaming.

My feet faltered as the first shreds of it reached my ears – muffled yet desperate, voices of men and women who were too far gone to manage a single coherent word. Another attack? Another battle? But Helenka strode on as if she didn't hear the distant cacophony at all, and Creon did not look perturbed in the least when he drew to a nonchalant halt alongside me and gestured for me to walk on.

What's that? I mouthed, unwilling to let Helenka find out how my stomach had rolled over.

Prisoners. He threw a quick glance at the red-haired nymph queen, then quickly added, *They don't kill. Matter of religious principle.*

I swallowed something bitter. 'So they take captives instead?'

Yes. A wry smile. *Fae tend to believe that's a weakness. Until they find themselves in a nymph prison, that is. Coming?*

Gods help me. I hurried after him and Helenka, mind spinning and unable to ignore the nameless pleas that came filtering through the foliage. Was the queen leading us past this spot on purpose, just a little reminder of what her people were capable of? Or had it not even occurred to her that her prison might be shocking to guests who had their fair share of fae blood on their hands, too?

A shiver ran down my spine. Death, yes, but whatever was happening to the poor souls who had ended up in her hands ... *Wolves against wolves.*

An idea sparked.

'Helenka?' How I managed to get out her name calmly and confidently was anyone's guess; the words were loose shreds of ideas before they found their way to my lips. 'Would you mind terribly if I borrowed a couple of your prisoners for a few hours?'

She turned around without slowing down, nimbly avoiding branches and stringy roots even as she dashed backwards. 'And what exactly would you need them for, Emelin Vedra?'

'A few things I need to figure out,' I said, pausing for a heartbeat or two to see whether that would be enough. When she merely continued looking at me, I sighed and added, 'About the bindings.'

Helenka stiffened mid-step.

'I'm trying to figure out how to break them.' In a flash of inspiration, I nodded at Alyra, who squeaked at that small acknowledgement. 'It's the reason Zera gave me this magic. But I'd prefer not to conduct any risky experiments on the magic of our allies, and I don't have *that* many test subjects around to—'

'Yes,' she interrupted me. Her voice had gone rough. 'I understand.'

It seemed I was still underestimating how much a mere mention of the bindings could accomplish. It was the future of her people on the line, too, of course – their fertility, and with that the fate of their entire race. And yet I was surprised when she turned back around with no further questions and said, 'I'll have a few of them sent to you. Are there any requirements they should meet?'

I glanced at Creon, who shrugged, looking amused. *Not overly insane, preferably.*

'It would be nice if they have something of a mind left,' I said cautiously, ignoring the next nervous flip of my stomach.

Helenka chuckled but gestured to our right without wasting another word on the matter. 'This way, please.'

We soon left the screaming behind. I couldn't say I was sorry to get away from it. The piercing whispers were a pleasant backdrop in comparison.

It took some ten more minutes of walking before familiar voices finally emerged from the tightly tangled forest around us.

'... *told* you to stay in bed!' That was Lyn, her high child's voice easiest to distinguish. 'And don't tell me Ylfreda allowed you to leave! You'll be darning socks for the next decade if she hears ...'

'Not sure I'd leave him alone with my socks, honestly,' Tared said dryly.

A grin broke out on my face all by itself. Edored was in the middle of making his furious retort – something about excellent sock darning skills, not that he'd ever touch anything that had come so close to Tared's smelly feet – when we stepped through the last curtain of flowering branches and into the large clearing where the others had gathered. There were more alves than I had expected, likely part of the small force Thorir had brought to the island. Edored, still covered in burn salves and bandages, ranted at Lyn, whose clothes showed a generous number of burn marks and soot stains.

'Your company,' Helenka said, stiffly and redundantly.

'Em!' Lyn cried out at the same moment, ignoring Edored entirely as she snapped around and sprinted towards me. Conversations around the clearing stilled abruptly as every head turned in unison. 'Inika have mercy, you're *soaked* – don't tell me you jumped off that gods-damned ship? And ...' She faltered as her amber eyes slid to Alyra on my shoulder. 'Oh, good gods.'

'You're faster than I was,' I said wryly, suppressing the urge to shrink away from the eyes staring in my direction. These were members of the Alliance, some of them alves I considered friends, and yet the brand new edge of unease in their gazes was achingly similar to the looks I'd gotten during my first days in the Underground. 'This is Alyra. Alyra, the family. Would you all mind ...' I gestured weakly at my drenched clothes. 'I could use a moment to recover before giving you the full report.'

'Right,' Thorir said from behind a group of comrades. I hadn't spotted him until that moment, but his grin at me was *almost* unchanged, and I could have hugged him for it. 'Time to get back to work, everyone. And nice work, Nosebreaker.'

Not a word of praise to Creon, of course. He may as well not have been standing there beside me while the group around Thorir mumbled some words of agreement and faded off. The only alf who clearly acknowledged his presence was Tared, and with the dagger-looks they exchanged across the clearing, I'd have preferred for Tared to follow the example of the others.

'I'm off as well,' Edored hastily informed us, vanishing before Lyn could get in another word about injuries and Ylfreda's wrath.

Helenka cleared her throat beside me, an obvious warning that she'd wasted enough time watching alves bickering. 'I trust you'll find all you need here, Emelin Vedra. I'll have your test subjects sent to you as soon as possible.'

She turned on her heel and strode off. Around her, vines and branches helpfully nudged themselves out of her way so as not to get tangled up in her curved horns.

'Test subjects?' Tared repeated, his eyebrows shooting up as he finally tore his gaze away from Creon to examine me and the bird on my shoulder. 'Even more ambitious plans, Em?'

Lyn sent Creon and me a look of mild despair, then whirled back to Tared. 'Let's get them some dry clothing first. Talking war strategy in wet rags is asking for trouble.'

Just beyond the clearing, a dozen small structures had been shaped out of branches and leaves – not exactly huts, but rather man-high domes, appearing to have grown straight from the earth rather than been built. The bag I'd left on the beach before the battle was standing beside one of the low doors; Creon's bag had been unceremoniously dumped on the path to the next.

He picked it up from the ground with no more than a shrug, sending me a quick smile as he disappeared through the delicate beaded curtain. Every fibre of me ached to follow him into that bloody hut, hold him for half an hour, then selflessly assist him with undressing ... but Tared's gaze itched between my shoulder blades, and nymphs were doubtlessly watching me from their hidden spots between the greenery.

I told Alyra to go take a look at the island and snuck into my dome on my own.

The large bowl of steaming hot water I found on the table inside was enough to make me forget about war and bindings for a moment. Next to it stood a small pile of soaps and lotions, and I took almost orgasmic pleasure in trying every single one of them before deciding on the lemony soap filled with dried flowers. I'd spent ages roaming forests without a bath in sight; I could take a few moments to spoil myself.

By the time I'd disposed of my salty, sticky dress and scrubbed every inch of my skin clean of blood, sweat, and seawater, I felt like a woman reborn. Rinsing the salt from my hair and rubbing a good handful of jasmine oil into the dry strands did the rest. Once I was clean and no longer smelled like a drowned corpse, I pulled the only non-black piece of clothing I'd brought along from the bottom of my bag – a cornflower-blue blouson dress I'd taken along because it was as light as it was comfortable. I doubted I'd need any red magic under Helenka's protection, and dressing myself in blue might give the hint I really wasn't here to harm anyone.

With my nails clipped and my hair tied into a loose braid, I felt significantly readier for the next task waiting for me. If I had to become the kind of person who conducted magical experiments on prisoners, at the very least I could do it stylishly.

Lyn and Tared were sitting in the clearing when I made my way back, heads close together as they discussed something in hushed tones. That first glimpse was all I caught. The moment I stepped towards them, something pink and honey-blonde flashed across my field of vision and slammed into my ribcage with a bone-rattling smack – Naxi, clutching her slender arms around me as she rattled off an elaborate monologue of gratefulness and squeezed all but the last puff of air from my lungs. I was seeing black spots by the time she finally let go of me, her blue eyes wet with almost-tears, her shoulders stiff with the panic of the past hours.

'Thank you so much,' she whispered for what had to be the twentieth time. Her voice still shook. 'You have no idea ... The bastards ...'

'It's alright,' I said, not sure what else I could tell her. She didn't look convinced, so I found a grin to throw at her and added, 'Wasn't much of an effort.'

She burst out laughing at that and skipped to the next dome with a little more of her usual liveliness. 'Creon! Creon, you'll have to come out – I need to hug you too!'

At least someone was acknowledging his part of the work. There was no sign of Creon yet, but Naxi looked staunchly determined as she positioned herself at his door, and I doubted it would take her much longer than a minute to drag him out.

Which gave me about two minutes to make sure Tared wouldn't get ideas about drawing a sword next time the two of them exchanged a look.

He and Lyn broke off their conversation when I walked over to them. Only halfway across the clearing did I notice the food spread out on a blanket before them – cheese and nuts and bread and a dizzying number of brightly coloured dips, divided between dozens of small bowls and plates. My stomach let out a single, heartfelt rumble at the sight of that abundance, and at once my legs were shaking with a ravenousness I hadn't allowed myself to feel yet.

'We thought you might be hungry,' Tared said dryly as I dropped down onto the moss beside him and grabbed the first white bun within arm's reach from its reed basket. There were tense lines around his lips, and he hadn't sheathed his sword yet, but his voice betrayed little of his worries. 'Take whatever you want. We had lunch with the others.'

I stuffed one cheek full of bread and swallowed without chewing much. 'I imagine Helenka was delighted with a surprise pack of hungry alves to feed.'

Lyn's chuckle said enough. Tared gave me an amused look and said, 'I don't hear you doubting our table manners, do I?'

'No doubt involved at all,' I said.

He shoved an elbow into my ribs. I considered chucking a handful of hazelnuts at him but decided I was much too hungry to waste good food, and he would probably consider it a victory anyway. Popping the nuts into my mouth instead, I nodded at the other side of the clearing and muttered, 'Is Naxi alright?'

'She will be,' Lyn said quietly. 'Old wounds coming up. She lost her mother and her mother's family in one of these attacks.'

Close to what I had suspected. It did explain a thing or two about how a half-demon with very little empathy had ended up loyal to the losing side in this war. The sound of her chipper chatting to Creon seemed jarring in comparison – what would I have felt beneath that cheerful shield had I looked for her with Zera's bag in my arms?

'So,' Tared said, interrupting my spiralling thoughts, 'are we getting the story of how in hell you walked out of that battle alive, or is that arcane godly knowledge that we simple immortals are not deigned worthy of having?'

I threw a hazelnut at him anyway. He chuckled, looking more relieved than I'd expected below that superficial amusement.

It took just a few minutes to summarise the madness of our fight – shells, velvet, Iorgas and his alf steel. They looked deeply satisfied by my account of how Silly Helmet had been crushed below a mast, and even more pleased with my description of Iorgas's undignified end. By the time I got to Alyra's arrival – tactfully leaving out the situation in which she'd interrupted us – even Creon's emergence from the hut on the other side of the clearing was not enough to wipe the wry smile from Tared's face.

'And then we convinced Helenka to allow us in,' I finished, again strategically skipping over the finer details and the questions she'd asked, 'and we passed a prison on our way here. Which made me realise ... Well, if I need to practise some untrained magic on people anyway, better a few fae captives than our own friends, right?'

'Yes,' Lyn admitted, hesitation obvious in that single word. 'I agree we shouldn't be using our own allies as test subjects ...'

'Although there are a few I wouldn't particularly miss,' Tared muttered, which earned him a hazelnut to the head from Lyn.

'... but are you sure this is something you want to do *now*?' she continued, turning back to me as if she hadn't heard him. 'Your day has been wild enough as is. If you just want to stay here a few days while we make sure the Mother doesn't try anything again, no one will begrudge you that.'

A damn tempting suggestion – just a few days of loitering around in a sun-streaked forest, with nothing on my mind except perhaps snacking on sweet berries and taking the occasional swim in the azure sea. Then again ...

I risked a glance at Creon, who was sauntering closer, Naxi bouncing along by his side. Helenka wanted him gone from Tolya by tomorrow, and his bargain mark gave him no choice but to obey that command. So that would be days on my own in this place. Days of pretending I wasn't missing him. Days of keeping secrets I desperately did not want to keep anymore.

'You very convincingly argued why we had limited time to go look for Zera,' I said, dipping a chunk of bread into something bright red that I suspected to be a pomegranate sauce. Against the white bread, it looked uncannily like blood, and I had to consciously stop my stomach from churning. 'I doubt the Mother will take things more slowly now that she knows Creon and I are capable of stopping whole fleets together.'

Lyn's tight lips told me that she hated to agree with me. 'Still, it won't help anyone if you work yourself to death.'

'Good gods,' Naxi said brightly, plopping down next to me. 'Are we already talking about dying again?'

I shifted aside a little so Creon could sit down between her and me – and just as importantly, not next to Tared. It took a constant effort to remind myself that their ill-conceived duel had taken place less than twenty-four hours ago in their timeline, but Tared's icy glares made the point convincingly enough. Creon, bless his heart, simply ignored him.

'I promise I'm not dying,' I said once everyone had sat down, speaking to Naxi as much as to Lyn. 'I'll just see how far I get, alright? Worst-case scenario, I don't figure it out today, and then I'll just try again later. But doing nothing for half a day when the Mother might attack another island tomorrow ...'

The smile abruptly dissolved from Naxi's face, and Lyn's muffled curse told me I'd won that argument. Next to me, ignoring the conversation entirely, Creon licked a drop of pomegranate sauce from his thumb, and my lower body erupted in a flurry of sparks even as I tore my gaze away from that unfairly enticing sight.

Hell, it really was about time we had this quest behind us. If I had to pretend for another week I was not madly, senselessly in love with him, I might spontaneously combust.

As if she'd heard that thought, a slim nymph with arms covered in silvery scales darted into the clearing at that moment, announcing that the first of Her Majesty's prisoners was ready to be delivered.

Chapter 27

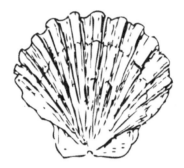

The emaciated fae male was dragged into the forest clearing in bonds of prickly greenbrier vines, held by four nymphs as if he was an unbroken horse to be restrained.

He did look broken, though.

If not for his guardians tugging him forward, I suspected he'd have collapsed onto the forest floor miles ago. His clothes hung in tatters around his body, and the skin below was drawn tight over his bones, the gauntness of the last days before death by starvation. Red welts marred his limbs, some of them superficial chafe, others deep enough to draw blood. His red hair was matted and hung to his shoulders in dishevelled clumps, and his wings were pale and cracked and tight with the effort of standing.

He crashed to his knees the moment the nymphs halted before us, air shrieking through his throat as he attempted to gather his breath.

'The prisoner you asked for, Vedra,' a red-eyed nymph proclaimed.

I stared at the wretched mess at my feet and considered changing my mind, taking Lyn's advice after all, and fleeing back into my hut for the next five days. *Wolves against wolves.* The others could handle this. Not me, the little lamb who had somehow gotten caught up in their predator games.

Then I remembered I'd put myself in the middle of those games, that I had claimed these powers despite all of Zera's warnings, and forced the gall back down my throat. Raising my chin ever so slightly, I said, 'Would you untie him, please?'

They blinked but went to work without questions. The vines slithered loose under their hands, pulling away from the motionless captive. Next to me, Lyn and Tared didn't move, watching our delivery with tight lips and cold eyes. Naxi looked like a young girl who'd just gotten a new puppy. Creon's left hand lay on his thigh – or rather on the black trousers covering that thigh – ready to intervene if there was any lust for fighting left in our unlucky prisoner.

'Thank you,' I said as the nymphs stepped back, squeezing every bit of politeness I could find within me into my voice. 'We'll manage from here. I'll let you know when I'm done.'

With a few quick nods, they vanished between the trees. Others would still be watching us from the shrubbery, I supposed, but this way at least I didn't need to worry about good courtly manners towards Helenka's envoys. The fae male before me didn't move, forehead pressed into the moss as if we'd all vanish if he wished for oblivion hard enough.

'Well,' Tared said, wry voice unperturbed as usual despite the chill in his grey eyes, 'there's not much left to ruin here.'

The prisoner rolled over at that, dull, half-lidded eyes trailing from me to Creon by my side. A spark of recognition flickered in his gaze – a relief I rarely saw in anyone laying eyes on the Silent Death.

'Please.' The word was barely audible, a ragged whisper. 'Hytherion – end this – *please*.'

Creon didn't move, watching him with the unimpressed calm of a man studying a fly trying to climb out of his beer. Lyn was chewing on a red curl, fists clenched tight. Tared breathed a curse but didn't say another word.

Waiting for me, all of them.

Fuck. I couldn't do this. Iorgas's warriors had at least been true opponents, charging at us with the arrogance of fighters used to easy victories. This broken shell of a soul, already halfway to hell and pleading with us to help him over the last leg ... How was I supposed to reduce him to even *less*?

'Oh, if you insist,' Naxi said impatiently, rolling her eyes at me before scowling at the crumpled fae male. He went slack in a heartbeat, eyes glazing over. 'There. He'll be out for a while. And before you start feeling sorry for him, he got here by attempting to chop down our trees and sell them for his own gain. He knew what he was in for.'

I blinked as I cautiously stepped closer. The tree thief didn't move. 'How do you know?'

'It's the only crime for which we're currently allowed to lock fae in the prisons,' she said, flopping down onto the moss in a flutter of pink skirts. 'The new ambassador agreed they're effectively stealing from the Mother, too, since those tree murders get in the way of the tribute harvest.'

The new ambassador – who had presumably gained that title after Creon killed the previous one. So much damn history on this small island alone. 'And what exactly did you do to him to knock him out?'

'Oh, bogged down his nervous system.' She beamed at me. 'That usually shuts them down for a bit. Remind me to teach you that trick, Creon. Anything else, or can we get to work?'

I sank to my knees beside the motionless body and studied the thief's face. He did not look like he was in pain right now. That, I supposed, was as good as I was going to get.

'I'll try,' I said quietly.

She clapped her hands like an eager toddler. 'Exciting!'

I wished I felt even a sliver of that enthusiasm as I reached out to the poor male's face and hesitated inches away from his gaunt cheeks. Perhaps I should have warned my audience in plainer terms that I had not the faintest idea what I was doing. Mind and magic, Zera had said, but by way of instruction, that was vague to the point of uselessness.

'Here's what we know,' I muttered, keeping my voice down for the ears hidden in the foliage. Perhaps some brilliant idea would come to me if I simply repeated all of it again. 'The Mother used a combination of iridescence and smoothness to bind you all. Iridescent magic to limit your powers, smooth magic to do it only when you're intent on harming her. But that whole condition of intention is optional – she would be able to bind people by taking *all* their magic, too, wouldn't she?'

She's done that, too, Creon signed when I looked up. *With people whose magic wasn't useful to produce tributes for the empire.*

'Of course.' I pulled a face. 'Any idea if the favourite pearl necklace was worn to the occasions of those bindings, too?'

He nodded, slowly. *Think so.*

'So that would essentially be a less sophisticated variety of the same thing.' Less sophisticated sounded good. Sounded doable, at least. 'Let's try that first, then. Does anyone happen to have a handful of pearls around?'

Creon chuckled as he dropped down to the ground, crossed his legs, and swung a flash of yellow at the moss around me. The plush green turned iridescent, shimmering like emerald pearls under my fingertips.

'Still feels like cheating,' I said, pressing my hands into that opalescent surface and focusing my gaze on the unconscious fae thief. Magic to change magic ... But where to start when there was only a limp body before me, rather than the sharply drawn rays of colour I had so easily diverted on the Sun ship?

Sheepishly, I added, 'Do we have any idea of where someone's magic is located?'

'There are dozens of different theories about that,' Lyn said, plopping down next to me with that small line between her brows that signalled the experiment had become an academic puzzle. Tared kept standing, his nonchalant stance against a tree not enough to conceal his wary glances at both Creon and the unconscious fae male. 'The current most popular thought is that magic is stored in the heart, but ...'

Her sentence died away, sounding dubious.

Truth be told, Creon signed with a lazy quirk of his eyebrows, *a knife to the heart does tend to limit one's magical capacities.*

I snorted a laugh, then caught Tared's look and decided I best swallow my amusement. With another sting of guilt, I bent over and lightly placed my fingertips against the fae male's chest. His heart fluttered like a caged bird below his ribs. I closed my eyes and thought of pearls and opals and bubbles of soap – enough to draw a tingle of magic from my left hand, but that power that stirred in me ...

It didn't go anywhere.

Like a trickle of water running into an obstacle, the magic halted, the pressure of it building in my right fingers, hand, forearm. I muttered a curse and pulled my left hand away from the pearly moss. The built-up pressure seeped out of me, leaving a sensation of cold water behind.

'Can't find a target to use it on.' I bit my lip, studying the unconscious fae male. 'Do you think I need to make him use his magic before I can take it?'

'Didn't need to do that when the Mother bound us,' Naxi offered with a light shrug. 'She just pointed a hand at us and I went all hollow and wobbly in my belly – took no more than—'

'Belly?' Tared interrupted, stiffening up against his tree. 'It was a headache for me.'

An abrupt, eerie silence fell. The two of them didn't move, frowning at each other over the fae body in the moss as each of them went over their memories again, found them accurate, and waited.

'Oh, gods,' Lyn said breathlessly. 'Why did we never talk about this? Lower belly for me, too – but does that mean ...'

The rest of her sentence drifted off.

I glanced at Creon, sudden suspicions sharpening in my mind, and found no laughter in his eyes as our gazes met. He nodded, reading my thoughts as usual as he tapped two fingers lightly against his throat.

His throat.

Because she'd taken his voice.

'Inika help us,' Lyn whispered. 'We're idiots. Of *course.*'

Her price had been her fertility – magic coming from her lower belly, or more specifically, from her womb. The same applied to Naxi. For Tared ...

I turned towards him, saw his thin lips and the steel gleam in his grey eyes, and hesitated. 'What ... what did she take from you?'

He did not smile, did not shrug, did not raise an eyebrow. None of those softening gestures that usually accompanied even the most unpleasant of truths from his lips. His voice was tight as a bowstring as he said, 'The memory of my parents.'

I stared at him.

'I know what the others have been able to tell me about them afterwards, of course.' Now he did force a smile onto his face – a wry, aching thing I felt like a blade to the guts. 'But I can't remember their voices. Or their faces.'

'Fuck.' I couldn't think of anything else to say. *Why did we never talk about this?* Lyn had asked, and the answer to that question seemed crystal-clear – because none of them had wanted to think about that hell of a day after the Last Battle, or about what they'd lost. 'I'm so sorry.'

He shrugged, averting his gaze. 'Best you can do is break the damn things.'

Right. I sucked in a breath for courage and turned back to my victim, that broken body covered in traces of torture. My voice shook only a little as I forced my attention to the question at hand. 'Alright, if you all felt the loss of your magic with the loss of whatever else she took ... Is that why she always takes something with the bindings, then? Not because she likes to hurt people, but because it's the only way to pull the magic out of others – by linking it to something else?'

I assume it's necessary in some ways, yes, Creon signed, pursing his lips. *She wouldn't force a price from her allies otherwise.*

A damn good point. 'So what are we going to take from this one?'

'His fingers?' Naxi suggested brightly.

'For fuck's sake,' Lyn said with a scoff. 'Whatever is easiest for you, Em. Just don't take his heartbeat. Helenka would be displeased.'

To hell with Helenka and her displeasure, I wanted to say, swallowing the words for the sake of diplomacy. I rubbed my hands over my face, then tapped them back against the moss and the fragile skin of the starving fae male. What was even left to be taken from him?

Except, perhaps ...

The idea did not so much spark as ambush me, latching on to me in the time it took to draw in a breath. I did have one decent option – one option that would still allow me to look myself in the eye when I was done. It *would* offend Helenka, though. She might accuse me of undermining her, and truth be told, she wouldn't be wrong.

Which meant I shouldn't do this. That I should just take the prisoner's voice or eyesight or whatever other cruel price and send him back to suffer the rest of his short life in chains of thorns.

But hell, I didn't *want* to.

Resolve solidified somewhere just below my midriff, a little core of stability that I could cling to even as my thoughts wavered. I couldn't give up everything for the fate of the world, Creon had said. And not being able to look myself in the eye ... that was not a sacrifice I wanted to make. Helenka might kick me out, Lyn and Tared might be furious for endangering this alliance, but I *had* to make choices.

And Creon would have my back.

I moved abruptly, forcing the decision before I had time to change my mind. Pearls and shells. I closed my eyes, focusing on that flimsy, many-coloured impression of iridescence in my mind's eye. This time I didn't aim it at a magic that I couldn't reach, concealed deeper than flesh and bone; instead, I dug for something far more accessible, something that was part of the outer layer of the skin under my hands. If I could just drag *that* out, enough a part of my victim to bring his magic with it ...

Power flushed through me, and this time it hooked onto its target.

My eyes flew open. A thin, shimmering line had spun itself between my fingers and his skin, spreading over his body like hoarfrost. I pulled at it in an odd but instinctive reverse drawing of magic, and the spread of the pearly hoarfrost slowed, halted, and reversed.

I dared to lift my hand an inch, two inches away from the fae male. The line didn't snap. I reeled it in with slow, gentle tugs, until with a strange, sucking sensation, the magic slipped out of him in a pulsing ball, fragile like a bubble of soap as it hung in the air between us.

For a moment, I didn't dare to breathe.

'Em?' Lyn said, her voice small with tension. 'Is it working?'

Oh. They couldn't see my new powers, then. I swallowed, unable to pull my gaze away from that throbbing bubble of magic, and whispered, 'I think so.'

None of them replied, but I could almost *feel* their widening eyes. I pulled my hand back until the magic was half an arm's length away from its former possessor, drew in a deep breath, and let go.

With a whoosh I felt rather than heard, the pulsing bundle dove back into the fae male's labouring chest.

'Fuck!'

'Trouble?' Tared said sharply.

'I *had* it.' I dropped back into the moss with a frustrated gesture as I looked up at him, suppressing the urge to curse again. 'The magic was pulling out. Just ... as soon as I let go, it shot back into him.'

'It's the first time you're doing this,' Lyn said reasonably. 'Give yourself a few chances to fail. Do you think it would help if you pulled it farther?'

'I don't know.' I gritted my teeth, facing the captive once more. 'Let me try.'

But even when I pulled the magic a full stride away, it found its way back to where it had come from; hell, even when Creon experimentally dragged the fae male's body to the other side of the clearing while I held his magic with me, it shot back to him in a flash of silver iridescence the moment I released my powers. Which didn't make sense. The Mother had not been standing half a mile away from the others while binding them.

Any last ties you can sever somehow? Creon signed after carrying our victim back to me and installing him in the grass and moss with just a little more care than expected. *Or perhaps there's something you can change about his magic?*

I tried and tried again, until the moss had gone flat green and we needed another dose of yellow to bring back its iridescent sparkle. None of my haphazard attempts had the desired effect. The magic pulsed and throbbed and shimmered wherever I sent it, but the moment I broke the line that connected it to me, it found its way back to its owner no matter how I tried to separate them.

'Perhaps it would be better to try again tomorrow?' Lyn cautiously suggested around attempt number twenty.

'I'm close,' I said curtly, wrestling with the magic between my hands. It wouldn't allow me to grasp it, like a wisp of smoke. But trying tomorrow meant trying without Creon, and I'd be damned if I put myself through this without his advice and suggestions to keep me sane. 'Just give me a few more tries. I'm pretty sure I can—'

She groaned, interrupting me. 'Then at the very least take a break for something to drink. Here, elderflower juice? Mint tea?' She held up a glass as she rose to her feet and tottered towards me – too close to me. 'Let the magic go for a bit and—'

'Watch *out*,' I blurted, trying to snatch the bubble of magic away.

Everything happened too fast to process. Lyn hastily yanked the glass aside, I lost control of my iridescence – and with that infuriatingly familiar sizzle, the magic shot back to the still motionless figure before me.

Except that Lyn was in its way.

And rather than circumventing her and returning to the nameless fae thief anyway, the iridescent flash flew straight into the glass in her chubby hands and dissolved within the blink of an eye.

I gaped at it, too baffled to curse for an infinite heartbeat.

'Em?' Lyn was saying. 'Em, are you—'

'Put that down. *Now.*' There was a hoarse edge of authority to my voice that I didn't recognise, and she blinked but did as I'd asked, questions buzzing in her amber eyes. 'And step away from it, before I accidentally pull out *your* magic.'

Her eyes widened. 'What?'

'I think ... I think I accidentally bound it to the glass.' I planted my left hand in the glistening moss again, aiming the fingers of my right at that innocent object before me. And there it appeared again, that familiar blob of magic – drawn from smooth crystal, now, rather than from skin.

A watery laugh escaped me. I let my magic go, and it slipped back where it had come from, dissolving into the glass.

'As if it's another body,' Lyn said dazedly, reading my expression

390

correctly. 'You gave that magic a new body to bind to.'

'But if that's the trick ...' I stared at the glass, shining innocently in the late afternoon sun. 'If that's the answer, that would mean she bound *your* magic to objects, too. Did she have a whole army of magic containers at hand when she—'

'Those damned pens,' Tared interrupted me, stepping forward so abruptly that Naxi jolted back with a little squeak. 'The pens Thysandra was using.'

Lyn frowned. 'What of it?'

'She used a different one for each name she wrote down.' He finally sank into a seat, his long legs folding in as if they'd run out of strength entirely. 'Orin's eye. Didn't you notice? I wondered about it for a moment, but then I figured I had better things to do than fret about administrative quirks ...'

'You're saying she bound our magic to *pens*?' Naxi said shrilly.

'Well, it does make sense,' I said, glancing at Creon. He'd gone dangerously taut, lips shaping a soundless curse. 'She doesn't want anyone to know how those bindings work, does she? Even if no one can break them, people could figure out ways to protect themselves against them. So *if* the method requires binding magic to objects, she needs objects that wouldn't draw too much attention during a giant administrative endeavour.'

'Like pens,' Lyn said, sounding numb.

'But that means she must have tens of thousands of pens lying around somewhere.' Naxi uttered a high-pitched chuckle. 'We should have noticed that, shouldn't we?'

They don't have to be pens anymore, Creon signed. His eyes were shooting from the glass to the fae thief and back again. *She could have changed them into anything more convenient with yellow magic. Also ...* He hesitated, fingers stiffening.

'She could have destroyed them,' I said.

He closed his eyes for a brief moment. *Yes.*

'But wouldn't the magic return to us if they're destroyed?' Lyn said, fidgeting with a red curl and audibly hoping she was right. 'From what we've seen so far ...'

'Who wants to test it?' Tared said wryly.

For a heartbeat or two, no one moved, five pairs of eyes glued to that innocent glass before me. Then Naxi muttered a curse, snatched it up, and chucked it against the nearest stone with more strength than I'd expected from her slender arms.

The glass shattered, elderflower juice spraying everywhere. Between the drops and the shards, two wisps of something else entirely drifted away from the rubble – a bubble of iridescence that had to be the fae male's magic, and something even more insubstantial, barely more than a breath of mist, floating in the perfect opposite direction.

Neither of them seemed to be aiming for their previous possessor.

With a curse, I grabbed for the iridescent moss again. My first attempt reached the magic and managed to pull it back in the direction of the unconscious fae – but that second, eerie bit that had escaped the crash grew even thinner at the same time, drifting farther away from us. When I tried to pull it back, it was instead the magic that swiftly wandered off.

'They've been separated.' I returned to the magic with a pounding heart, only to lose my grip on the other element again when I pulled at it. 'His magic and his ... the thing I linked it to. I can't get them both to return to him ... Oh, *damn* it—'

'It's fine, Em.' Lyn rubbed her eyes with a joyless chuckle. 'I doubt he'll have much use for his powers anymore.'

True, admittedly – but he'd need that other little part of him even less. I bit out a curse and yanked the magic back towards me, back towards our test subject, dragging it below his skin the way I'd accidentally sent it into the glass before.

It slipped back, shimmering for a last moment before seeping into his gaunt body. At the same moment, that insubstantial element I'd pulled from just below his skin dissolved into the moist autumn air, never to be seen again.

I stared at the spot where it had last been, not daring to believe the consequences of this experiment for a moment. 'If you break it – if you break the new container of the magic – I think you can only get one of two back. Unbound magic or whatever else you lost.'

'Orin's fucking eye,' Tared muttered.

'And it doesn't return to its rightful possessor by itself,' I added, feeling like screaming. 'So for all we know, she just snapped all those pens in two the moment you turned your backs.'

Ophion told us she can reverse the bindings, though, Creon signed.

'Oh. Yes.' I bit my lip, clinging to that thought. 'That suggests she may have kept them, then?'

'Not just that,' Lyn said, although she had gone pale. 'She's been promising some communities that they may get back their fertility if they prove themselves loyal to the empire. I doubt it's ever been her intention to let all of the magical world go extinct. Just to let the rebels die out and keep the lineages willing to bend to her rule.'

'But then she must have tens of thousands of pens – or whatever else – in storage,' I said slowly. '*Somewhere.*'

'Yes.' Lyn glanced at Creon. 'Any ideas?'

He shook his head slowly, thoughts spinning behind his eyes.

'If they're somewhere at the Crimson Court, you'd have known,' I said, hoping that was at least true. 'Are there any other places large and safe enough to keep them hidden? Mysterious underground caves? Towers with lots of "do not enter" signs around the entrance?'

Half a smile grew around his lips. *Not that I've ever seen or heard of, but then again ...*

'You wouldn't be the first person she'd tell,' I finished bleakly.

His shrug suggested agreement.

'Well, fuck,' Lyn said, glowering at the broken glass. 'Anyone else we could ask? Iorgas might have known, but ...'

Tared let out a grim chuckle.

I suspect Thysandra knows, Creon signed with a near-imperceptible glance at Naxi. Her pensive frown stiffened only for a moment. *She did most of the administration around the bindings as far as I know. Apart from her ...* His soundless groan betrayed he wasn't too happy about his own suggestion. *Agenor?*

'Don't you think he'd have told us?' I said.

I don't think he knows where the bindings are stored. But he might be able to give us a few well-defended locations he's never been allowed to enter for the past eight centuries.

'Well,' Tared said coldly, clearly loath to go along with any idea proposed by the Silent Death, 'it's not as if we have any better sources at hand. Any chance we can get him to Tolya? I'd prefer not to let the island out of sight for a few more hours.'

Lyn groaned. 'Helenka is going to skin us alive if we bring him here.'

'Don't think she'll do worse than a few scratches,' Naxi said gleefully, jumping up. 'I'll have a word with her. Good luck with that thief of yours, Em – I think he'll wake up in a few minutes once I'm no longer keeping him under.'

And with that meagre warning, she skipped off, her dancing pink skirts swallowed by the forest within a heartbeat or two.

CHAPTER 28

THE THIEF DID INDEED wake up in a few minutes, dizzy and disoriented as he clawed the forest floor to haul himself upright.

Then he froze, staring at his own bony fingers where they lay curled around a clump of grass.

Lyn and Tared did not appear to think much of that little gesture of bewilderment; they studied the nameless fae with morbid academic curiosity, as if he might succumb to the consequences of my binding magic any moment. But Creon's eyes narrowed with the thief's catching breath, his demon senses picking up on the oddities in the other's sensory perception at the very same moment.

The wounded fae male released the grass with stiff, staggering motions, then cautiously pushed his palm back against the earth, like a farmer testing the quality of his soil. For one more moment he lay motionless. Then, scrambling up into a sitting position, he pressed the nails of his right hand into his left forearm for a long three seconds, leaving crescent-shaped cuts between the wilts and scrapes when he pulled away.

He stared at the marks in disbelief for another heartbeat before his head jerked up, bloodshot eyes seeking Creon. 'What ... what did you *do*?'

Creon merely nodded at me, his face expressionless.

'What?' Lyn said sharply. 'Em?'

'*You*?' the fae thief rasped, gaping at me as he half-crawled, half-leaned towards me. In the corners of my sight, the nymph guards loomed from between the trees, making no effort to hide their colourful presence. They'd never been far away, presumably. They knew we were as good as done with our work, and any moment, the greenbrier vines would come out again.

No time for elaborate explanations, then.

'Don't let them know,' I hissed, bending over to the male before me to hide both the sound of my words and the motions of my lips. He smelled of stagnant water and sulphur – as if he'd already started rotting. 'Do you understand? We'll both be in trouble if they figure out what I did, alright?'

'My ... my lady.' The breathless gratitude in his voice made my skin itch. His dull gaze clung to me; bony, spider-like hands clawed at my wrist, trembling with emotion. 'Thank you – gods bless you – *thank you*—'

Behind me, the red-eyed nymph said, 'Vedra?'

I did not look up. Wrapping my hands around the captive's wrist in turn, as if to pull him away, I breathed, 'Do you *understand*?'

'I understand.' The word came out on a whispered sob. 'I'll be silent as the grave, I swear – I—'

'Good.' I pulled myself from his powerless grip, managing only with the greatest effort not to scrub the feel of his dirt-stained hands from my skin. The nymphs were striding closer, thorny vines in their hands as I'd expected.

Behind me, the others were suspiciously quiet.

'Vedra,' the red-eyed nymph repeated, bowing her head a fraction. 'You're done with him? Do you need another one?'

'No, thank you.' As long as I had to be diplomatic, I didn't want to think about numbers – about how many of these living corpses they'd have paraded before me if I'd asked for them. 'We found what we needed for now. Please pass on my gratitude to the queen once again. This has been very helpful.'

She nodded, turning towards their prisoner without another word. The vines lashed from her hands like whips, thorns digging deep into the fae male's fragile skin as the greenbrier twisted around his arms and ankles.

He screamed in very convincing agony.

Even so, I didn't dare to face the others. No one spoke up. It was only after his cries and moans had melted into the stirring of the forest, minutes later, that I found the courage to meet their gazes again, feeling like a convict stepping onto the scaffold as I turned. They hadn't moved, although the shadows in their eyes proved it was not for lack of thoughts.

I braced myself for defence. 'I thought—'

'You took away his ability to feel pain,' Lyn interrupted me quietly – too quietly for nearby nymphs to hear. 'To feel anything at all.'

Somehow, she didn't look furious.

If anything, she looked unbearably sad, and my defiant speech about Zera's wishes and damn our allies' preferences froze on the tip of my tongue. I parted my lips, then realised I had no idea what to say anymore. The touch of those powerless fingers lingered on my skin. Like a reminder of what I might become – like an accusation.

My shoulders sagged, the absence of resistance turning my bones to lead. 'Well ...'

'Oh, Em,' she said, sounding smothered. 'That was once again not your responsibility.'

'Might be wise not to tell Naxi,' Tared said and sent me a mirthless grin. No anger burning in his eyes, either. 'She's capable of sneaking into that prison and cutting off his fingers anyway. Not that the poor sod would feel it, at this point, but ...'

Lyn let out a mirthless chuckle. I blinked at Creon, who smiled – that insufferable, smug smile that said, *I told you so.*

397

Told me that I could make choices. That I could piss people off. That maybe, just maybe, Zera had been right to trust me.

A surge of gratefulness washed over me, bringing heavy exhaustion in its wake.

'I'll be in my hut for a bit,' I forced out, deliberately averting my eyes from Creon while I spoke that sentence. I'd be damned if I let Tared think this was some sort of invitation. 'Let me know if my dear father shows up.'

'Will do,' Tared said dryly. 'Although I suspect he might announce himself as soon as he hears of your latest shenanigans.'

Or as soon as Alyra tries to clip his wings, Creon added.

That at least pulled something like a laugh from my depleted mind. Then I staggered off and lay in a soft nymph bed for the rest of the afternoon, resting my limbs, staring at the roof of braided branches, unable to stop thinking of hands that could no longer feel.

I didn't remember falling asleep, but it must have happened at some point, given that I was woken up abruptly by the double alarm of Alyra's squealing and Agenor's deep voice.

'*What* did she ...'

I was given about half a heartbeat to jolt up in bed – 'She might be sleeping!' Lyn cried in that moment – before all six-foot-something of my father's winged stature burst through the beaded curtain that covered the doorway of my nymph dome. With his smooth silk shirt and his hair brushed into meticulous locks, he looked like he'd been pulled straight from a routine day of meetings and strategizing – but his familiar green-brown eyes were wide like saucers in the low light of early evening.

And something about him was different.

Not the hard set of his jaw or the keys around his neck or the agitated spread of his wings behind his shoulders ... but his *hands*. My gaze, travelling down, latched on to his fingers, or more particularly, on to the faint shine that glowed around the tips of them, shrouding his well-kept nails in a hint of gold.

Gold – the colour of the gods' blood.

His gaze had hooked onto my hands, too, which lay curled into my blankets. I saw no trace of that strange glow around them, but his eyes grew impossibly wider.

'Good gods.' That tone would have been called shrill for any lighter voice. 'Good gods.'

Alyra scurried in after him, shaking her little white-grey head irritably against the clay beads. The look she threw me was the look a weary governess might send the parents of her most hopeless subjects: *I tried so hard to explain the situation*, it said with an air of righteous indignation, *but of course you can't expect a fool with such an excessive wingspan to make sense of this.*

'Oh, good,' Lyn said, a little out of breath as she slipped in after my familiar. 'You're awake.'

'Not much choice,' I said sourly, swinging my legs to the floor and rubbing the sleep from my eyes. 'Evening, Agenor. I gather they told you about my latest feats?'

He just stared at me blankly – a little more blankly, really, than I thought reasonable for a male who had one day drunk Korok's blood from his veins to achieve the exact same thing.

'Just trying to fit in with the family traditions,' I added, pulling a face and shoving to the edge of the mattress. With a fae lord, a phoenix, and a bird hovering beside the bed, the nymph dome was about as full as it could be without bursting at the seams. 'Could you all give me a moment to get up, perhaps?'

Lyn modestly retreated, but Agenor seemed to have taken root where he stood, and Alyra merely fluttered up to the table containing my soaps and washing bowl. I snorted and got to my feet nonetheless. Smells of frying onions and fresh bread reached me from outside, and I wasn't going to let a bewildered father stand between me and dinner.

'What did Korok give you?' I said as to him as I tugged the first sweater I could find from my bag. I might as well use the occasion to learn a little more about common divine practices. 'You don't have the other types of colour magic, right?'

He let out a baffled chuckle. '*Other* types of colour magic?'

'That sounds like a no.' I pulled the sweater over my head and beamed at him. 'Surface magic, Zera called it. The Mother has it, too. It's how she binds people. What did you get – just the snakes?'

'Just the snakes, yes,' he grunted, looking like he might faint any moment. 'Em, do you have any idea ... Zera has never sworn in anyone she hasn't known for decades. *None* of them ever did something like ...'

'Well,' I said practically, 'she *has* known me for decades, hasn't she? I just didn't know her back. Also, this is quite an extraordinary situation, you must admit that. Also, I suppose it helps that I carried that bag.'

He went grey – actually *grey* – in the dimming light. 'You did *what*?'

'Carried the bag of grief.' I flung some yellow at the shoulder of my dress, turning the light fabric thick and sturdy. 'Let's go get dinner. Alyra?'

The little falcon squealed and jumped from the table top, surged towards me, and landed clumsily on my shoulder. The warmth of her feathery body against my cheek was a comfort, the immediate connection so strong I almost flinched.

'Em,' Agenor said again, sounding like he was holding himself together with rapidly unravelling stitches, 'lifting that bag is impossible.'

'Yes, so it turned out.' I stepped into the honeysuckle-scented world outside and held aside the bead cords for him. 'She forgot to tell me that until I'd already done it, though. Oh, and she sends you her regards. And her compliments for that lovely spine you uncovered recently.'

Lyn laughed out loud. Agenor made a somewhat choked sound as he followed me onto the path, an unhealthy pallor still dulling the bronze of his skin.

'Anything else?' he said, sounding like he was telling a healer that he might as well amputate all his limbs at once, if they needed to be chopped off anyway.

'Zera didn't know where she is,' I said. 'Allie.'

His wings and shoulders sagged a fraction. I'd correctly guessed that

that was the question he hadn't dared to ask, then.

'I see.' His voice had gone flat and deep again.

'She did say your magic was still unbound by the time of Korok's death, though,' I quickly added. A small comfort, but it was all I had to offer – that, and the knowledge that he was not the only one whose heart sank two inches every single time my mother's name was uttered. 'So at least we know that.'

He muttered something like a thanks, and I knew in that instant that he wouldn't care much about being a coward – hell, that he'd *welcome* the scorn and the self-loathing of never stepping in to stop the Mother all those years – if it brought back the woman he'd loved and lost twenty years ago.

I wasn't sure what more to say, the way I never quite knew what to tell my father as soon as either of us started feeling something. We walked the rest of the way in silence, Lyn a tactful ten strides ahead of us, to where a roaring campfire was burning and the others were busy distributing plates and cutlery to a messy circle of diners.

'Is fire even allowed in nymph forests?' I muttered.

'As long as you use dead wood,' Agenor said immediately, seeming equally glad for a less inflammatory topic to revive our conversation. 'But yes, cutting off fresh branches would land you in their prisons, which ...'

I shivered. 'Yes. No.'

He gave me a grim smile of understanding, hand coming up a few inches as if he was about to squeeze my shoulder. Alyra huffed, ruffling her feathers, and his arm dropped again.

There was little room for feelings around the fire, where Tared and Beyla were exchanging rapid remarks on the future defence of Tolya and Naxi was monologuing to Creon about the convenience of over-burdened nervous systems. I lifted Alyra off my shoulder, allowed her to flutter off, and dropped down next to Creon, which earned me a habitual side-glance from Tared and Agenor. Ignoring them, I accepted the plate Naxi offered me and said, 'Any new ideas on the bindings?'

Several, Creon signed with a shrug. *All of them nonsensical. Haven't asked Agenor yet.* His lips trembled into a smile that could have melted stone. *He seemed a tad distracted by something when Beyla faded him in.*

'Must have been the pretty nymph scenery,' I said earnestly.

Creon chuckled. Naxi's grin at me suggested no one had told her about the prize I'd taken from the fae thief yet.

We summarised our discoveries for Agenor while we ate grilled vegetables drenched in smoky date sauce and baked handfuls of dough into crispy rolls over the fire. My father had recovered his unwavering composure; he didn't bat an eye at the sentient nature of Zera's forest, only allowed himself a slight frown at the mention of living dragons, and accepted the news of Iorgas's death with a raised eyebrow and a nod. But he shot up straighter at our theory on the Mother and her pens, and went so far as to mutter a curse when we finally arrived at the question for which we'd dragged him away from the besieged Golden Court.

Where were the bindings?

'We're talking about immense quantities of objects, I presume,' he said slowly, eyes darting around the circle as if he was waiting for more information. They lingered on Creon, who shrugged and signed, *Tell him he knows the numbers better than I do.*

I passed on the message. Agenor groaned, rubbed his temple, and said, 'All magical peoples put together, we would be speaking about hundreds of thousands of items. Unless Achlys and Melinoë bound all of you to a grain of sand ...'

'Considering that she can reverse individual bindings,' Lyn said, 'it stands to reason the objects must at least be sizeable enough to be separable.'

'Yes. Let's assume dice-sized at the minimum. And I assume there would need to be some sort of organisation.' Agenor stared at the forest for a moment in sharp concentration. 'I can't think of any location at the Crimson Court that would lend itself to that sort of collection. Which was your conclusion, too, I'm guessing?'

'What about her throne?' I suggested, the idea already past my lips before I could think it through.

'They already had that thing long before the Last Battle,' Agenor said, his brows drawing together. 'And I doubt it would offer enough space to store that many bindings. Even if they used every individual bone ... Not enough of them by far, I'd say. Interesting idea, though.'

Now that I considered the matter a moment longer, I was inclined to agree with him. My hunch had hardly been based on any evidence, but rather on the persistent annoyance of not knowing why in hell she was so protective of the damn thing. There had to be *some* reason, even if Zera had said ...

I pushed the matter aside. Another question, another day.

'How about the Borython complex?' Lyn was saying, fidgeting with her curls. 'It's about as well-defended as I'd expect for a binding storage area.'

'I've been there often,' Agenor murmured as he shook his head. 'I know the place well, and I've never noticed anything that might fit what we're looking for. There's the Khepri caves, of course, and Achlys and Melinoë have always been rather secretive of their reasons for keeping us out of there ...'

'It's not the caves,' Beyla said, her eerie voice hardly audible over the crackling of the fire. 'They're mostly empty, save for a couple of old blood altars I suppose she inherited from Korok.'

Agenor blinked at her. 'How in hell did you get into that place?'

'With a sharp sword,' she said a little smugly.

Even Agenor allowed himself a chuckle, although it sounded somewhat bewildered. 'Well. Not the caves, then. I can't really think of any other closely guarded locations – there are a few places where no one ever goes anymore, of course, but that's usually for far more innocent reasons.'

'Any examples?' Lyn said.

He pursed his lips. 'Oskya was destroyed by a volcanic explosion a few centuries ago. The line of Castor Thenes died out, and since their lands are as infertile as a damn desert, no one has ever tried to make the house inhabitable again. A few islands were ravaged by battle, and then there's ...'

His sentence halted in its tracks. For one silent heartbeat, the world remained motionless save for the flames, which danced joyfully under the paling evening sky.

'And then there's the Cobalt Court, of course,' Agenor finished slowly. Another silence rippled across the clearing.

On the other side of the fire, Lyn's eyes had widened. Tared stiffened beside her. In the corner of my sight, Creon did not so much perk up as sharpen, his shoulders and wings relaxing in that deceptively controlled way that betrayed the tension beneath.

I felt infuriatingly young, suddenly, surrounded by people who knew, people who understood, people whose breath had a reason to catch in their throats.

All I knew about the Cobalt Court ... 'Wasn't that destroyed during the War?'

'It was.' Agenor raked a hand through his hair, jaw tight with concentration. 'About half of the castle is gone, and the rest is a ruined mess. I didn't think of it as a place of great secrecy at all – that is to say, we *know* why she doesn't want anyone around there. But the fact remains that no one has set foot on the island for centuries, and even if it's not terribly well-defended—'

'It is quite well-defended,' Beyla interrupted – calmly, quietly, but in a tone that left no room for arguments.

Agenor raised his eyebrow. 'Beg your pardon?'

'*Some* people did set foot on the island, you see.' Again that little smile, a spark of wanderer's joy burning through the pale mask of her grief. 'I tried to reach the castle a few decades ago. There's a shield of sorts around it – looks like nothing but air, but I couldn't get through it when I tried. I assumed at the time it had something to do with that damn memorial and didn't think much about the place anymore, but—'

'Whose memorial?' I said, anxious suspicions rising in me.

'Her son.' Agenor was very deliberately not looking at Creon. 'The Cobalt Court was the last place where she saw him alive before he left for the Continent and got killed by human mages. She hasn't allowed anyone to visit the place since he died – wandering alves aside, that is.'

Beyla huffed a quiet laugh. I glanced at Creon, who had gone still in that most deadly of ways, the glass-edged quiet of a predator readying to strike. What was he thinking of – the day that same grieving mother had cast him out to die in a muddy bay at the Golden Court and told him he'd served his purpose?

'We're idiots', Lyn said before I could figure out how to ask, wrapping her arms around her face with a pained groan. 'She's been so loudly sentimental about keeping the place untainted and preserving those memories that I never even considered there might be *other* reasons to keep everyone away from the island.'

'It might still just be the memorial, of course', Tared said. His slender fingers were rubbing slow circles over his thigh – signs of a mind in deep thought. 'If she was willing to battle gods over the little prick, a magic shield or two wouldn't be the strangest she's done in his memory.'

It's not just a magic shield, though, Creon signed. That undercurrent of tension below his movements had intensified, leaving an impression of a coil about to snap even on the lazy, elegant motions of his fingers. *It's a magic shield she didn't tell her most trusted people about, not even those technically responsible for protecting the place.*

Tared's lip curled up at the correction, but he restrained himself to a cold, 'Yes.'

I had to fight to stay calm as Lyn quietly translated the point to spoken language for my father's benefit. Creon's agitation was infectious. I knew that way his wings drew taut against his spine, knew the way his almond eyes narrowed in cold concentration, and he never allowed himself to be so affected by anything less than spectacular breakthroughs. The Cobalt Court – a tightly guarded fortress masquerading as an innocent memorial. That *was* odd, wasn't it?

'Have you ever been there?' I said, forcing myself to keep breathing slowly.

Creon shook his head with a minuscule shrug. *I'm the very last person she would ever allow into the place.*

Right. One son lost; as much as she had treated the second as a convenient tool of her own making, she wasn't making the same mistake a second time.

Or, just as likely, she hadn't trusted the powerful mage she'd forcibly bound anywhere near the secrets of his own lost powers.

405

'Memorial or not', I said slowly, 'it sounds like we should go take a look, then.'

'I'm not terribly bothered about memorials for murderers', Tared said with a grimace. 'The Mother is allowed to complain about grave sanctuary by the time she's arranged a proper burial for every human he killed. That shield may be an issue, though – do you think you could break through it, Em?'

'From the long and extensive study I've made of my new magic', I said, pulling a scholarly face at him. 'I don't have the faintest damn clue.'

He laughed. 'Brat.'

'I mean, I could try.' I pulled up my knees, rested my chin on them, and gave the matter some serious thought. 'It sounds like it might be soft magic – limiting movement, not allowing people to step through. If it's possible to make a shield of that, the Mother presumably figured it out, and if I have enough iridescence at hand, I may be able to cancel out her magic.' Now that I put it like that, it began to sound surprisingly doable. Agenor was staring at me with blank eyes, though. I grimaced and finished, 'I'll just have to try.'

'All we can do, isn't it?' Beyla said philosophically.

But hell, I wanted more. I wanted to tear the Mother's shields to shreds. I wanted to find the damn bindings, pens or whatever else they might be. I wanted to drain every last drop of magic out of them, restore all my friends had lost, then burn what was left of the cursed things to dust and ashes. Restless impatience was creeping into my limbs, a desperate urge to jump up and go, go, *go* ...

'What about Tolya, though?' Naxi said, her voice small. 'Who says she won't attack again if we leave now?'

'If they attack again, it won't be within the week', Agenor immediately said, rubbing those gold-glowing fingers over his temple. 'They'll need a moment to decide what they're going to do with an unbound godsworn mage on our side. That said, once they've determined their plan ...' A small, bitter pause. 'I wouldn't expect them to stall for much longer.'

Faces turned hard and grim in that deafening silence.

Stall. Ships around the Golden Court, threatening but not attacking. Envoys on the islands, spreading rumours but nothing worse – yet. Now that the full extent of my new magic had been revealed, however … The Mother would realise that every day of delay gave us the chance to gather more strength.

No more time to prepare. No more time to look for bindings or allies. The next attack would be a genuine one.

'All the more reason to go as soon as possible', I said, breaking the ominous silence. *Move,* my limbs were hissing at me, *move, move, move.* 'Helenka wants to have us gone tomorrow anyway. Might as well leave straight for the Cobalt Court.'

There was a hint of relief in the murmured confirmations and agreements, just enough to tell me I was not the only one teetering on the brink of reckless movement. Agenor alone drew his brows together, glanced at the azure bargain mark lodged into Creon's wrist, and slowly said, 'How did you even convince her to let you in for a single minute?'

Creon merely shrugged as he bent over to tear off a bite of bread, the very picture of uncaring, unmannered boredom.

The atmosphere shifted like a gust of cold wind as Agenor's doubt morphed into annoyance. 'You didn't threaten her, I hope?'

With an unimpressed raised eyebrow, Creon stuck half of the bread into his mouth and held the rest out to Alyra, watching her as she excitedly picked it from between his fingers. The high-strung silence lasted two, three seconds before Lyn quietly said, 'Did you tell her the truth? About Zoya's death?'

Agenor frowned. 'What truth?'

Without so much as a glance at him – or at Lyn, or even at me – Creon rose to his feet, brushed the dried leaves off his shirt, and sauntered off.

He was gone so swiftly I didn't have time to object. Even Alyra's alarmed squeal didn't stop him as he vanished between the trees, the shadows of dusk wrapping around his dark wings unnaturally fast. Lost for words, I stared at the spot where he'd disappeared and felt for a moment as if I was back at the Crimson Court, back at the pavilion, where he would shrug and walk off whenever my questions dug just a little too deep.

Demon powers. Dangerous ground to tread.

'For fuck's sake,' Tared muttered, audibly rolling his eyes.

I dragged my eyes from the dusky forest, managing only with the greatest of efforts not to jump up and run after him. What in hell had sparked this flight? Should the story have remained a secret from this company in particular, for whatever reason?

'Forgive me,' Agenor said stiffly, clearly of the opinion that someone rather owed *him* forgiveness, 'but I don't see what—'

'It's about his demon magic,' Lyn interrupted in hushed tones, throwing me an apologetic look. 'He used his powers to soothe Zoya's pain when he killed her, you see. Took it for himself instead. I suppose if Helenka—'

'What?' Agenor blinked at her with a sharp, incredulous laugh. 'Good gods. Lyn, that's a lovely story, but he cut Zoya to *pieces*.'

'Bold of you to assume we aren't perfectly aware,' Tared said coldly, and I recalled my father had admitted the whole mission had been executed under his command.

'Thank you, Thorgedson,' Agenor bit out. 'That's not what I'm ... Look, Creon would effectively have killed himself if he'd taken her pain the way you're suggesting. Do you really think *he* would make that sort of sacrifice? What madman would ...'

And there it was – the reason Creon had walked. My confusion melted into razor-sharp clarity, a sensation so bitter it made me wince. He must have known this was coming. The scorn, the anger, the disbelief. The nettling remarks. The brand new stabs at a vulnerable wound he hadn't chosen to bare here or now or to these people.

Something snapped inside me, the reckless fury drowning out the rest of my father's words. 'A madman with ten times the integrity you always assumed, perhaps?'

Agenor stared at me.

'He's been doing it for all of them,' I added sharply, shoving my plate aside to get to my feet. Damn my father's good opinions, then. 'Not just Zoya – everyone the Mother made him kill. It was the only way he could mitigate—'

'Em.' His tone was too firm – the tone of a male who has no choice but to be firm, because the alternative is to slip into flailing hysterics. 'He's killed thousands upon thousands of people since the Last Battle.'

'So?'

He didn't move. The fire crackled and spat sparks into the darkening sky; a cool night breeze blew through the clearing, drawing goosebumps over my bare arms.

'He did not take all of that pain,' Agenor finally said, audibly struggling to convince himself and me at once. 'You must have misunderstood. He might have done it for a few people, perhaps, but—'

I scoffed. 'Glad to see it's still your first instinct to assume the rest of the world must have gotten it all wrong.'

He winced as if I'd struck him in the face. 'That's *not* what I meant, Em.'

'Then you're being unusually sloppy with your wording.' I rose to my feet, careful not to step on Alyra in my restless anger. The others were quiet around us, a tense, uncomfortable silence. 'What were you trying to say, then, in all your sage wisdom?'

'You …' He closed his eyes, drew in a deep breath, opened them again. 'Em, you haven't seen those lists of names. You haven't read the reports. I'm not fully sure it's physically *possible* to torture yourself to death that many times, and as much as I see the appeal of—'

'Is it more impossible than lying under a bargain of truth?' I said coldly.

He stiffened. 'I beg your pardon?'

'Did you assume Helenka believed him on the basis of his pretty blue eyes? He just told her the whole story this afternoon, under a bargain of truth. Go ask her, if you need someone else's word for it.'

He didn't move. Something almost *helpless* flickered in his eyes as he parted his lips, closed them, seemed to think better of it, and opened his mouth again. Naxi chuckled behind me – that ruthless, melodious laugh.

'Why for the gods' sakes did I not know about this?' Agenor finally ground out.

'Not my secret to tell,' I said stiffly and squatted down to scoop Alyra from her spot beside my feet. She found her balance on my shoulder with a contented squeak. 'If you want to know what he's actually been doing all this time, maybe stop waiting for me to tell you and just go have a word with him for once?'

His jaw tensed. 'Like you're about to do, I gather?'

Did it make sense to deny it? The reflex was frighteningly strong, a testament to weeks and weeks of stifling those addictive stutters of my heart, of trying to play by my guardians' rules at least in the public eye. But no one would believe I was about to go to sleep, and what was the sense in lying if it would only fan their suspicions?

Oh, to hell with it. Let them be unhappy with me. Let them worry about my poor unblemished innocence. Creon needed me, and choices had to be made.

'Just want to make sure he's alright,' I said – such a mind-blowingly simple sentence, tumbling over my lips so mind-blowingly easily. 'Let me know if you come up with any other ideas about the Cobalt Court.'

I heard them resume their conversation as I walked off through the darkening forest. Heard my name, Creon's name, something about the defences of the Mother's memorial. Tared sounded unhappy. Agenor sounded politely aggrieved.

I'd deal with their displeasure later. For now, I had better things to do.

CHAPTER 29

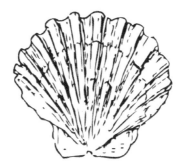

CREON'S HUT WAS IDENTICAL to mine, although his bed had not been made before our arrival and the washing bowl on his table was accompanied by a significantly smaller assortment of soaps than I had received.

It was also empty.

I muttered a curse and stepped back outside, considering whether this was enough of an emergency to stumble around a rapidly darkening forest to find him. Before I could come to a decision, Alyra launched herself from my shoulder and flapped to my own little dome of braided branches, then peered at me with a look that said, *so much head, so little brain.*

Oh. Of course.

I rolled my eyes at her, threw a last glance over my shoulder, and when no one appeared to be following me, slipped through my own beaded curtain.

Creon had collapsed into the wool and linen of my bed, his eyes closed, his hair unbound and brushing loosely over his shoulders. His wings lay spread out over the abundance of pillows and blankets, the black velvet so dark in the falling twilight that it seemed they were sucking up the last sunlight that fell through the wall. As I tiptoed in, he looked up and smiled – but it was a faint smile, a fragile thing that could shatter at the first nudge.

This, I decided, was not going to be a conversation for birds.

'Alyra,' I said quietly. The thin walls did not give the impression they would conceal any sound louder than a deep sigh. 'Would you do me a very important favour and make a quick flight around the island? I want to be sure the fae aren't unexpectedly coming back.'

Alyra proudly and fearsomely puffed out her chest, then hopped out-side and soared out of sight. Creon gave another unconvincing smile but didn't move. The slump of his shoulders was a disconcerting sign – a hint that I still didn't fully understand his reasons for walking, that he was plagued by more than the possibility of an unkind word or two.

'What's the matter?' I whispered, cautiously arranging the beads before I stepped deeper into the dusky little dome.

He sat up with a soundless groan, tucking in his left wing to make room for me on the bed. *Agenor.*

'I figured, yes, but what exactly did he do to—'

Ask his fucking questions, Creon signed, pulling a face. His signs were sloppy and exhausted; he barely lifted his hand more than an inch from the blankets.

I blinked. 'His questions?'

Why can't the bastard just assume I pressed a knife under Helenka's nose and keep his mouth shut? He averted his face in the dusk, wings rising and falling with the deep breath he took. It did not appear to calm him down much; his fingers still moved restlessly as he lifted his hand, hesitated, and added, *Did you tell him?*

'Lyn did.' I sat down beside him and folded my legs to my chest. 'But I told Lyn, so I suppose ...'

He gave a heavy shrug. *Don't worry about it.*

'Of course I'm worrying about it, you idiot', I said, wrinkling my nose at him. 'You're not making sense. It's *good* if he realises at some point you're not the unfeeling bastard he's always assumed you were, isn't it? That's supposed to be progress?'

Creon looked like I'd twisted his balls two full rounds and called it a caress.

'That's a no,' I concluded wryly. 'Help me out here, Your Highness. You're panicking because he finally figured out you weren't merely slaughtering people for the fun of it for the past thirteen decades? Why for the gods' sakes would you—'

Helenka wasn't going to spread the word, he signed hurriedly. *But if Agenor knows, the whole Golden Court will hear in a few days. And possibly half of the magical world, too.* He rubbed a hand over his face, the ink scars on his fingers twisting like macabre worms in the falling darkness. *I feel ... naked.*

I huffed a laugh. 'I've never known you to be terribly troubled by nakedness.'

He shrugged. *Skin is just skin.*

'Rather pretty skin, in your case.' I studied the way his lips twitched up, a barely perceptible motion that looked like a performance for my benefit, not like an expression meeting even the lowest threshold to be counted as a smile. 'You're actually frightened, aren't you?'

Terrified, he signed, a blunt honesty in the shapes of his fingers that left me lost for words for a moment. Before I could recover, he added, *It's alright. I knew it was going to happen when I told Helenka. But knowing they know what I did makes me feel like someone's flaying me alive to take a look at what lies beneath.*

Coming from one of the few people in the world who actually knew what it felt like to be flayed alive, that was enough to send a cold shiver down my spine. I considered wrapping my arms around him, then decided against it. Whatever twists of that shadowy mind were coming to the surface here, I suspected they were important; physical contact would only give him an excuse to quickly shove any accidental revelations back into the shadows.

These glimpses of vulnerability were rare enough. Better to allow them every opportunity to free themselves.

'And why would that be so bad?' I said, slowly, quietly. 'If they took a look at what's below?'

Creon closed his eyes, sagging against the wall. *They stopped looking centuries ago, when they decided they knew all there was to know about me. Now that they've figured out the first secret, they'll start ...* He hesitated. *Reconsidering.*

I cocked my head at him. 'As they should.'

He flinched – actually *flinched*.

'Why does that bother you so much?' Gods help me. I'd known he was loath to open up about his secrets, that he'd staunchly refused any effort to soften that cold hatred of the rest of the world ... but I hadn't expected *this*, ugly and bitter fear as the revelations slipped from his control. 'You were the one who told me to stop worrying about everyone's opinions, for hell's sake. Not exactly a shining example you're setting here.'

His chuckle was about as joyful as a frosty winter morning. *That's different.*

'Why?'

If they think anything unfavourable about you, at least ... His fingers froze in mid-air for a single but all-telling moment. *At least they would be wrong.*

The sight of those signs sunk into my guts like a sip of pungent liquor, leaving a trace of burning, aching understanding behind.

Of course.

Of *course*.

Months of playing the cruel fae murderer he didn't even want to be, months of infuriating our allies rather than offering any hope of peace or even a meagre ceasefire ... Because trying would open the door to the possibility of failure – that much I'd always gathered. Only now did I realise it was not so much the possibility of failure but rather the *expectation* of it – the full and honest assumption that as soon as anyone took a closer look at whatever hid below his skin, they would inevitably conclude he was still exactly as rotten as two centuries ago.

Killing his last hope of ever being anyone else.

It wasn't uncertainty creeping up on him, now. It was a sense of inevitable doom. And yet he *had* told Helenka, he *had* sat there by that fire and waited for someone to bring up the topic ... Oh, Creon.

'I see,' I said, my choked whisper just loud enough to rise above an orchestra of crickets outside the thin wood walls. 'The problem is not that everyone else may hate you. It's that you still hate yourself far too much.'

I don't. He averted his eyes, fingers clenching and unclenching in the falling darkness. *I'm just trying to be realistic about myself.*

I huffed a laugh. 'Edored is more realistic about himself than you are.'

A meagre grin crossed his face. *Stop trying to convince me I'm not a fucking prick, Em. You're not helping yourself by picking an impossible stance to defend.*

'You *are* a fucking prick,' I said, leaning over to tuck a strand of hair behind his pointed ear. He shivered at the touch. 'I've never argued otherwise. And you're a vain, reckless idiot, you have a terrible tendency towards melodrama, and you don't have the faintest clue how to deal with people when you can't threaten or infuriate or seduce them. None of that is a lie. It's just that you forget to be realistic about the other side of you.'

Ah. He rested his head against the braided twigs. *Like my pretty face.*

I scoffed. 'Skin is just skin.'

This time his grin looked significantly more like a true grin. *It's rather impolite to turn my own weapons against me, cactus.*

'Shouldn't have started training me, then,' I said and stuck out my tongue. That, too, seemed to cheer him up better than expected. 'But fine, I can wield a weapon of my own if you insist. Tell me something pleasant about yourself.'

Had I told him to go hug Tared, his watery grin couldn't have evaporated any faster. *Something ... what?*

'Something positive.' I could feel a smile grow on my face as I scrambled up in the abundance of soft pillows and crossed my arms. 'You know, realism. Or did you want to convince me there's not a single nice thing to be said about you?'

He blinked. *Well—*

'Because in that case you'll have to assume that Lyn and Naxi and I are all utter fools to think you might be salvageable at all,' I interrupted as briskly as I could in my hushed voice, 'and that doesn't sound terribly realistic to me, either. So?'

The way his eyes darted to the curtain-covered doorway and back to my face was vaguely reminiscent of a trapped animal looking for escape.

I climbed into his lap just in case he was earnestly considering fleeing, straddling his powerful thighs so that he would at the very least cause an unhelpful lot of noise if he tried to storm out. His muscles strained tight beneath me, mocking my attempts to keep him in place. He smelled of blood and summer – a strange, wild fragrance that made my stomach clench in anticipation. I swallowed and tried to focus on his face instead of the sensation of his hard muscles pressing into me, tried not to think of those quiet moments on the ship and all the places where his hands had wandered ...

He had stopped looking at the door. His eyes had swept back to my face with the full intensity of his demon senses, aware of every unwelcome spark that burned through me.

Damn it. This was not the moment to get distracted, no matter how delightful the temptation. I cocked my head at him, holding his ink-black gaze, and slowly repeated, 'Say something pleasant about yourself, Creon. I promise I'll adequately reward you.'

Something flared in his eyes – something that made me expect for one breathless moment that he'd flip me over in the blankets and kiss the next sentence on my lips to oblivion. But he slumped against the wall without any seductive attempts to distract me and flatly signed, *I suppose I can be reasonably intelligent at times.*

I snorted. 'You suppose?'

Yes. He clenched his jaw. *Not enough?*

'I suppose I love you,' I said, pulling a face. 'Hear how convincing that sounds?'

For fuck's sake. He forced a quiet laugh over his lips. *This is torture, Em.*

Not much of an exaggeration, probably – he may have been trained to suffer the sting of blades and knuckles without flinching, but the ragged edges of his own mind were an adversary he'd happily avoided for most of his life. I shrugged and said, 'I learned from the best. Try again, and make it sound a little more convincing, please.'

I'm ... He sucked in an unsteady breath. His fingers paused, twitching into several signs they never ended up finishing, before they finally settled on a weak, *Intelligent enough?*

Still barely passable, but at least it was progress. I leaned over and pressed a kiss to his forehead, breathing in the metallic tang of blood that had mixed with the familiar scent of his body. His breath caught at the first contact of skin to skin, and again it took all I had not to tear off his shirt and find the far easier, far more immediate comfort of pleasure in his arms.

But this was not about comfort. This was not about the easy road.

I made myself move away from him, bringing a much-needed foot of cool air between our faces, and whispered, 'Tell me another thing.'

He swallowed audibly. His gaze followed me with hawkish focus, but his hands lay unmoving in the blankets, as if he hadn't even heard me.

'Creon.' If not for the flimsy walls, my voice may have grown louder. 'You convinced yourself this battle was lost before you even started fighting it. To hell with that. There *is* a reason I love you, and if I have to punch that insight into you, so be it. Try to see yourself through my eyes. Tell me another thing.'

His lips shaped a curse, but his hand came up. *I don't suppose you fell in love with me because of the pretty face and the impressive title?*

I snorted. 'Rather despite the title, I think. Stop trying to talk your way out of it.'

I ... He rose up a fraction, jaw clenching. *I'm not some backstabbing bastard to the people I care about? I mean* – he'd interpreted my unimpressed eyebrow correctly – *I suppose I can be loyal. I mean*—

I burst out laughing, unable to help myself. He followed the example a moment later, dropping his arm back into the blankets – wry, apologetic laughter, but laughter all the same, a thousand miles removed from the gloomy pit in which I'd found him. I slumped chuckling against his chest, drinking in the boom of his heartbeat, and wondered if it was possible to love him hard enough to make him understand, hard enough to crack through that inhuman armour of his self-loathing.

Could demon senses do that?

His fingers wrapped around my chin, tugging my face up to his. Suddenly his lips were dangerously close, parting ever so slightly, beckoning me closer with nothing but their seductive curve. His eyes had gone fierce – gone *hungry*. A storm was raging in the depth of that gaze, thunderclouds drawing together ... But no storm would ever harm me with his arms around me, and my body screamed at me to lean into that safety, into the blissful, all-encompassing presence of him.

So much for my attempts at torture.

'This is unfair,' I breathed, unwilling to surrender, unable to move away. 'Using your body to get what your words can't.'

Mischief gleamed in his eyes, a glimpse of almost boyish amusement that made my heart stutter pathetically. *Didn't I earn a second kiss with my point about loyalty?*

Oh. Gods help me. He had.

I pressed a single kiss to his sharp jaw – a chaste virgin's peck, but if I lingered just a moment longer, I doubted I'd ever pull away again. He *knew*, of course. A satisfaction far too close to smugness shone in his eyes, a gleam of self-assured triumph that made it almost impossible to believe this was the same male who could not compliment himself to save his own damn life.

'This is not how any of this works, Your Highness,' I informed him in a husky whisper, planting a finger in his chest. The tremble of his suppressed laughter did not help, damn him. '*You* were the one in trouble here. You can't just start kissing me without doing anything to deserve it.'

Even his wings were shaking now, but his face remained gravely serious apart from that twinkle in his eyes, lighting up the bottomless black. *I wouldn't dare to start kissing you. I have the greatest respect for your honour and innocence.*

My honour and innocence had slipped out of the window hours ago, I suspected, and run off for a night of carousing in dubious establishments. At the very least, they were nowhere to be found as I clenched my teeth, jutted up my chin, and tersely said, 'Well, I'm not kissing you either.'

A most respectable decision. How did he manage to look like he was laughing when those sensuous lips of his didn't so much as twitch? And why did I feel like *I* was losing this game all of a sudden, when I'd started out in a position of guaranteed victory?

'Unless you give yourself another compliment first,' I added quickly – perhaps a little too quickly. There. That should give him something to feel a tad humbler about, shouldn't it?

Except that he didn't look humble at all, or flinch, or stop smiling that infuriatingly satisfied smile at me.

I have excellent taste in partners, he signed dryly. *As opposed to you, if I may be so free as to make that point.*

'That's not a compliment! You can't just—'

His left hand fisted in my hair, and then his lips were on mine – claiming, triumphing. I was too late to object. Too late to think. His tongue brushed against my lower lip, seeking entrance, and I gave in before my good sense could override my instincts, opening my mouth to him. His tongue swept in, and the world blurred, turned liquid. I moaned before I could help myself, clutching my hands around his jaw. He tasted like freedom. Like starry nights and velvet wings flaring wide, and I drank him in like an addict, unable to get enough of every single breath and moan.

His hand in my hair pulled me back, breaking our kiss.

I gasped, disoriented, as I came back to myself in that darkening nymph dome, surrounded by braided twigs and the continuous sounds of a forest full of life. My hands had left Creon delightfully ruffled below me, his hair tousled and his lips a bright, gleaming red – but that little smirk on his face was far too controlled, and far too content.

'You said ...' I almost forgot to keep my voice down. 'You weren't going to kiss me, you ...'

His innocent blink was about as convincing as floating gold. *I was just collecting my prize.*

'You weren't going to get a prize for that sorry excuse for a compliment!'

He lazily ran his tongue over his lips, holding my gaze. *If this is how you kiss when you're unimpressed, I think I'll stop trying to impress you.*

Heat bloomed in my lower belly, radiating all the way to my cheeks in a blush so fiery it must have been visible even in the dusk. A dazed laugh fell over my lips. 'Creon ...'

Look at me. He sat up straighter, the motion swift and sudden like a viper's attack. There was no moving back with his left hand still tangled in my hair; all that still separated us was his right hand, signing the words with breathless speed. *I can't see myself through your eyes, cactus. It feels too close to a lie. But I can feel you see me.*

Oh, gods.

Demon eyes, again.

I couldn't have looked away even if I'd wanted to, drawn into the abyss of his eyes like a sailor lured into the depths by sirens' songs. So many contradictions in that one look – a plea and a challenge, self-hatred and arrogance ... I swallowed and made myself take in the sight of him, the cruel scar cutting through his eyebrow, the sharp slashes of his cheekbones. His full lips, capable of such glorious smiles. The silk-black hair I played with when he was falling asleep in my arms. The sharp tips of his ears, which would show dark blue smudges after long days of reading, when he'd tucked back dark strands with ink-stained fingers a little too often.

Warmth flushed through me, and this time, it had very little to do with lust.

Look at me. He mouthed the words. Smouldering eyes drank in the breathless stutters of my heart as he leaned closer; warm breath brushed over my lips, and I forgot about prizes, forgot about compliments and rewards. His right hand wrapped around my hip, tugging me closer. His left hand drew a torturous line down my spine. I didn't dare close my eyes beneath those worshipful caresses, even as pleasure slowly unfolded through me.

But at last his lips found mine, and my eyelids fluttered shut.

His kiss was warm and slow, but full of dangerous promise. Sensation swallowed me in a heartbeat. His tongue teased the seam of my lips, and I opened for him with a greed I couldn't deny – unsure whether I'd lost or won the game, and no longer able to care. Captured by the deepening intensity of his kiss, I could do nothing but feel. I could do nothing but want. His hand slid up along my spine, into my hair, and for one moment I was afraid he'd pull away and force me to think sensibly again.

Instead, he tilted back my head and moved his mouth to the vulnerable skin just below my jaw, kissing a slow line down the side of my neck.

A moan escaped me.

With a silent laugh, he moved back and rested a single strong finger against my lips.

Right. Silence. I gulped in a breath, his finger a heavy brand against my mouth. These branch walls would betray every sound we made – it was madness, to follow the fiery need pulsing below my skin under those circumstances ... But every touch we shared was like the release of a breath I'd held for days, like loosening muscles I no longer even realised were cramped. Just the two of us – such simple, instinctive freedom.

'I'll be silent', I breathed. 'Don't flee me now.'

His finger slid down my chin, then up my cheek, tracing the line of my cheekbone. His gaze followed, as if committing every inch of my features to memory. Even in the near-dark, the black of his eyes radiated a raw, cautious vulnerability – as if the curtains had lifted and revealed every broken shard below, every flaw and imperfection, every aching scar.

Look at me, he'd said.

'Do you feel me?' I whispered.

A shudder ran through him. I lifted my hand and gently dragged my fingertips over the edge of his pointed ears, savouring his gaze like the rich burn of a fine wine, savouring the next tremble that shook him to the very tips of his wings. My mind whirled in a warm, lazy tangle of images, laughter and the glow of magic and strong, unyielding arms around me. My body burned like hellfire, equal parts love and sin.

'I once hated you', I added quietly, brushing down over his temple. 'Do you understand? I don't just want you to know how I feel about you now. I want you to remember and feel the difference. I want you to realise in the very marrow of your bones that last time you showed yourself to the world, you became the world to someone.'

He was shaking now, as if I was breathing frost and cutting winter winds into his face. I lowered my hands to his shirt and slowly, infinitely slowly, pried open the first button in the shadowy dark, resting my fingers against the taut skin just below his collarbones.

'Don't forget that I once saw the worst of you, too', I whispered, leaning over to the silhouette of his face. 'And then I found the rest of you, and everything changed. I'm not an idiot, Creon. I know courage and dedication and empathy and selflessness when I see them. So don't *ever* tell yourself again that you're being realistic, hating yourself, because—'

His lips silenced me.

He kissed me like a drowning man, like a soul hanging over a bottomless chasm by the tips of his fingers. I'd felt that dark pit inside him with Zera's bag in my arms, the howling void of loneliness and guilt; now I felt it again, tasted the abyss on his lips as he wrapped his arms around me and dragged me against his shivering chest. Blood rushed to my head, to my fingers, to every place where our bodies met. I clawed into his shirt and rose to meet his kiss, finally surrendering to the hunger that clawed through me.

I *would* keep him from plummeting again, damn it all.

He broke away without warning, planting ravenous kisses along my jaw, my throat, my shoulder. Biting down hard on my lip was all I could do not to cry out. In the dark, we were reduced to wandering limbs and hot, frantic breath; I moved on instinct, unable to see more than outlines as I reached for his wings and found the smooth surface on my first try. Creon growled a breath, and I repeated the motion, brushing a long line to that spot just behind the shoulder I knew to be more sensitive than any other place.

He flipped me around in the blankets.

Hands moved feverishly in the night, bunched up my skirt, parted my thighs. Rough fingers slid below my underlinen, and I whimpered as he stroked the slick flesh without mercy, finding the core of my pleasure effortlessly as if no gods or magic had ever separated us. Gritting my teeth, I arched into him, into that heavenly friction of his touch, desperate for more. He pressed a first finger into me in response, and my moans fought a desperate battle for freedom on my tongue.

The world had grown too dark to read signs or the shapes of words on lips. I could barely even distinguish his silhouette against the backdrop or braided twigs and vines, the shape of him kneeling between my thighs. It was torture not to see his face, torture not to know his thoughts, and somehow those unknowns only heightened the sensations I *did* feel, his fingers thrusting into me, his thumb rubbing that most sensitive spot, his free hand stroking and kneading my half-bared bottom. I dug my nails deep into my blankets and struggled to be silent, struggled to swallow every sob and cry, as he coaxed me to my breaking point with the ease of a male who knew my body better than myself.

I had to clasp my hands over my mouth as I came, smothering my unstoppable moans in the warmth of my own palms.

Wings whooshed through the darkness as he lowered himself over me, pulled my hands aside, and kissed me as if he could not help himself, as if he had to taste the remnants of my whimpers for himself. I spread my legs wider, and he ground the bulge of his erection against my slit with a single demanding roll of his hips.

Good sense unravelling, I yelped into his kiss.

He nipped at my bottom lip, hard, an unmistakable punishment. Fuck. Yes. Silence. But how in hell was I supposed to be silent when he once again rubbed himself against me, or when he slipped his hand between our bodies and freed his straining erection with a flick of his fingers? Bodily reflexes had taken over, and my limbs and lungs didn't care about secrets and alliances. I fought the very breath in my throat, fought my parting lips, fought the cries and declarations crowding up against the flimsy shields of my self-control ...

Like they must do for him.

I stiffened for a single breathless moment.

Was this forbidding cage of silence so very different from the restraints in which he'd lived for over a century? Hadn't he felt this a hundred thousand times before, the frustration of words not allowed to come through? Perhaps this was the perfect levelling of our playing field, the *both* of us forced into a quiet that went against every instinct and desire – and perhaps it would teach me, if nothing else, to understand.

His cock prodded my inner thigh, hot and heavy and slick with arousal, and I clenched my jaw against the moan that had been about to escape me. I might have trouble keeping silent for others, but I *would* be silent with him.

Even as his broad tip settled against my entrance and pleasure pulsed through every nerve in my body.

Even as he entered me in one deep thrust, hard and full of unbridled passion, filling me until I could barely breathe around him.

He gave me no time to adjust, to brace myself. His breath turned to a low growl as he slid out and buried himself back into me, a relentless claiming I welcomed eagerly. My fingers gripped his shoulders, knotted in his hair. His fingers dug deep into the flesh of my hips. Faster and faster he moved, fucking me with the frenzy of the beast who'd stood on that deck and brought down an army, with the fury of a lover who'd do a hundred times worse for me, with the bottomless despair of a heart that could not forgive itself. There was no sweetness to this release. No grace or control. Something raw and wild grew between us, something unhinged that unfurled in the darkness and sank its hooks and nails deep below my skin, and I gave myself over to it in that perfect, horrible, impenetrable silence.

He clawed his way up my body, fingers finding my belly, breasts, throat. I wrapped my legs around his slender hips and arched even closer to his ruthless thrusts. The quiet, desperate harmony of panting breath and skin slapping together filled my ears, mingling with the thunder of my heartbeat; senses bled together until I could taste the pressure of his fingers, smell the darkness of the night. He grazed his teeth over my ear. I scraped a nail over his wing. He snarled and slammed into me even harder, and I just had the presence of mind to repeat that caress a last time as every muscle in my body clenched in surrender.

We blew apart together, one silent creature of teeth and nails and convulsing limbs in that soft, narrow bed.

I clung to him throughout our shared release, biting my tongue so hard I tasted blood, the pain nothing but a faint, discordant note amidst the ecstasy. Creon's lips never left my skin. He kissed my jaw as I clenched around him, my throat, my shoulder, until at last my climax faded and he slowly pulled out of me, lowered himself to his side, and tucked me against his chest so tightly I could feel his heartbeat through the thin layers of shirt and dress.

I closed my eyes, struggling for breath, for composure, for the sense to care about anything beyond the feel of his body against mine. His breath was rough against my ear. His arms were warm and powerful. One wing curled around me, invisible but recognisable by the soft brush of velvet in the night, and I realised we hadn't shared a moment like this since the last night we'd slept in the Underground, not so much lust but simple, unhurried intimacy.

A sigh of contentment escaped me as I nestled even closer against him.

Time thickened to a slow, syrupy substance. Far away, I could hear the voices of the others for a while until they eventually became silent, too. The crickets had gone to sleep. In their place rose the sounds of a forest at night, the hooting of owls and the scurrying of small animals. Barely audible and yet infinitely reassuring, I could distinguish the distant rustle of the sea. I hadn't realised until that moment how much I'd missed that familiar backdrop of my old life in the quiet Underground and on the middle of the endless continent.

'If we're lucky', I murmured drowsily, stroking the wrist he'd locked around my waist, 'we'll be having conversations in the dark tomorrow night.'

He stiffened for an instant, then let out a long, unsteady breath and released me to roll over. I fumbled for his body in the dark and found his half-hard cock first, still sticky with the traces of his pleasure.

'Oh, damn it', I grumbled, and he breathed an audible laugh. 'Perhaps we do need a little light.'

A spark of yellow broke through the darkness, and my blanket glowed up – a change to create luminescence, the same technique that was used to create the orbs illuminating the fae courts. In that eerie, silvery shine, Creon's half-naked glory became even more inhuman, more *other*, his sharp features highlighted by the shadows. His cock stirred under my appreciative gaze, and I chuckled and patted it before he could button up again.

Much as I cherish your good opinion, he signed dryly after he'd finished that task, *you should probably get some sleep before you save the world tomorrow.*

I should. My day had been too long already, with the afternoon shifted into morning after I'd returned from Zera; I suspected I'd sleep within a heartbeat the moment I allowed my body to soften into my bed. But it was with some apprehension that I glanced at my rumpled blankets and muttered, 'You're not staying here.'

He did not avert his gaze, watching me with those inscrutable demon eyes. In the silver light, the black of his pupils sparkled like a star-flecked night sky. *Do you want me to stay?*

Yes. No. The usual conundrum, want versus should, desire versus strategy; of course I wanted him to stay, but what if Helenka's spies would see him slip from my dome tomorrow morning? I swallowed and whispered, 'If we're right about the Cobalt Court ...'

There was no need to finish that sentence. If we were right, *everything* would change. He'd have his voice and his magic. We'd stand a chance to win this war. And unless that mysterious shield gave us more trouble than expected, we'd be back in the Underground by nightfall.

Where I could come clean to Tared and Beyla and Agenor without spending gods knew how much time locked in the same small travel company.

We could handle one last night, after the many we'd spent apart.

'Tomorrow', I said quietly, which was by no means a sensible continuation of my sentence, but brought a small smile to his lips regardless. He held out a hand. I crawled into his lap, flung my arms around his shoulders, and kissed him with that word still pulsing in my thoughts, warm and silky like a promise – *tomorrow, tomorrow, tomorrow.*

For a single perfect moment, nothing existed except his hands and mouth on me and his strong legs below me, our tongues dancing together in the intoxicating rhythm of our hearts. One moment in which I was simply here, simply his, touches muting all worries and concerns,

blurring the thoughts of battles and challenges to come ...
Then Tared's voice said, 'Em? Are you—'
And silence.
Deadly, damning silence.

CHAPTER 30

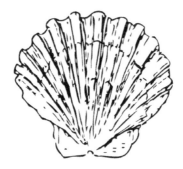

A BUCKET OF ICE water could not have been more effective to separate us.

With a gasp I tore away from Creon and jumped back, a lightning-quick movement that would have been reason for praise during any training session. Away from the bed. Away from that glaring, incriminating transgression of our kiss. For one last moment I dared to hope – *had* to hope – that I'd been fast enough, that the world had been dark enough, that Tared's familiar voice hadn't truly sounded as close as it had seemed through the panicked rush of my thoughts ...

And then I whipped around and found him standing in the low doorway, frozen mid-step, his gaze fixed on Creon like an arrow about to fire.

Oh no.

Oh no oh no oh no oh—

'Tared?' I choked out. 'Tared, it's not – I'm not ...'

He didn't even glance my way, narrowed eyes examining the fae male on my bed in a silence that swelled to a roar in my ears. Outside, nymphs were chattering. Insects buzzed through the humid darkness. None of it broke the frozen impasse between these braided walls, this high-strung moment between lust and disaster. In the silvery light, Creon's face could have been a statue's, a perfectly sculpted sneer on his lips, his eyes cold as the deepest sea.

The memory of whooshing blades welled up in me without warning, of blood spattering on moss and fire roaring through Zera's wood.

'Tared,' I hissed, more desperately now. 'Please don't—'

'Get out,' Tared said softly.

His voice didn't rise. His hand didn't so much as twitch in the direction of the sword on his back. But there was an iciness to his tone, like the cold and deadly undercurrents below a perfectly still body of water, and it got the hairs rising on the back of my neck even though those two words had not been aimed at me.

'He's *not* getting out,' I snapped.

Now Tared finally turned, eyes narrowing in unmistakable warning. 'Em—'

'He's not going anywhere.' My chest constricted, as if laced into a too-tight corset; the words spilled out without thought or reason. *Mine*, something inside me growled, on that knife-edged line between claiming and giving in – a choice I hadn't wanted to make yet made instinctively, driven by every promise I'd made. *I'll have your back.* 'You are one who just came barging in! Not exactly your place to tell anyone to go anywhere, and—'

His arm closed around my shoulder before I could jerk away.

Night and silver blurred around me, and when the world returned to its own colours, we were standing in the empty forest outside, not a living soul to be seen or heard. Stars sparkled between the branches overhead. The night breeze brushed my cheeks. I wrenched myself out of Tared's grip and took a step back, hurriedly gazing around – no huts or nymphs or anything else to be seen, nothing but the alf before me and rows and rows of dark trees.

My heart sped up to a dizzying rattle. 'Where are we?'

'Alone.' His words were perfectly calm and jarringly unthreatening.

'Away from Helenka's spies. What—'

'Take me back!'

'Into his claws?' His eyes narrowed in the dark. 'Not until you we've had a *very* good word. What exactly is going on here, Em?'

I should have been more diplomatic, more defensive, more appreciative of his concern … But what did he think he was doing, for fuck's sake, dragging me around like a child without a mind of her own? I bit out a laugh. 'If you need me to explain to you what's going on, the state of your love life is significantly worse than I thought.'

He didn't bat an eye. 'Em, what has he been doing to you?'

'Nothing!' I burst out, hushed voice cracking. 'Nothing that I didn't want him to do, at least!'

'Hardly a defence,' Tared said coldly, a hint of gritted teeth breaking through the unnatural calm of his façade for the first time. In the white and grey moonlight, his slender face was pale as snow. 'He should know *so* much better than to take advantage of—'

'He did no such thing, for fuck's sake!'

We glared at each other, breathing heavily, neither of us willing to back down. He was the first to avert his face, releasing a heavy groan as he did, visibly forcing himself to lower his shoulders. Two, three more seconds went by as he opened his mouth, looked for words, closed it again, and struggled a moment longer to compose himself.

Then, with flat, unnatural composure, he said, 'I'm not sure how to put this, Em.'

I swallowed several more unpleasant retorts. 'How to put what?'

'Creon.' He made a sharp gesture at the forest to his right, hesitating a last moment before he continued. 'Look, he knows how to manipulate people, do you understand? He knows how to make himself likeable when he needs to be. I don't blame you for feeling … hell, *infatuated*, if he's been making an effort to—'

'He has *not*.'

'No, of course that is what he—'

'Could you stop treating me like a gods-damned *child*, Tared?' I was so very sick of this – of walking on eggshells every moment of the day, of having to defend my own damn choices at every bend in the road. 'I can determine for myself how I feel about him, thank you very much, and—'

Something twitched at his temple. 'Em.'

'You're doing exactly what you accused Agenor of doing!' The words were speaking themselves now, weeks and weeks of unspoken frustration hurtling over my lips. 'Don't you see that? Telling a grown woman where to go, what to think, how to deal with—'

'And what else am I supposed to do?' he hissed, the shield of composure not so much breaking as wavering. 'Would you prefer for me to observe this very real threat to your wellbeing and just leave you to deal with it yourself?'

'He's not a threat to me!'

A scoff-like laugh broke from his lips. 'He's a threat to everyone.'

'Oh, for the bloody gods' sakes.' I was no longer keeping my voice down. I could no longer care about keeping my voice down. He stood no more than five feet away from me, every inch my friend, every inch the unshakable, imperturbable alf who had all but adopted me into his home, and yet I felt like I was shouting at him over a gaping chasm. 'Listen, I *know* he's been an utter prick to you, I *know* how much he's ruined for you, but did you ever consider that perhaps he wouldn't be nearly so much of a threat if you could stop kicking him down on every possible occasion?'

The silence reverberated between us as he drew in a long, steadying breath – a desperate attempt not to drag me back into the Underground and lock me far away from any intruding fae princes, I suspected.

'Em,' he said. Curt and clipped. 'Please don't start about his poor misunderstood soul to me.'

'But you won't understand if you refuse to understand *this*!' Would physically shaking him improve anything? Unlikely, and yet my hands itched to try. 'He did not make an effort to seduce me, alright? He stayed away from me to make sure nothing of the sort would happen until *I* forced him to stop running from me, and if I hadn't done that, we would never have ...'

I faltered, unsure how to finish that sentence. The only options I came up with were options I very, very much did not want to speak out loud for Tared to hear. *We'd never have kissed. We'd never have fucked against that wall. We'd never have fallen in love.*

His voice had gone flat and low again. 'And when, exactly, did all of this happen?'

Oh, fuck.

'I ...' I stammered. *Months. I've been keeping secrets from you since the very first time we met.* 'It depends on what you—'

'Before or after the Golden Court?' he interrupted.

Hell take me. I'd planned to prepare for this conversation, to come up with some version of the story that, while staying true to the general outcome of things, would put a little less emphasis on weeks and weeks of sneaking around. I'd planned to figure out first how many harmless lies would be acceptable.

But there was no time to think here, in the face of those merciless questions, and if he found out later I'd been lying ... Would he ever trust me again?

'Before,' I whispered weakly.

His jaw tightened. 'Before or after we brought you to the Underground?'

The steel in his voice could have drawn blood. I felt myself shrink under his gaze, pathetically tempted to burst out crying and plead for forgiveness and hope that would put a stop to his questions. But I had *some* pride left, and my knees wouldn't buckle even as the silence swelled to deadly proportions in the night air between us.

'Before.' I had to force the word over my lips.

'I see.'

Still there was no spark of fury – hell, couldn't he at the very least have shouted a little? Anything was better than this unbearable flatness, no trace of the friend I knew and joked around with, no clue of what was happening below that undisturbed surface.

I started, 'Tared—'

'And you didn't think,' he cut in, a whetted edge to every individual word, 'that it would be helpful to inform us of the situation at some point?'

I grasped for the answer – the *true* answer – as if I was drowning. 'I was going—'

'Do you have *any* idea what this has been doing to me, Em? To let the fucker back into our lives after everything?' There was no sign he'd even heard the start of my answer, and only then did I realise his question had not been a true question, either. His outburst came from behind clenched teeth, washing over me in with the unstoppable force of a tidal wave. 'I haven't had a single decent night of sleep since he weaselled his way back into the Underground, for Orin's gods-damned sake – haven't stopped looking over my shoulder for a minute. Did you ever spend the *faintest* thought on how much I've been worrying about you and your starry eyes? About ... about ...'

He fell silent, breathing heavily. Something wolfish tightened in his expression, something even his tense lips and clenched jaw could not conceal – a glimpse of wildness crawling from behind his easy-going exterior, howling for justice.

I'd felt the emotion behind that stoic calm, standing with Zera's bag in my arms.

'About Lyn,' I finished numbly.

He swallowed visibly, jaw not loosening. 'Yes.'

'I ... I didn't know you were still worried about that.' I couldn't breathe. Understanding seeped through me like ice water, driving gall up my throat. *Not a decent night of sleep.* 'I thought you talked with Lyn. I thought—'

'If someone were to keep his hands wrapped around your neck day after day,' he snarled, 'ready to squeeze the very fucking air you breathed from your lungs, would you feel terribly reassured by people telling you the bastard surely doesn't mean any harm? I've been hovering over my own damn grave for months, and *this* is how you decide to inform me it was never Lyn he was preying on? You never thought that may have been worth mentioning before?'

I gaped at him, stunned into silence. His eyes were cold chips of grey in the moonlight, glittering like hoarfrost.

'But ...' My thoughts had scattered like leaves in the wind. 'But it wasn't just ... Even Naxi told you that you didn't have to worry! She's a *demon*! I didn't realise—'

His eyes widened abruptly. 'Naxi knew about this?'

Oh, fuck. *Not* the right thing to say. 'Well, she ...'

'... is a demon,' he finished, his voice biting like acid. 'Anyone else you told? Or do I at the very least have the honour of being the second to figure out your little secret?'

And only then did the full extent of my stupidity hit me.

Because Lyn knew.

Lyn, who had to realise just how much he had suffered because of my secrets; Lyn, who had gently suggested I tell the family, but hadn't pushed, hadn't pressed past the limits of my fear. Who was, once again, at the centre of this tangled web in a way I'd never comprehended until half a minute ago.

And *she* hadn't told him.

The silence stretched out too long as I grasped for words. I could see it in Tared's face – anger making way for exhaustion, the look of a male wondering how many more times he'd have to brace himself.

'Who knew, Em?'

'I – I ...'

Gods help me, what could I say? *Why* hadn't Lyn told him? Not my responsibility, a weight she hadn't wanted to place on my shoulders – but that meant she'd left it on his, and was that the sort of disloyalty an alf teetering on the edges of his sanity could wave aside?

I'd *felt* it, the raw agony of that unfulfilled bond between them. Would I have been able to wave it aside, had it been my pain to live with?

Tared was too fast for my spiralling thoughts, his words hard and sharp, but not enough to hide the festering fear below the surface. 'Does Lyn know?'

I should have denied it immediately.

But I hesitated, unsure for one moment how many lies I could afford to tell, and I knew in that moment that he knew – the answer a leaden invisibility between us, too heavy to be spoken out loud. Betrayal flashed in his eyes, shock baring his hurt and anger for one brief instant – the feelings not aimed at me, this time, or even at Creon.

'I made her promise not to tell anyone!' I blurted out, breathlessly.

No. *No.* He couldn't go blame Lyn for my stupidity now – I may have messed up my own secrets, perhaps, but I was *not* going to cause any more trouble between them, was not giving that gods-damned bond a chance to drag Tared into whatever hell awaited heartbroken alves. 'I made her keep it quiet! Don't blame her. I ... I thought ...'

The sentence dried up on my lips. What for hell's sake had I thought?

'I'm sorry,' I breathed, the painful inadequacy of the apology audible in every syllable. 'I wasn't trying to hurt anyone.'

He stared at me for an endless heartbeat, expression unreadable in the moonlight. Around us, the forest had tensed, too, branches holding still in the midnight breeze like silent sentinels. As if the trees themselves were holding their breath with me, waiting for him to speak, waiting for my knees to buckle.

Then his shoulders abruptly slumped. He stepped back, parting his lips with a chuckle that seemed to have been drawn straight from a corpse's lips.

'Go to hell, Emelin.'

And without waiting for a response, he faded.

The moist forest floor was cold to the touch when I sank down against the nearest tree, staring up at the star-flecked sky with numb, unseeing eyes.

Fuck.

For minutes on end, that seemed to be the only thought my mind was capable of forming.

I ought to get up and look for help – that awareness was still vaguely present in the back of my mind. I should try to draw someone's attention and find my way back to familiar territory. But my body refused to oblige, limbs making the unhelpful point that being stranded in the middle of an unknown forest wasn't the worst of my problems by far.

As opposed to …

Go to hell, Emelin.

I flinched, stomach rolling violently as I curled my knees to my chest and buried my face between them, breathing in short, shallow gasps. Gods help me, what had I done? What had I been thinking? All those weeks of keeping secrets for the sake of peace, and one moment of stupidity had unleashed more trouble than I could have imagined – more than honestly might have done. Why couldn't I have kept my hands off Creon for a few more days – kept up pretences until I was prepared for this conversation?

Why had I somehow failed *again*?

A shudder ran through me as memories mingled, different voices and different faces, but their gut-punch effect so very similar. *You embarrass me, Emelin.* Once again, I'd tried so damn hard. Once again, I'd miscalculated. And here I was, sitting shivering and close to tears in the thicket of a nymph forest, dreading the fact that I'd have to get back up at some point, that I'd have to face them all again and find out just how much I'd ruined with one stolen kiss too many.

Would Tared tell Beyla? Would he, gods help me, tell Edored?

I was back at the pavilion at the Crimson Court, Valter's letter in my trembling hands – *Don't look for us.* What if we returned to the Underground tomorrow to find the people I'd called my family would no longer look me in the eyes? What if Lyn was furious with me for betraying the secret in such a foolish way? What if Agenor heard about this catastrophe and decided I wasn't worth the family name after all, and—

A squeak broke through the silence, mere strides away.

I jolted up, only just suppressing a shriek. Red shot from my fingertips before I even realised I was drawing magic, and a slash of crimson cut through the moonlit darkness, lighting up moss and bark and leaves and sending a flurry of blossoms swirling down.

Only then did I recognise the small, feathery shape that had landed at my feet, glaring indignantly at me.

'Alyra?' My voice wobbled dangerously as I jerked back my hand. 'Oh, gods. Sorry. Didn't mean to attack you. I'm not … I'm not feeling my best.'

She could see that, her unimpressed glower informed me, and she was of the strong opinion that I was whining needlessly. Sure, it would be somewhat inconvenient if the man-with-a-sword-in-stead-of-wings were to stay angry forever, but then again, I still had her. And I didn't think she'd be going anywhere, did I?

I blinked against the deluge of thoughts welling like my own, my panic faltering in favour of surprise. Did I expect her to go anywhere?

'Well,' I said, sounding defensive, 'you think I'm an idiot, too.'

Which was exactly why she wasn't going to leave me alone, for the goddess's sake; a bird had to know her responsibilities, and clearly I was the sort of little fledgling that needed some guidance so as not to drop out of the metaphorical nest.

'Ah,' I said sheepishly. *Metaphorical?* Did birds even know what metaphors were, or was that my own mind's interpretation of whatever was coming down this bond between us? 'Well. That is reassuring, I suppose?'

Alyra hopped impatiently up and down, waiting for me to get up and follow. Minutes ago, the very concept of moving had paralysed me, but I found myself scrambling to my feet now, driven by the wish not to disappoint her more than by any inherent desire to get out of this patch of moss. Moss couldn't shout at me. Moss wouldn't be embarrassed by my presence. But she was right, I couldn't sit here wallowing for the rest of the night – and if nothing else, Creon would probably be looking for me.

If he wasn't breaking Tared's bones, at least.

I bit down a curse and walked a little faster.

Alyra either knew the way or was very confidently lost; I didn't have the heart to question her as she flapped before me, her white feathers starkly visible even in the darkest shadows. The nymph forest was quieter at night, but never completely still. Trees whispered around us like gossiping old ladies, and night birds flitted from branch to branch, their songs shattering the quiet at irregular intervals. Now and then, I thought I heard footsteps, but whether they were Helenka's spies or just figments of my imagination, I didn't dare guess.

Then finally, looming up between the trees and the silver glow of moonlight, that winged silhouette I knew better than my own hands.

'Creon!'

He'd pulled me into his arms the next moment, squeezing me against his chest as if to press every last huff of breath for my lungs. I buried my face against his shoulder, dug my hands deep into his sides. When I breathed his name a second time, my voice was laced with involuntary sobs, and every muscle in his body seemed to stiffen at that sound.

I knew that stillness. If I so much as thought of violence a little too loudly, he would have his knife against Tared's throat before I could draw my next breath.

'Stay here,' I whispered, forcing myself to be rational. Violence was the last thing we needed now. 'Please. I need you with me.'

His arms relaxed, although not much. Moving half a step away from me, he wrapped the fingers of his left hand around my chin, tilting up my face for inspection. With his right, he signed, *What did the bastard do?*

The gestures were barely visible in the dark, and yet his straining fingers left no doubt of the emotion behind them: both worry and the tight fury of a male wrestling with himself not to tear down half an island in his wrath.

I blinked back tears and managed a muffled, 'He wasn't happy.'

Em. His jaw clenched, the cold moonlight sharpening the edges of his face. *You're crying.*

'I didn't want to hurt him!' I gabbled, unable to avert my face with my chin still caught in the vice of his fingers. 'You were right, I should have told him weeks ago. I should have ...'

What did he do, Em?

The first tears came dripping over my face, like drizzling rain, pathetic and useless. I couldn't stop them from spilling out no matter how hard I tried. Alyra squeaked beside me, a reproachful sound. *Have you still not learned that honesty makes everything easier?* my thoughts translated, and I caved.

'He figured out Lyn knew and didn't tell him.' The words poured out like an unstoppable waterfall. 'I told him to blame me, and then he told me to go to hell and vanished, and ... and ...'

Creon had gone icily still before me.

'What if I ruined *everything*?' Sobs tore out with my words. 'What if he never wants to see me again and I can't live with them anymore and they start whispering about me all over again and—'

Cactus. His fingers gripped my face so hard it hurt – ungentle, but the shock brought the escalating spiral of my thoughts to an immediate halt. *Listen to me. Him being angry doesn't equal him hating you. He'll come to his senses, or else Lyn will bring him to his senses, and then you'll have a chance to explain yourself. Give him time to cool down. No use in trying to reason with a furious alf.*

'But what if—'

What if the ocean freezes over tonight?

'Sounds more likely than Tared deciding tomorrow morning that he is perfectly happy to have a little fae whore living in his house,' I muttered defiantly.

Creon quirked up an unamused eyebrow. *Did he call you any such thing?*

'No, but—'

Good. His lip curled up a fraction. *Otherwise I would have to conduct some elaborate experiments on all the different directions his knees can bend. Give it a night, Em. You may find out tomorrow morning it's all much more manageable than you expected.*

Tomorrow. The Cobalt Court. Golds help me, how was I going to deal with a single binding if I hadn't settled this fight by that time?

But my knees were trembling. A headache was building behind my eyes, threatening to break through my skull. The day had gone on for too long and brought too much trouble with it, and no matter how hard my instincts were screaming at me that the foundations of my life were slipping from beneath my feet with every second I wasted here, my rational mind had to admit that any solution I tried in this state would just make everything worse.

'I don't want to see them right now,' I whispered.

Creon released my chin and hoisted me into his arms without a word. Cradling me against his firm chest, he stepped over a small circle of mushrooms and past a tangled bush of thorny vines before he sank down on the forest floor to rest his back against a sturdy oak. His wings fidgeted restlessly for a moment, then folded around me in his lap, darkening the silver-streaked night to an impenetrable black.

Vaguely, I realised that even Alyra did not object.

Sleep washed over me suspiciously easily. I was too far gone to care. Let it be demon magic. Let it be whatever powers this forest possessed. Let it be the strong arms around me and the wings shielding me from every angry word, the beat of Creon's heart against my cheek and the warm, spiced smell of male skin. My thoughts grew hazy and bottom-less, and I gave in to the lure of temporary oblivion – to the desperate and unfounded faith that the world would mysteriously have rectified itself by the time morning came around.

CHAPTER 31

THE WORLD HAD NOT rectified itself by morning.

I woke alone in my own bed, below a ceiling of intricately braided twigs. Creon was nowhere to be seen. Alyra perched on the foot board of my bed, sleeping, her small head turned below her wing. She woke the moment I moved, ruffled her feathers, then hopped off her seat and peered at me with a clear expectation of movement in her beady eyes.

I didn't want to move.

But I couldn't hide myself in this little hut forever, and the longer I waited, the harder it would be to face the world again. I swung my legs out of bed, braced myself for one last moment, then pushed myself to my feet and grabbed the first more-or-less clean dress I could find from my bag. A black one, today – whatever we were going to find at the Cobalt Court, I suspected my colours would come in handy.

The sun had only just risen, and the bright colours of the nymph forest were shrouded in a deep golden glow. Dew sparkled on every leaf and petal, reflecting the first rays of light in a dazzling display as I cautiously made my way to the clearing where we had eaten together last night.

It was almost deserted now.

Agenor must have gone home before Tared's unfortunate discovery, or at least I hoped he had; if he had to be informed about my escapades, I preferred to do it myself. Tared himself was nowhere to be seen either, quite to my relief. But I did find Beyla in that wide open space between the fragrant trees, and the frosty look she sent me as I tiptoed closer crushed my last hopes of cushioning the blow of this news for her.

'Morning, Emelin,' she said flatly and returned her attention to the rumpled notebook she had been reading. Her bag lay beside her, fully packed already. 'Might be best if you prepared to leave as soon as possible.'

Not the moment for elaborate apologies, the glaring message between the lines said. I swallowed, stomach twisting, and made a single unwise attempt anyway.

'I just wanted to say I'm sorry for not telling you—'

She lowered her notebook so swiftly it was almost a slap, and it took every bit of self-restraint I possessed not to jump back like a frightened rabbit. Her glare at me was the sharpest I had ever seen her wield, the ever-present hollow grief in her pale blue eyes all but eclipsed by the sheer force of her anger.

'You're *sorry*?'

'I was just … you know, hoping everyone would be getting along a little better by the time I told you …'

My voice died away. Against the memory of Tared's frigid anger, my hopes of the last weeks sounded so pathetically small, so humiliatingly childish. Get along better? While half of our company still expected Creon to charm Lyn away at any moment?

'You fell in love with a fae executioner,' Beyla said, her frail voice biting, 'then didn't tell us about it for months on end. How did you ever expect that to end well, Emelin?'

End. The word echoed through my mind with the force of a reverberating hammer blow to an anvil. Was this an *end*, then?

'I didn't realise I was hurting anyone by staying silent,' I mumbled – all I had left to say to defend myself. 'If someone had *told* me—'

'Oh, don't worry.' She scoffed, shaking her silvery braids over her shoulders. 'You're not the only one I'm blaming here. Which doesn't make this entire situation any less ridiculous. Now go pack your bags. I refuse to let your questionable judgement get in the way of the work we've got to do.'

I retreated to my hut, feeling impossibly more hopeless than when I'd stepped out of bed, Alyra darting after me like a feathery little chaperone.

You're not the only one I'm blaming. Was she talking about Lyn? About Naxi? Both of them could likely have told me how much pressure Tared was under, even if they didn't want to spill my secrets to him themselves. But Naxi had her rules, forbidding her to spread information about the inner lives of others, and Lyn ...

I threw a look over my shoulder, found Beyla bent over her notebook again, and changed course just before I reached my own little dome. Lyn slept in the structure farthest from the clearing. A risk, to go see her now – hell, if I was unlucky, I would find Tared waiting for me in her company – but there would be little time to talk once we had left for the Cobalt Court, and if I had to spend our entire journey guessing at her opinions, I might just go mad. A little delay in packing was the better alternative.

No sounds came from behind the thin wall of branches. That seemed a hopeful sign.

'Lyn?' I whispered, not daring to raise my voice.

Only silence answered me for a moment. Then, equally quietly and unnervingly numbly, she said, 'Come in, Em.'

I ducked through the bead curtain. She had started packing, too; half-folded clothes and the occasional dagger covered the bed. She was sitting cross-legged on the floor herself, still wearing the same shirt and loose linen trousers she had worn yesterday, her red hair an unusual mess. The smile she forced at me was about as cheerful as a threatening thunderstorm.

'Morning.' A powerless gesture at the bed. 'Sit down.'

443

Nudging a few shirts aside, I obliged.

Lyn grabbed a hairbrush from the floor, glared at it for a moment as if she could not quite remember why it was here in the first place, then shoved it firmly into her bag and turned to face me. With a grunt, she added, 'Well.'

Out of nowhere, tears were stinging behind my eyes again.

'Don't feel guilty, Em,' she said, reading my expression with unnerving accuracy. Her voice was tired. 'It's a miracle you managed to keep it hidden for so long. Sooner or later, it was bound to go wrong.'

'Did you know?' Not the words I had planned to speak, but the ones that forced themselves over my lips with no regard for my more diplomatic plans. 'That Tared still thought Creon might try to run off with you at any moment?'

She groaned. 'Strong suspicions. I told you we are extremely experienced at not talking about Creon when we can avoid it.'

'Why didn't you tell me?'

She was quiet for a moment, fidgeting with a fuzzy red curl. Then, slowly, she said, 'What would you have done with the knowledge?'

I frowned, taken aback. 'I ... I'm not sure? I suppose it would have seemed rather cruel to me to keep the secret if I'd known ...'

'Yes,' she said flatly. 'There are quite a lot of things that could be considered cruel to bonded alves, as a matter of fact.'

There was too much weight in that sentence, too much meaning in her gaze. Oh, hell. 'I didn't mean to say *you're* cruel for ... you know.'

'Not blindly shrugging off everything he's ever messed up and just declaring my undying love to him already?' she suggested wryly.

'Well. Yes.' I gave a helpless shrug. 'Obviously you shouldn't be forced to feel anything.'

'No. There has to be a limit, hasn't there?' Her smile was too small for her face, a closely guarded expression so very different from her usual radiant warmth. 'Look, this is his tragedy, Em. Our tragedy, possibly. I refuse to extend it beyond that – to make the responsibility of the rest of the world to do away with all personal preferences and accommodate a bond that shouldn't have been there in the first place.'

A few more pieces of the puzzle fell into place. I swallowed and said,

'I think Beyla might disagree with you on that.'

'Oh,' she said sourly, 'Beyla is absolutely furious with me, of course.'

I blinked, the readiness and weary acceptance of that statement equally surprising. 'Of course?'

'She always is when these things come up,' Lyn said with an unconvincing shrug. 'Maintains that I should be more careful, that I don't understand the utter torture of a broken bond, and so on and so forth. Which is true, of course – but then again, I maintain she doesn't have the faintest idea what it's like to unwillingly become the target of a bond, either. So it's a bit of a stalemate.'

'*Unwillingly?*' The word sounded ominous. I tried to imagine Tared forcing a bond on any unwilling partner – calm, easy-going Tared, who would rather join a suicidal quest to a plague-stricken continent than infringe on my autonomy by stopping me – and failed even after last night's reveal of brimming anger.

'He didn't do it on purpose.' She didn't look me in the eyes, focusing her gaze instead on her small, intertwined hands in her lap. Even her fingers were freckled. 'I don't blame him – he wanted this as much as I did. But that still doesn't mean I'm happy to be in this position after trying very explicitly not to end up there, and it also doesn't mean I'll suddenly agree with Beyla that nothing could be more important than soothing broken alf hearts.'

Nervousness stirred in my guts, a sensation close to nausea. They had always been there, hadn't they, these slow undercurrents of disagreement between my friends? I'd seen them in Ylfreda's anger when we first came to the Underground. Edored's attempts to remove Creon from the library, and his fury at Lyn when she stopped him.

But they'd been undercurrents for over a century, and I was bringing all of it to the surface. Lyn could tell me it wasn't my responsibility a hundred times over, but they *wouldn't* be in this mess if not for me.

'Stop blaming yourself, Em,' Lyn said softly, watching me closely with those bright amber eyes. 'We wouldn't have a chance at winning this war without you, either.'

It felt like a cheap excuse, a cop-out rather than an honest judgement. I opened my mouth to ask if there was anything I could do, realised she likely wouldn't tell me even if there was, and settled for the second question burning on my lips. 'Is he going to forgive me for this?'

She sighed, hesitating just a moment too long for my pounding heart. 'It's not you he needs to forgive. Give him some time to figure that out.'

Which was no comfort at all, coming from the person who was always the first to offer a reassurance if there was even the slightest trace of one to be found.

'Right,' I said numbly.

'Time to go pack your bag. And go pull Creon out of bed, if he isn't up yet.' A wry smile flitted around her lips. 'At least you won't have to worry about everyone and their sister volunteering to be chaperones.'

That was the opposite of a consolation, somehow. I made myself smile anyway and trudged out, finding Creon – awake, dressed, and packed – in his own hut.

'Morning,' I said, attempting levity but achieving none.

His smile was equally convincing. An unsettling awkwardness lingered in the air as I sank down beside him, not quite sure why that foot of empty air was still between us, why I hadn't yet jumped into his lap like I'd have done in our bedrooms in the Underground. There was no one here to see us, for the gods' sakes! There was absolutely no reason to feel like we had to find a brand new balance merely because other people – who I had always known would be unhappy about the revelation – would not have liked to know where I was spending my time right now.

And yet it was there, that minimal hesitation as I forced myself to roll over into his lap.

It was the abrupt vanishing of the separation, I realised. The Emelin I was with him had always been a secret, almost a different person from the Emelin people knew and had opinions about – someone who did not have to care about common propriety and other headaches. Now Creon's Emelin *was* the public Emelin, at least to the people who mattered to me – and didn't that mean that I had somehow brought the public into this little world that had always been ours alone?

My heartbeat quickened, accelerating from agitation into the first stages of panic. What if I had somehow ruined even *this*, the only damn thing that had always been easy all this time?

I was working myself into a spiral. I knew I was, and yet it took an almost inhuman effort to draw in a deep breath, hold it for five seconds, and force my heartbeat down. Hell's sake, I could be more sensible than this. Was I hoping to restore anyone's good opinion of me by showing up at the Cobalt Court as a shivering mess, unable to make even a dent in the Mother's magical shields?

It was only when I looked up that I became aware of Creon's eyes on my face, observing me in silence. Seeing everything, as usual. Knowing me, as usual.

'I'm a bit of a mess,' I breathed, lowering my gaze to his hands so I would not need to look at him.

Don't suppose you want me to carve some artistic marks into anyone? he signed, so carelessly that it had to be a deliberate provocation.

I took the bait. It was better than feeling hopeless. 'You know damn well that would make everything worse.'

He chuckled without sound, chest straining against his black shirt. *It's so annoying when your good sense and reason get in the way of my dramatics.*

And just like that, the ice was broken, the strange tension between us gone. I snorted a laugh and dropped my head back onto his powerful thigh. 'Yes, I can see the annoyance on your face, Your Highness.'

The emotions on his face had very little to do with annoyance – the small wrinkles around his almond eyes, the skewed grin playing around his lips. He flicked a finger against my cheek, a gesture as playful as it was reprimanding, and I had to bite my lip not to laugh out loud.

What do you want? he signed.

One day I would be ready for that question. Today, as usual, I was not.

'Hide away and never look any of them in the eyes again,' I muttered, all lust for laughter withering. 'Which I suppose comes with some practical obstacles.'

He grimaced. *Could get rid of their eyes for you.*

'Oh, for fuck's sake.' I glared up at him, unable to suppress a chuckle, but noticing it sounded suspiciously like a sob of despair. 'I think that might hinder them on the battlefield, if nothing else.'

The amused twitch of his lips told me he agreed.

'Do you know if Tared told others? Except for Beyla, that is?'

Don't think so. He nodded at the forest outside. *He knows better than to inform Helenka and risk our alliance again, and if the rest of the alves had known, Edored would already have shown up to duel me over your honour.*

A cold fist clenched around my heart. Of course Edored's first instinct would be to blame Creon – that was virtually a national sport among the alves. But sooner or later, even he would have to accept that I wasn't an innocent victim here, and if Beyla's reaction gave any indication of what I could expect ...

I doubted I'd spend much of my time at card tables in the coming months.

'Let's be a little discreet, then,' I said, voice small. 'No need to spread the news to the nymphs yet. And it's probably better for everyone's nerves if I don't spend half of our time in public glued to your face.'

A shadow slid across his face even as he nodded – just a glimpse, like a cold draft sneaking in through closed curtains. Out of nowhere, Zera's words returned to me. *Love doesn't like to be taken for granted ...*

I firmly shoved that thought away. It was just for a few days. Just to minimise the imminent damage. Just to keep our allies happy.

Which sounded suspiciously like the other arguments I'd been repeating to myself for weeks.

I pushed that thought aside, too.

'I should start packing,' I said, sitting up and shoving to the edge of the bed with a hand on his thigh. 'Don't want to make them wait for me.'

His smile had an edge of bitterness to it. *Naxi is still sleeping. You'll be fine.*

But Naxi hadn't lied to her friends for months or potentially ruined their already fraught relationships and opened the gates to all the disastrous consequences of broken alf bonds. I packed my bag with trembling hands, flinching at every voice that passed by outside. Tared showed up, sounding curt. Naxi's melodious rattling emerged from her hut minutes later. Creon, of course, never made a sound, and yet I knew the exact moment he came out by the silence that rippled across the clearing – a silence filled with icy glares that I could feel even through my safe shield of intertwined branches and beaded curtains.

My stomach turned again as I pressed my last belongings into my backpack and tied it shut.

I had to step out – I *had* to. But moving my legs felt no more doable than moving Zera's bag of grief, and I postponed it until Naxi loudly declared she was ready to go and I truly couldn't wait a minute longer.

The looks were the worst part.

I could feel Tared and Beyla's gazes on me the moment I stepped into view – the two of them watching me like hawks even as they pretended to be deep in conversation, taking note of my every movement and every glance with entirely new eyes. Watching me like I was Emelin the liar, suddenly, rather than Emelin the innocent, infatuated child; Emelin the wrecker of peace rather than the saviour of the world. The empty air between Creon and me seemed to have become a physical, living thing, and every single person in that forest clearing was studying it as I dragged myself towards them, unsure of where to look or what to say or how to move.

'Morning, Emelin!' Naxi said cheerfully – bless her heart.

Alyra squeaked a welcome too as she flapped out from between the trees and landed clumsily on my shoulder. Tared grumbled some sort of greeting, received a sharp glare from Lyn, and produced something suspiciously close to an eyeroll as he averted his gaze to check the knots on his bag again. Lyn's freckled face darkened, but she remained silent.

I didn't dare to look Creon's way for fear that would be enough to ignite the fuse. *My fault. My fault. My fault.* The words sung through my mind like a lullaby.

'So,' said Naxi in that same unperturbed tone. I wondered how many times she must have played this role in the past, perfectly aware of the storms raging in the minds around her and utterly unaffected by any of it. 'We're ready to go, then?'

Without a word, Tared grabbed her wrist and Lyn's shoulder, then vanished. Beyla muttered a curse at where he had stood, raised her thin eyebrows at Creon and me, and coldly said, 'Waiting for something?'

'A promise you won't stick a sword through me, mostly,' I said as I stepped towards her.

She let out an unamused huff but held out her hand. I grabbed her wrist, then turned to Creon to wrap my other hand around his elbow.

There was nothing reassuring about the touch with Beyla's eyes on us. *I feel naked*, Creon had said, and gods help me, now I understood.

No one spoke another word, and the bright colours of the forest distorted around us as Beyla faded. Away from Tolya – away from the nymph prisons and the spies and the remainders of the Sun fleet – and towards what I desperately hoped would be the endpoint of our journey.

The Cobalt Court.

CHAPTER 32

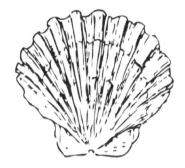

WE EMERGED IN A landscape unlike any other I'd seen before.

When the colours dripped back into their natural slots and the ground turned solid beneath my feet again, we were standing on an ink-black beach surrounded by smooth cliffs and elegant sea arches, shreds of mist clinging to the dark stone like fine silk to skin. The air tasted of salt and eucalyptus. Before us, the deep blue expanse of the ocean stretched towards the horizon, where – so faint I didn't dare to trust my eyes – a broad stretch of land was just visible in the pale sunlight.

The continent.

I drew in a slow breath and turned around. A low mountain range rose farther inland, hiding the sun from view at this time of the day. Waterfalls tumbled from the cliffs, shrouding that side of the bay in plumes of spray and creating the eerie impression that these wild, imposing rock formations had grown from a sky of clouds.

A silent, almost *serene* place, like the still surface of a lake hiding unfathomable depths.

Alyra fluttered from my shoulder and soared along the shoreline. Only when I turned to follow her did I notice Tared, Lyn, and Naxi, who had appeared a few hundred strides away on the other side of the bay. Beyla was already marching towards them. I risked a glance at Creon beside me and found him studying the crystalline rocks around us with soft, almost wistful eyes.

'You've never been here,' I murmured, unwilling to disturb the peaceful silence.

He shook his head, then sighed and nodded at the others, jaw tightening. *Let's tell them we're getting out of here.*

I blinked. 'Beg your pardon?'

To explore the island, he clarified as he started walking, signs sloppy enough to be unreadable from a distance. *Don't think we need to trudge around the place with the full group, and I'm not in the mood to tolerate Tared's face a moment longer than necessary.*

'Right. Yes.' I forced a chuckle and tried not to think of Tared's face if I were to announce that I was about to set out with Creon and only Creon as my company. 'Do you have a rough idea of where to find the castle ruins?'

He shrugged. *Wings help.*

Of course.

I was still bracing myself when we reached the rest of the group. It turned out not to be necessary. The moment we came within hearing distance, Lyn said in that firm tone that did not allow for objection, '... so if Em and Creon go take a look at whatever that shield is ...'

I could have kissed her, but I managed to keep my expression carefully neutral. 'What would you be doing instead?'

'See if we can find any traces of recent fae activity.' She shrugged at Beyla, whose cold nod contained equal parts annoyance and agreement. 'You've been to the east side of the island, too, I presume?'

'Yes.' Beyla sighed. 'I'll take that side. Naxi, coming with me?'

The reasonable grouping, assuming that Lyn and Tared would stick together even through their disagreements of the day. But Beyla and

Naxi faded off without further discussion, and that left me alone with Creon and the two people whose doomed love I had potentially blown up – the four of us standing on that glittering black beach in a long moment of stifling silence, threads of excruciating tension stretching back and forth between each and every one of us.

Was this a moment to apologise yet again, or would that only make everything worse?

'Well.' Tared flatly broke the silence before I could remember how to move my lips. 'Let us know if you need any help with that shield, I suppose.'

Get the hell out of my sight, the undertone suggested.

Not the moment for apologies, then.

'Will do,' I forced myself to say, sliding my bag off my shoulders and dropping it in the sand. 'Do we meet you here when we're done?'

They barely had time to nod before Creon scooped me into his arms and took off into the pale blue morning sky, Alyra following us in a blur of fluffy white and grey. Infinitely familiar arms around me, strong and reassuring as always, and yet I couldn't suppress a twinge of dread at the thought of the people we'd left behind – of the way Tared would be re-evaluating every touch I shared with the male holding me, every moment we'd spend alone.

What an irony, that a week ago I would have been overjoyed at this moment of freedom, the lack of alves running after us to protect my honour and innocence. Now I felt the accusing glares weighing like millstones on my shoulders, lingering even after we'd passed the first mountain ridge and disappeared from the others' view.

Give him time, Lyn had said, but how much time was it going to take?

Below us, the breathtaking landscape of the island unfolded, and its sheer untamed beauty was enough to break through the smothering haze of my worries for a moment. The rugged mountain slopes stretched across most of the inland, valleys cut between them like deep claw marks in black stone. Windswept olive trees and the occasional sturdy cypress covered the slopes. Deep pools on the higher plateaus mirrored the blue sky, surrounded by wisps of vapor that made me wonder whether the water rising from the depths of the earth was warm in those spots; creeks and waterfalls ran from those wells, sparkling across the slopes and terraces like a crystal spider web.

It wasn't pretty the way a meticulously kept garden would be pretty; it wasn't lush or colourful or sweet. But there was a magnificence to the panorama below us, a sense of tranquillity, as if we were treading on the last patch of earth that hadn't been tainted by war and bloodshed.

Until the castle loomed up before us, at least.

Perched atop a cliff on the northwest edge of the island, the Cobalt Court was a grand vision of a bygone age – a mess of crumbling turrets and gaping archways, surrounded by rubble and overgrown with ivy. Once it must have been an idyllic place, a labyrinth of corridors and grand halls surrounded by extensive gardens. The last blue-grey granite walls and their high, vaulted windows still suggested a soothing place full of light and peace – a place of healing, even, and I had a sudden vision of long library halls and bright flowers and slow sunsets over the whispering sea ... But the gardens had turned into wilderness, barely a quarter of the building was still standing, and even the remaining towers stretched towards the sky like skeletal fingers.

A shiver ran down my spine, nervousness and a strange, twisted admiration for this grandiose, forgotten place.

'It must have been beautiful,' I breathed, clutching Creon's labouring shoulders as we flew. 'How could she ruin a place like this?'

He didn't reply as he began his slow descent, his arms beneath my knees and armpits, his gaze focused on the ruins ahead. But as we landed at the foot of the castle's cliff, on a narrow path that winded upwards to our destination, he averted his eyes and signed, *Destroying beautiful things is what she's always done best.*

Too much weight, too much meaning. I rubbed my face and muttered, 'She didn't destroy you.'

A wry smile broke through as he folded his wings against his shoulders and turned back towards me. *Did you just call me beautiful, cactus?*

I burst out laughing, hooking my hand through his left arm as I started walking up the path. No others in sight here, and gods, the world was easy again. 'Beautiful and a vain prick, yes. Why did you land here and not closer to the castle?'

Wasn't sure if that shield would be visible to you, he signed, amusement dancing in his dark eyes. *Slamming into walls mid-flight is a good way to lose teeth.*

'Bad for the pretty face.'

He let out a silent laugh. *Quite.*

We didn't speak or sign much as we climbed the gradual slope, Alyra darting in wide circles around us like a feathery moon orbiting its planet. Creon pointed out the hot springs in the plain east of the castle. I remarked on the abundance of succulents and small cacti growing along the path. When we reached the plateau at the top of the cliff, he was the first to notice the remaining shards of stained glass in the vaulted windows and their multi-coloured impressions on the rocky ground, and once again I found myself wondering what the Cobalt Court had looked like at the height of its glory, before an arrogant half god had the unwise idea of getting himself killed nearby.

We passed into what must have been the gardens of the castle itself – muddy ponds, crumbling fountains, and a surprisingly lush orchard of apple trees. There was still no shield to be seen, and worry snuck back into my thoughts. What if Beyla had been mistaken? What if the Mother had predicted our next step and removed the bindings? What if we walked straight to the front gate of the castle – an iron-plated colossus that hung askew on its hinges – and found the hall behind filled with nothing but cobwebs and dust?

But there, between the branches and golden leaves ...

A shimmer.

I ground to a halt, squinting at what looked so deceptively like the cloudy sky of an early autumn afternoon. There it was again, not unlike the faint iridescence of very fine organza – a flicker of colour against the pale blue, and then nothing.

Creon had stood still as well, watching me closely.

'You don't see it, do you?' I already knew the answer. None of this strange surface magic had been visible to my companions. 'Five, six strides before you— Alyra, please be careful not to fly into it ...'

She threw me an indignant look as she looped around us once again. *I'm a bird*, that glare said, *not an idiot.*

Due to lack of such confidence, I walked slowly, hand stretched out before me to make sure I didn't accidentally rid myself of my front teeth. I felt the magic the moment it collided with my fingertips – cool and silky, but as unbreachable as a massive castle wall. More unbreachable, perhaps. Most walls could be brought down as long as one had plenty of red at their disposal. This one ...

I took a step back, lowered my hand to my black skirt, and sent an experimental spark of red magic into the invisible shield. It yielded a small crackle, a flash like a colourful lightning bolt, and no useful result whatsoever.

'Interesting,' I muttered, prodding the shimmering wall again.

Creon chuckled. When I glanced over my shoulder, he had sat down in the grass, legs crossed and wings lazily spread out behind his shoulders – quite like an audience member at a theatre preparing himself for a highly anticipated show.

I scowled at him. 'Enjoying yourself?'

Oh, don't mind me. His smile – dazzling, inhumanly gorgeous, and untamed like the landscape around us – said otherwise. *Always a pleasure to see you work when you're determined to solve something.*

That took all the bite out of the offense I'd planned to take, damn him. I turned back to my target, cocked my head at the soft shimmer of magic, and contemplated my options. I could just let loose a storm of my own iridescence and hope that would break through whatever defences the Mother had created here. That would hardly be subtle, though, and knowing the bitch, it might be dangerous, too. What if the shield reflected my attacks right back into my face?

So I had to be careful – and to my own surprise, I didn't mind much. There was something deeply intriguing about this application of magic I possessed but barely understood, a tempting taste of what I might one day be able to do.

'I'm going to need softness,' I said absently. 'And iridescence. A lot of it.'

In a flicker of yellow, my dress turned a pearly sort of velvet – a fabric I was quite sure no one had ever dreamed up before.

'We might just start a new fashion before this war is over,' I added as

I smoothed my fingers over the surface.

The rhythm of Creon's breath betrayed a laugh, but I didn't turn around to see his response. Using a brush of soft magic for movement, I lifted a fallen apple some fifteen feet away and flung it as hard as I could into the Mother's shield.

It bounced back, the place of impact bruised as if someone had dropped a hammer on it.

That suggested I'd been wise not to use my fists to test the barrier. Breaking my fingers and wrists was not in the plans for that afternoon.

I spent a good hour experimenting, testing the properties of the Mother's safety measures in any way I could imagine. The shield contained a lot of movement magic, I concluded after a while; nothing, not even air, seemed capable of breaking through it. Obviously, there was iridescence to cancel out my attacks, too, considering that none of my common colour magic had the slightest effect on the wall. I tried to figure out if it had any influence on the thoughts of passers-by – what if Beyla's decision to shrug off her discovery and continue her journey was not entirely her own? But if there was any mind magic involved in the mix, I didn't seem to be terribly susceptible to it. At no point was I suddenly overcome by a deep conviction that I was wasting my time in this place.

Creon, who had spent his time refreshing my magic sources and eating apples, looked content when I summarised my findings for him, then handed me an apple, too.

'The question,' I said, only now realising how hungry I'd grown, 'is how I'm going to get through it.'

Did you try cancelling out her magic entirely? he suggested.

I tried and tried and tried, exhausting several dresses of pearly iridescence in my efforts. It was like trying to dry a well. Whenever I managed to block a small patch of the shield, magic seemed to flow back in from all four sides, restoring the defences before I could so much as stick a finger through the hole I'd created.

After half an hour of trying with increasing force to break through, I had to admit defeat.

'It's like trying to punch a hole in a waterfall,' I grumbled, falling down next to Creon to devour another apple. The damn things were surprisingly sweet, and frustration made me ravenous. 'What else can we try? If it's like water, I could see if I can ... let's say, redirect it?'

Creon's shrug did not betray any tension – as if he didn't realise with every fibre of his body that this impenetrable wall of magic may be all that separated him from the voice he'd fiercely missed for over a century. *Your guess is as good as mine.*

'What use are ancient fae princes if they can't even unravel magical mysteries for me?' I said, rolling my eyes at him.

He gave me a dramatically pained look. *Ancient? You wound me, Em.*

'Slightly antique,' I corrected myself leniently.

Experienced, he spelled.

'Historical,' I suggested.

He quirked up a stern eyebrow. *Mature.*

I snorted a laugh. 'You're as mature as any person who's never been allowed to be a child. Who wanted to duel me the moment I showed up with godsworn powers?'

Matter of strategic intelligence, he signed dryly. *I need to know how much of a threat you are.*

But I didn't feel much like a threat as I glowered at the Mother's shield for another solid hour, trying to direct the magic elsewhere and failing hopelessly at every attempt. I tried to slowly bend the barrier inward – no luck. I tried to pull it towards me and let it envelop me so that I would end up on the other side of it – again, nothing. I tried to let the magic flow aside to create a small tear I would be able to step through, and smashed another dozen apples with my tests before I concluded that strategy was coming to naught, too. The protective force seemed fixed in the dome-like shape she'd erected over the Cobalt Court, a structure so massive I could only guess how many pearl necklaces she'd used in the process.

The sun had passed its highest point by the time I reached that conclusion, sinking slowly to the west and making an eerie silhouette out of the castle ruins. I plopped down next to Creon, who had wandered off to find a creek in the meantime and collected water in a drinking bag shaped from a handful of fall leaves and plenty of yellow magic. A few gulps lessened the dry ache in my throat but did nothing to soothe my frustration.

The more time I spent fighting this wall, the more certain I felt that something of essential importance was hidden behind it. Why couldn't I figure out the trick, damn it?

I've started thinking we might be going about this the wrong way, Creon signed as he considered the pile of bruised apples my efforts had produced. Alyra was cheerfully picking at them.

'You think?' I said sourly.

I'm trying to figure out the logistics. He rubbed a scarred hand over his face, eyes narrowed in concentration. The bright blue bargain mark he'd exchanged with Helenka was gone, I noticed only then – dissolved after he'd fulfilled his promise to leave today. *We know the Mother did reverse bindings in a few cases, yes?*

'Yes, that's what Ophion said. Do you ... *Oh.*' I blinked at him. 'Oh. You said she's never left the Crimson Court since the Last Battle?'

If she left, she did it very quietly, at least.

'But then – if the bindings are not stored at the Crimson Court – she must have sent someone else to retrieve the ones she needed in those cases.'

Exactly. His smile was tired yet satisfied. *You see where I'm going?*

'If others had to be able to step through this shield, they can't have needed divine magic to do so,' I said slowly. 'The Mother is – was – the only one with those powers. So that suggests we don't need to do anything to the *shield* to get through, because she wouldn't have been able to do that from a distance.'

He combed his fingers through his hair, then signed, *Could she change anything about the envoys she sends? Make them undetectable to the shield, something like that?*

Energy buzzed through my veins as I jumped up, my wavering resolve restored. Trying to change the shield – that vast, incomprehensibly powerful display of magic – had been not unlike trying to change the colour of the ocean with little drops of paint. Changing one person, in whatever way, seemed a far more achievable goal.

I started with apples, though. They seemed safer test subjects.

Over the course of an hour and a half, I created apples that could not move no matter how hard I tried to throw them, floating apples, apples making disconcerting sizzling sounds, and apples that absorbed magic in a way that vaguely reminded me of alf steel. Not even that last category made it through the Mother's shield, however.

'For fuck's sake,' I said as my most hopeful attempt yet bounced back and nearly hit me square in the face.

Give yourself time, Creon signed, looking sourly amused. *She studied this magic for centuries. You're at two days.*

'I was hoping destruction would be easier than construction,' I grumbled. 'Alright. Help me think this through again. The shield stops all movement – we can be sure of that, yes?'

He nodded, pursing his lips at the invisible barrier of magic.

'So what we need is something that … doesn't move. To make sure the shield doesn't detect it. Except that if it doesn't move' – I glowered at the three motionless apples I'd created, which had taken root in the grass and could not be carried off or kicked aside no matter how hard we tried – 'it can't move through the shield, either.'

So we need something that's both movable and immovable.

I let out a long groan. 'It sounds like one of those terrible riddles from a fairy tale. Does it have three legs in the morning, too?'

Four, he corrected me with a grin. *Three in the evening.*

'I'm pretty sure I've felt you wake up with three legs on regular occasions,' I said, snorting.

He threw back his head, that damned soundless laugh bursting out of him. *I'm trying to dutifully save the world here, Em.*

'Oh, fine.' I fell down next to him and crossed my legs. 'You're better at riddles. How do we solve this one?'

Perhaps … He stared at Alyra with unseeing eyes as she pecked at the motionless apples. *Perhaps you could attach the immovability to something that's still capable of movement?*

I blinked.

Like air to our planet, he added, looking sheepish. *Do you remember what I told you about that fae researcher who flew some seven miles up and found he couldn't breathe up there? Seems like the oxygen is clinging to our world's surface, which means it's motionless in that sense. But we're still moving around the sun. So ...*

'Moving,' I finished numbly.

Yes.

'So if we could create a ... a shield of motionlessness around one of those apples – not *on* the apple, but *around* it ...' I swallowed. 'Good gods. Let me try.'

The hardest part was learning how to attach motion magic to a surface without affecting the surface itself. It wouldn't stay stable no matter how carefully I wrapped it about the apple in my lap, unravelling the moment I took my left hand away from the soft velvet of my dress.

Just be quick, Creon suggested. *Don't wait to see if it's taken hold.*

So I tried once again, folded a firm layer of motionlessness around the cheerful red fruit before me, and hissed, '*Now!*'

Creon snatched the apple from my lap and swung it at the shield before I'd let the magic go.

There was a crackle.

A faint, sucking sound.

And then – a small blot of red against the sun-streaked grass of the unkept garden – the apple lay on the other side of the shield, blushing innocently at us from ten unreachable feet away.

We stared at it in silence for half a minute, as if the damn thing might change its mind and turn back on its own just to torment us. But even as I blinked and pinched myself and blinked again, there was no denying it – it *had* crossed the shield.

'You're a gods-damned genius,' I breathed, eyes still clinging to the miracle.

For coming up with dozens of ideas, most of them terrible? His signs forced me to avert my eyes. *You did the work here, cactus.*

I swallowed as the heady triumph finally made its way into my chest, my throat. 'I ... I just need to find a way to sustain it for a moment longer.'

Yes. Now, for the very first time, the tension betrayed itself, just a small shudder in his deep inhale. *And then we could cross.*

The words lingered between us for a moment, temptation itself

461

shaped in the signs of those scarred, nimble fingers.

'Should we?' I whispered. 'Or should we ... you know ... warn the others first?'

He closed his eyes, jaw clenching at the mention of them. I felt the same tightening in my gut, a sensation somewhere between dread and nervousness – the others, who would look at us with those accusing eyes and turn every shared touch between us into something guilty and shameful. But not telling them meant putting ourselves in danger without any rear-guard in case things went awry. And accidentally locking myself behind the shield of the Cobalt Court was not a risk I was happy to take.

I doubt sneaking in without telling them will soothe their bruised feelings, Creon eventually signed.

Yes. That, too.

'Let's go warn them, then.' I got up, finding to my surprise that the sun hung just above the horizon. We had spent half a day here on nothing but magical experiments, and I'd barely noticed the time going by. 'We can always decide to go together, but then at least they can't complain we left them entirely in the dark.'

He gave a wry smile, holding out his hands to me as he rose. I grabbed his wrist to press a kiss to his palm, then stepped into his embrace and braced myself for flight.

CHAPTER 33

WE LEFT THE APPLE carnage behind – Alyra looked displeased but followed nonetheless – and soared back towards the black-sanded bay where we'd arrived.

In the light of the setting sun, the island seemed an entirely different place. The shadows of the valleys and ridges had shifted, so it seemed like the mountains had moved over the course of the afternoon; peering down, I noticed the hollows of caves I hadn't seen at all during our morning flight. The waterfalls looked almost golden in the dusk, as if molten metal was flowing across the rugged slopes.

Did the rocks or the water have any magical powers? The Crimson Court had the hounds and the Labyrinth, and the Golden Court had the pixies; surely Korok must have had a reason to claim this island for the third of his courts.

A question for later. Before us, the little bay enclosed by cliffs and high stone arches appeared, the water deep blue and threaded with coppery foam in the sunlight.

It was empty.

I almost asked if this was the right bay – Beyla would not be back from her explorations until the last moment, of course, but surely Lyn and Tared would have concluded their search by now? Then again, Creon was better at navigating than me, and as we descended, I recognised the peculiar forms of the rock formations – the one stretching deep into the sea, resembling a bulging fist planted between the waves, and the three sharp peaks that rose from the water around it.

Right bay. No Lyn and Tared.

We landed on the beach, which similarly reflected the light of the sinking sun – small, golden crystals flickering amidst the black sand whenever I moved my head. I opened my mouth to ask where Creon thought we'd find the others, then caught a glimpse of light in the corner of my eye and turned toward it.

The source was another cave, receding deep into the rocks farthest from the sea. There was no sign of Lyn and Tared, but the glow of fire clearly reflected off the smooth, dark stone.

Of course. They had finished their task of the day and made a start at preparing dinner. My belly produced a rumble of approval, and for a moment, I didn't even care much about Tared's disappointed glances. Everything would be easier to handle with a full stomach.

'Ready?' I muttered to Creon as we started walking.

He didn't smile this time.

I was still figuring out an appropriate facial expression – content and innocent? But clearly I wasn't that innocent after all, and maybe trying too hard would only make me look like I'd spent most of the afternoon fucking my brains out – when the first shred of conversation reached us.

Or rather, of a fight.

Lyn's voice, high-pitched and agitated, was the first to cross the distance. '... making such a point of it! She was *scared*, for fuck's sake! What was I supposed to ...'

I froze so abruptly Creon nearly bumped into me. Tared's answer, in a lower tone, was impossible to make out.

'Well, that's pretty rich, isn't it,' Lyn snapped at whatever his defence had been, 'coming from the person who didn't dare to tell his own gods-damned bonded mate that he'd bonded to her?'

The silence could have cut through steel.

My heart stopped beating for a moment, then thudded wildly against my ribs. I stared at the cave entrance with unseeing eyes, only just feeling Creon's hand around my shoulder, only just hearing Tared's much louder reply – 'We decided we were *not* going to talk about—'

'Yes, because we were the only ones involved! Do you want me to keep biting my tongue when you're making this everyone else's problem?'

Creon's hand was pulling me back.

'*Lyn*,' Tared said, and it was the jagged sharpness in that one word that brought the memory soaring back with the intensity of hellfire – the plea that lay beneath the surface of it, a sensation of something slowly, agonisingly slowly tilting over an edge. I'd *felt* that plea with Zera's bag in my arms. Felt that fierce, scalding need that bordered on insanity, a bond he could let go as easily as he could claw out his own heart. I knew what that one word was saying better than I'd ever wanted to know: *Don't go there. Don't open that door. Don't you know you might kill me – that you'll undo me?*

'I know!' Lyn's cry was almost a sob. 'Inika help me, I know! But you're being an arse all the same, and I'm sick of excusing every—'

'Lyn, please *stop*!' There was a crack in his voice, in that imperturbable voice of the male who'd called himself my family.

I broke.

This could not be happening – not because of *me*. Beyla's hollow eyes. Words Lyn had spoken an eternity ago – *he would crumble* ... She wasn't going to risk that just because I had been a naïve fool, for the bloody gods' sake! I would tell them so, if I had to. I would tell them it was all my fault, that they ought to be furious with me and unite in their righteous anger, that I didn't deserve—

Creon's arm hooked around my waist.

'Hey!' The word broke out like the lash of a whip. 'You can't—'

His fingers settled over my mouth next.

I fought to pull free as he unceremoniously hauled me off like a bundle of old rags. Even my most violent efforts came to nothing. His arms didn't give way as I struggled, his fingers didn't so much as twitch even when I set my teeth into them, and in the end I gave up and went furiously, panickily still. The voices of my friends died away as Creon put distance between us. My heart was still trying to crawl up my throat and choke me. What if Lyn was saying more? What if she was saying worse? What if Tared was falling apart *right now* and there was absolutely nothing I could do …

What if I had ruined *everything*?

Creon released me so suddenly I gasped and nearly tumbled over in the sand. My words came out on a shriek – 'What for the gods' sakes do you think you're *doing*?'

He had always been taller than me, but in that moment, he positively towered over me, a dark, ominous silhouette against the pink- and orange-streaked sky. His demon eyes seemed to be measuring me, his piercing gaze so intense I could barely breathe.

I fought the urge to look away and snapped, 'Well?'

Creon pulled up an eyebrow, unflinching. *I'd rather ask what you thought you were doing.*

'They're breaking down everything!' Dread blurred my words together; I swung a wild gesture at the fire-lit cave. 'I can't just … We can't just—'

And do you really think, he interrupted, his signs sharp and biting in that unmistakable way of words remaining unsaid, *that anything you say or do will be enough to save them from themselves after decades of this? Short of wiping their memories clean, that is?*

'At least I can try!'

He sighed. *And how were you planning to go about that?*

'I … I …'

There was no finishing that sentence. My mind was a blank slate, or not so much a blank slate as a churning sea of panic from which no sensible thought could escape. I was *ruining* them. After they'd given me a home and a family. After they'd risked their lives for me. I was being an ungrateful, disgraceful little wench, and there had to be *something* I could do ...

'She's angry because he is, right?' I blurted, words tumbling over my lips without consulting my rational thoughts on their way out. Vaguely, I was aware I was gabbling. It didn't stop my tongue from pressing on. 'So if we can just calm him down – if we can stop him from being pissed with us for a moment ...'

Which is what you've been trying to achieve for weeks, Creon reminded me.

'Can't we ... can't we tell him it was all a mistake?' My mind clung to that thought with hooks and nails – mollify Tared. Save Tared. 'What if we just tell them we've broken up! That would help, wouldn't it? That would—'

No.

Just one sign, one snappish gesture, yet it was enough to smother every word I'd been planning to utter.

He had gone still in the deep golden light, a stark contrast to the emotions turning my mind into a whirlpool of fright – his face a sharp mask, his muscles straining tight. Only his wings flared ever so slightly behind his shoulders, an involuntary reflex not even his steely self-control could suppress.

Fuck.

That had *not* been the right thing to say.

'I didn't mean ...' The sand seemed to be swaying beneath my feet like a ship's deck. Oh, no. Oh, *no.* 'Creon, I was not suggesting we break up! Just that we *tell* them—'

I heard you. Something twitched in his jaw. *And I was rejecting the suggestion.*

'But—'

I said no, Em.

I blinked, heart skipping a beat. 'I'm just trying to understand—'

—that I can't do this anymore? he burst out, the signs wide, uncontrolled swings as he took half a step towards me. *What do you need to understand – that I'm sick of these lies? Sick of this secrecy? Sick of sneaking around like I'm committing some gods-damned crime, loving you?*

'Wait ... *wait.*' My voice shot up. 'I mean, that much is clear, but—'

If it is, then why are we still doing this? He signed the words at dizzying speed, as if they'd itched below his skin for weeks, building pressure until they finally broke free. *I understand the stress you're under, I really do. I understand you've been trained all your life to care about everyone else before you care about yourself. But you can't keep telling me to make myself vulnerable and then continue to treat me like something you're ashamed of, or—*

'I'm not ashamed of you!' I staggered towards him, hands coming up to grab the collar of his shirt and falling back down before they could complete the motion. 'I'm just trying not to let everything fall apart before we even get *close* to saving the world! You *know* I am!'

Which is no excuse to destroy yourself, he signed, not moving even an inch towards me.

I let out a shrill laugh. 'You're one to talk. Who kept torturing himself for a hundred and thirty years on the off chance he might kill the Mother one day?'

My alternative was death. His lip curled up. *Your alternative is happiness.*

'How many times do I have to tell you that I won't be happy if I mess this up, either!' My voice cracked. 'If you know it all so damn well, why don't you just tell me how I'm going to keep the phoenixes from shoving us out and the nymphs from cancelling our alliance and my fucking *friends* from destroying themselves while I'm living my best life and ignoring everyone else's wants and needs?'

Ringing silence.

The two feet between us seemed a distance of miles, suddenly, a chasm not even words could cross. Creon's hands had clenched into fists. His breath was coming in slow, overly controlled inhalations, strangling back a fitting reply to my outburst.

'Creon ...'

What you need to do, he interrupted, signs strained and unnatural, *is finally realise you're not a pawn in this game. That every single one of them, even the ones who pretend they don't care, even the ones who bluff and act like they're in a position to make demands, will be utterly fucking lost without you. You're the queen here, Em. You're not the piece to be sacrificed. Start acting like it instead of bowing to their idle threats.*

468

'Fine, but that's not—'

And also, he continued as if he hadn't heard me, *figure out what you want from me.*

A tight cage seemed to be compressing my ribs, squeezing the air from my lungs. 'You know exactly what I want from you.'

Unconditional support combined with convenient invisibility? he suggested sharply, wings giving another involuntary shudder. *My truths bared to the world while you cling to every lie you find useful at that moment? Anything else I'm forgetting?*

I stared at him.

Anything else?

No sound came out when I parted my lips. Dark spots were dancing on the edges of my sight, my eyes focused on his strong fingers, on the sight of those motions I would never be able to scrub from my mind's eye again. I'd forgotten how to speak. I might just have forgotten how to breathe, too.

I love you so much it fucking hurts, Em. How could even those signs look, somehow, like a door about to slam in my face? *You've taken that ugly black heart of mine and brought it back to life, and I'm not sure it can even beat without you anymore. But I can't have half of you. I can't let you go every single time someone so much as looks at us with an unkind eye. And I definitely* – that sign was a wide swing – *am not going to listen to you telling the world we've broken up for whatever ungodly reason you come up with, true or not.*

The air was ice in my lungs, cold seeping slowly into my guts, my limbs. I wrestled open my mouth and managed to ground out a hoarse, 'I ...'

So tell them whatever you want. He stepped back, sucking in the sort of breath one takes before diving into cold, deep water without knowing what's waiting at the bottom. *But I'll be taking it for the truth.*

And before I could find the presence of mind to reply – before I could figure out just what I was supposed to reply to – he was gone.

The sand was still warm when I sank down onto the beach, or perhaps rather collapsed onto it, my knees unable to carry my own weight a moment longer.

The truth.

The gods-damned *truth*.

How for the gods' sakes had we ended up here – how had *I* ended up here, one lie removed from losing the one person I couldn't, *couldn't* stand to lose?

In hindsight ... Gods, in hindsight everything was clearer. Looking back now, eyes clenched shut and head buried in my arms, I could see the warning signals I'd firmly ignored in my zeal for the greater good, the mirthless smiles I'd shoved aside, the discomfort I'd argued away. One bad choice at a time. One cowardly decision at a time.

Love doesn't like to be taken for granted, Zera had said, and then ... then I'd gone forth and done exactly that, hadn't I?

A helpless, powerless curse slipped over my lips.

Something warm and soft rubbed against my bare lower leg, the touch accompanied by a faint chirp I recognised in that disconcerting, instinctive way. I lifted my head – not because I felt much like lifting my head, but rather because I suspected a sharp peck to the ankle would follow if I didn't pay my familiar the proper attention.

She'd settled into the sand next to my boot, wings folded and little talons tucked in beneath her body, watching me with dark eyes that almost seemed to contain a glimmer of sympathy. That only deepened the pit in my stomach. If even *Alyra* was feeling sorry for me, I had to be a bigger mess than I had realised.

'I fucked up, didn't I?' I muttered to her, resting my chin on my knees.

That was true, the tilt of her small white head admitted, but then again, I had been trying my best, fae were so very dramatic about these things, and the weight of the world on my shoulders was a fine reason for the occasional lapse in judgement.

I groaned, rubbing my face. 'You're starting to sound like Lyn.'

Lyn was small and winged, my thoughts informed me through whatever mental bond existed between us, and therefore an excellent advisor to follow on most occasions. Had I considered just waiting for her to solve everything?

'I'm not even sure she can solve her own problems,' I said bleakly. 'Let alone mine.'

Alyra ruffled her feathers, a gesture much like a shrug, and gently rested the side of her little head against my boot as she waited for my thoughts to unfold. Before me, half of the sun had already vanished behind that thin outline of the continent, and coppery flames danced over the sea and the sky. Too much beauty – far too much beauty – for this miserable night of anger and heartbreak.

'I can't lose him,' I whispered.

A certainty, and yet it wasn't a comfort. Because if I wanted Creon – and hell take me, I *did* want him – that meant the time for careful manoeuvring was over. No more diplomatic little lies. No more strategic distance. I would be his for the entire damn world to see, and if that meant pissing off people we couldn't do without, if that meant ruining my friends' love lives and losing the home I'd created for myself in this world of wolves against wolves ... Well, those would have to be the natural consequences.

Could I live with so much selfishness?

But what was my alternative – to stop wanting him? I gave myself one painful heartbeat to contemplate the option, to imagine my world without him in it, or worse, to imagine my world with him in it, but not as *mine*.

Even a flash of that thought made me feel like committing bloody murder.

Which meant I had to anger people. Which meant I was not, after all, good enough to do what my friends and allies and humanity needed me to do – which meant Valter and Editta may just have been right when they suspected, young as I had been, that I would one day be the death of them. Which meant—

'Emelin!'

My head snapped up, my heart in my throat.

Naxi came hurrying towards me over the dusky beach, tiptoeing so lightly that she left no footprints behind in the sand. Her blonde hair fluttered wildly around her face in the sea breeze, and so did her flowery pink skirts, a sweetness that did not fit the rugged, serene beauty of the Cobalt Court in the slightest.

'What's the matter?' I said, alarmed. She *had* to know she wasn't disturbing me at the most tactful moment. Had something happened with Lyn and Tared? With Creon?

'Oh, don't panic,' she said with a chuckle, dancing the last steps towards me and shaking her hair out of her face. 'Very sorry to interrupt your wallowing, but we just saw a small flock of fae arrive at the other side of the island. Something needs to be done about them.'

'Oh. Right.' My stomach sank. *Something.* I'd have to go after them with Creon, then – more death, more bloodshed, and I hadn't even figured out what I was going to say to him. 'How many of them?'

She shrugged. 'About thirty.'

That suggested they weren't here for us – the Mother would have sent a larger force, after what had happened to the Sun fleet. I hauled myself to my feet with a suppressed groan, picked Alyra up, and settled her on my shoulder.

'That should be doable, shouldn't it?' I said slowly, attempting to give the impression I had even a tenth of a brain left to devote to this newest complication.

'Should be,' Naxi said brightly, and I recalled with a shiver what Creon had said. *Very little empathy.* 'The important thing is that none of them escape.'

Because even one fae getting away could tell the Mother we had been spotted around the Cobalt Court, and she might just react to that news by simply destroying the bindings before we could get our hands on them.

'Right,' I said, bracing myself. 'Does that mean we're going after them with our full company?'

She gave me a knowing grin. 'Not excited?'

There seemed to be no need to answer; she knew very well that my level of excitement lay far below zero. Nonetheless ... She might well be the only truly unbiased member of the group I had left at this point, and even if her rules forbade her from telling me much, she might be able to help me just a little.

I cleared my throat as we walked across the beach, a straight line to the entrance of the cave, where Creon and Beyla now stood ignoring each other. 'Naxi?'

'Hm?' She sounded amused.

'I just wanted to ask – Tared and Lyn ...'

'They're not fighting because of you,' she said with a careless shrug. 'They're fighting because of them. Not your problem to worry about.'

I was getting pretty damn sick of that line. 'Fine, but it's still a problem, and I *am* worried.'

She muttered something about us poor sods with morals, and didn't offer any other response. We arrived at the cave in high-strung silence, Beyla's impatient looks not half as hurtful as Creon's utter lack of looks.

I'll be taking it for the truth.

The knots in my guts pulled tighter. Until I got a moment alone with him – until I figured out what exactly my answer was to his thinly veiled ultimatum – I'd have to be very damn careful with my words.

'Alright,' Beyla said, her nod at me her only greeting. 'What is the plan?'

The plan was made in two minutes and boiled down to a simple "let's go find them and take them down". No one seemed to have the patience or peace of mind to work out a more nuanced approach.

By the time the alves faded us one ridge away from the Cobalt Court – which was judged the most likely destination for the newly arrived fae – I still hadn't fully grasped the reality of this new threat. Three quarters of my mind had stayed behind on that dark beach, struggling to make choices I didn't want to make. The muttered conversations between the others largely slid past me, as did most of our surroundings; had any fae jumped out from behind a eucalyptus tree with malicious intent in that moment, I may have been too slow to save myself.

Thankfully, no winged silhouettes leaped at us from the shadows.

Habit and instinct were all that kept me moving, around a low hill and then up the last slope that separated us from the cliff that held the castle. The ruins looked even more desolate under a quickly darkening sky. With my gaze on the ragged stone walls and the crumbling towers, I failed to notice our targets for a moment or two – the small group of fae standing at the foot of the cliff, chatting carelessly to each other. They lit their torches as we approached, unaware of any watching eyes.

I swallowed a bitter twinge of regret. Couldn't we just leave them alone? But no, they would find the traces of my attempts to break through the Mother's shield, and worse, the one fresh apple that had made it through. More than enough evidence of what I was able to do.

Which meant they had to die.

I wanted nothing more than to crawl into my bed in the Underground and hide below my blankets for the next five years or so.

Tared and Beyla had quietly drawn their swords as we walked; Creon's blade already lay in his hand. A hundred feet left between us. Ninety. Eighty. It was almost a miracle they still hadn't noticed us, fully absorbed in their conversations and whatever chores they had to finish for the night ...

A little *too* much of a miracle, really.

'Wait,' Naxi hissed behind me, her voice quiet but urgent. 'Something's wrong. They're tense as bowstrings. This is not—'

And as if they'd heard her, the group of fae parted.

The manoeuvre was perfectly coordinated, a clean split through the middle followed by a swift motion backwards, like a flower unfolding its petals. Suddenly the haphazard flock had become three rows of battle formation, torches a straight line of flames. Swords and daggers glinted in the firelight. Hands pressed against black and red shirts. Eyes found us, all thirty pairs of them, staring us down as if gazes alone could wound.

I froze in place, my thoughts solidifying back into the here and now so abruptly I winced.

'For fuck's sake,' Tared hissed as he ground to a halt as well. 'Should we get out?'

'Wouldn't help,' Lyn said, her voice small. 'They already know that we're here and why. If the Mother hears ...'

Tared cursed again but didn't move, fingers tightening around the hilt of his blade. On the left edge of my sight, I could see Creon move towards me without sound. Yellow flickered between us, and the texture of my black dress changed ever so slightly, turning a plush velvet.

On my right, Beyla drew her second sword, her lips a wafer-thin line. 'Do we attack?'

'Let's see what they do first.' Lyn didn't turn to look at us as she spoke. 'I'd like to know if the Mother sent them herself, because in that case—'

She didn't finish her sentence, didn't need to. If the Mother had sent these fae to the Cobalt Court, even their deaths would not conceal the fact that we had been here. We'd have to be swift, very swift, to get as many of the bindings out as we possibly could.

I pressed my nails into my palms and whispered, 'What are they waiting for?'

Behind me, Naxi squeaked.

For one moment, I thought it may have been her demon senses again, noticing some looming menace before any of us could. Then I saw the movement among the ranks of our opponents, wings and torches edging aside as one solitary figure made her way to the front of the formation.

One distressingly familiar, tall, black- and golden-haired figure.

Oh, gods.

Oh, *gods.*

Panic and hysterical laughter fought for preference as Thysandra stepped from the rows of warriors, looking casually deadly as always, and alarmingly gorgeous, too. She was dressed in aggressive red, her scarred, gold-flecked wings tucked in tight, gold rings and bracelets contrasting starkly with the dark umber of her skin. A curved dagger flipped back and forth between her fingers as she sent us an icy smile and started, 'I thought you would be—'

She faltered there, mid-sentence.

From the abruptness of her silence, she may have stopped breathing, too.

Her knife stopped circling. Her eyes – those dark, calculating eyes – went wide and round at something behind me. Her mouth sagged open a fraction, dark red lips struggling to form words – a sight that would have been comical if not for the tension weighing down the air between us, the burden of a battle threatening to explode.

'Thysandra?' I heard a fae male behind her mutter.

I risked a glance over my shoulder despite knowing exactly what I would find. Face pale in the torchlight, Naxi had frozen where she stood, staring at her war-time opponent, would-be murderer, and passionate obsession of decades as if a ghost had just emerged from the ruins of the Cobalt Court.

CHAPTER 34

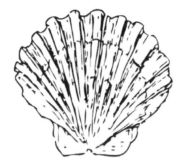

'Oh,' Naxi said, breaking the breathless silence with a voice sounding nothing like her own – taut and husky, as if someone was squeezing his hands around her throat. Her chuckle bore no resemblance to her usual melodious laugh, either. 'Of *course* it's you.'

Our presence seemed to have been forgotten. So had the presence of the fae standing guard behind Thysandra, who exchanged nervous glances amongst each other as their commander remained silent and motionless. Naxi wandered two steps forward, seemingly without noticing she would have bumped into me if I hadn't hastily scurried aside; her blue eyes stayed fixed on their mark with the same hungry ferocity. As if the two of them were back on that battlefield of decades ago – as if blinking at the wrong moment may end in death.

'Yes,' Thysandra said slowly, icily, chin jutting up. 'Of course.'

Naxi released another one of those bone-chilling giggles. 'Heard about Emelin's brand new powers, I suppose? Realised they were suspiciously similar to the powers the old bitch told you about and that—'

'Do *not*,' Thysandra interrupted, her voice a lash of fire, 'speak about my High Lady in such a way, you little menace.'

Two steps away from me, Creon let out a huff. It was the only reaction from our side. No one appeared inclined to come between the two lovers – or mortal enemies or whatever they were – and for good reason, presumably. Individually, they were deadly enough. To end up caught between their clashing powers ... I suppressed a small shiver.

'Oh,' Naxi said softly, and although her tone was still strained, some of the usual razor-sharp breeziness shimmered through again, 'you mean that High Lady you served so flawlessly during the Last Battle? Or when Emelin escaped?'

Thysandra's eyes flicked to my face – just one glance, but the fury burning in it felt like a punch to the jaw. How many nights had she lain awake over her betrayal that day, the choice to let me go in return for delivering her message?

Her cold voice betrayed nothing. 'My loyalties have never shifted.'

'No,' Naxi retorted, almost purring now as she cocked her head. 'Except the bitch still doesn't seem to realise just how exceptional your loyalty is, does she? Still doesn't see how much you're doing for her or how much she's relying on you. So the moment you realised we'd be here, of *course* you grabbed your weapons and your people and ran off for glory without telling anyone else – because you didn't tell anyone else, did you, darling?'

Beyla breathed a curse next to me. Fifty feet away, visible unease had crept up the rows of fae warriors, harrowed whispers snaking back and forth between them as they threw unnerved looks at Naxi and her beaming face.

Thysandra's spine stiffened even further, her damaged wings tensing dangerously. 'I had to act quickly,' she bit out. 'That was my only concern.'

'Of course,' Naxi said dreamily. 'Must be just a happy coincidence that it also means no one else will be able to get here first and claim the credit for your hard work. As usual.'

The flash of hurt on Thysandra's face was all too visible even through the mask of her fury – a strike straight into that festering wound I'd felt myself, the quiet resentment of the Crimson Court's unsung hero. Perhaps, I realised with a start, this was why she'd been alone, that morning she'd come down to the Labyrinth's exit and tried to stop me from fleeing the island – not because she had already been planning to let me go, but because it meant no one else could lay claim to her achievements for once.

'You seem quite sure of yourself and your dubious deductions,' Thysandra was saying, the tremor of anger *just* noticeable beneath the veneer of her composure. A dangerous tremor. She was finally clawing her way out of her shock, and a counter-attack was coming. 'As usual.'

Naxi shrugged. 'Am I wrong?'

'First of all, you are underestimating me.' She jutted up her chin a fraction, and it was that gesture that made me recall, with a sudden sinking sensation in my guts, that she had somehow *bested* a murderous little nymph with demon powers and no empathy during the Last Battle. 'If you truly think I'll hand over the victory for your pretty promises—'

'Oh, I don't,' Naxi said dryly. 'I was planning to leave the fighting part to our fae mages, to tell you the truth.'

Thysandra's glare at Creon glinted with unmistakable hatred. 'I see.' A mirthless laugh. 'Here for your voice, I presume, Hytherion?'

He didn't react, didn't even blink.

'I'm getting a little tired of this,' Tared said flatly. 'If we keep her ladyship alive, Naxi, do you mind if we just get to work and talk out the details later?'

'I strongly recommend you don't,' Thysandra cut in before Naxi could open her mouth. Her low voice had gone unnervingly sweet. 'Assuming you'd ever like to get those memories back, Thorgedson.'

A shiver of unease rippled through the silence.

Those memories. I stared at Thysandra – clever, stoic Thysandra, whose lips were now showing the faintest hint of a smug smile – and felt my heart ever so slowly sink towards the soles of my feet. She had been waiting here for us. She had known that Creon and I had almost single-handedly taken down the full force of the Sun fleet. Which meant she must have prepared for us some other way – of *course* she had.

And we had, indeed, underestimated her.

'There exist keys to the defences of the Cobalt Court, you see,' she added, every single word drenched in poisonous honey, 'one of which happens to be mine. As we speak, one of my people is inside the castle, keeping an eye on this pleasant conversation from afar and keeping a good dose of red at hand. The moment anything happens to us' – her smile broadened a fraction – 'you've lost the bindings forever.'

The fresh sea air had gone thick and oppressive, burning in my throat as I tried to keep breathing without gasping. So they *were* here, the bindings. So we *had* been right – about the physical forms of the damn things, about the location, even about the right way to breach the shield around the castle ruins. Yet if we made one wrong move now, if we miscalculated for even a moment ...

They wouldn't hesitate to destroy the bindings. Taking all of that magic with them. Taking all of those sacrifices, too.

'You're threatening the entire magical world with irrevocable extinction,' Lyn said, her voice shaking. 'Do you even realise that?'

Thysandra shrugged, unimpressed. 'To be fair, you are currently threatening *my* people with extinction.'

'That's ...' Lyn interrupted herself, drawing in a shivering breath. 'Hell take every single one of you. What do you want?'

'Your surrender.'

No one moved.

'I can guarantee your safety until the moment we reach the Crimson Court,' Thysandra added dryly – as if *that* would be anyone's greatest worry. 'Don't worry, I'm not the one in the habit of gutting prisoners ... or skinning them ... or taking their tongue and fingers for my amusement ...'

'Yes, thank you,' Tared interrupted sharply. 'A great relief. I don't suppose you can offer us any reassurance that the Mother will be equally mild?'

She raised her dark eyebrows. 'I'm not a liar, Thorgedson.'

'And would you agree to any other compromise to leave the bindings alone?'

'Not killing you on the spot *was* the compromise,' she said dryly, and behind her, some of her warriors risked chuckles and grins. Gone was the earlier confusion. They had us where they'd planned to have us from the start, before their commander had momentarily been brought off balance by the drivelling of some little demon, and that high of triumph was enough to make them forget about those moments of uncertainty.

Naxi looked as though Thysandra had just slapped her in the face, cheeks burning and eyes feverishly wide.

'I see,' Tared said, and the flatness of his voice made my stomach turn. He wasn't going to *agree*, was he? There had to be *something* we could do to get out of this trap? 'In that case ...'

To my surprise, it was Creon he turned to as his words drifted off, his eyebrows raised in an unspoken question.

Without looking at me, Creon signed two words. *Em. Key.*

'Yes.' Tared sighed, sounding even more defeated now – was that an act? I could hardly ask, nor could I ask what in hell the two of them were cooking up. Before I could even catch Creon's gaze, Tared calmly added, 'Bey, get Em to safety.'

Fingers dug into my upper arm.

The colours of the world warped around me, fire-yellow mingling with the dark blue of night. It lasted for barely the blink of an eye. Then I stood wavering on a familiar mountain path, the starry sky overhead, Alyra's talons digging so hard into my shoulder it hurt even through the thicker patch of fabric. In the distance, I heard the echo of something suspiciously similar to Thysandra's voice; the glow of torches lit up the mountain slopes behind the ridge just before us.

Beyla hastily let go of my arm and pressed a meaningful finger against her lips.

I gave a numb nod, still desperately trying to catch up with whatever the others were planning – their clues offering no more than meagre glimpses into their minds, but apparently enough for people who'd spent centuries strategising together. *Em. Key.* The magical key currently with the person Thysandra had sent into the Cobalt Court to destroy the bindings ...

Behind the shield.

Pieces clicked into place.

'Oh, fuck,' I breathed. 'But I never even tried—'

Beyla glared a warning over her shoulder as she slunk towards the low ridge separating us from the others. I could make out Thysandra's voice now – '... don't *want* to destroy them, but if another one of you disappears, I won't have a choice but to give the sign ...'

That was what Beyla had been looking for, apparently. She turned on her heel and strode back to me with brisk steps, again grabbing my arm without a word of explanation.

We emerged on a pitch-dark cliff this time, the purple-and-orange glow at the western horizon the only source of light. Four steps away from us, the world seemed to end in nothingness as the jagged edges of stone broke off sharply towards the sea. Below, waves roared against the rocks with that loud, primal force that broke ships and pulled men into its depths, never to be seen again.

'What are you *doing*?' I hissed as quietly as I could while still being audible over the noise. I didn't seem able to look away from the edge.

'We can speak here,' Beyla said, although her eerily thin voice wasn't much louder. 'This is the other side of the Cobalt Court. Thank Orin's merciful heart that I took the time to climb the cliff last time I visited the island – don't know what we would have done if I hadn't been able to fade here.'

I threw a glance at the cliff and swallowed, suppressing the urge to step away from it as I turned around. On the other side, both majestic and broken in the starlight, the Cobalt Court rose from the rocky ground, the walls on this side of the castle still mostly standing. Five feet away, the shield shimmered silvery between me and the bindings – between me and the lives of my friends.

'Right,' I said, drawing in a deep breath to steady myself. Thysandra's voice still echoed in my ears – *Your surrender* ... Would she have surprised us so easily if we had not all been thoroughly occupied with untangling our messy love lives? 'Let me make sure I understand your plan. We try to break through the shield here, get rid of the fae who's waiting for their sign to destroy the bindings, then take down Thysandra and the others?'

'That sounds like a plan, yes.' No matter how much she may have disagreed with me all day, there was no trace of annoyance on her face now – only calm, ruthless resolve. 'Creon seemed to think you could get inside.'

'I've managed with an apple.' My voice was a hair's breadth away from cracking. 'Not with any living creatures, let alone two.'

Alyra pecked at my ear with a furious squeak.

'Oh, fuck – three.' I shook her from my shoulder and glared at her as she flapped into the air. 'But you'll have to promise me you'll be *extremely* quiet. If I hear so much as a single squeak from you to warn that bastard with the key, I'll ... I'll ...'

'Pluck you like a soup chicken?' Beyla suggested without a spark of humour in her eyes.

'Find someone with larger wings to accompany me on future adventures,' I finished instead, to be rewarded with a quiet squeak of outrage. 'Do you understand?'

Alyra grumpily fluttered back onto my shoulder and pointedly jutted her closed beak into the air.

'Good.' I rubbed my left hand over the velvet of my dress as I stepped closer to the shield. *Softness for movement.* Thank the gods for Creon's presence of mind, providing me with that extra source of magic the moment our opponents appeared ready for battle. But it was only a single dress, and I would not be able to restore the plush surface myself ...

One attempt. No time to mess this up.

'Stay just behind me,' I muttered to Beyla, lifting my right hand. 'I'll try to get us both through the shield. If it doesn't work, we'll have to return to our luggage and get every woollen piece of clothing we can find for another try.'

She nodded, face nearly as pale as her silvery braids. 'Understood.'

I closed my eyes and thought about apples.

Thought about the magic I'd woven around their blushing surface that afternoon, in what seemed to have been another world entirely –

Creon by my side, laughing and joking, as if he wouldn't tell me half an hour later that he was over and done with my waffling. Thought about motionlessness, a magic trick to fool the shield into believing we weren't moving through it at all. *Stillness, stillness, stillness ...*

Power trickled up my arm, drawn from the lush velvet of my dress, seeping from the fingertips of my right hand as I drew the magic around me.

I stepped forward and met no resistance.

Another step. Another flow of magic. I *was* the key now – I was moving immobility, not so much breaking through the wall but rather oozing in, as invisible to the shield as it was for those around me ... One more step, and a deafening silence closed around me, as if the thunderous sea and the whispering breeze had all at once ceased to exist.

At the same moment, the magic dried up beneath my fingers.

I staggered forward and tore open my eyes, barely able to believe what I had done. Before me, the wild gardens of the Cobalt Court stretched out, no shield left between me and the crumbling walls of the castle. Behind me, a thin, silvery dome rose all the way overhead to cover the granite ruins of the court on all sides.

And Beyla stood on its other side.

No!

I almost cried out her name, then recalled just in time I'd threatened Alyra over the same mistake and snapped my mouth shut. In the pressing silence beneath the dome, the slap of teeth on teeth reverberated jarringly loudly.

A single glance down confirmed what I'd feared – the softness of my dress had been exhausted.

It took an effort to keep down a string of curses. Beyla's lips were moving on the other side, but not a sound came through, and I could only read loose words from the shape of her mouth. *Reach you. Too fast. Alone.*

Alone.

In a spur of inspiration, I raised my right hand and formed the familiar shapes with my fingers, much more slowly than Creon by lack of practice. *I can't hear you through the shield.*

She abruptly stopped talking, then nodded, lips tight. Her signs were even slower, and half of them got a finger position or direction wrong – but the general message was clear enough. *I couldn't get through with you. Can't get you any more soft things this way.*

My thoughts were whirling so fast that the fear had no time to catch on. No way for her to join me. No way for her to provide me with more magic fuel. And meanwhile, Thysandra was forcing the people I loved to surrender to her armed forces – bringing them closer to the Crimson Court with every minute I wasted here.

I'm on my way, I signed, stepping back. *Hide near the others. I'll let you know when I'm done.*

And without waiting for her answer, I turned and ran – Alyra on my shoulder, heart in my throat, and the survival of the magical world once again pressing on my every step.

In the dark, it was hard to see where my legs were moving. I stumbled over granite rubble, got my feet tangled in vines thick as ropes, bashed my knee against a broken fountain so hard I had to bite my lip to tatters not to scream. Alyra flew ahead of me most of the time, her bright plumage a beacon in the night, but even her guidance couldn't save me from a nasty fall or two.

I didn't slow down, damn the scrapes burning on my shins and knees. The image of those rows of torches had scorched into my mind's eye like a white-hot brand; visions of what might be happening to the others played out again and again as I ran, the scenarios more unpleasant at each turn. Creon, handing over his knives. Tared, handing over his sword. Naxi, once again at Thysandra's mercy – and with dozens of fae to witness the scene, Thysandra wouldn't let her go a second time ...

My foot caught on a block of stone and I lost my balance once again, reflexively bracing myself and rolling over. Sharp pebbles welcomed my bare skin to the ground, and when I pushed back to my feet with gritted teeth, the wet warmth of blood came trickling down my knee.

I'd look at the wounds later. I wasn't going to risk any blue magic here; in the darkness, the flash of colour might give my presence away.

I half ran, half staggered on. The Cobalt Court loomed over me from so close, its outlines visible by the stars it eclipsed – stumps of towers, broken windows, the once smooth walls pocked and scarred by violence. The silence below the dome was stifling, a silence that smelled of dust and stale water and rot.

This should have been a triumph, I thought bitterly as I avoided a pile of splintered wooden beams, then almost walked face-first into a dead tree – it should have been a moment to savour. At long last, I'd reached the destination I hadn't even known was there when we set out on this mad quest. The bindings were within my reach, the culmination of months of work.

Yet there was no triumph, no joy or excitement – just the sensation of sand slipping through an hourglass and death waiting as my time ran out.

Would Thysandra have shackled them at this point? Would she try and force Tared to fade all of them to the Crimson Court?

The others would try to stall, wouldn't they?

Before me, a faint blue glow broke through the darkness. I pivoted and ran towards it; it grew stronger as I crossed the distance. A skewed doorway gaped in the granite wall, wooden door ajar and rotting off its hinges. Behind it ...

I staggered to a halt, unable to hold back my gasp.

The bindings.

Here they lay, mere steps away from my eager hands ... and once again, we had underestimated the Mother's malicious genius.

Wooden shelves stretched into the darkness, like bookcases in some twisted library of souls. Narrow aisle after narrow aisle filled the vaulted hall of the Cobalt Court, a room so expansive I couldn't see the back wall from where I stood. And on those endless shelves, glowing blue and silver like stars on a winter night, lay thousands upon thousands of flawless crystal spheres.

Hollow spheres.

The Mother had known as well as I did how catastrophic it would be for the bindings to be destroyed.

And so, in a decision so cruelly self-evident I should have seen it coming, she'd made them as fragile as possible.

CHAPTER 35

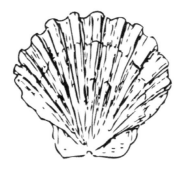

I WAS HOLDING MY breath as I took my first steps into the grand hall of the Cobalt Court, afraid that even a violent sigh would be enough to shatter the delicate crystal around me. Alyra landed cautiously on my shoulder, peering around for a pair of eyes to set her claws into.

No one showed up to fight us. Yet.

It wasn't just this room, I realised. To my right, another low doorway led away from this first archive of bindings, the blue light evidence that even more shelves would be waiting for me in the next hall. The gods knew how many of these rooms there were – *hundreds of thousands of people*, Agenor had said, and I felt myself getting a little light-headed as I tried to do the maths. If I had to search every aisle in every room for my fae opponent, I might still be wandering around these ruins by the time Thysandra had already presented her captives to the Mother.

Alyra rubbed the side of her small head against my cheek – comfort as much as a proposal.

'Be very careful,' I breathed, barely more than mouthing the words. 'We don't want to alarm them. Or break any bindings.'

She hopped onto the ground and rolled her eyes at me.

'Alright, alright.' I forced a smile. 'I'll wait here.'

With an inaudible whoosh, she twirled off, climbing slowly to the height of the upper shelves. Once there, she began exploring the room in greater and greater circles, slowly and meticulously to make sure not a single aisle would escape her attention. Every time she dipped from my view, my heart would stutter to a standstill for a moment, then pound on as she returned to the vaulted space above the endless cabinets – still safe, still unnoticed.

Eventually, after five minutes that felt like five hours, she soared back towards me and landed on the smooth granite floor, looking aggravated.

'Let's find the next room, then,' I whispered.

She allowed me to carry her to the small doorway I'd seen, then took off again. Thank the gods for those small, nimble wings, I thought as I saw her dart through the narrow aisles without brushing a single crystal ball. Some burly eagle would never have been able to help me here.

I'd barely finished the thought before Alyra swirled around in mid-air, racing back to me as fast as she'd left. Jumbled, excited thoughts rushed at me through our bond – fae male, waiting near the window, looking out. He hadn't seen her, focused on the view of his comrades outside.

I had to bite my tongue not to heave a sigh of relief. If he was still looking, the others must still be there. They hadn't yet left for the Crimson Court.

'Guide me,' I mouthed.

We snuck through the blue-lit darkness together, spheres of glass twinkling at me from every corner of my sight, reflecting like sapphires in the smooth granite of the floor. One of these had to contain Creon's voice. One contained Agenor's memories of that fated day after Korok's death; one contained the faces and voices of Tared's parents. But there were so many of them, and they had no name plates, no labels except for the numbers scratched into their shelves – how were we ever going to find everyone's individual bindings in this treasury of magic?

Trouble for later. Right now, we needed our fae male with the key.

As we navigated the rows of open shelves, I caught glimpses of a large window in the south wall – looking out over the garden and the meeting of the others. We were approaching the fae male from wingside, Alyra's thoughts informed me, and yet I was holding my breath as I finally tiptoed around those last corners, fully expecting to hear the catastrophic clattering of breaking glass swell to a roar around me.

No such thing happened.

The fae was sitting with his large wings towards us, blue light reflecting in his short dark hair and his snowy pale hands. A thick rope had been attached to the upper corner of the cabinet to his right, the other end clenched between his fingers – in position to yank down this first set of shelves at the smallest sign of trouble.

And with it ...

Oh, gods.

One cabinet going down would take the next one with it, and the next one, and the next one, reducing at least half of the room to shards and lost magic before he even made his second move. Even if I had been willing to sacrifice a single cabinet of bindings to the surprise effect, I would inevitably destroy thousands and thousands of other crystal spheres with it.

It took all I had to keep my breath shallow and quiet. No room for mistakes, then. I'd have to kill him on my first try, before he even had the chance to yank that gods-damned rope ...

But I couldn't hit him in the throat or heart from where I stood, and the back of his neck would not be nearly fast enough. He'd still have time to pull before he died. He'd still have time to ruin everything.

Cold sweat pearled in the small of my back. What other options did I have? Use red magic to cut the rope? But he'd be warned and retaliate, and the gods knew how many shelves may be wiped empty in the fight that would follow. Aim for the hand holding that rope? But if he had any presence of mind – and I'd have to work on the assumption my opponent was actually capable here – he'd pull with his other hand before I had time to target that one, too, and then we were back at the same catastrophe.

And meanwhile, Thysandra was killing my friends.

Fuck. I had to *think*, and think fast – but my mind had gone blank, my thoughts filled with the vision of glass ball after glass ball diving towards the granite floor. Perhaps I had to take the risk, but what if I was overlooking something? What if the solution was actually dead simple, and everyone would be furious with me for missing it, and—

You're not a pawn in this game.

My spine straightened itself.

The storm subsided, thoughts settling down like rowdy children called to order. Hell, I *wasn't* a pawn. I was saving the day here, damn it. I was the one standing in the heart of the Cobalt Court, behind a shield no other mortal or immortal could have crossed, and ...

And I had my magic.

My godsworn magic.

At once, everything was clear. A risk, yes, but safe choices rarely led to victory – and what alternatives did I have, when every familiar option likely ended with shattering crystal and magic lost?

Freezing him in his spot would have worked, but I had no softness left, and no time to go look for it. So instead, I quietly sank to my knees and firmly planted my left fingertips against the granite floor. *Smoothness for mind.* Stretching out my right hand at the tense fae male twenty feet away from me, I focused my thoughts on the most soothing, calming phrases I could think of, anything peaceful that welled up in me: *All is well. The others are safe. I no longer need to keep watch. I am surrounded by friends.*

I can let go.

Magic burst from my fingertips, gleaming like silk and steel as it enveloped the fae male before me. He didn't so much as twitch. This power was invisible to him, like all divine magic to those who couldn't wield it. He raised no alarm as I drew more and more smoothness from the endless expanse of the floor and sang that silent lullaby to him through the power that connected us.

I'm safe. We're all safe. I can step away from the bindings now.

His hand tensed around the rope. His shoulders stiffened, preparing for physical effort.

My magic faltered as I bit back a gasp. Fuck. Had I gone about this the wrong way? Did mind magic not work like this at all? Had I alarmed him, confused him, somehow driven him to pull that gods-damned rope anyway?

All is well all is well all is well all is—

He loosened his shoulders with an audible sigh, drawn from the very bottom of his lungs, and let the rope go.

My knees almost buckled with relief – but no, I couldn't start slacking yet. Was this where I killed him? But I didn't *want* to kill the poor sod, no matter how many times I told myself he had been here to single-handedly doom every magical people but faekind to slow extinction – not when he started humming a dreamy, happy melody, sauntering towards the wide open window with his hands in the pockets of his trousers. Like a happy child. Like the male he might have been if not for centuries among the cutthroat masses at the Crimson Court.

I thought of Iorgas, drifting down towards the deadly ocean, and squeezed my eyes shut. *Stop.*

The humming abruptly ceased.

My eyes flew open. He was still standing where he'd stood a moment ago, shoulders slumping deep, head lolling gently to one side. When I cautiously pulled my left hand away from the smooth floor, he didn't move.

I rose to my feet, not making a sound. No reaction.

One cautious step forward. Two more. Two more. Still no reaction. I tiptoed a few yards further, until I was close enough to jump on top of him and physically restrain him if necessary, then let out a small, polite cough.

No reaction.

Bolder now, I slid past him to where I could see his face. He stared back at me with glassy, unseeing eyes, not registering my presence or movement in the slightest.

A shrill, mirthless laugh slipped over my lips. No reaction. I steadied him with a hand on his shoulder and whispered, 'You don't mind me searching your pockets for a bit, do you?'

There was no spark of understanding in his eyes – nothing that suggested he even remembered what pockets were, let alone cared about their contents. I patted him on the shoulder and went to work, feeling the sides of his well-tailored linen coat, then his broad thighs. In the left pocket, something rustled as cloth brushed over parchment, and I slipped my hand in to retrieve the note he was carrying.

West hall, it said, *F413*.

And below that, in another, messier hand, *(CH)*.

CH.

Creon Hytherion.

Was I going mad? This *had* to be the west hall of the two. F413 – one of the glass balls to my right carried the number 413 on its shelf, indeed. When I darted to the head of the aisle, I found a large, copper F nailed to the side of the cabinet.

My breath quickened to shallow gasps. It made sense, didn't it? Thysandra had handled the administration surrounding the bindings, Creon had said – so it stood to reason that she would know which of these thousands and thousands of glass balls was his. Would she send her agent that way, too? It *could* be. There was enough old animosity between them, she'd sounded particularly venomous when inquiring if he was here to get his voice, and if push came to shove, it may have given extra weight to her threats. She could not have been sure the Silent Death would care much about the sacrifices the rest of the world had made. His own binding, though ... That was guaranteed to make an impression.

So she'd handed this note to her subordinate. *West hall, F413*. And he had, nervous about forgetting anything or messing anything up, added that clarification later – *Creon Hytherion*.

I shoved the note aside, heart a fluttering mess now. In the fae male's right pocket, I found what I had originally been looking for – a heavy key, an *actual* key, forged from gold and the bow inlaid with mother of pearl. No one could argue the Mother didn't have style when it came to prisons and reigns of terror.

Then I had all I needed, didn't I?

493

I threw a glance at the window. Far away, in a circle of torchlight, I could see the others moving around at the foot of the cliff, fae binding Lyn's hands behind her back as I squinted. I should hurry the hell up. But that damned note, *CH* ...

His *voice.*

'Alyra?' Of course she was right behind me. 'Could you fly out ahead of me and draw as much attention as possible? Make sure Beyla sees you.'

The little falcon was already on her way, squeaking in elation as she shot out through the window and into the open air beyond. I drew in two slow, deep breaths and slipped the key into the pocket of my own dress. With that weight pulling on one hip, I leaned over ever so slightly and tapped my fingers against ball number 413.

It didn't shatter on the spot. I dared to release my breath, slowly.

Should I use yellow magic to strengthen the material? But the gods knew what unintended side effects that may have; if I was going to experiment, I shouldn't do it with what might very well be the key to Creon's magic. Which meant I'd have to be careful out there. But the orb would illuminate my path, diminishing the risk of surprise rubble, and ...

His *voice.*

I may have muddled my priorities for weeks, if not months, but this I could get right.

The glass was so very light when I lifted it and cradled it against my chest like a newborn child, heart pounding in my ears. I walked as if I were carrying a cup of water filled to the brim, trying not to spill a single drop; every single step was a conscious decision, the safety of the ground a relief each time my feet settled back on the granite. Out of the hall. Through the first doorway I found. Onto a crumbled terrace, collapsed rooms to my right, a line of still trees to my left. Down the slope of the cliff on this side of the castle, to where the others were waiting.

Or rather, fighting.

Hell had broken loose since the last glance I'd thrown their way, the whirling movements hard to follow from this distance. Beyla was there, fading back and forth, swords slashing around her in silvery flashes as she cut through wings and limbs and throats. Judging by the wild gestures and frantic movements, people were shouting. Around Naxi, fae were dropping to the earth like fall leaves. Lyn's binds lay smouldering on the ground while she frantically worked to free Tared's wrists, and Creon seemed to be well on his way to killing a dozen opponents without even unbinding his hands at all. Alyra raced around in excited circles on our side of the Mother's shield, squeaking in joyful triumph with every fae to go down.

I had to restrain myself from walking any faster, determined not to fall into a jog. I'd done my part. They'd manage without me for another minute or two.

The glass binding burned in my hands, pulsing with the promise of a goal achieved.

Alyra slowed down as I finally reached her, settling back into her familiar spot on my left shoulder. On the other side of the shield, Creon and the alves were busy sticking knives into every fallen opponent, double-checking for their lack of heartbeat; only Thysandra was still standing, alf steel chain around her wrists. Naxi stood beside her with a wolfish grin upon her face. Lyn was talking, gesturing wildly at the scene.

Crossing the barrier was bafflingly easy with the key in my pocket. A shimmer of magic, a ripple of light, and the sounds of the world crashed over me again. Frantic voices. Shrieking blades. The smell of ripe apples, the brush of the cool wind over my face, and—

'Em!'

They all snapped around at Lyn's cry, abrupt silence descending over the battlefield.

I should have greeted them. Should have given some reassurance, *any* reassurance, on the fate of the hundreds of thousands of bindings I'd left behind. But the smooth glass in my hands brimmed with three months' worth of pent-up frustration, and my gaze was drawn to Creon like a river finding the sea – every fibre of my being honing in on his presence as if nothing else in the world would ever matter again.

He stood a few strides away, frozen in place, hands covered in ink and blood. His eyes had blazed with wild fury a moment ago, yet now they'd gone still – the fight seeping out of him like the last grains of sand trickling through an hourglass. An expression blank with disbelief, his heart and cautious, scheming mind unable to agree on just what they were seeing.

His lips moved. *Em?*

My grin came from somewhere fathoms deep inside me. 'Got you something.'

For one last moment, he merely stood there, knife drooping in his hands, unmoving except for the free locks of hair fluttering in the sea breeze.

Then he smiled.

A smile like a sunrise, spreading over his face with slow, almost timid radiance – all wistful wonder, all heartfelt relief, melting every mask of pride or cruelty away. A smile I'd *never* seen before in the company of others, no trace left of the Silent Death they knew. This was just Creon, *my* Creon, every twisted, dramatic, vulnerable, irresistible inch of him.

A flood of words surged through me, every apology I'd been unable to articulate on that bloody beach suddenly flying to my lips with perfect clarity – *I'm sorry. I don't know what I was thinking. Of course you're mine. Of course I'm yours. Let's go eat each other's faces off in front of the bloody phoenix elders.*

But that conversation on the beach had taken place an hour ago, and he'd waited a hundred and thirty years for the treasure I was holding in my hands. So I beamed back at him, hoping that smile would convey most of the message, and managed to sound almost composed as I said, 'Shall I just get to work, then?'

'No,' Thysandra ground out somewhere close. '*No!* You have no idea what you're ... You can't just ...'

'I don't think she was asking you for permission, Sashka,' Naxi said, sounding like a cat locked in with a hundred saucers of cream.

'*Don't* call me that!'

Naxi just giggled.

'Do whatever you can, Em,' Lyn said, amusement sparkling below the thin veneer of reasonable business. 'I suggest the rest of us focus on removing our traces for now – if the Mother doesn't yet know about this visit to the Court, I'd like to keep it that way.'

Thysandra made a choked, strangled sound.

'I suggest staging a fight on some other island and dropping the bodies there,' Beyla said, finally sheathing her swords. 'How about Oskya? Guaranteed to have no witnesses. Then if we get rid of that apple mess Em left behind, it's as if we've never been here.'

There were mutters of general agreement. I looked back at Creon, who quirked up an eyebrow and dryly signed, *You can go ahead and help cleaning up corpses, if you prefer.*

'Oh, go to hell,' I said, bursting out laughing as I held out the crystal ball to him. 'Hold this, will you? I'm going to need my hands.'

He mindlessly changed my dress to glittering mother of pearl, then curled his fingers around the glass with slow, painstaking care. In the pale blue light, the sharp angles of his face were tense – with concentration, anticipation, a tremor of something close to fear. But he held the binding as if it were the most precious thing in the world, and his dark eyes never lifted from the glittering surface.

'Ready?' I muttered.

His throat bobbed, but he nodded.

I lowered my left hand to my iridescent dress, pressing my fingers into the smooth fabric to calm myself. Around us, the others scurried from body to body, muttering observations at each other; even Tared had tactfully turned away. I drew in a last breath, the smells of sea and stone and blood mingling in the back of my throat, and allowed the iridescent magic to travel up, up, up through my left arm—

Something red lunged forward on the edge of my sight.

And then everything happened much, much too fast.

Thysandra dove at us with the desperate strength of a hunted animal, wings bursting wide, arms stretched out to grab the glowing orb. Creon reacted before I could shout a warning. A knife appeared in his free hand as he took a swift step sideways, arm swinging back to aim and throw.

Naxi cried, '*No!*'

Creon went slack mid-swing, dagger clattering down as his knees buckled.

And the glass ball fell.

It seemed to be plummeting for an eternity as I stood there, horrified, paralysed, unable to figure out what for hell's sake was happening for one catastrophic moment too long. Demon magic. Bogged down nervous system. Catch it, *catch it*—

The fragile glass sphere shattered as it met the rocky ground.

The world moved in brusque, jerky flares around me. Beyla had jumped forward, blades forcing Thysandra away from me and the glass shards. Lyn was shouting at Naxi. Naxi's high voice wailed melodious apologies laced with sobs, something about defending, something about death.

I stared at the broken binding, knowing what was about to happen yet unwilling to believe it.

There they were, two small wisps of magic, rising from the rubble just like they had done from that shattered glass on Tolya. One containing Creon's unbound magic, powers so deadly they might single-handedly decide the outcome of this war. One containing the price he'd paid – his voice.

Drifting in separate directions.

'Em!' Tared's voice, rough and hurried. *Panicked.* 'Fuck, Em, we need his magic. I'm sorry – I'm *sorry* – but please—'

'I'm sorry,' Naxi moaned, as if echoing him, 'I'm *sorry*!'

'Em?' Beyla said behind me, warnings clinging to the sound of my name. 'Orin's eye, don't be stupid now, Em. He can't talk the Mother to death. *He* wants to kill her too, doesn't he?'

Make good choices, Emelin.

Tared was saying more. Lyn's voice was climbing higher and higher. I absorbed none of it, staring at Creon's blank face as he lay there on the rocky ground, the roar of my thoughts numbing that ever-present chorus of needs and expectations. Through the iridescent cloth of my skirt, my nails dug deep lines into my thigh, the pain a blessing to keep me focused.

Make good choices.

We did need that cursed magic. He did want to kill the Mother. He had sacrificed more than a voice to win this war. All true, all so very true. Emelin the hopeful symbol wouldn't hesitate. The Underground's perfect unbound mage knew her duties. And yet—

I didn't want to make that choice.

I'd promised to protect him.

He had suffered enough. He had lost too much already. These split seconds before choosing brought a clarity that even hours of deliberation could never rival – the perfect, razor-sharp understanding that I was never going to be Emelin the hopeful symbol. I was not an obedient weapon. I was not everyone's smiling saviour.

And that did not make me a failure.

They would be angry, and that was fine. I didn't need to please them to save them. If they thought me an idiot, I was still going to save the gods-damned world.

But I was going to do it on *my* terms.

The magic drew itself, a burst of iridescence so vigorous it left me light-headed. *Make good choices*, and here was my choice – my powers lashing out and snatching one of those tendrils of binding magic just before it could dissolve. A single flick of my wrist, and I dragged my catch into Creon's throat with the full strength of my fury.

It spread over his bronze skin with a pearly glow, then sank in, like raindrops absorbed by the earth. The second fleck of magic was gone, and I couldn't bring myself to mourn it.

The world had gone icily quiet around me.

But at my feet, Creon shuddered.

I fell to my knees without thinking, grabbed his shoulder, shook it. His wing twitched in response. I sharply said, 'Creon?' and again a tremble ran through him, eyelashes fluttering against his cheeks.

'*Creon.*'

He shot up without warning, gulping in a lungful of air as he doubled over and grabbed for his throat. Somewhere behind me, I could hear Tared's cursing. Shrill laughter, too – Thysandra was laughing, a maniacal sound nearly drowning out Beyla's furious objections. But Creon was here, alive, gasping for breath, coughing his lungs out, and why would I bother with grumbling allies if there were dramatic fae princes

499

to be saved?

'Creon, breathe.' I grabbed his other shoulder, too, and he nodded on another wheezing inhale, one hand releasing his throat to clutch my elbow. Dark hair cascaded around his temples, obscuring his face in the firelit dark. 'It's alright. You're alright. Take a sip of water and try to—'

His head abruptly jerked up, frantic gaze meeting mine. Ink-black eyes darted over my face with an intensity that could set the bare rock beneath our feet ablaze, and my heart skipped a beat as the words dried to dust on my lips. His fingers squeezed my arm with the force of a vice. It took me a moment to realise that he was fighting to keep his hands from shaking.

'Creon?' I whispered again, like a prayer.

He sucked in a hoarse, guttural breath. His lips parted, and for one heartbeat I could swear even the wind itself was holding its breath.

'Em,' he rasped. 'Emelin.'

The end...
for now

Queens of Mist and Madness, the fourth (and final) Fae Isles book, is not yet up for pre-order. If you want to be notified once it becomes available, you can:

- Add the book <u>on Goodreads</u>

- Follow me <u>on Amazon</u> (make sure you allow release updates)

- Follow me <u>on BookBub</u>

- Subscribe to my newsletter (www.lisettemarshall.com/sign

-up)

- Follow me on Instagram (@authorlisettemarshall)

ACKNOWLEDGMENTS

Over the course of my writing career, I've found that the longer a book is, the more I struggle with the writing process. *Ruins of Sea and Souls* is the longest book I've ever written, so unsurprisingly, it came quite close to defeating me.

I owe the victory to a number of friends whose support and advice has been indispensable while I wrestled with health issues, day job stress, and general author despair. So in no particular order, I would like to thank Colleen (for sending me to bed), Elsie (for teaching me how to be an asshole), Amber (for sharing her wisdom about singing at night), Vela (for being a care bear and, at times, an intensive care bear), and Christine (for kicking me whenever I'm being an eldest daughter again).

And of course, my special thanks to Erin (for sharing her faery dust and being the most patient editor in the world) and to Steph (who glitter-bombs into my life whenever I'm running out of words).

Finally, as always, all my gratitude to W., who continues to love me no matter how often I forget to close the kitchen cabinets. You have my whole heart.

Printed in Great Britain
by Amazon

26337985R00290